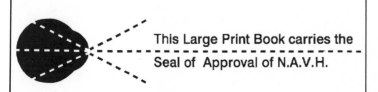

THE SERPENT'S TALE

THE SERPENT'S TALE

ARIANA FRANKLIN

THORNDIKE PRESS
A part of Gale, Cengage Learning

GALE
CENGAGE Learning™

Detroit • New York • San Francisco • New Haven, Conn • Waterville, Maine • London

GALE
CENGAGE Learning·

Copyright © 2008 by Ariana Franklin.
Thorndike Press, a part of Gale, Cengage Learning.

Thorndike Press® Large Print Historical Fiction.
The text of this Large Print edition is unabridged.
Other aspects of the book may vary from the original edition.
Set in 16 pt. Plantin.
Printed on permanent paper.

LIBRARY OF CONGRESS CATALOGING-IN-PUBLICATION DATA

Franklin, Ariana.
  The serpent's tale : by Ariana Franklin.
    p. cm. — (Thorndike Press large print historical fiction)
  ISBN-13: 978-1-4104-0622-4 (hardcover : alk. paper)
  ISBN-10: 1-4104-0622-9 (hardcover : alk. paper)
    1. Women forensic pathologists — Fiction. 2. Henry II, King of England, 1133–1189 — Fiction. 3. Mistresses — Fiction. 4. London (England) — Fiction. 5. Large type books. I. Title.
  PR6064.O73S47 2008b
  823'.914—dc22   2008002074

Published in 2008 by arrangement with G. P. Putnam's Sons, a member of Penguin Group (USA) Inc.

Printed in the United States of America
1 2 3 4 5 6 7 12 11 10 09 08

*To Dr. Mary Lynch, M.D., FRCP, FRCPI,
consultant cardiologist.*

My literally heartfelt thanks.

PROLOGUE

The two men's voices carried down the tunnels with reverberations that made them indistinguishable but, even so, gave the impression of a business meeting. Which it was. In a way.

An assassin was receiving orders from his client, who was, the assassin thought, making it unnecessarily difficult for himself, as such clients did.

It was always the same; they wanted to conceal their identities, and turned up so masked or muffled you could hardly hear their instructions. They didn't want to be seen with you, which led to assignations on blasted heaths or places like this stinking cellar. They were nervous about handing over the down payment in case you stabbed them and then ran off with it.

If they only realized it, a respectable assassin like himself *had* to be trustworthy; his career depended on it. It had taken time,

7

but Sicarius (the Latin pseudonym he'd chosen for himself) was becoming known for excellence. Whether it was translated from the Latin as "assassin" or "dagger," it stood for the neat removal of one's political opponent, wife, creditor, without suspicion being provable against oneself.

Satisfied clients recommended him to others who were afflicted, though they pretended to make a joke of it: "You could use the fellow they call Sicarius," they'd say. "He's supposed to solve troubles like yours."

And when pressed for information: "I don't know, of course, but rumor has it he's to be contacted at the Bear in Southwark." Or Fillola's in Rome. Or La Boule in Paris. Or at whatever inn in whichever area one was plying for trade that season.

This month, Oxford. In a cellar connected by a long tunnel to the undercroft of an inn. He'd been led to it by a masked and hooded servant — oh, really, *so* unnecessary — and pointed toward a rich red-velvet curtain strung across one corner, hiding the client behind it and contrasting vividly with the mold on the walls and the slime underfoot. Damn it, one's boots would be *ruined.*

"The . . . assignment will not be difficult for you?" the curtain asked. The voice behind it had given very specific instructions.

"The circumstances are unusual, my lord," the assassin said. He always called them "my lord." It pleased them. "I don't usually like to leave evidence, but if that is what you require . . ."

"I do, but I meant spiritually," the curtain said. "Does your conscience not worry you? Don't you fear for your soul's damnation?"

So they'd reached that point, had they, the moment when clients distanced their morality from his, he being the low-born dirty bastard who wielded the knife and they merely the rich bastards who ordered it.

He could have said, "It's a living and a good one, damned or not, and better than starving to death." He could have said, "I don't have a conscience, I have standards, which I keep to." He could even have said, "What about *your* soul's damnation?"

But they paid for their rag of superiority, so he desisted. Instead, he said cheerily, "High or low, my lord. Popes, peasants, kings, varlets, ladies, children, I dispose of them all — and for the same price: seventy-five marks down and a hundred when the job's done." Keeping to the same tariff was part of his success.

"Children?" The curtain was shocked.

Oh, dear, dear. *Of course* children. Children inherited. Children were obstacles to the stepfather, aunt, brother, cousin who would come into the estate once the little moppet was out of the way. And more difficult to dispose of than you'd think . . .

He merely said, "Perhaps you would go over the instructions again, my lord."

Keep the client talking. Find out who he was, in case he tried to avoid the final payment. Killing those who reneged on the agreement meant tracking them down, inflicting a death that was both painfully inventive and, he hoped, a warning to future clients.

The voice behind the curtain repeated what it had already said. To be done on such and such a day, in such and such a place, by these means the death to occur in such and such a manner, this to be left, that to be taken away.

They always want precision, the assassin thought wearily. Do it this way, do it that. As if killing is a science rather than an art.

Nevertheless, in this instance, the client had planned the murder with extraordinary detail and had intimate knowledge of his victim's comings and goings; it would be as well to comply. . . .

So Sicarius listened carefully, not to the instructions — he'd memorized them the first time — but to the timbre of the client's voice, noting phrases he could recognize again, waiting for a cough, a stutter that might later identify the speaker in a crowd.

While he listened, he looked around him. There was nothing to be learned from the servant who stood in the shadows, carefully shrouded in an unexceptional cloak and with his shaking hand — oh, bless him — on the hilt of a sword stuck into a belt, as if he wouldn't be dead twenty times over before he could draw it. A pitiful safeguard, but probably the only creature the client trusted.

The location of the cellar, now . . . it told the assassin something, if only that the client had shown cunning in choosing it. There were three exits, one of them the long tunnel, down which he'd been guided from the inn. The other two might lead anywhere, to the castle, perhaps, or — he sniffed — to the river. The only certainty was that it was somewhere in the bowels of Oxford. And bowels, as the assassin had reason to know, having laid bare quite a few, were extensive and tortuous.

Built during the Stephen and Matilda war, of course. The assassin reflected uneasily on the tunneling that had, literally, undermined England during the thirteen years of that unfortunate and bloody fracas. The strategic jewel that was Oxford, guarding the country's main routes south to north and east to west, where they crossed the Thames, had suffered badly. Besieged and re-besieged, people had dug like moles both to get in and to get out. One of these days, he thought — and God give it wasn't today — the bloody place would collapse into the wormholes they'd made of its foundations.

Oxford, he thought. A town held mainly for King Stephen and, therefore, the wrong side. Twenty years on, and its losers still heaved with resentment against Matilda's son, Henry Plantagenet, the ultimate winner and king.

The assassin had gained a deal of information while in the area — it always paid to know who was upside with whom, and why — and he thought it possible that the client was one of those still embittered by the war and that the assignment was, therefore, political.

In which case it could be dangerous. Greed, lust, revenge: Their motives were all one to him, but political clients were usually of such high degree that they had a tendency to hide their involvement by hiring yet another murderer to kill the first, *i.e., him.* It was always wearisome and only led to more bloodletting, though never his.

Aha. The unseen client had shifted, and for a second, no more, the tip of a boot had shown beneath the curtain hem. A boot of fine doeskin, like one's own, and *new,* possibly recently made in Oxford — again, like one's own.

A round of the local boot makers was called for.

"We are agreed, then?" the curtain asked.

"We are agreed, my lord."

"Seventy-five marks, you say?"

"In gold, if you please, my lord," the assassin said, still cheerful. "And similarly with the hundred when the job's done."

"Very well," the client said, and told his servant to hand over the purse containing the fee.

And in doing so made a mistake which neither he nor the servant noticed but which the assassin found informative. "Give Master Sicarius the purse, my son," the client said.

In fact, the clink of gold from the purse as it passed was hardly less satisfactory than that the assassin now knew his client's occupation.

And was surprised.

ONE

The woman on the bed had lost the capacity to scream.

Apart from the drumming of her feet and the thump of her fists against the sheets, her gyrations were silent, as if she were miming agony.

The three nuns, too, kneeling at either side, might have been aping intercession; their mouths moved soundlessly, because any noise, even the sibilance of a whispered prayer, set off another convulsion in the patient. They had their eyes closed so as not to see her suffering. Only the woman standing at the end of the bed watched it, showing no expression.

On the walls, Adam and Eve skipped in innocent tapestried health among the flora and fauna of the Garden while the Serpent, in a tree, and God, on a cloud, looked on with amiability. It was a circular room, its beauty now mocking the ghastliness of its owner: the fair hair that had turned black and straggled with sweat, the corded veins in the once-white neck, lips stretched in the terrible grin.

What could be done had been done. Candles and burning incense holders heated a room where the lattices and shutters had been stuffed closed so as not to rattle.

Mother Edyve had stripped Godstow, her convent, of its reliquaries in order to send the saints' aid to this stricken woman. Too old to come herself, she had told Sister Havis, Godstow's prioress, what to do. Accordingly, the tibia of Saint Scholastica had been tied to the flailing arm, droplets from the phial containing Saint Mary's milk poured on the poor head, and a splinter of the True Cross placed into the woman's hand, though it had been jerked across the room during a spasm.

Carefully, so as not to make a noise, Sister Havis got up and left the room. The woman who had been standing at the end of the bed followed her. "Where you going?"

"To fetch Father Pol. I sent for him; he's waiting in the kitchen."

"No."

Like the stern but well-born Christian she was, Havis showed patience to the afflicted, though this particular female always made

16

her flesh creep. She said, "It is time, Dakers. She must receive the viaticum."

"I'll kill you. She ain't going to die. I'll kill the priest if he comes upstairs."

It was spoken without force or apparent emotion, but the prioress believed it of this woman; every servant in the place had already run away for fear of what she might do if their mistress died.

"Dakers, Dakers," she said — always name the mad when speaking to them so as to remind them of themselves — "we cannot deny the rite of holy unction's comfort to a soul about to begin its journey. Look . . ." She caught hold of the housekeeper's arm and turned her so that both women faced into the room where their muttered voices had caused the body on the bed to arch again. Only its heels and the top of its head rested on the bed, forming a tortured bridge.

"No human frame can withstand such torment," Sister Havis said. "She is dying." With that, she began to go down the stairs.

Footsteps followed her, causing her to hold fast to the banister in case she received a push in the back. She kept on, but it was a relief to gain the ground and go into white-cold fresh air as she crossed to the kitchen that had been modeled on that of

17

Fontevrault, with its chimneys, and stood like a giant pepper pot some yards away from the tower.

The flames in one of the fireplaces were the only light and sent leaps of red reflection on the drying sheets that hung from hooks normally reserved for herbs and flitches of bacon.

Father Pol, a mousy little man, and mousier than ever tonight, crouched on a stool, cradling a fat black cat as if he needed its comfort in this place.

His eyes met the nun's and then rolled in inquiry toward the figure of the house-keeper.

"We are ready for you now, Father," the prioress told him.

The priest nodded in relief. He stood up, carefully placed the cat on the stool, gave it a last pat, picked up the chrismatory at his feet, and scuttled out. Sister Havis waited a moment to see if the housekeeper would come with them, saw that she would not, and followed Father Pol.

Left alone, Dakers stared into the fire.

The blessing by the bishop who had been called to her mistress two days ago had done nothing. Neither had all the convent's trumpery. The Christian god had failed.

Very well.

She began to move briskly. Items were taken from the cupboard in the tiny room that was her domain next to the kitchen. When she came back, she was muttering. She put a leather-bound book with a lock on the chopping block. On it was placed a crystal that, in the firelight, sent little green lights from its facets wobbling around the room.

One by one, she lit seven candles and dripped the wax of each onto the block to make a stand. They formed a circle round the book and crystal, giving light as steady as the ones upstairs, though emitting a less pleasant smell than beeswax.

The cauldron hanging from a jack over the fire was full and boiling, and had been kept so as to provide water for the washing of the sickroom sheets. So many sheets.

The woman bent over it to make sure that the surface of the water bubbled. She looked around for the cauldron's lid, a large, neatly holed circle of wood with an iron handle arched over its center, found it, and leaned it carefully on the floor at her feet. From the various fire irons by the side of the hearth, dogs, spits, etc., she picked out a long poker and laid that, too, on the floor by the lid.

"Igzy-bidzy," she was muttering, "sishnu

shishnu, adony-manooey, eelam-peelam . . ."
The ignorant might have thought the repetition to be that of a child's skipping rhyme; others would have recognized the deliberately garbled, many-faithed versions of the holy names of God.

Dodging the sheets, Dame Dakers crossed to where Father Pol had been sitting and picked up the cat, cradling and petting it as he had done. It was a good cat, a famous ratter, the only one she allowed in the place.

Taking it to the hearth, she gave it a last stroke with one hand and reached for the cauldron lid with the other.

Still chanting, she dropped the cat into the boiling water, swiftly popping the lid in place over it and forcing it down. The poker was slid through the handle so that it overlapped the edges.

For a second the lid rattled against the poker and a steaming shriek whistled through the lid's holes. Dame Dakers knelt on the hearth's edge, commending the sacrifice to her master.

If God had failed, it was time to petition the Devil.

Eighty-odd miles to the east as the crow flew, Vesuvia Adelia Rachel Ortese Aguilar was delivering a baby for the first time — or trying to deliver it.

"Push, Ma," said the fetus's eldest sister helpfully from the sidelines.

"Don't you be telling her that," Adelia said in East Anglian. "Her can't push til the time comes." At this stage, the poor woman had little control over the matter.

And neither do I, she thought in desperation. *I don't know what to do.*

It was going badly; labor had been protracted to the point where the mother, an uncomplaining fenwoman, was becoming exhausted.

Outside, on the grass, watched by Adelia's dog, Mansur was singing nursery rhymes from his homeland to amuse the other children — all of whom had been delivered easily with the aid of a neighbor and a bread knife — and it was a measure of Adelia's desperation that at this moment she relished neither his voice nor the strangeness of hearing a castrato's angelic soprano wafting minor-key Arabic over an English fenland. She could only wonder at the endurance of the suffering woman on the bed, who managed to gasp, "Tha's pretty."

The woman's husband remained uncharmed. He was hiding himself and his concern for his wife in the hut's undercroft with his cow. His voice came up the wooden

21

flight of stairs to the stage — part hayloft, part living quarters — where the women battled. "Her never had this to-do when Goody Baines delivered 'em."

Good for Goody Baines, Adelia thought. But those babies had come without trouble, and there had been too many of them. Later, she would have to point out that Mistress Reed had given birth to nine in twelve years; another would probably kill her, even if this one did not.

However, now was not the moment. It was necessary to keep up confidence, especially that of the laboring mother, so she called brightly, "You be thankful you got me now, bor, so you just keep that old water bilin.' "

Me, she thought, *an anatomist, and a foreigner to boot. My speciality is corpses. You have a right to be worried. If you were aware of how little experience I have with any parturition other than my own, you'd be frantic.*

The unknown Goody Baines might have known what to do; so might Gyltha, Adelia's companion and nursemaid to her child, but both women were independently paying a visit to Cambridge Fair and would not be back for a day or two, their departure having coincided with the onset of Mistress Reed's labor. Only Adelia in this isolated part of fenland was known to have medical knowledge and had, therefore, been called to the emergency.

And if the woman in the bed had broken her bones or contracted any form of disease, Adelia could indeed have helped her, for Adelia was a doctor — not just wise in the use of herbs and the pragmatism handed down from woman to woman through generations, and not, like so many men parading as physicians, a charlatan who bamboozled his patients with disgusting medicines for high prices. No, Adelia was a graduate of the great and liberal, forward-thinking, internationally admired School of Medicine in Salerno, which defied the Church by enrolling women into its studies if they were clever enough.

Finding Adelia's brain on a par with, even excelling, that of the cleverest male student, her professors had given her a masculine education, which, later, she had completed by joining her Jewish foster father in his department of autopsy.

A unique education, then, but of no use to her now, because in its wisdom — and it *was* wisdom — Salerno's School of Medicine had seen that midwifery was better left to midwives. Adelia could have cured Mistress Reed's baby, she could have performed a postmortem on it were it dead and revealed what it died of — but she couldn't birth it.

She handed over a basin of water and cloth to the woman's daughter, crossed the room, and picked up her own baby from its wicker basket, sat down on a hay bale, undid her laces, and began to feed it.

She had a theory about breast-feeding, as she had for practically everything: It should be accompanied by calm, happy thoughts. Usually, when she nursed the child, she sat in the doorway of her own little reed-thatched house at Waterbeach and allowed her eyes and mind to wander over the Cam fenland. At first its flat greenness had fared badly against the remembered Mediterranean panorama of her birth, with its jagged drama set against a turquoise sea. But flatness, too, has its beauty, and gradually she had come to appreciate the immense skies over infinite shades of willow and alder that the natives called carr, and the richness of fish and wildlife teeming in the hidden rivers.

"Mountains?" Gyltha had said once. "Don't hold with mountains. They buggers do get in the way."

Besides, this was now the homeland of the child in her arms, and therefore infinitely beloved.

But today, Adelia dared not indulge either her eyes or her mind for her baby's sake. There was another child to be saved, and be damned if she was going to let it die through her own ignorance. Or the mother, either.

Silently apologizing to the little thing in her arms, Adelia set herself to envisaging the corpses she'd dissected of mothers who'd died with their fetuses yet undelivered.

Such pitiable cadavers, yet when they were laid out on the marble table of the great autopsy hall in Salerno, she'd withheld compassion from them, as she'd learned to do with all the dead in order to serve them better. Emotion had no place in the art of dissection, only clear, trained, investigative reasoning.

Now, here, in a whiskery little hut on the edge of the civilized world, she did it again, blanking from her mind the suffering of the woman on the bed and replacing it with a map of interior organs, positions, pressures, displacements. *"Hmm."*

Hardly aware she was doing it, Adelia withdrew her baby from her left, now empty, breast and transferred it to the other, still calculating stresses on brain and navel cord, why and when suffocation occurred, blood loss, putrefaction . . . *"Hmm."*

"Here, missis. Summat's coming." The daughter was guiding her mother's hands toward the bridle that had been tied to the bed head.

Adelia laid her child back in its basket, covered herself up, and went to the bottom of the bed.

Something was indeed emerging from the mother's body, but it wasn't a baby's head, it was a baby's backside.

Goddamn. A breech birth. She'd suspected it but, by the time she'd been brought in, engagement in the uterus had taken place and it was too late to insert her hand and revolve the fetus, even if she'd had the knowledge and daring.

"Ain't you going to tug it out?" the daughter asked.

"Not yet." She'd seen the irreparable damage caused by pulling at this stage. Instead, she addressed the mother. *"Now* you push. Whether you want to or not, *push."*

Mistress Reed nodded, put part of the bridle in her mouth, clamped her teeth on it, and began pushing. Adelia gestured to the girl to help her drag the mother's body farther down the bed so that her buttocks hung over the edge and gravity could play its part.

"Hold her legs straight. By the ankles, behind me, *behind* me, that's right. Well done, mistress. Keep pushing." She herself was on her knees, a good position for delivering — and praying.

Help us, Lord.

Even so, she waited until a navel appeared with its attached cord. She touched the cord gently — a strong pulse. *Good, good.*

Now for it.

Moving quickly but with care, she entered her hand into the mother's cavity and released one leg, then the other, flexing the tiny knees.

"Push. *Push,* will you."

Oh, beautiful, sliding out by themselves *without having to be pulled* were two arms and a torso up to the nape of the neck. Supporting the body with one hand, Adelia laid the other on the little back and felt the tremor of a pulse.

Crucial now. Only minutes before suffocation set in. *God, whichever god you are, be with us now.*

He wasn't. Mistress Reed had lost strength, and the baby's head was still inside.

"Pass over that pack, *that* pack." In seconds, Adelia had extracted her dissection knife, always kept clean.

"Now." She placed the daughter's hand on Mistress Reed's pubic region. "Press." Still supporting the little torso, she made a cut in the mother's perineum. There was a slither and, because the knife was still in her fingers, she had to catch the baby in the crook of her elbows.

The daughter was shouting, "That's out, Dadda."

Master Reed appeared at the head of the ladder in a smell of cow dung. "Gor dang, what is it?"

Stupid with relief, Adelia said, "It's a baby." Ugly, bloodied, soapy, froglike, with its feet tending toward its head as they had in the womb, but undamaged, breathing, and, when tapped on its back, objecting to life in general and its emergence into it in particular — to Adelia, as beautiful a sight and sound as the world was capable of producing.

"That's as may be, but what *is* it?"

"Oh." Adelia put down the knife and turned the miracle over. It was male, quite definitely male. She gathered herself. "I believe the scrotum swelling to be caused by bruising and will subside."

"He's a'going to be popular if it don't, ain't he?" Master Reed said.

The cord was severed, Mistress Reed was stitched and made decent for visitors, and the baby was wrapped in a fleece and put into his mother's arms.

"Here, missis, you got a name as we can call him after?" her husband wanted to know.

"Vesuvia Adelia Rachel Ortese Aguilar," Adelia said apologetically.

There was silence.

"What about him?" Master Reed pointed at the tall figure of Mansur, who had come up with the siblings to view the miracle.

"Mansur bin Fayîî bin Nasab Al-Masaari Khayoun of Al Amarah."

More silence.

Mansur, whose alliance with Gyltha was enabling him to understand English even if it gave him little chance to speak it, said in Arabic, "The prior comes, I saw his boat. Let them call the boy Geoffrey."

"Prior Geoffrey's here?" Adelia was down the ladder in a trice and running to the tiny wooden platform that served as a quay — all homes in the fenland had access to one of its innumerable rivers, its children learning to maneuver a coracle as soon as they could walk.

Clambering out of his barge with the help of a liveried oarsman was one of Adelia's favorite people. "How are you here?" she said, hugging him. "*Why* are you here? How is Ulf?"

"A handful, but a clever handful. He thrives." Gyltha's grandson, and, so it was said, the prior's as well, had been set to serious study at the priory school and would not be allowed to leave it until the spring sowing.

"I am so pleased to see you."

"And I you. They told me at Waterbeach where you were gone. It appears that the mountain must come to Mohammed."

"It's still too mountainous," Adelia said, standing back to look at him. The prior of Saint Augustine's great canonry in Cambridge had been her first patient and, subsequently, her first friend in England; she worried about him. "You have not been keeping to my diet."

"*Dum vivimus, vivamus,*" he said. "Let us live while we live. I subscribe to the Epicureans."

"Do you know the mortality rate among Epicureans?"

They spoke in fast and classical Latin because it was natural to them, though it caused the men in the prior's barge to wonder why their lord was concealing from them what he was saying to a woman and, even more wondrous, how a woman could understand it.

"Oh, but you are well come," Adelia said, "just in time to baptize my first delivery. It will comfort his parents, though he is a healthy, glorious child."

Adelia did not subscribe to the theory of Christian infant baptism, just as she didn't subscribe to any of what she regarded as barbarous tenets held by the world's three major faiths. A god who would not allow that baby upstairs into the Kingdom of Heaven if it died before being sprinkled with certain words and water was not a god she wanted anything to do with.

But his parents regarded the ceremony as vital, if only to ensure the boy a Christian burial should the worst happen. Master Reed had been about to send for the shabby, peripatetic priest who served the area.

The Reed family watched in silence as bejewelled fingers wetted their son's forehead and a voice as velvety-rich as its owner's vestments welcomed him into the faith, promising him life eternal and pronouncing him "Geoffrey in the name of the Father, and of the Son, and of the Holy Ghost, amen."

"Fen people never say thank you," Adelia apologized, as, carrying her baby, she joined the prior in his barge, the dog called Ward scrambling in with her, leaving Mansur to follow in their rowing boat. "But they never forget, either. They were grateful but amazed. You were too much for them, as if archangel Gabriel had come down in a shaft of gold."

"*Non angeli, sed angli,* I fear," Prior Geoffrey said, and such was his fondness for Adelia that he, who had lived in Cambridgeshire for thirty years, remained complacent at being instructed in the ways of the fens by this woman from southern Italy.

Look at her, he thought, *dressed like a scarecrow, accompanied by a dog that will necessitate fumigation of the bench it sits on, the finest mind of her generation hugging her bastard for joy at having delivered a brat into a hovel.*

Not for the first time, he wondered about her parentage, of which she was as ignorant as he. Brought up by a Salernitan couple, a Jew and his Christian wife, who'd found her abandoned among the stones of Vesuvius, her hair was the dark blond sometimes seen on Greeks or Florentines. Not that anybody could see it at the moment, hidden in that unspeakable cap.

She is still the oddity she was when we first met on the road to Cambridge, Prior Geoffrey thought. *I returning from the pilgrimage to Canterbury, she in a cart, accompanied by an Arab and a Jew. I put her down as their trull, not recognizing the virginity of a scholar. Yet when I began to bawl in pain — Lord, how I bawled, and Lord, what pain it was — despite all my company of Christians, only she played the Samaritan. In saving my life that day she reduced me,* me, *to stammering adolescence by manipulating my most intimate parts as if they were mere tripes to be cooked. And still I find her beautiful.*

She had been obeying a summons even then, brought from her work with the dead of Salerno to be part of a team in disguise led by the investigating Jew, Simon of Naples, to find out who was killing Cambridge's children — a matter that seriously bothered the King of England because it was leading to riot and, therefore, a depletion of his taxes.

This being England and not freethinking Salerno, it had been necessary for Mansur, Adelia's servant, to set up as the doctor, with Adelia herself pretending to be his assistant during their investigation. Poor, good Simon — even though a Jew, the prior remembered him in his prayers — had been murdered in his search for the killer, and Adelia herself had nearly lost her life, but the case had been resolved, justice imposed, and the king's taxes restored to his treasury.

In fact, so useful had been Adelia's forensic skill in the matter that King Henry had refused to let her return to Italy in case he should need her again. A miserly and greedy ingratitude typical of kings, Prior Geoffrey thought, even while he rejoiced that it had made the woman his neighbor.

How much does she resent this exile? It wasn't as if she'd been rewarded. The king had done nothing — well, he'd been abroad — when Cambridge's doctors, jealous of a successful interloper, had driven her and Mansur out of town and into the wilderness of the fens.

Sick and suffering men and women had followed them, and still did, not caring if treatment was at the hands of foreign unbelievers but only that it made them well.

Lord, I fear for her. Her enemies will damn her for it. Use her illegitimate child as proof that she is immoral, take her before the Archdeaconal Court to condemn her as a sinner. And what can I do?

Prior Geoffrey groaned at his own guilt. *What friend have I been to her? Or to her Arab? Or Gyltha?*

Until he had himself teetered on the edge of death and been dragged back by Adelia, he had followed the Church's teaching on science that only the soul mattered, not the body. Physical pain? It is God's purpose, put up with it. Investigation? Dissection? Experiments? *Sic vos ardebitis in Gehenna.* So will ye burn in hell.

But Adelia's ethos was Salerno's, where Arab, Jewish, and even Christian minds refused to set barriers on their search for knowledge. She had lectured him: "How can it be God's purpose to watch a man drowning when to stretch out one's hand would save him? *You* were drowning in your own urine. Was I to fold my arms rather than relieve the bladder? No, I knew how to do it and I did it. And I knew because I had studied the offending gland in men who'd died from it."

An oddly prim little thing she'd been then, unsophisticated, curiously nunlike except for her almost savage honesty, her intelligence, and her hatred of superstition. She had at least gained something from her time in England, he thought — more womanliness, a softening, and, of course, the baby — the result of a love affair as passionate and as unsuitable as that of Héloïse and Abelard.

Prior Geoffrey sighed and waited for her to ask why, busy and important man that he was, he had sailed forth to look for her.

The advent of winter had stripped the fens of leaves, allowing the sun unusual access to the river so that its water reflected back exactly the wild shapes of naked willow and alder along the banks. Adelia, voluble with relief and triumph, pointed out the names of the birds flying up from under the barge's prow to the stolid baby on her lap, repeating their names in English, Latin, and French, and appealing to Mansur across the water when she forgot the Arabic.

How old is my godchild now? the prior wondered, amused. *Eight months? Nine?* "Somewhat early to be a polyglot," he said.

"You can't start too soon."

She looked up at last. "Where are we going? I presume you did not come so far on the chance of baptizing a baby."

"A privilege, *medica,*" Prior Geoffrey said. "I was taken back to a blessed stable in Bethlehem. But no, I did not come for that. This messenger" — he beckoned forward a figure that had been standing, cloaked and transfixed, at the barge prow — "arrived for you at the priory with a summons, and since he would have had difficulty finding you in these waters, I volunteered to bring him."

Anyway, he'd known he must be at hand when the summons was delivered; she wouldn't want to obey it.

"Dang bugger," Adelia said in pure East Anglian — like Mansur's, her English vocabulary was being enlarged by Gyltha. *"What?"*

The messenger was a skinny young fellow, and Adelia's glare almost teetered him backward. Also, he was looking, open-mouthed, to the prior for confirmation. "This *is* the lady Adelia, my lord?" It was, after all, a name that suggested nobility; he'd expected dignity — beauty, even — the sweep of a skirt on marble, not this dowdy thing with a dog and a baby.

Prior Geoffrey smiled. "The lady Adelia, indeed."

Oh, well. The young man bowed, flinging back a cloak to show the arms embroidered on his tabard, two harts rampant and a golden saltire. "From my most reverend master, the lord Bishop of Saint Albans."

A scroll was extended.

Adelia didn't take it. The animation had leeched out of her. "What does *he* want?" It was said with a frigidity the messenger was unused to. He looked helplessly at the prior.

Prior Geoffrey intervened; he had received a similar scroll. Still using Latin, he said, "It appears that our lord bishop needs your expertise, Adelia. He's summoned you to

Cambridge — something about an attempted murder in Oxfordshire. I gather it is a matter heavy with political implications."

The messenger went on proffering his scroll; Adelia went on not taking it. She appealed to her friend. "I'm not going, Geoffrey. I don't want to go."

"I know, my dear, but it is why I have come. I'm afraid you must."

"I don't want to see him. I'm happy here. Gyltha, Mansur, Ulf, and this one . . ." She dandled the child at him. "I like the fens, I like the people. Don't make me go."

The plea lacerated him, but he hardened his heart. "My dear, I have no choice. Our lord bishop sends to say that it is a matter of the king's business. The *king's.* Therefore, you have no choice, either. You are the king's secret weapon."

Two

Cambridge hadn't expected to see its bishop again so soon. Eighteen months ago, after his appointment to the see of Saint Albans, the town had turned out for him with all the pomp due a man whose word ranked only a little below that of God, the Pope, and the Archbishop of Canterbury.

With equal pomp, it had seen him off on an inaugural circuit of his diocese that, because it was huge, like all England's sees, would take him more than two years to complete.

Yet here he was, before his time, without the lumbering baggage train that had accompanied him when he left, and with gallopers coming only a few hours ahead to warn of his arrival.

Still, Cambridge turned out for him. In strength. Some people fell on their knees or held up their children to receive the great man's blessing; others ran at his stirrup, babbling their grievances for him to mend. Most just enjoyed the spectacle.

A popular man, Bishop Rowley Picot. One of Cambridge's own. Been on Crusade. A king's appointee to the bishopric, too, not the Pope's. Which was good, King Henry II being nearer and more immediately powerful than the Vatican.

Not one of your dry-as-a-stick bishops, either: known to have a taste for hunting, grub, and his drink, with an eye for the ladies, so they said, but given all that up since God tapped him on the shoulder. And hadn't he brought to justice the child murderers who'd terrorized the town a while back?

Mansur and Adelia, followed disconsolately by the bishop's messenger, had insisted on scouring Cambridge's fair for Gyltha, and now, having found her, Mansur was holding her up so that she could peer over the heads of the crowd to watch the bishop go by. "Dressed like a Christmas beef, bless him," Gyltha reported down to Adelia. "Ain't you going to let little un look?"

"No," Adelia said, pressing her child more closely to her.

"Got a crosier and ever'thing," Gyltha persisted. "Not sure that hat suits un,

40

though."

In her mind's eye, Adelia saw a portly, portentous, mitered figure representing, as most bishops did, the hypocrisy and suffocation of a church that opposed not only herself but every advance necessary for the mental and physical health of mankind.

There was a touch on her shoulder. "If you would follow me, mistress. His lordship is to grant you an audience in his house, but first he must receive the sheriff and celebrate Mass."

"Grant us a audience," Gyltha mimicked as Mansur lowered her to the ground. "That's rich, that is."

"Um." The bishop's messenger — his name had turned out to be Jacques — was still off-balance; Saracens and fishwives were not the sort of people he was in service to deal with. Somewhat desperately, he said, "Mistress, I believe my lord expects his interview to be with you only."

"This lady and gentleman come with me," Adelia told him, "or I don't go."

Being in Cambridge again was distressing her. The worst moments of her life, and the best, had passed in this town; the place was haunted by spirits whose bones rested in peace while others still shrieked to a god that hadn't heard them.

"The dog, too," she added, and saw the poor messenger's eyes roll. She didn't care; it had been a concession to come at all. When she'd stopped off at her house on the way in order to pack suitable winter clothing for them all, she had gone so far as to wash her hair and change into her best dress, shabby though it now was. Further than that, she would not go.

The episcopal residence — the bishop had one in every major town in the diocese — was in Saint Mary's parish, a building now abuzz with servants preparing it for unexpected habitation.

Followed by the dog, Ward, the three were shown into a large upstairs chamber where dust sheets were now being whisked off heavy, ornate furniture. An open door at its far end revealed the gilt and plaster of a bedroom where footmen were hanging brocade drapes from the tester of a magnificent bed.

One of them saw Mansur looking in and crossed the room to shut the door in his face. Ward lifted his leg and piddled against the door's carved arch.

"Tha's a good dog," Gyltha said.

Adelia hefted the rush basket holding her sleeping baby onto a brassbound chest, fetched a stool, undid her bodice laces, and began the feed. *What a remarkable child,* she thought, gazing down at it, accustomed to the quiet of the fens yet showing no fear, only interest, amid the hubbub that had been Cambridge today.

"Well," Gyltha said to her. The two women hadn't had a moment until now in which to talk privately.

"Exactly."

"What's his lordship want with you, then?"

Adelia shrugged. "To look into an attempted murder in Oxfordshire, so Prior Geoffrey said."

"Didn't think you'd come for that."

"I wouldn't have, but it's on the king's orders, apparently."

"Oh, bugger," Gyltha said.

"Indeed." Henry Plantagenet's was the ultimate command; you could squirm under it, but you disobeyed it at your peril.

There were times when Adelia resented Henry II bitterly for marooning her on the island of Britain so that, having discovered her talents at reading the secrets of the dead, he could use them again. There were other times when she didn't.

Letters had originally passed between the English king and his royal kinsman, William of Sicily, requesting help for the problem in Cambridge that only Salerno's investigative tradition could provide. It had been a shock to everybody that Salerno obliged by sending a mistress of the art of death rather than a master, but things had turned out well — for Henry II, at least. So much so that other letters had passed between him and King William requesting — and granting — that Adelia stay where she was awhile longer.

It had been done without her request or permission, an act of naked piracy, typical of the man. "I'm not an object," she'd shouted at him. "You can't borrow me, I'm a human being."

"And I'm a king," Henry told her. "If I say you stay, you stay."

Damn him, he hadn't even *paid* her for all she'd done, for the danger, for the loss of beloved friends — to the end of her days, she would mourn for Simon of Naples, that wise and gentle man whose companionship had been like a second father's. And her dog, a much lesser loss but, nevertheless, a grief.

On the other hand, to weight the scale, she had retained her dear Mansur, gained an affection for England and its people, been awarded the friendship of Prior Geoffrey, Gyltha and her grandson, *and,* best of all, acquired her baby.

Also, although the Plantagenet was a

crafty, hot-tempered, parsimonious swine, he was still a great king, a *very* great king, and not just because he ruled an empire of countries stretching from the borders of Scotland to the Pyrenees. The quarrel between him and his Archbishop of Canterbury, Thomas à Becket, would damn him forever, ending as it had in the archbishop's murder. But Henry'd had the right of it, in Adelia's opinion, and it had been disastrous for the world that the Jew-hating, self-aggrandizing, backward-looking Becket's refusal to allow any reform of the equally backward-looking English Church had driven his king into uttering the dreadful cry *"Who will rid me of this turbulent priest?"* For immediately it had been taken up by some of his knights with their own reasons for wanting Becket dead. They'd slipped away across the Channel to Canterbury and committed a deed that had resulted in making a martyred saint out of a brave but stupid and blinkered man while, at the same time, giving the Church every excuse to scourge a king who'd wanted to curb its power and allow greater justice to his people with laws more fair, more humane than any in the world.

Yes, they called Henry Plantagenet a fiend, and there were times when Adelia thought he probably was, but she also knew that his ferocious blue eyes saw further into the future than any other man's. He'd succeeded to the throne of an England blasted and impoverished by civil war and given it a secure prosperity that was the envy of other lands.

It was said his wife and his sons resented and had plotted against him and, again, Adelia could see why — he was so far ahead of everybody else, so quick, that their relationship with him could provide no more than metaphorically clinging to his stirrup as he rode.

Yet when the Church would have put Adelia on trial during her search for the murderer of Cambridge's children, it was this busy king who'd found time to step in and exonerate her.

Well, so he should, she thought. *Wasn't I saving him trouble and money? I'm not his subject, I am a Sicilian; he has no right to coerce me into his service.*

Which would have been an unquestionably reasonable sentiment if, sometimes, Adelia didn't feel that to be in the service of Henry II of England was a privilege.

Nevertheless, she damned his eyes for him and, for the sake of her child's digestion, tried to clear him from her mind. Trouble was, the vast room around her reflected a Church that made her angrier than Henry ever could. Here was nothing that was not rigidly and opulently religious — the bishop's massive chair, a cushioned, gold-inlaid prie-dieu where his lordship could kneel in comfort to the Christ, who'd died in poverty, air stuffy with incense. Urging herself to despise it, Adelia contrasted it with Prior Geoffrey's room at the priory, which was all the holier for its reminders of the profane — fishing rods in a corner, the smell of good food, an exquisite little bronze Aphrodite brought back from Rome, the framed letter from a pupil he was proud of.

She finished feeding. Gyltha took the child from her to burp it, an occupation both women vied for — there was no more satisfying sound than that tiny belch. Because the newly lit brazier had not yet begun to warm the room, Gyltha added another blanket to the basket before she put it in the shadows to let the baby sleep. Then she went to stand by the brazier and looked around with complacence. "Murder, eh? Old team and old days back again."

"*Attempted* murder," Adelia reminded her. "And no, they aren't."

"Do make a change to go travelin', though," Gyltha said. "Better'n a winter iced into they bloody fens."

"You love winter in the fens. So do I."
Adelia had learned to skate.

"Don't mean as I can't enjoy somewheres
else." Old as she was, Gyltha had an adventurous spirit. She gave a rub to her backside
and nodded toward the basket. "What's his
lordship going say to our little treasure,
then?"

"I can only hope," Adelia said, "that he
won't ask whose it is."

Gyltha blinked. "Ooh, that's nasty. He's
not a'goin' to do that, 'course he not a'goin'
to do that. What's set your maggots bitin'?"

"I don't want us to be here, Gyltha.
Bishops, kings, they've got no right to ask
anything of me. I won't do it."

"You got any choice, girl?"

There was a step on the landing outside.
Adelia gritted her teeth, but it was a small
priest who came in. He carried the holder
of a lit candle in one hand and a slate book
in the other, raising the light high and making a slow arc with it, peering at each face
with shortsighted eyes.

"I am Father Paton, his lordship's secretary," he said. "And you are . . . yes, yes." To
make sure, he put his book on a table,
opened it, and held the candle near. "An
Arab male and two females, yes." He looked

48

up. "You will be provided with transport, service, and provisions to Oxford and back, a winter cloak each, firing, plus a rate of a shilling a day each until such time as his lordship is satisfied the work be done. You will have no expectation beyond that."

He peered at his slate once more. "Ah, yes, his lordship has been informed of a baby and expressed his willingness to give it his blessing." He waited for appreciation. Getting none, he said, "It can be conveyed to him. Is it here?"

Gyltha moved to stand between him and the basket.

The priest didn't see his danger; instead, he looked once more at his slate and, unused to dealing with women, addressed Mansur. "It says here you are some sort of doctor?"

Again, there was no reply. Apart from the priest, the room was very still.

"These are your instructions. To discover the culprit whom, three days ago" — he checked the date — "yes, it was the celebration of Saint Leocadia . . . three days ago, made an attempt on the life of the woman Rosamund Clifford of Wormhold Tower near Oxford. You will require the help of the nuns of Godstow in this endeavor." He tapped the slate with a bony finger. "It must

49

be pointed out that, should the aforesaid nuns offer you free accommodation at the convent, your payment shall be reduced accordingly."

He peered at them, then returned to the main thrust. "Any information is to be sent to his lordship immediately as it is gained — a messenger to be provided for the purpose — and you will tell no one else of your findings, which must be unearthed with discretion."

He scanned his book for more detail, found none, and clapped it shut. "Horses and a conveyance will be at the door within an hour, and food is being prepared in the meantime. To be provided without charge." His nose twitched at his generosity.

Was that all? No, one more thing. "I imagine the baby will prove a hindrance to the investigation; therefore, I have commissioned a nurse to look after it in your absence." He seemed proud to have thought of it. "I am informed the going rate is a penny a day, which will be deducted . . . Ow, *ow,* put me down."

Dangling by the back of his surplice from Mansur's hand, he had the appearance of a surprised kitten.

He's very young, Adelia thought, *although he will look the same at forty. I would be sorry for him if he didn't frighten me so much; he'd have taken my baby away without a thought.*

Gyltha was informing the struggling kitten. "You see, lad," she said, bending to put her face close, "we come to see Bishop Rowley."

"No, no, that is impossible. His lordship departs for Normandy tomorrow and has much to do before then." Somehow, horizontally, the little priest achieved dignity. "I attend to his affairs. . . ."

But the door had opened and a procession was entering in a blaze of candles, bearing at its center a figure from an illuminated manuscript, majestic in purple and gold.

Gyltha's right, Adelia thought immediately, *the miter doesn't suit him.* Then she took in the set of jowls, the dulled eyes, so changed from the man she remembered.

No, we're wrong: It does.

His lordship assessed the situation. "Put him down, Mansur," he said in Arabic.

Mansur opened his hand.

Both pages carrying his lordship's train leaned out sideways to peer at the ragbag of people who had floored Father Paton. A white-haired functionary began hammering on the tiles with his wand of office.

Only the bishop appeared unmoved. "All right, steward," he said. "Good evening,

51

Mistress Adelia. Good evening, Gyltha, you look well."

"So do you, bor."

"How's Ulf?"

"At school. Prior says as he's doing grand."

The steward blinked; this was lèse-majesté. He watched his bishop turn to the Arab. "Dr. Mansur, *as-salaam alaykum.*"

"Wa alaykum as-salaam."

This was worse. "My lord . . ."

"Supper will be served up here as quickly as may be, steward, we are short of time."

We, thought Adelia. The episcopal "we."

"Your vestments, my lord . . . Shall I fetch your dresser?"

"Paton will divest me." The bishop sniffed, searching for the source of a smell. He found it and added, "Also, bring a bone for the dog."

"Yes, my lord." Pitiably, the steward wafted the other servants from the room.

The bishop processed to the bedroom, the secretary following and explaining what he had done, what *they* had done. "I cannot understand the antagonism, my lord, I merely made arrangements based on the information supplied to me from Oxford."

Bishop Rowley's voice: "Which seem to

have become somewhat garbled on the journey."

"Yet I obeyed them as best I could, to the letter, my lord. . . . I cannot understand. . . ." Outpourings of a man misjudged came to them through the open door as, at the same time, Father Paton divested his master of cope, dalmatic, rochet, pallium, gloves, and miter, layer after layer of embroidered trappings that had employed many needle-women for many years, all lifted off and folded with infinite care. It took time.

"Rosamund Clifford?" Mansur asked Gyltha.

"You know her, you heathen. Fair Rosa-mund as they sing about — the king's pet fancy. Lots of songs about Fair Rosamund."

That Rosamund. Adelia remembered hear-ing the ha'penny minstrels on market days, and their songs — some romantic, most of them bawdy.

If he's dragged me here to involve me in the circumstances of a loose woman . . .

Then she reminded herself that she, too, must now be numbered among the world's loose women.

"So she've near been murdered, has she?" Gyltha said, happily. "Per'aps Queen Eleanor done it. Tried to get her out of the way, like. Green jealous of Rosamund,

Eleanor is."

"The songs say that as well, do they?" Adelia asked.

"That they do." Gyltha considered. "No, now I think on't, can't be the queen as done it; last I heard, the king had her in prison."

The mighty and their activities were another country, *in* another country. By the time reports of what they were up to reached the fens, they had achieved the romance and remoteness of myth, nothing to do with real people, and *less* than nothing compared to a river flooding or cows dead from the murrain or, in Adelia's case, the birth of a baby.

Once, it had been different. During the war of Stephen and Matilda, news of their comings and goings was vital, so you could know in advance — and hopefully escape — whichever king's, queen's, or baron's army was likely to come trampling your crops. Since much of the trampling had taken place in the fens, Gyltha had then been as aware of politics as any.

But out of that terrible time had emerged a Plantagenet ruler like a king from a fairy tale, establishing peace, law, and prosperity in England. If there *were* wars, they took place abroad, blessed be the Mother of God.

The wife Henry brought with him to the

throne had also stepped out of a fairy tale — a highly colored one. Here was no shy virgin princess; Eleanor was the greatest heiress in Europe, a radiant personality who'd ruled her Duchy of Aquitaine in her own right before wedding the meek and pious King Louis of France — a man who'd bored her so much that the marriage had ended in divorce. At which point nineteen-year-old Henry Plantagenet had stepped forward to woo the beautiful thirty-year-old Eleanor and marry her, thus taking over her vast estates and making himself ruler of a greater area of France than that belonging to its resentful King Louis.

The stories about Eleanor were legion and scandalous: She'd accompanied Louis on crusade with a bare-breasted company of Amazons; she'd slept with her uncle Raymond, Prince of Antioch; she'd done this, done that. . . .

But if her new English subjects expected to be entertained by more naughty exploits, they were disappointed. For the next decade or so, Eleanor faded quietly into the background, doing her queenly and wifely duty by providing Henry with five sons and three daughters.

As was expected of a healthy king, Henry had other children by other women — what ruler did not? — but Eleanor seemed to take them in her stride, even having young Geoffrey, one of her husband's bastards by a prostitute, brought up with the legitimate children in the royal court.

A happy marriage, then, as marriages went.

Until . . .

What had caused the rift in the lute? The advent of Rosamund, young, lovely, the highest-born of Henry's women? His affair with her became legendary, a matter for song; he adored her, called her *Rosa Mundi,* Rose of all the World, had tucked her away in a tower near his hunting lodge at Woodstock and enclosed it in a labyrinth so that nobody else should find the way through. . . .

Poor Eleanor was in her fifties now, unable to bear any more children. Had menopausal jealousy caused her rage? Because rage there must certainly have been for her to goad her eldest son, Young Henry, into rebellion against his father. Queens had died for much less. In fact, it was a wonder her husband hadn't executed her instead of condemning her to a not uncomfortable imprisonment.

Well, delightful as it was to speculate on these things, they were all a long way away.

Whatever sins had led to Queen Eleanor's imprisonment, they had been committed in Aquitaine, or Anjou, or the Vexin, one of those foreign places over which the Plantagenet royal family also ruled. Most English people weren't sure in what manner the queen had offended; certainly Gyltha was not. She didn't care much. Neither did Adelia.

There was a sudden shout from the bedroom. "It's *here?* She's brought it *here?*" Now down to his tunic, a man who looked younger and thinner but still very large stood in the doorway, staring around him. He loped to the basket on the table. "My God," he said, "my God."

You dare, Adelia thought, *you* dare *ask whose it is.*

But the bishop was staring downward with the awe of Pharaoh's daughter glimpsing baby Moses in the reeds. "Is this him? My God, he looks just like me."

"She," Gyltha said. "*She* looks just like you."

How typical of church gossips, Adelia thought viciously, that they would be quick to tell him she'd had his baby without mentioning its sex.

"A daughter." Rowley scooped up the child and held her high. The baby blinked from sleep and then crowed with him. "Any fool can have a son," he said. "It takes a man to conceive a daughter."

That's *why I loved him.*

"Who's her daddy's little moppet, then," he was saying, "who's got eyes like cornflowers, so she has — yes, she has — just like her daddy's. And teeny-weeny toes. *Yumm, yumm, yumm.* Does she like that? Yes, she does."

Adelia was helplessly aware of Father Paton regarding the scene. She wanted to tell Rowley he was giving himself away; this delight was not episcopal. But presumably a secretary was privy to all his master's secrets — and it was too late now, anyway.

The bishop looked up. "Is she going to be bald? Or will this fuzz on her head grow? What's her name?"

"Allie," Gyltha said.

"Ali?"

"Almeisan." Adelia spoke for the first time, reluctantly. "Mansur named her. Almeisan is a star."

"An Arab name."

"Why not?" She was ready to attack. "Arabs taught the world astronomy. It's a beautiful name, it means the shining one."

"I'm not saying it isn't beautiful. It's just that I would have called her Ariadne."

"Well, you weren't there," Adelia said nastily.

Ariadne had been his private name for her. The two of them had met on the same road, and at the same time that she'd encountered Prior Geoffrey. Although they hadn't known it then, they were also on the same errand; Rowley Picot was ostensibly one of King Henry's tax collectors but privately had been clandestinely ordered by his royal master to find the beast that was killing Cambridgeshire's children and thereby damaging the royal revenue. Willy-nilly, the two of them had found themselves following clues together. Like Ariadne, she had led him to the beast's lair. Like Theseus, he had rescued her from it.

And then, like Theseus, abandoned her.

She knew she was being unfair; he'd asked, begged, her to marry him, but by this time he'd earned the king's approbation and was earmarked for an advancement that needed a wife devoted to him, their children, his estates — a conventional English chatelaine, not a woman who neither would nor could give up her duty to the living and dead.

What she couldn't forgive him for was doing what she'd told him to do: leave her, go away, forget, take up the king's offer of a rich bishopric.

God torment him, he might have *written.*

"Well," she said, "you've seen her, and now we are leaving."

"Are we?" This was Gyltha. "In't we going to stay for supper?"

"No." She had been looking for insult from the first and had found it. "If someone has attempted to harm this Rosamund Clifford, I am sorry for it, but it is nothing to do with me."

She crossed the room to take the baby from him. It brought them close so that she could smell the incense from the Mass he'd celebrated clinging to him, infecting their child with it. His eyes weren't Rowley's anymore, they were those of a bishop, very tired — he'd traveled hard from Oxford — and very grave.

"Not even if it means civil war?" he said.

The pork was sent back so that the smell of it should not offend Dr. Mansur's nose and dietary law, but there were lampreys and pike in aspic, four different kinds of duck, veal in blancmange, a crisp, golden polonaise of bread, a sufficiency for twenty and — whether it displeased Mohammedan nostrils or not — enough wine for twenty

60

more, served in beautiful cameo-cut glass bowls.

Once it had all been placed on the board, the servants were sent from the room. Father Paton was allowed to remain. From the straw under the table came the crunch of a dog with a bone.

"He *had* to imprison her," Rowley said of his king and Queen Eleanor. "She was encouraging the Young King to rebel against his father."

"Never understood that," Gyltha said, chewing a leg of duck. "Not why Henry had his boy crowned king along of him, I mean. Old King and Young King ruling at the same time. Bound to cause trouble."

"Henry'd just been very ill," Rowley told her. "He wanted to make sure of a peaceful succession if he died — he didn't want a recurrence of another Stephen and Matilda war."

Gyltha shuddered. "Nor we don't, neither."

It was a strange dinner. Bishop Rowley was being forced to put his case to a Cambridgeshire housekeeper and an Arab because the woman he needed to solve it would not look at him. Adelia sat silent and unresponsive, eating very little.

He's a different creature, there's nothing of

61

the man I knew. Damn him, how was it so easy for him to stop loving me?

The secretary, disregarded by everybody, ate like a man with hollow legs, though his eyes were always on his master, as if watching for further unepiscopal behavior.

The bishop explained the circumstances that had brought him hurrying from Oxford, part of his diocese, and tomorrow would take him to Normandy to search out the king and tell him, before anybody else did, that Rosamund Clifford, most beloved of all the royal mistresses, had been fed poisonous mushrooms.

"Mushrooms?" Gyltha asked. "Could've been mischance, then. Tricky things, mushrooms, you got to be careful."

"It was deliberate," the bishop said. "Believe me, Gyltha, this was not an accident. She became very ill. It was why they called me to Wormhold, to her sickbed; they didn't think she'd recover. Thanks to the mercy of Christ, she did, but the king will wish to know the identity of the poisoner, and I want, I *have*, to assure him that his favorite investigator is looking into the matter. . . ." He remembered to bow to Mansur, who bowed back. "Along with his assistant." A bow to Adelia.

She was relieved that he was maintaining

the fiction in front of Father Paton that it was Mansur who possessed the necessary skills for such an investigation — not her. He had betrayed himself to a charge of immorality by saying that Allie was his, but he was protecting her from the much more serious charge of witchcraft.

Gyltha, enjoying her role as interrogator, said, "Can't've been the queen sent her them mushrooms, can it? Her being in chains and all?"

"I wish she *had* been in bloody chains." Rowley was Rowley again for a moment, furious and making his secretary blink. "The blasted woman escaped. Two weeks ago."

"Deary dear," Gyltha said.

"Deary dear indeed, and was last seen heading for England, which, in everybody's opinion bar mine, would give her time to poison a dozen of Henry's whores."

He leaned across the table to Adelia, sweeping a space between them, spilling his wine bowl and hers. "*You* know him, you know his temper. *You've* seen him out of control. He loves Rosamund, truly loves her. Suppose he shouts for Eleanor's death like he shouted for Becket's? He won't mean it, but there's always some bastard with a reason to respond who'll say he's doing it

63

on the king's orders, like they did with Becket. And if their mother's executed, *all* the boys will rise up against their father like a tide of shit."

He sat back in his chair. "Civil war? It'll be here, everywhere. Stephen and Matilda will be nothing to it."

Mansur put his hand protectively on Gyltha's shoulder. The silence was turbulent, as if from noiseless battle and dumbed shrieks of the dying. The ghost of a murdered archbishop rose up from the stones of Canterbury and stalked the room.

Father Paton was staring from face to face, puzzled that his bishop should be addressing the doctor's assistant with such vehemence, and not the doctor.

"Did she do it?" Adelia asked at last.

"No." Rowley wiped some grease off his sleeve with a napkin, and replenished his bowl.

"Are you sure?"

"Not Eleanor. I know her."

Does he? Undoubtedly, there was tender regard between queen and bishop; when Eleanor and Henry's firstborn son had died at the age of three, Eleanor had wanted the child's sword taken to Jerusalem so that, in death, little William might be regarded as a holy crusader. It was Rowley who'd made

64

the terrible journey and lain the tiny sword on the high altar — so *of course* Eleanor looked on Rowley kindly.

But like everything else in royal matters, it was King Henry who'd arranged it, Henry who'd given Rowley his orders, Henry who'd received the intelligence of what was going on in the Holy Land that Rowley'd brought back with him. Oh, yes, Rowley Picot had been more the king's agent than the queen's sword carrier.

But still claiming special knowledge of Eleanor's character, the bishop added, "Face-to-face, she'd tear Rosamund's throat out . . . but not poison. It's not her style."

Adelia nodded. She said in Arabic, "I still don't see what you want of me. I am a doctor to the dead. . . ."

"You have a logical mind," the bishop said, also in Arabic. "You see things others don't. Who saved the Jews from the accusation of child murder last year? Who found the true killer?"

"I had assistance." That good little man Simon of Naples, the *real* investigator who had come with her from Salerno for the purpose and had died for it.

Mansur, unusual for him, struck in, indicating Adelia. "She must not be put in such danger again. The will of Allah and only the will of Allah saved her from the pit last time."

Adelia smiled fondly at him. Let him attribute it to Allah if he liked. Actually, she had survived the child killer's lair only because a dog had led Rowley to it in time. What neither he, nor God, nor Allah *had* saved her from were memories of a nightmare that still reenacted themselves in her daily life as sharply as if they were happening all over again — often, this time, to young Allie.

"Of course she won't be in danger again," the bishop told Mansur with energy. "This case is completely different. There's been no murder here, only a clumsy attempt at one. Whoever tried to do it is long gone. But don't you see?" Another bowl tipped as he thumped the board. "*Don't you see? Everybody* will believe Eleanor to be the poisoner; she hates Rosamund *and* she was possibly in the neighborhood. Wasn't that Gyltha's immediate conclusion? Won't it be the world's?" He took his eyes away from Mansur and to the woman opposite him. "In the name of God, Adelia, *help me.*"

With a jerk of her chin toward the door, Gyltha nudged Mansur, who nodded, rose, and took an unwilling Father Paton by the scruff of his neck.

The two who remained seated at the table didn't notice their going. The bishop's gaze was on Adelia; hers on her clasped hands.

Stop resenting him, she was thinking. *It wasn't abandonment; mine was the refusal to marry, only mine the insistence we shouldn't meet again. It is illogical to blame him for keeping to the agreement.*

Damn him, though, there should have been something *all these months — at least an acknowledgment of the baby.*

"How are you and God getting along?" she asked.

"I serve Him, I hope." She heard amusement in his voice.

"Good works?"

"When I can."

She thought, *And we both know, don't we, that you would sacrifice God and His works, me and your daughter, all of us, if doing so would serve Henry Plantagenet.*

He said quietly, "I apologize for this, Adelia. I would not have broken our agreement not to meet again for anything less."

She said, "If Eleanor *is* proved guilty, I won't lie. I shall say so."

"Ya-*hah.*" Now *that* was Rowley, the energy, the shout that shivered the wine in its jug — here, for an instant, was her joyous lover back again.

"Couldn't resist, could you? Are you taking the baby with you? Yes, of course, you'll still be breast-feeding — damned odd to think of you as lactating stock."

He was up and had opened the door, calling for Paton. "There's a basket of mushrooms in my pack. Find it and bring it here." He turned to Adelia, grinning. "Thought you'd want to see some evidence."

"You devil," she said.

"Maybe, but this devil will save its king and its country or die trying."

"Or kill me in the process." *Stop it,* she thought, *stop sounding like a wronged woman; it was your decision.*

He shrugged. "You'll be safe enough, nobody's out to poison *you.* You'll have Gyltha and Mansur — God help anyone who touches you while they're around — and I'm sending servants along. I presume that canine eyesore goes, too?"

"Yes," she said. "His name's Ward."

"One more of the prior's finds to keep you safe? I remember Safeguard."

Another creature that had died saving her life. The room was full of memories that hurt — and with the dangerous value of being shared.

"Paton is *my* watchdog," he said conversationally. "He guards my virtue like a bloody chastity belt. Incidentally, wait until you see Fair Rosamund's labyrinth — biggest in Christendom. Mind you, wait til you see Fair Rosamund herself, she's not what you'd expect. In fact —"

She interrupted. "Is it at risk?"

"The labyrinth?"

"Your virtue."

All at once, he was being kind. "Oddly enough, it isn't. I thought when you turned me down . . . but God was kind and tempered the wind to the shorn lamb."

"And when Henry needed a compliant bishop." *Stop it, stop it.*

"And the world needed a doctor, not another wife," he said, still kind. "I see that now; I have prayed to see it; marriage would have wasted you."

Yes, yes. If she had agreed to marriage, he'd have refused the bishopric the king had urged on him for political expediency, but for her, there had been the higher priority of her calling. She'd have had to abandon it — he'd demanded a wife, not a doctor, especially not a doctor to the dead.

In the end, she thought, *neither of us would bestow the ultimate, sacrificial gift on the other.*

He got up and went to the baby, making

the sign of the cross on her forehead with his thumb. "Bless you, my daughter." He turned back. "Bless you, too, mistress," he said. "God keep you both safe, and may the peace of Jesus Christ prevail over the Horsemen of the Apocalypse." He sighed. "For I can hear the sound of their hooves."

Father Paton came in carrying a basket and gave it to his lordship, who then gestured for him to leave.

Adelia was still staring at Rowley. Among all this room's superfluity of wealth, the turmoil she'd experienced in it as shades of the past came and went, one thing that should belong to it — its very purpose — had been missing; she had just caught its scent, clear and cold: sanctity, the last attribute she'd expected to find in him. Her lover had become a man of God.

He took the chair beside her to give her details of the attempt on Rosamund's life, putting the basket in front of her so that she could examine its contents. In the old days, he couldn't have sat beside her without touching her; now it was like sitting next to a hermit.

Rosamund loved stewed mushrooms, he told her; it was well known. A lazy servant, out gathering them for her mistress, had been handed some by an old, unidentified woman, a crone, and had taken them back without bothering to pick more.

"Rosamund didn't eat them all, some had been kept for later, and while I was with her I took the remainder to bring with me. I thought you might be able to identify the area they came from or something — you know about mushrooms, don't you?"

Yes, she knew about mushrooms. Obediently, Adelia began turning them over with her knife while he talked.

It was a fine collection, though withering now: boletes that the English called Slippery Jack, winter oysters, cauliflower, blewits, hedgehogs. All very tasty but extraordinarily, *most* extraordinarily, varied; some of these species grew exclusively on chalk, some under pine trees, others in fields, others in broadleaf woodland.

Deliberately or not, whoever gathered these had spread the net wide and avoided picking a basketful that could be said to come from a specific location.

"As I say, it was quite deliberate," the bishop was saying. "The crone, whoever she was, made a point of it — they were for the Lady Rosamund, nobody else. Whoever that crone was, she hasn't been seen since. Disappeared. Slipped in a couple of malignant ones, do you see, hoping they'd poison the

71

poor woman, and it's only through the mercy of God . . ."

"She's dead, Rowley," Adelia said.

"What?"

"If these fungi duplicate what Rosamund ate, she's dead."

"No, I told you, she recovered. Much better when I left her."

"I know." Adelia was suddenly so sorry for him; if she could have changed what she was going to say, she would have. "But it's what happens, I'm afraid." She speared the killer with her knife and lifted it. "It's a feature of this one that those who eat it apparently get better for a while."

Innocuous-looking, white-gilled, its cap now aged into an ordinary brown but still retaining a not unpleasant smell. "It's called the Death Cap. It grows everywhere; I've seen it in Italy, Sicily, France, here in England; I've seen its effect, I've worked on the corpses who ate it — too many of them. It is always, *always* fatal."

"No," he said. "It can't be."

"I'm sorry, I'm so *sorry,* but if she ate one of these, even a tiny bite . . ." He had to know. "Sickness and diarrhea at first, abdominal pain, and then a day or two when she'd seem to be recovering. But all the while the poison was attacking her liver and kidneys. There's absolutely no cure. Rowley, I'm afraid she's gone."

THREE

No question now of the bishop crossing from England to Normandy in order to calm a turbulent king. The king's beloved was dead, and the king would be coming to England himself, riding the air like a demon to ravage and burn — maybe, in his rage, to kill his own wife if he could find her.

So, at dawn, the bishop rode, too, another demon loose on the world, to be ahead of the king, to find the queen and get her away, to be on the spot, to locate the real culprit, to be able to say: "My lord, hold your hand; *this* is Rosamund's killer."

To avoid Armageddon.

With the bishop went those for his purpose, a pitiful few compared to his lordship's usual train: two men-at-arms, a groom, a secretary, a messenger, a carriage, horses, and remounts. Also an Arab doctor, a dog, two women, and a baby — and to hell if they couldn't keep up.

They kept up. Just. Their carriage, Father Paton's "conveyance," was splendidly carved, enclosed against the weather by purple waxed cloth with matching cushions among the straw inside, but it was not intended for speed. After three hours of it, Gyltha said that if she stayed in the bugger much longer she'd lose her teeth from rattling, and the poor baby its brains.

So they transferred to horses, young Allie being placed and padded into a pannier like a grub in a cocoon; Ward, the dog, was stuffed less gently into the other. The change was made quickly to stay up with the bishop, who wouldn't wait for them.

Jacques the messenger was sent ahead to prepare the bishop's palace at Saint Albans for their brief stay overnight and, then, next day, to the Barleycorn at Aylesbury for another.

It was cold, becoming colder the farther west they went, as if Henry Plantagenet's icy breath were on their neck and getting closer.

They didn't reach the Barleycorn, because that was the day it began to snow, and they left the roads for the Icknield Way escarpment, where avenues of trees and the chalk under their horses' hooves made the going easier and therefore faster.

There were no inns on these high tracks, and the bishop refused to waste time by descending to find one. "We'll make camp," he said.

When, eventually, he allowed them to dismount, Adelia's muscles protested as she struggled to get off her horse. She looked with anxiety toward Gyltha, who was struggling off hers. "Are you surviving?" Tough as leather the fenwoman might be, but she was still a grandmother and entitled to better treatment than this.

"I got sores where I wou'n't like to say."

"So have I." And stinging as if from acid.

The only one looking worse than they did was Father Paton, whose large breakfast at Saint Albans had been jolting out of him, amidst groans, for most of the way. "Shouldn't have gobbled it," Gyltha told him.

Baby Allie, on the other hand, had taken no harm from the journey; indeed, snuggled in her pannier, she appeared to have enjoyed it, despite her hurried feeds when Bishop Rowley had permitted a stop to change horses.

Carrying her with them, the two women retired to the cart and ministered to their wounds with salves from Adelia's medicine chest. "The which I ain't letting Father Fus-

76

tilugs have any," Gyltha said vengefully of Father Paton. She'd taken against him.

"What about Mansur? He's not used to this, either."

"Great lummox . . ." Gyltha liked to hide her delight in and love for the Arab. "He'd not say a word if his arse was on fire."

Which was true; Mansur cultivated stoicism to the point of impassivity. His sale as a little boy to Byzantine monks who'd preserved the beauty of his treble singing voice by castration had taught him the futility of complaining. In all the years since he'd found sanctuary with Adelia's foster parents and become her bodyguard and friend, she'd never heard him utter a querulous sentence. Not that he uttered many words in strange company anyway; the English found him and his Arab dress outlandish enough without the addition of a child's squeaky speaking voice issuing from a man six feet tall with the face of an eagle.

Oswald and Aelwyn, the men-at-arms, and Walt, the groom, were uneasy in their dealings with him, apparently crediting him with occult powers. It was Adelia they treated like dirt — though never if Rowley was looking. At first she'd put their discourtesies down to the rigors of the journey, but gradually they became too marked to be disregarded. Unless the bishop or Mansur was nearby, she was never assisted onto a horse nor down, and the occasions when she went off into the trees to answer a call of nature were accompanied by low, offensive whistles. Once or twice she heard Ward yelp as if he'd been kicked.

Nor had she and Gyltha been provided with sidesaddles. Rowley had ordered them, but somehow, in the haste, they'd been forgotten, leaving the women perforce to ride astride, an unseemly posture for a lady though, actually, one that Adelia preferred because she considered sidesaddles injurious to the spine.

Nevertheless, the omission had been uncivil and, she thought, intended.

To church servants like these, she was a harlot, of course; either the bishop's trull or the Saracen's, perhaps both. For them it was bad enough to be chasing across country in bad weather to attend the funeral of a king's mistress without dragging another whore along with them.

"What's she with us for?"

"God knows. Clever with her brains, so they say."

"Clever with her quim more like. Is that his lordship's bastard?"

"Could be anybody's."

The exchange had been made where she could overhear it.

Damn it, this would harm him. Rowley had been appointed by Henry II against the wishes of the Church, which had wanted its own man to fill the post of Saint Albans and still hoped for a reason to dismiss the king's candidate. Knowledge that he'd fathered an illegitimate child would give his enemies their chance.

Damn the Church, Adelia thought. *Our affair was over before he became a bishop. Damn it for imposing impossible celibacy on its people. Damn it for hypocrisy* — Christendom was littered with priests wallowing in varieties of sin. How many of *them* were condemned?

And damn it for its hatred of women — an abuse of half the world's inhabitants, so that those who refused to be penned into its sheepfold were condemned as harlots and heretics and witches.

Damn you, she thought of the bishop's men, *are you so innocent? Are all your children born in wedlock? Which of you jumped over the broomstick with a woman rather than legally marry her?*

And damn you, Bishop Rowley, for placing me in this situation.

Then, because she was feeding Allie, she

damned them all again for making her angry enough to damn them.

Father Paton escaped her curses; unlovable as he was, he at least treated her like he treated everybody else — as a sexless and unfortunate expense.

The messenger, Jacques, a gauche, large-eared, somewhat overeager young man, seemed more kindly inclined to her than the others, but the bishop kept him on the gallop with taking messages and preparing the way ahead, so she saw little of him.

With imperceptible difference, the Icknield Way became the Ridgeway. The cold was gaining an intensity that leeched strength out of humans and horses, but they were at least approaching the Thames and the Abbey of Godstow, which stood on one of its islands.

Jacques rejoined the company, appearing from the trees ahead like a mounted white bear. He shook himself free of snow as he bowed to Rowley. "Abbess Mother Edyve sends greetings to your lordship and her joy to accommodate you and your party whenever you will. Also, I was to say that she expects the body of the Lady Rosamund to be brought to the convent by river today."

Rowley said heavily, "So she is dead."

"I trust so, my lord, for the nuns intend to

bury her."

His bishop glared at him. "Go back there. Tell them we should arrive tonight and that I am bringing a Saracen doctor to examine Lady Rosamund's corpse and determine how she died." He turned to Adelia and said in Latin, "You'll want to see the body, won't you?"

"I suppose so." Though what it could tell her, she wasn't sure.

The messenger stopped long enough to stuff bread, cheese, and a flask of ale into his saddlebag before remounting.

"Shouldn't you rest first?" Adelia asked him.

"Don't mind for me, mistress. I sleep in the saddle."

She wished *she* could. To stay in it at all took strength. Father Paton's provision of cloaks had been of the cheapest wool and, wearing them, she, Gyltha, and Mansur would have frozen to death on horseback if it hadn't been for the rough mantles of beaver fur they had brought with them. The fenland was full of beaver, and these were gifts from a grateful trapper Adelia had nursed through pneumonia.

That afternoon the travelers descended from the hills to the village of Thame and the road leading to Oxford. It was getting dark, still snowing, but the bishop said, "Not far now. We'll press on with lanterns."

It was terrible going; the horses had to be rugged even though they were kept moving. Soon they had to be fitted with headbands that fringed their eyes, usually a device to keep off flies, so they would not be blinded by the thick flakes that swirled and stuck to the lashes.

It was impossible to see beyond a yard. If the road hadn't run between hedges, they would have lost their way, lanterns or no lanterns, and ended in a field or river. When the hedges disappeared at a crossroads, Rowley had to call a halt until they found the right track again, which meant the men had to search for it, all the time calling to each other in case any one of them blundered away — an error that, in this cold, would cost him his life.

For the baby's sake as well as their own, the women were forced to reenter the carriage and stay there. Father Paton had already done so, complaining that if he stayed in the cold he would lose the use of his secretarial writing hand.

They hooked one of the lanterns to the arch over their heads and began heaping straw to make a bed, tucking Allie between them to benefit from the heat of their bodies. The cold lanced in like needles through the eyelets where the canopy was tied to its struts, so icy that it nullified the smell of the straw and even of the dog at their feet.

They were going at walking pace — Mansur was leading the horses — but deep pits in the track concealed by snow caused the carriage to fall and tip with bone-jarring suddenness so that rest was impossible. In any case, anxiety for what the others were suffering outside precluded sleep.

Gyltha said admiringly of Rowley, "He ain't a'going to stop, is he?"

"No." This was a man who'd pursued a murderer across the deserts of Outremer. An English blizzard wasn't going to defeat him. Adelia said, "Have no concern for him: He's showing none for . . ." There was a lurch of the carriage, and she grabbed at a strut with her right hand and her baby with her left to stop them being thrown from one side to the other. The lantern swung through an arc of one hundred eighty degrees, and Gyltha lunged upward to snuff out its candle in case it set fire to the canopy.

". . . us," Adelia finished.

In the darkness and at an angle, they could hear Father Paton praying for deliverance while, outside, screeching Arabic curses rained on horses that refused to pull.

One or another was effective; after another grinding jerk, the carriage went on.

"You see," came Gyltha's voice, as if resuming a conversation, "Rowley, he remembers the war betwixt Matilda and Stephen. He's a youngster compared to me, but he was born into it, and his parents, they'd have lived through it, like I did. King Stephen, he died natural in his bed. And Queen Matilda, she's still going strong. But the war betwixt them . . . weren't so for us commoners. We died over and over. It was like . . . like we was all tossed in the air and stayed there with nothing to hold to. The law went, ever'thing went. My pa, he was dragged off his fields one day to build a castle for Hugh Bigod. Never came back. Took three years a'fore we heard he was crushed flat when a stone fell. We near starved without un."

Adelia heard the deep intake of breath, heavier than a sigh. Simple sentences, she thought, but what weight they carried.

Gyltha said, "We lost our Em an' all. Older than me she was, about eleven. Some mercenaries came through and Ma ran with my brothers and me to hide in the fen, but they caught Em. She was screaming when they galloped off with her, I can hear her now. Never did find out what happened, but

84

she was another as didn't come back."

It was a lecture. Adelia had heard Gyltha talk about the thirteen-year war before, but only in general terms, never like this; as witness to its chaos, the old woman was calling up specters that still gave her pain. Feudalism might be harsh for those at its bottom end, but it was at least a protection. Adelia, who had been brought up both protected and privileged, was being told what happened when order crumbled and civilization went with it.

"Nor it weren't no good praying to God. He weren't listening."

Men gave way to basest instincts, Gyltha said. Village lads, decent enough if controlled, saw those controls disappear and themselves became thieves and rapists. "Henry Plantagenet, now, he may be all sorts, but with him a'coming king it stopped, d'you see. It stopped; the ground was put back under us. The crops grew like they had, the sun come up of a morning and set of nights, like it should."

"I see," Adelia said.

"But you can't *know*, not really," Gyltha told her. "Rowley do. His ma and pa, they was commoners, and they lived through it like I did. He'll move mountains so's it don't happen again. He's seeing to it so's my Ulf, bless him, can go to school with a full belly as nobody'll slit open. Bit of traveling? Few snowflakes? What's that?"

"I've only been thinking of myself, haven't I?" Adelia said.

"And the baby," Gyltha said, reaching over to pat her. "And a fair bit of his lordship, I reckon. Me, I'll follow where he goes and happy to help."

She had raised their venture to a plane that left Adelia ashamed and exposed to her own resentment. Even now, she couldn't give credence to the reasoning that caused them to be doing what they were doing, but if the bishop, who did, was right and they could prevent civil war by it, then she, too, must be happy to give of her best.

And I am, she thought, grimacing. *Ulf is safe at school; Gyltha and Mansur and my child are with me. I am happy that Bishop Rowley is happy in a God who has taken away his lusts. Where else should I be?*

She shut her eyes and gave herself up to patient endurance.

Another great lurch woke her. They'd stopped. The canvas was lifted, letting in a draft of wicked cold and showing a face blue and bearded by ice. She recognized it as the messenger's; they had caught up with him. "Are we there?"

"Nearly, mistress." Jacques sounded excited. "His lordship asks, will you come out and look at this?"

It had stopped snowing. A moon shone from a sky full of stars onto a landscape almost as beautiful. The bishop and the rest of his entourage stood with Mansur in a group at the beginning of a narrow, humped stone bridge, its parapets perfectly outlined in snow. Loud water hidden by the drop on the left suggested a weir or millrace. To the right was the gleam of a smooth river. Trees stood like white sentinels.

As Adelia came up, Rowley pointed behind her. She looked back and saw some humped cottages. "That's the village of Wolvercote," he said. He turned her so that she was now facing across the bridge to where the stars were blanked out by a complexity of roofs. "Godstow Abbey." There was a suggestion of light coming from somewhere among its buildings, though any windows on this side were dark.

But it was what was in the middle of the bridge that she must look at. The first thing she saw was a saddled horse, not moving, head and reins drooping downward, one leg bent up. The groom, Walt, stood at its head, patting its neck. His voice came shrill and querulous through the stillness. "Who'da

87

done this? He's a good un, this un, who'da done it?" He was more concerned for the horse than for the dead man sprawled facedown in the snow beside it.

"Robbery and murder on the King's Highway," Rowley said quietly, his breath wreathing like smoke. "Plain coincidence and nothing to do with our purpose, but I suppose you'd better look, bodies being your business. Just be quick about it, that's all."

He'd kept everyone else back like she'd taught him; only the groom's footprints and his own showed going *to* the bridge in the snow, and only his returned. "I had to make sure the fellow was dead," he said. "Take Mansur with you for the look of it." He raised his voice. "The lord Mansur can read traces left on the ground. He speaks little English, so Mistress Adelia will interpret for him."

Adelia stayed where she was for a moment, Mansur beside her. "What time is it, do you know?" she asked in Arabic.

"Listen."

She unbound her head from its muffler. From the other side of the bridge, solitary, faraway, but clear over the rush of noisy water, came a sweet female voice raised in a monotone. It paused and was answered by the disciplined response of other voices.

She was hearing a chime of the liturgical clock, an antiphon. The nuns of Godstow had roused from their beds and were chanting Vigils.

It was four o'clock in the morning, near enough.

Mansur said, "Was not the galloper here earlier? He may have seen something."

"When were you here, Jacques? The doctor wants to know."

"In daylight, mistress. That poor soul wasn't lying there then." The young man was aggrieved and upset. "I delivered his lordship's message to the holy sisters and rode straight back across the bridge to rejoin you all. I was back with you before the moon came up, wasn't I, my lord?"

Rowley nodded.

"When did it stop snowing?" From what she could see of the body, there were only a few flakes on it.

"Three hours back."

"Stay here."

Mansur took up a lantern, and they went forward together to kneel by the body. "Allah, be good to him," Mansur said.

As her foster father had taught her, Adelia took a moment to pray to the spirit of the dead man who was now her client. "Permit your flesh and bone to tell me what your voice cannot."

He lay facedown, too neatly for someone who'd fallen off a horse, legs straight, arms splayed above the head, cloak and tunic down over his hams. His cap, like his clothes, was of good but slightly worn wool, and it lay a few inches away, the brave cockpheasant feather in it broken.

She nodded to Mansur. Gently, he raised the wavy brown hair from the neck to touch the skin. He shook his head. He'd attended on enough corpses with Adelia to know it would be impossible to estimate the time of death; the body was frozen — had begun to freeze the moment life left it, would stay frozen long enough to delay the natural processes.

"Hmm."

Expertly, acting together, they turned the corpse over. Two half-shut brown eyes regarded the sky with disinterest, and Mansur had to force the frozen lids down over them.

He was young: twenty, twenty-one, perhaps less. The heavy arrow in his chest came from a crossbow and had gone deep, probably being driven farther in by the fall that had broken its flights. Mansur held the lantern so that Adelia could examine the wound; there was blood around it but only a few smears on the snow occupying the space that the body had vacated when it was turned.

She guided Mansur's hand so that the lantern illuminated the corpse's neck. *"Hmmm."*

A scabbard with a sword still in it was attached to a belt with a tarnished buckle engraved with a crest. The same crest had been embroidered on a gaping, empty purse.

"Come along, Doctor. You can do all this when we take him to the nunnery." Rowley's voice.

"Be quiet," Adelia told him in Arabic. He'd hurried her all the way from Cambridge; now he could damn well wait. There was something wrong here; perhaps it was why Rowley had called for her to investigate it, some part of his mind noticing the anomalies even while part was intent on another murder altogether.

There was an anguished plea from Walt, the groom. "This here poor bugger's in pain, my lord. Naught to be done. 'S time he was finished."

"Doctor?"

"Wait, will you?" Irritably, she got up and

91

went over to where the horse and the groom stood, regarding the ground as she went. "What's the matter with it?"

"Hamstrung. Some godless swine cut his tendon." Walt pointed to a slash across the horse's leg just above the hock. "See? That's deliberate, that is."

The snow here was bloodied black and showed that the animal had thrashed around before managing to rise on its three uninjured legs.

"Can it be mended?" All she knew about horses was which end you faced.

"He's hamstrung." Answering stupid questions from a woman no better than she should be added to Walt's anger.

Adelia returned to Mansur. "The animal has to be dispatched."

"Not here," he said. "The carcass will block the bridge." And bridges were vital; not to repair them, or to render them unusable, was a hostile act causing such hardship to the local economy that the law came down heavily on those who committed it.

"What in *hell* are you two about?" Rowley had come up.

"There's something wrong here," Adelia told him.

"Yes, somebody robbed and killed this poor devil. I can see that. Let's load him up and get on."

"No, it's more than that."

"*What* is?"

"Give me time," she shouted at him, and then, realizing, "the doctor needs time."

The bishop blew out his cheeks. "Why did I bring her, Lord? Answer me that. Very well, let's at least see to his horse."

Adelia insisted on going first, slowly leading the way past Walt and the crippled animal and down the other side of the bridge, Mansur beside her holding the lantern so that light fell on the ground at each step.

Everything that was not white was black; boot marks, hoofprints, too jumbled to be distinguished from one another. There'd been a lot of activity where the bridge rejoined the road near the great gatehouse of the convent. A lot of blood.

Mansur pointed.

"Oh, well done, my dear," she said. Under the shadow of heavy oak branches lolling over the convent wall, clear prints led to others — writing a story for those who could read it. "*Hmm.* Interesting."

Behind her, the bishop and groom soothed the jerkily limping horse as they led it, discussing where it should be put down. Would the nuns want the carcass? Good eating on a horse. But butchery and skinning would be arduous in this weather; better to cut its throat among the trees where the convent wall bent into a forest. "They can get it later if they want it."

"Doubt there'll be much left by then, my lord." It wasn't only humans that appreciated the eating on a horse.

Walt relieved the animal of its tack. There was a roll attached to the saddle protected by oilcloth. "Oo-op now, my beauty, oo-op." Murmuring gentle equine things, he led it toward the trees.

"Could we hide the body there as well?" Adelia wanted to know.

"If we do, there will be not much left of that, either," Mansur said.

Rowley joined them. "Will you hurry *up,* you two. We'll all be bloody icicles in a minute."

Adelia, who had shivered from cold all the way from Cambridge, was no longer aware of it. "We don't want the body discovered, my lord."

The bishop tried for patience. "It *is* discovered, mistress. *We* discovered it."

"We don't want the killer to find it."

Rowley cleared his throat. "You mean, let's not tell him? He knows, Adelia. He shot a bolt into the lad's chest. He's not coming back to make sure."

"Yes, he is. You'd have seen it yourself if you hadn't been in such a rush." She nudged Mansur. "Look as if you're instructing."

With Rowley between them, Mansur speaking of their findings in Arabic, and Adelia, on the other side, appearing to translate, they told him the story of a killing as the marks in the snow had told it to them.

"We can't be sure of the time. *After* it stopped snowing is all we can guess. Anyway, late enough this night for nobody to be about. They waited for him here, near the gates."

"They?"

"Two men." Rowley was pulled into the shadow of the oak. Footprints were just visible in the snow. "See? One wears hobnails, the other's boots have bars across the soles, maybe clogs bound with strips. They arrived here on horseback and took their horses into those trees, where Walt has gone. They came back on foot and stood here. They ate as they waited." Adelia retrieved a crumb of something from the ground, and then another. "Cheese." She held them to the bishop's nose.

He recoiled. "As you say, mistress."

Vigils over, the convent was silent again.

From deeper in among the trees of the forest came Walt's prayer, "And the Lord have mercy on thy poor soul, if thee have one."

A long scream like a whistle, a heavy crash. Silence.

Walt emerged, simultaneously wiping his dagger on his cloak with one hand and his eyes with the other. "Goddamn, I hates a'doing that."

The bishop patted him on the shoulder and sent him to join the others on the far side of the bridge. To Adelia and Mansur, he said, "They knew he was coming, then?"

"Yes. They were waiting for him." Even the most desperate robber didn't loiter in the hope of a passerby in the early hours of a freezing night.

They must have thought themselves lucky that the blizzard had passed, she thought, not knowing they were imprinting their guilt in the resultant snow for Vesuvia Adelia Rachel Ortese Aguilar, *medica* of the renowned School of Medicine in Salerno, expert on death and the causes of death, to happen along and decipher it.

For which they were going to be sorry.

It had been a cold wait; they'd stamped their feet to keep warm. In her mind, Adelia waited with them, nibbling phantom cheese. Perhaps they had listened to the sound of

Compline being sung before the nuns retired to bed for the three hours until Vigils. Apart from that it would have been quiet except for an owl or two, perhaps, and the shriek of a vixen.

Here he comes, the rider. Up the road that leads from the river to the convent, his horse's hooves muffled by the earlier snow but still audible in the silence.

He's nearing the gates, slowing — does he mean to go in? But Villain Number One has stepped out in front of him, the crossbow cocked and straining. Does the rider see him? Shout out? Recognize the man? Probably not; the shadows are dark here. Anyway, the bolt has been loosed and is already deep in his chest.

The horse rears, sending its rider backward and tumbling, breaking the bolt's flights as he falls. Villain Number Two snatches at the reins, leads the terrified horse to the trees, and tethers it there.

"He's on the ground and dying — a crossbow quarrel is nearly always fatal wherever it hits," Adelia said, "but they made sure. One or other of them — whoever he was has big hands — throttled him as he lay on the ground."

"God have mercy," the bishop said.

"Yes, but here's the interesting thing,"

Adelia told him, as if everything else had been commonplace. "*Now* they drag him to the center of the bridge. See? The toes of his boots make runnels in the snow. They throw his cap down beside him — dear *Lord*, they're stupid. Did they think a man fallen from his mount looks so tidy? Legs together? Skirts down? You saw that, didn't you? And then, *then,* they fetch his horse to the bridge and slice its leg."

"They do not take him into the trees," Mansur pointed out. "Nor the horse. Neither would have been found if they'd done that, not until the spring, and by then, no one could see what had happened to them. But no, they drag him to where the first person across the bridge in the morning will see him and raise the hue and cry."

"Not giving the killers as much time to get away as they might have." The bishop was reflective. "I see. That's . . . eccentric."

"*This* is what's eccentric," Adelia said. They'd come up to the body again. At the bottom of the bridge where the others were gathered, somebody had made a makeshift brazier and lit a fire. Faces, ghastly in the reflection of the flames, turned hopefully in their direction. "You goin' to be much longer?" Gyltha shouted. "Little un's due a feed, and we'm dyin' of frostbite."

Adelia ignored her. She still didn't feel the cold. "Two men," she said, "and they are poor, judging from their footwear. Two men kill our rider. Granted, they take the money from his purse, but they leave the purse, a good one that has his family crest on it. They leave his boots, his cloak, the silver buckle, his fine horse. What thief does that?"

"Perhaps they were disturbed," Rowley said.

"Who disturbs them? Not us. They are long gone before we come up. They had time to strip this poor soul of everything he . . . had. They do not. Why, Rowley?"

The bishop thought it through. "They want him found."

Adelia nodded. "It is vital to them."

"They want him to be identified."

Adelia's exhaled breath was a stream of satisfaction. "Exactly. It must be known who he is and that he is dead."

"I see." Rowley considered. "Hence the suggestion that we hide his body. I don't like it, though."

"But that will bring them back, Rowley," Adelia said, and for the first time she touched him, a tug on his sleeve. "They've taken pains to have this poor young man's death declared to the world. They'll come back to find out why it isn't. We can be waiting for them."

Mansur nodded. "Some fiend intends to profit by this killing, Allah ruin him."

Adelia jiggled the bishop's sleeve again. "But not if the boy seems merely to have gone away, just disappeared."

Rowley was doubtful. "There'll be someone at home, worrying for him."

"If so, they'll want his murderers found."

"He ought to be buried with decency."

"Not yet."

Pulling his arm from her grasp, the bishop went away from her. Adelia watched him go to the parapet of the bridge and lean over it, looking at the roaring water that showed white in the moonlight.

He hates it when I do this, she thought. *He was prepared to love the woman but not the doctor. Yet it was the doctor he invited along, and he must bear the consequences. I have a duty to that dead boy, and I will* not *abandon it.*

Now she was cold.

"Very well." He turned round. "You may be fortunate in that Godstow possesses an icehouse. Famous for it."

While the body was being wrapped in its cloak and its possessions collected, Adelia went to the fire to feed her baby.

The Bishop of Saint Albans gathered his

men round him to tell them what Dr. Mansur had discovered from reading the signs in the snow.

"With the mercy of God, we may hope to catch these killers. Until then, not one of you — I say again, *nobody* — is to mention what we have seen this night. We shall keep this body reverently, but secretly, hidden in order to find out who comes back for it — and may God have mercy on their souls, for we shall not."

It was well done. Rowley had fought in Outremer on Crusade and found that men responded better for knowing what their commander was about than those merely given reasonless commands.

He drew an assenting growl from the circle about him, the messenger's particularly fervent — he and the others spent much of their lives on the road, and they saw the rider on the bridge as any one of themselves fallen to the predators infesting the highways. As Good Samaritans, they had been too late to save the traveler's life, but they could at least bring his killers to justice.

Only Father Paton's frown suggested that he was assessing how much the corpse was going to cost the ecclesiastical purse.

Baring their heads, the men took the body

up and put it in the cart. With everybody walking beside it, leading their horses, they crossed the bridge to Godstow nunnery.

FOUR

Godstow Abbey with its surrounding grounds and fields was actually a large island formed by curves of the Thames's upper reaches and tributaries. Although the porter who unbarred its gates to the travelers was a man, as were the groom and ostler who saw to their horses, it was an island ruled by women.

If asked, its twenty-four nuns and their female pensioners would have insisted that it was the Lord God who had called them to abandon the world, but their air of contentment suggested that the Lord's wish had coincided exactly with their own. Some were widows with money who'd heard God's call at their husband's graveside and hurried to answer it at Godstow before they could be married off again. Some were maidens who, glimpsing the husbands selected for them, had been overwhelmed by a sudden vocation for chastity and had taken their dowries with them into the convent instead. Here they could administer a sizable, growing fiefdom efficiently and with a liberal hand — and they could do it without male interference.

The only men over them were Saint Benedict, to whose rule they were subject and who was dead these six hundred and fifty years; the Pope, who was a long way away; the Archbishop of Canterbury, often ditto; and an investigative archdeacon who, because they kept their books and their behavior in scrupulous order, could make no complaint of them.

Oh, and the Bishop of Saint Albans.

So rich was Godstow that it possessed *two* churches. One, tucked away against the abbey's western wall, was small and acted as the nuns' private chapel. The other, much larger, stood on the east, near the road, and had been built to provide a place of worship for the people of the surrounding villages.

In effect, the abbey was a village in itself, in which the holy sisters had their own precincts, and it was to these that the travelers were taken by the porter. A maid carrying a yoke squeaked at the sight of them and then curtsied, spilling some milk from the buckets. The porter's lantern shone on passageways and courtyards, the sudden, sculptured pillars of a cloister where the shutters of the porter's windows opened to show white-coifed heads like pale poppies whispering, "Bishop, the bishop," along the row.

Rowley Picot, so big, so full of energy and intent, so loudly male, was a cockerel erupting into a placid coop of hens that had been managing happily without him.

They were met by the prioress, still pinning her veil in place, and begged to wait in the chapter house where the abbess would attend them. In the meantime, please to take refreshment. Had the ladies any requirements? And the baby, such a fine little fellow, what might be done for him?

The beauty of the chapter house relied on the sweep of unadorned wooden crucks and arches. Candles lit a tiled floor strewn with fresh rushes and were reflected back in the sheen of a long table and chairs. Besides the scent of apple logs in the brazier, there was a smell of sanctity and beeswax — and now, thanks to Ward, the stink of unsavory dog.

Rowley strode the room, irritated by the wait, but, for the first time since the journey began, Adelia fed young Allie in the tranquillity the baby deserved. Its connection with Rosamund Clifford had made her afraid that the abbey would be disorderly, the nuns lax and no better than they should be. She still had bad memories of Saint Radegund's in Cambridge, the only other religious English sisterhood she'd encountered until now — a troubled place where, eventually, a participant in child killing had been unmasked.

Here at Godstow the atmosphere spoke of safety, tidiness, discipline, everything in its place.

She began to doze, lulled by the soporific mutterings of Father Paton as he chalked the reckonings onto his slate book. "To cheese and ale on the journey . . . to provender for the horses . . ."

A nudge from Gyltha got her to her feet. A small, very old nun, leaning on an ivory-topped walking stick, had come in. Rowley extended his hand; the nun bent creakily over it to kiss the episcopal ring on his finger. Everybody bowed.

The abbess sat herself at the head of the board, took trouble to lean her stick against her chair, clasped her hands, and listened.

Much of Godstow's felicity, Adelia realized within minutes, was due to this tiny woman. Mother Edyve had the disinterested calm of elderly people who had seen everything and were now watching it come around for the second time. This young bishop — a stripling compared to her — could not discompose her, though he arrived with a Saracen, two women, a baby, and an unprepossessing dog among his train, telling her that he had found a murdered man outside her gates.

Even the fact that the bishop wished to conceal the corpse in her icehouse was met calmly. "Thus you hope to find the killer?" she asked.

"Killer*sss*, Abbess," the bishop hissed impatiently. Once again, he went over the evidence found by Dr. Mansur and his assistant.

Adelia thought that Mother Edyve had probably grasped it the first time; she was merely giving herself time to consider. The wrinkly lidded eyes embedded into a face like creased calfskin closed as she listened, her veined hands reflected in the high polish of the table.

Rowley ended with, "We are assured that there are people who wish the young man's death and name to be broadcast; when there is only silence, they may return to find out why."

"A trap, then." It was said without emphasis.

"A trap is necessary to see justice done," Rowley persisted, "and only you to know about it, Abbess."

He is asking a great deal of her, Adelia thought. To conceal a body unmourned and unburied is surely against the law and certainly unchristian.

On the other hand, according to what Rowley had told her, this old woman had kept both her convent and her nuns inviolate during thirteen years of civil war, much of it waged in this very area, a feat suggesting that the rules of men, and even God's, must have been tinkered with somewhere along the line.

Mother Edyve opened her eyes. "I can tell you this, my lord: The bridge is ours. It is our convent's duty to maintain its structure and its peace and, by extension therefore, to catch those who commit murder on it."

"You agree, then?" Rowley was taken aback; he'd expected resistance.

"However," the abbess said, still distantly, as if he hadn't spoken, "you will need the assistance of my daughter prioress." Sliding it along her belt from under her scapular, Mother Edyve produced the largest chatelaine Adelia had ever seen; it was a wonder it didn't weigh her to the floor. Among the massive keys attached to it was a small bell. She rang it.

The prioress who had first greeted them

came in. "Yes, Mother?"

Now that she could compare them, Adelia saw that Sister Havis had the same flat face and the same calfskin, though slightly less crinkled, complexion as the abbess. "Daughter prioress," then, was not a pious euphemism; Edyve had brought her child with her to Godstow when she took the veil.

"Our lord bishop has with him a consignment for our icehouse, Sister Havis. It will be stored there secretly during Lauds." A key was detached from the great iron ring and handed over. "There shall be no mention of it to any soul until further notice."

"Yes, Mother." Sister Havis bowed to her bishop, then to her mother, and left. No surprise. No questions. Godstow's icehouse, Adelia decided, must have stored more than sides of beef in its time. Treasure? Escapers? Situated as it was between the town of Wallingford, which had held out for Queen Matilda, and Oxford Castle, where King Stephen's flag had flown, there might well have been a need to hide both.

Allie was wriggling, and Gyltha, who was holding her, looked interrogatively at Adelia and then at the floor.

Adelia nodded, clean enough. Allie was put down to crawl, an exercise she was refusing to perform, preferring to hitch herself along on her backside. Wearily, the dog Ward disposed himself so that his ears could be pulled.

Rowley wasn't even thanking the abbess for her cooperation; he had moved on to a matter more important to him. "And now, madam, what of Rosamund Clifford?"

"Yes, the Lady Rosamund." It was spoken as distantly as ever, but Mother Edyve's hands tightened slightly. "They are saying it was the queen poisoned her."

"I was afraid they would."

"And *I* am afraid it may precipitate war."

There was a silence. Abbess and bishop were in accord now, as if they shared a foul secret. Once again, trampling horsemen milled around the memories of those who had known civil war, emitting to Adelia a turbulence so strong that she wanted to pick up her baby. Instead, she kept an eye on her in case the child made for the brazier.

"Has her corpse arrived?" Rowley asked abruptly.

"No."

"I thought it had been arranged; it was to be carried here for burial." He was accusatory, the abbess's fault. *Whereas,* thought Adelia, *any other bishop would have commended a convent that refused to inter a notorious woman in its ground.*

Mother Edyve looked down the side of her chair. Allie was trying to pull herself up by one of its legs. Adelia rose to go and remove her but the abbess held her back with an admonishing finger, then, without a change of expression, took the little bell from her chatelaine and passed it down.

You know babies, Adelia thought, comforted.

"Our foundation is indebted to the Lady Rosamund for many past kindnesses." Mother Edyve's voice tweeted like a distant bird. "We owe her body burial and all the services for her soul. It was arranged, yet her housekeeper, Dakers, refuses to release the corpse to us."

"Why not?"

"I cannot say, but without her consent, it is difficult to amend the situation."

"In the name of God, *why* not?"

Something, and it might have been a gleam of amusement, disturbed the immobility of the abbess's face for half a second. From the floor by her chair came a tinkling as Allie investigated her new toy. "I believe you visited Wormhold Tower during the lady's illness, my lord?"

"You know I did. Your prioress . . . Sister Havis fetched me from Oxford to do so."

"And both of you were led through the

111

labyrinth surrounding the tower?"

"Some crackbrained female met us at the entrance to it, yes." Rowley's fingers tapped on the table; he hadn't sat down since entering the room.

"Dame Dakers." Again, the suggestion of amusement like the merest breath on a pond. "I understand she will admit nobody since her mistress died. She adored her. My lord, I fear without she guides you through the labyrinth, there is no way of gaining the tower."

"I'll gain it. By God, I'll gain it. No body shall remain unburied whilst I am bishop here. . . ." He stopped, and then he laughed; he'd brought one through the gates with him.

It is his saving grace, Adelia thought as she melted and smiled with him, to see the incongruity of things. She watched him apologize to the abbess for his manner and thank her for her amiability — until she saw that the nun's pale old eyes had turned and were watching *her* watching *him.*

The abbess returned to the subject. "Dame Dakers's attachment to her mistress was" — the adjective was carefully considered — "formidable. The unfortunate servant responsible for bringing in the fatal mushrooms has fled from the tower in fear of her life and has sought sanctuary with us."

"She's here? Good. I want to question her." He corrected himself. "With your *permission,* madam, I should like to question her."

The abbess inclined her head.

"And if I may trespass on your kindness a little more," Rowley went on, "I would leave some of my party here while Dr. Mansur and his assistant accompany me to Wormhold Tower and see what may be done. As I say, the good doctor here has investigative abilities that can enable us . . ."

Not yet. Not today. For God's sake, Rowley, we've traveled hard.

Adelia coughed and caught Gyltha's eye. Gyltha nudged Mansur, who stood next to her. Mansur looked round at them both, then spoke in English and for the first time. "Your doctor advise rest first." He added, "My lord."

"Rest be damned," Rowley said, but he looked toward Adelia, who must go with him when he went, or why was she here?

She shook her head. *We need rest, Rowley. You need it.*

The abbess's eyes had followed the exchange and, if it had told her nothing else, though it probably had, she'd learned

113

enough to know the matter was settled. "When you have disposed of the unfortunate gentleman's body, Sister Havis will see to your accommodation," she said.

It was still very dark and very cold. The nuns were chanting Lauds in their chapel, and everybody else with a duty to do was performing it within the complex of buildings, out of sight of the main gates, where a covered carriage containing a dead man had been left just inside them.

Walt and the men-at-arms were guarding it. They stood, stamping and slapping their arms to keep warm, stolidly ignoring the inquisition of the convent porter, who was leaning out of a bottom window in the gatehouse. Sister Havis told him sharply to withdraw his head, close the shutters, and mind his own business. "Keep thy silence, Fitchet."

"Don't I?" Fitchet was aggrieved. "Don't I always keep it?" The shutters slammed.

"He does," Sister Havis said. "Mostly." Holding the lantern high, she stalked ahead of them through the snow.

Walt led the horses after her, the bishop, Oswald, and Aelwyn marching beside him, with Adelia and Mansur above them on the cart's driving seat.

Rowley, aware now that he had tired her, would have left Adelia in the room that had been prepared for her and Gyltha and the baby in the guesthouse, but this dead young man was *her* responsibility. However good the reason, his body was being treated disgracefully at her behest; she must accord it what respect she could.

They were following the wall that ringed the convent's extensive buildings and gardens to where it ran into the woods in which, on the other side, lay the dead man's dead horse.

The rush of water that they'd heard from on the bridge became loud; they were close to the river, either the Thames itself or a fast stream running into it that gushed up even colder air. The noise became tremendous.

Mansur pointed; he and Adelia were seated high enough on the cart to see over the wall and, when trees allowed, across the water itself. There was their bridge and, on its far side, a water mill.

The Arab was saying something — she couldn't hear him — perhaps that the mill had been in darkness when they'd stood on the bridge so that they hadn't noticed it. Now light came through tiny windows set in its tower, and its great wheel was being turned by the race.

They'd pulled up. Sister Havis had stopped at a large stone hut built flush with the wall on this side and was unlocking its door.

The nun's lantern showed the inside of the hut to be empty apart from a ladder and a few tools. The floor was slabbed with stone, but most of its space was taken up by a great curve of iron set with handles, like the lid of an immense pot.

Sister Havis stood back. "It will need two to lift it." She had the same emotionless voice as her mother.

Aelwyn and Oswald exerted themselves to raise the lid, displaying the blackness of a hole and releasing a chill that was palpable even in the air of the hut, and with it a smell of straw and frozen meat.

The bishop had taken the lantern from the prioress and was down on his knees by the side of the hole. "Who built this?"

"We do not know, my lord. We discovered it and maintain it. Mother Abbess believes it was here long before our foundation."

"The Romans, I wonder?" Rowley was intrigued. The ladder was carried over and put in place so that he could descend. His voice came up with an echo, still asking questions, Sister Havis answering them with detachment.

Yes, its position so far from the convent butchery was inconvenient, but presumably its builders had placed it here to be close to a part of the river that was embanked so that the chamber would suffer no erosion while yet benefiting from the cooling proximity of running water.

Yes, the convent still pickled and salted most of its animals after the Michaelmas slaughter, since even Godstow could not provide feed for them all during the winter, but freezing some carcasses enabled its people to have occasional fresh meat into the spring, or later.

Yes, of course, the mill pond over the way needed a very cold winter to turn to ice, but all winters were cold these days and the last freeze had been exceptional, providing them with sufficient frozen blocks to last until summer. Yes, his lordship would see a drain that took away any melted water.

"Marvelous."

Adelia coughed with intent. Rowley's head appeared. "What?"

"The obsequies, my lord."

"Oh, of course."

The body was lain on the slabs.

Rigor mortis had passed off, Adelia was interested to see, but that would be from the comparative warmth provided by the wrapping of straw and the shelter of the cart; down in that freezing hole, it would return.

The sure, strong voice of the Bishop of Saint Albans filled the hut. "*Domine, Iesu Christe, Rex gloriae* . . . Free the souls of all faithful departed from infernal punishment and the deep pit . . . nor let them fall into darkness, but may the sign-bearer Saint Michael lead them into the holy light which you promised . . ."

Adelia silently added her own requiem prayer: *And may those who love you forgive me for what we do.*

She went down the pit ahead of the body, joining Oswald and the bishop. A dreadful place, like the inside of an enormous brick egg insulated throughout by thick, netted straw over which more netting held the ice blocks. On their hooks, butchered sides of beef, lamb, venison, and pig, whitened by frost, hung so close together that she could not pass through without brushing her shoulders against them.

She found a space and straightened, to have her cap caught in the talons of game birds hanging from their own gallows.

Teeth chattering — and not just from the cold — she and the others guided the feet of the dead man as Aelwyn and Walt lowered him.

Together they laid him down under the birds, positioning him so that if there were drips, they would not fall on his face.

"I'm sorry. I'm so sorry." When the others had climbed out of the hole, she stayed by the dead man for a moment to make him a promise. "Whether we catch your killers or not, I will not leave you here for long."

It was almost too long for her; she was so cold she couldn't manage the ladder and Mansur had to hoist her out.

The abbess gave up her house to Rowley, saying it was a relief to do so; its steep steps to the front door had become difficult for her. In that he was her superior in God, she could do no less, although it gave him access to the inner courtyard with its cloister, chapel, refectory, and nuns' dormitory, which were otherwise barred to men overnight. Having taken a look at Father Paton and deciding that he wasn't a sexual threat, either, she put the secretary in with his master.

Jacques, Walt, Oswald, and Aelwyn were accommodated in the male servants' quarters.

Mansur was given a pleasant room in the

men's guesthouse. Gyltha, Adelia, the baby, and the dog were accommodated just as pleasantly in the females' wing next to the church. Angled outside steps led up to each guest's private door, which, since they were on the top floor, gave the two women a view westward over the track to Oxford and the abbey's fields where they sloped down to the Thames.

"Duck down," said Gyltha, examining a large bed. "An' no fleas." She investigated further. "And some saint's put hot bricks to warm it."

Adelia wanted nothing so much as to lie down on it and sleep, and, for a while, all three of them did just that.

They were awakened by bells, one of them tolling as if in their ear and setting the water ewer shivering in its basin on the room's table.

Ready to flee, Adelia picked up Allie where she lay between her and Gyltha. "Is it a fire?"

Gyltha listened. The massive strokes were coming from the church tower nearby, and with them came the chime of other bells, tinnier and much farther away. "It's Sunday," she said.

"Oh, to *hell*. It's not, is it?"

However, courtesy and Adelia's consciousness of their indebtedness to the abbess demanded that they attend the morning worship to which Godstow was summoning its people.

And more than just its own people. The church in the outer courtyard was open to everybody, lay and religious — though not, of course, to infidels and the smellier dogs, thus leaving Mansur and Ward still in their beds — and today everybody within walking range was struggling through snow to get to it. The village of Wolvercote came across the bridge en masse, since its own church had been allowed to fall into ruin by the lord of the manor.

The attraction was the bishop, of course; he was as miraculous as an angel descended. A view of his cope and miter alone was worth the tithes everybody had to pay; he might be able to cure the little un's cough; for sure he could bless the winter sowing. Several poorly looking milch cows and one limping donkey were already tied up by the water trough outside, awaiting his attention.

The clergy entered by their own separate doorway to take their seats in the glorious stalls of the choir under the church's equally glorious fan-vaulted roof.

By virtue of his tonsure, Father Paton sat next to the nuns' chaplain, a little dormouse of a man, opposite the rows of nuns that included among their black ranks two young women in white veils who had a tendency to giggle; they found Father Paton funny.

Most bishops used their homilies to wag a finger at sin in general, often in Norman French, their mother tongue, or in Latin on the principle that the less the congregation understood, the more in awe it would be.

Rowley's was different, and in an English his flock could understand. "There's some buggers are saying poor Lady Rosamund has died at the Queen Eleanor's hand, which it is a wickedness and a lie, and you'll oblige our Lord by giving it no credit."

He left the pulpit to stride up and down the church, lecturing, hectoring. He was here to discover what or who had caused Rosamund's death, he said, "For I do know she was dearly loved in these parts. Maybe 'twas an accident, maybe 'twasn't, but if it weren't, both king and queen'll see to it the villain be punished according to law. In the meantime, 'tis beholden on us all to keep our counsel and the precious peace of our Lord Jesus Christ."

Then he kneeled down on the stones and straw to pray, and everyone in church kneeled with him.

They love him, Adelia thought. *As quickly*

as that, they love him. Is it showmanship? No, it isn't. He's beyond that now. Beyond me, too.

When they rose, however, one man — the miller from across the bridge, judging from the spectral whiteness with which flour had ingrained his skin — raised a question. "Master, they say as how the queen be up-sides with the king. Ain't going to be no trouble twixt 'em, is there?"

He was backed by a murmur of anxiety. The civil war in which a king had fought a queen was only a generation in the past; nobody here wanted to see another.

Rowley turned on him. "Which is your missus?"

"This un." The man jerked a thumb at the comfortable lady standing beside him.

"And a good choice you made there, Master Miller, as all can see. But tell me you ain't been upsides with her along the years some'eres, or her ain't been upsides with you, but you diddun start a war over it. Reckon as royalty ain't no different."

Amid laughter, he returned to his throne.

One of the white-veiled girls sang the responsory in honor of the bishop's presence and sang it so exquisitely that Adelia, usually deaf to music, waited impatiently through the congregation's answers until

123

she sang again.

So it was nice to find the same young woman waiting for her in the great court-yard outside after the clergy had filed out. "May I come and see the baby? I love babies."

"Of course. I must congratulate you on your voice; it is a joy to hear."

"Thank you. I am Emma Bloat."

"Adelia Aguilar."

They fell into step, or, rather, Adelia stepped and Emma bounced. She was fifteen years old and in a state of exaltation over something. Adelia hoped it was not the bishop. "Are you an oblate?"

"Oh, no. Little Priscilla is the one taking the veil. *I* am to be married."

"Good."

"It *is,* isn't it? Earthly love . . ." Emma twirled in sheer joie de vivre. "God must reckon it as high as heavenly love, mustn't he, despite what Sister Mold says, or why does He make us feel like this?" She thumped the region of her heart.

" 'It is better to marry than to burn,' " quoted Adelia.

"Huh. What I say is, how did Saint Paul know? He didn't do either."

She was a refreshing child and she did love babies, or she certainly loved Allie, with whom she was prepared to play peep-bo longer than Adelia had believed possible without the brain giving way.

It seemed that the girl must have privilege of some kind, since she was not called back to join the sisters' afternoon routine. *Wealth or rank?* Adelia wondered. *Or both?*

She showed no more curiosity about this influx of strangers to the convent than if they had been toys provided for her amusement, though she demanded that they be curious about her. "Ask me about my husband-to-be, ask me, ask me."

He was beautiful, apparently, *oh* so beautiful, gallant, wild with love for her, a writer of romantic poems that rivaled any Paris might have sent to Helen.

Gyltha raised her eyebrows to Adelia, who raised her own. This was happiness indeed, and unusual to be found in an arranged marriage. For arranged it was; Emma's father, she told them, was a wine merchant in Oxford and was supplying the convent with the best Rhenish to pay for having her educated as befitted a nobleman's wife. It was he who had procured the match.

At this point, Emma, who was standing by the window, laughed so much that she had to hold on to the mullion.

"Your intended's a lord, then?" Gyltha

asked, grinning.

The laughter went, and the girl turned to look out of the window as if its view could tell her something, and Adelia saw that when the exuberance of youth went, beauty would take its place.

"The lord of my heart," Emma said.

It was difficult for the travelers to forgather in order to discuss and plan. Lenient as Godstow was, it could not tolerate the step of a Saracen into its inner courtyard. For the bishop to visit the women's quarters was equally out of place. There was only the church, and even there a nun was always present at the main altar, interceding with God for the souls of such departed as had paid for the privilege. However, it had a side chapel devoted to Mary, deserted at night yet lit by candles — another gift from the dead that they might be remembered to the Holy Mother — and the abbess had given her permission for its use as a meeting place, as long as they were quiet about it.

The day's large congregation had left no warmth behind. Blazing candles on the shrine sent out light and heat only a few feet, leaving the ogival space around them in icy shadow. Entering by a side door, Adelia saw a large figure kneeling before the altar, his cowled head bowed and the fingers of his hands interlaced so tightly that they resembled bare bone.

Rowley got up as the women entered. He looked tired. "You're late."

"I had to feed the baby," Adelia told him.

From the main body of the church came the drone of a nun reading the commemorations from the convent register. She was being literal about it. *"Lord, in Thy mercy, bless and recognize the soul of Thomas of Sandford, who did provide an orchard in Saint Giles's, Oxford, to this convent and departed this life the day after Martinmas in the year of our Lord 1143. Sweet Jesus, in Thy Mercy, look kindly on the soul of Maud Halegod, who did give three silver marks . . ."*

"Did Rosamund's servant tell you anything?" Adelia whispered.

"Her?" The bishop didn't bother to lower his voice. "The female's rattle-headed; I'd have got more out of the bloody donkeys I've had to bless all bloody afternoon. She kept bleating. I swear, like a sheep."

"You probably frightened her." In full regalia, he'd have been overwhelming.

"Of course I didn't frighten her. I was charming. The woman's witless, I tell you. You see if you can get some sense out of her."

"I shall."

Gyltha had found some hassocks piled in a cupboard and was distributing them in a circle, where the candlelight fell on them, each one displaying the blazon of a noble family that didn't want to dirty its knees when it came to church.

"Hassocks are sensible," Adelia said, putting one under the sleeping Allie's basket in order to keep it off the stones. Ward settled himself on another. "Why don't the rich endow hassocks for the poor? They'd be remembered longer."

"The rich don't want us comfortable," Gyltha said. "Ain't good for us. Give us ideas above our station. Where's that old Arab?"

"The messenger's fetching him."

He came, having to stoop through the side door, wrapped in a cloak, Jacques behind him.

"Good," Rowley said. "You can go, Jacques."

"Ummm." The young man shifted in complaint.

Adelia took pity on him. Messengers had an unenviable and lonely job, spending their time crisscrossing the country with a horse as their only companion. Their masters were hard on them: letters to be delivered quickly, replies brought back even quicker; excuses, such as bad weather, falls, difficult country, or getting lost, discounted in favor of the suspicion that the servant had been wasting his time and his employer's money in some tavern.

Rowley, she thought, was being particularly hard on this one; there was no reason why the young man should not be included in their discussions. She suspected that Jacques's sin lay in the fact that, though he wore the sober Saint Albans livery, he compensated for his lack of height by wearing raised boots and a high plume in his hat, which led to the suspicion that he was following the trend introduced by Queen Eleanor and her court for males as well as women to subscribe to fashion — an idea welcomed by the young generation but condemned as effete by men, like Rowley, like Walt and Oswald, whose choice of clothing material had always been either leather or chain mail.

Walt had been heard to describe the messenger, not inaccurately, as looking like "a stalk of celery wi' roots attached," and Rowley had grumbled to Adelia that he feared his messenger was "greenery-yellery" and "not good, plain old Norman English," both epithets he reserved for men he regarded as effeminate. "I shall have to send him away. The boy even wears scent. I can't have my missives delivered by a popinjay."

This, thought Adelia, *from a man whose ceremonial robes dazzled the eye and took half an hour to put on.*

She decided to intercede. "Are we taking Master Jacques with us to Rosamund's tower tomorrow?"

"Of course we are." Rowley was still irritable. "I may need to send messages."

"Then he'll know as much as we know, my lord. He already does."

"Oh, very well."

From the altar beyond the screen that separated them, the ceaseless muttering of prayer for the dead went on as, with different nuns taking up the task, it would go on all night.

"*. . . of your mercy, the soul of Thomas Hookeday, hayward of this parish, for the sixpence he did endow . . .*"

Rowley produced the saddle roll that had belonged to the dead man on the bridge. "Hasn't been time to look through it yet." He unbuckled the straps and put it on the floor to unroll it. With Jacques standing behind them, the four sat round and considered its contents.

Which were few. A leather bottle of ale.

130

Half a cheese and a loaf neatly wrapped in cloth. A hunting horn — odd equipment for a man traveling without companions or dogs. A spare cloak with fur trimming, surprisingly small for what had been a tall man — again, carefully folded.

Wherever the youngster had been heading, he was banking on finding food and lodging there; the bread and cheese wouldn't have sustained him very far.

And there was a letter. It appeared to have been pushed just under the flap between the buckles of the leather straps that secured the roll.

Rowley picked it up and smoothed it out.

" 'To Talbot of Kidlington,' " he read. " 'That the Lord and His angels bless you on this Day that enters you into Man's estate and keep you from the Path of Sin and all unrighteousness is the dearest hope of your affct cousin, Wlm Warin, gentleman-at-law, who hereby sends: two silver marks as an earnest of your inheritance, the rest to be Claimed when we do meet. Written this day of Our Lord, the sixteenth before the Kalends of January, at my place of business next Saint Michael at the North Gate of Oxford.' "

He looked up. "Well, there we are, then. Now we know our body's name."

Adelia nodded slowly. *"Hmm."*

"What's wrong with *that?* The boy's got a name, a twenty-first birthday, and an affectionate cousin with an address. Plenty for you to work on. What he hasn't got is two silver marks. I imagine the thieves took those."

Adelia noted the "you"; this was to be her business, not the bishop's. "Don't you think it odd," she asked, "if the family arms on his purse were not to tell us who he was, here is a letter that does. It gives us almost too much information. What affectionate writer calls his cousin Talbot of Kidlington rather than just Talbot?"

Rowley shrugged. "A perfectly standard superscription."

Adelia took the letter from him. "And it's on vellum. Expensive for such a brief, personal note. Why didn't Master Warin use rag paper?"

"All lawyers use vellum or parchment. They think paper is *infra dignitatem.*"

But Adelia mused on. "And it's crumpled, just shoved between the buckles. Look, it's torn on one of them. Nobody treats vellum like that — it can always be scraped down to use again."

"Perhaps the lad was in a rush when he received it, stuffed it away quickly. Or he

132

was angry because he was expecting more than two marks? Or he doesn't give an owl's hoot for vellum. Which" — the bishop was losing his patience — "at this moment, I don't, either. What is your point, mistress?"

Adelia considered for a moment.

Whether the body in the icehouse was that of Talbot of Kidlington or not, when alive it had belonged to a neat man; his clothing had told her that. So did the care he'd expended on wrapping the contents of his saddle roll. People with such tidy habits — and Adelia was one of their number — did not carelessly thrust a document on vellum into an aperture with the flat of the hand, as this had been.

"I don't think he even saw this letter," she said. "I think the men who killed him put it there."

"For the Lord's sake," Rowley hissed at her, "this is overelaboration. Adelia, highway villains do not endow their victim with correspondence. What are you saying? It's a forgery to put us off the track? Talbot of Kidlington isn't Talbot of Kidlington? The belt and the purse belong to someone else entirely?"

"I don't know." But something about the letter was wrong.

Arrangements were made for the next

day's excursion. Adelia would accompany bishop, messenger, groom, and one of the men-at-arms on a ride upriver, using the towpath to Rosamund's tower while Mansur and the other man-at-arms would travel by water, bringing a barge on which to carry back the corpse.

While discussion went on, Adelia took the opportunity to examine the blazons on all the hassocks. None of them matched the device on the young man's purse or belt.

Rowley was talking to Gyltha. "You must stay here, mistress. We can't take the baby with us."

Adelia looked up. "I'm not leaving her behind."

He said, "You'll have to, it won't be a family outing." He took Mansur by the arm. "Come along, my friend, let's see what the convent has in the way of boats." They went out, the messenger with them.

"I'm not leaving her," Adelia shouted after him, causing a momentary pause in the recital of souls from beyond the screen. She turned to Gyltha. "How *dare* he. I won't."

Gyltha pressed on Adelia's shoulders to force her down onto a hassock, then sat beside her. "He's right."

"He's not. Suppose we get cut off by snow, by anything? She needs to be fed."

"Then I'll see as she is." Gyltha took Adelia's hand and bounced it gently. "It's time, girl," she said. "Time she was weaned proper. You're a'drying up; you know it, the little un knows it."

Adelia was hearing the truth; Gyltha never told her anything else. In fact, the weaning process had been going on for some weeks as her breast milk diminished, both women chewing food to a pap and supplementing it with cow's milk to spoon into Allie's eager mouth.

If breast-feeding, which the childless Adelia had considered would be an oozing embarrassment, had proved to be one of life's natural pleasures, it had also been the excuse to have her child always with her. For motherhood, while another joy, had burdened her with a tearing and unexpected anxiety, as if her senses had been transferred into the body of her daughter, and, by a lesser extension, into that of all children. Adelia, who'd once considered anyone below the age of reason to be alien and had treated them as such, was now open to their grief, their slightest pain, any unhappiness.

Allie suffered few of these emotions; she was a sturdy baby, and gradually Adelia had become aware that the agony was for herself, for the two-day-old creature that had been abandoned by an unknown parent on a rocky slope in Italy's Campania nearly thirty years before. During her growing up it had not mattered; an incident, even amusing in that the couple who'd discovered her had commemorated an event all three had considered fortunate by giving her Vesuvia as one of her names. Childless, loving, clever, eccentric, Signor and Signora Aguilar, both doctors trained in the liberal tradition of Salerno's great School of Medicine, he a Jew, she a Catholic Christian, had found in Adelia not only a beloved daughter but a brain that superseded even their intelligence, and had educated it accordingly. No, abandonment hadn't mattered. It had, in fact, turned out to be the greatest gift that the real, unknown, desperate, sorrowing, or uncaring mother could have bestowed on her child.

Until that child had given birth to a baby of her own.

Then it came. Fear like a typhoon that wouldn't stop blowing, not just fear that Allie would die but fear that she herself would die and leave the child without the mercy that had been bestowed on her. Better they both die together.

Oh, God, if the poisoner was not content merely with Rosamund's death . . . or if the killers from the bridge were waiting en route . . . or if she should leave her child in a Godstow suddenly overwhelmed by fire . . .

This was obsession, and Adelia had just enough sense to know that, if it persisted, it would damage both herself and Allie.

"It's time," Gyltha said again, and since Gyltha, most reliable of women, said it was, then it was.

But she resented the ease with which Rowley demanded a separation that would cause her grief and, however unfounded, fear as well. "It's not up to him to tell me to leave her behind. I hate leaving her, I hate it."

Gyltha shrugged. "His child, too."

"You wouldn't think so."

The messenger's voice came from the door. "My apologies, mistress, but his lordship asks that you will interview Bertha."

"Bertha?"

"Lady Rosamund's servant, mistress. The mushrooming one."

"Oh, yes."

Apart from the unremitting prayers for the dead in the church and the canonical hours, the convent had shut down, leaving it in a total, moonless black. The compass of light from Jacques's lantern lit only the bottom of walls and a few feet of pathway lined by snow as he led the two women to their quarters. There Adelia kissed her baby good night and left Gyltha to put her to bed.

She and the messenger went on alone, leaving the outer courtyard for open ground. A faint smell suggested that somewhere nearby were vegetable gardens, rotted now by the frost.

"Where are you taking me?" Her voice went querulous into the blackness.

"The cowshed, I'm afraid, mistress." Jacques was apologetic. "The girl's hidden herself there. The abbess put her to the kitchens, but the cooks refused to work with her, seeing it was her hand that fed the poison to the lady Rosamund. The nuns have tried talking to her but they say it's difficult to get sense from the poor soul, and she dreads the arrival of the lady's housekeeper."

The messenger chatted on, eager to prove himself worthy of inclusion into his bishop's strange, investigative inner circle.

"About the blazon on the poor young man's purse, mistress. It might profit you to consult Sister Lancelyne. She keeps the convent's cartulary and register, and has a record of the device of every family who's made a gift at some time or another."

He'd been making good use of his time. It was a messenger's attribute to persuade himself into the good books of the servants of households he visited. It got him better food and drink before he had to set off again.

Walls closed in again. Adelia's boots splashed through the slush of what, in daytime, must be much-used lanes. Her nose registered that they were passing a bakehouse, now a kitchen, a laundry, all silent and invisible in the darkness.

More open land. More slush, but here and there footprints in a bank of snow where someone had stepped off the path.

Menace.

It came at her, unseen, unaccountable, but so strong that she hunched and stood still under its attack as if she were back in the alleys of Salerno and had seen the shadow of a man with a knife.

The messenger stopped with her. "What is it, mistress?"

"I don't know. Nothing." There were footprints in the snow, valid, explicable footprints no doubt, but for her, remembering those on the bridge, they pointed to death.

She forced herself to trudge on.

The acrid stink of hot iron and a remnant

of warmth on the air told her they were passing a smithy, its fire banked down for the night. Now a stable and the smell of horse manure that, as they walked on, became bovine — they had reached the cowshed.

Jacques heaved open one of the double doors to reveal a wide, bespattered aisle between partitioned stalls, most of which were empty. Few beasts anywhere survived the Michaelmas cull — there was never enough fodder to see herds through the winter — but farther up the aisle, the lantern shone on the crusted backsides and tails of the cows that had been left alive to provide winter milk.

"Where is she?"

"They said she was here. Bertha," Jacques called. *"Bertha."*

From somewhere in the dark at the far end of the shed came a squeak and rustle of straw as if an extra-large mouse were making for its hole.

Jacques lit their way up the aisle and shone the lantern into the last of the stalls before hanging it from the hook of an overhead beam. "She's there, I think, mistress." He stood back so Adelia could see inside it.

There was a big pile of straw against the

stall's back wall. Adelia addressed it. "Bertha? I mean you no harm. Please talk to me."

She had to say it several times before there was a heave and a face was framed in the straw. At first, with the lantern sending downward light on it, Adelia thought it was a pig's, then saw that it belonged to a girl with a nose so retroussé as to present only nostrils, giving it the appearance of a snout. Small, almost lashless eyes fixed on Adelia's face. The wide mouth moved and produced sound high up the scale. "Non me faux," it sounded like. "Non me faux, non me faux."

Adelia turned back to Jacques. "Is she French?"

"Not as far as I know, mistress. I think she's saying it was not her fault."

The bleat changed. "Donagemme."

" 'Don't let her get me,' " Jacques translated.

"Dame Dakers?" Adelia asked.

Bertha hunched in terror. "Turmein-amouse."

" 'She'll turn me into a mouse,' " Jacques said helpfully.

The irresistible thought came, shamefully, that in the case of this child, the dame's powers to turn her into an animal would not be stretched very far.

141

"Antrappi." Bertha was becoming less frightened and more confidential, poking forward now to show a thin upper neck and body under head and hair colored the same as the straw that framed them. Her gaze became fixed on Adelia's neck.

" 'And catch I in a trap,' " Jacques said.

Adelia was getting the hang of Bertha's speech. Also, she had become angry, as she always did at the suggestion of magic, appalled that this girl should be terrorized by black superstition. "Sit up," she said.

The porcine little eyes blinked and Bertha sat up instantly, spilling straw. She was used to being bullied.

"Now," Adelia said, more quietly, "nobody blames you for what happened, but you *must* tell me how it came about."

Bertha leaned forward and poked at Adelia's necklet. "What be that purty thing?"

"It's a cross. Haven't you seen one before?"

"Lady Ros do have similar, purtier nor that. What be for? Magic?" This was awful. Had nobody taught the girl Christianity?

Adelia said, "As soon as I can, I shall buy you one of your own and explain it to you. Now, though, you must explain things to *me*. Will you do that?"

Bertha nodded, her eyes still on the silver cross.

So it began. It took infinite labor on Adelia's part and wearisome, evasive repetition on Bertha's, pursuing the theme that it wasn't her fault, before any relevant information could be teased from her. The girl was so ignorant, so credulous, that Adelia's opinion of Rosamund became very low — no servant should be so deprived of education. *Fair Rosamund,* she thought. Not much fairness in the neglect of this sad little thing.

It was difficult to estimate her age; Bertha herself didn't know it. Between sixteen and twenty, Adelia guessed, half-starved and as unaware of how the world wagged as any mole in its run.

Jacques, unnoticed, had slid a milking stool against her hocks, allowing her to sit so that she and Bertha were on a level. He remained standing directly behind her in shadow, saying not a word.

Ever since she'd heard of Rosamund's death, Adelia had believed that what she would eventually uncover was the tale of a sad accident.

It wasn't. As Bertha gained confidence and Adelia understanding, the story that emerged showed that Bertha had been the accomplice, albeit unwittingly, to deliberate

143

murder.

On the fatal day, she said, she'd gone into the forest surrounding Wormhold Tower to gather kindling, not mushrooms, pulling a sledge behind her to pile it with such dead branches as could be reached with a crook.

Lowest of all Rosamund's servants, it had already been a bad morning for her. Dame Dakers had walloped her for dropping a pot and told her that Lady Rosamund was sick of her and intended to send her away, which, Bertha being without family to turn to, would have meant having to tramp the countryside begging for food.

"Her's a dragon," Bertha whispered, looking round and up in case Dame Dakers had flown in, flapping her wings, to perch on one of the cowshed's beams. "Us calls her Dragon Dakers."

Miserably, Bertha had gathered so much fuel — afraid of Dragon Dakers's wrath if she didn't — that, having tied the bundled wood to the sledge, she found it impossible to pull, at which point she had sat down on the ground and bawled her distress to the trees.

"And then *her* come up."

"Who came?"

"*Her* did. Old woman."

"Had you ever seen her before?"

144

" 'Course not." Bertha regarded the question as an insult. "Her didn't come from our parts. Second cook to Queen Eleanor, she was. The queen. Traveled everywhere with un."

"That's what she told you? She worked for Queen Eleanor?"

"Her did."

"What did this old woman look like?"

"Like a old woman."

Adelia took a breath and tried again. "How old? Describe her. Well-dressed? In rags? What sort of face? What sort of voice?"

But Bertha, lacking both observation and vocabulary, was unable to answer these questions. "Her was ugly, but her was kind," she said. It was the only description she could give, kindness being so rare in Bertha's life that it was remarkable.

"In what way was she kind?"

"Her gave I them mushrooms, didn't her? Magic, they was. Said they'd make Lady Ros look on I with" — Bertha's unfortunate nose had wrinkled in an effort to recall the word used — "favor."

"She said your mistress would be pleased with you?"

"Her did."

It took time, but eventually something of the conversation that had taken place in the forest between Bertha and the old woman was reconstructed.

"That's what I do for my lady, Queen Eleanor," the old woman had said. *"I do give her a feast of these here mushrooms, and her do look on me with favor."*

Bertha had inquired eagerly whether they also worked on less-exalted mistresses.

"Oh, yes, even better."

"Like, if your mistress were going to send you off, she wouldn't?"

"Send you off? Promote you more like."

Then the old woman had added, *"Tell you what I'll do, Bertha, my duckling, I like your face, so I'll let you have my mushrooms to cook for your lady. Fond of mushrooms, is she?"*

"Dotes on 'em."

"There you are, then. You cook her these and be rewarded. Only you must do it right away now."

Amazed, Adelia wondered for a moment if this was a fairy tale that Bertha had concocted in order to conceal her own guilt. Then she abandoned the thought; nobody had ever bothered to tell Bertha fairy tales in which mysterious old women offered girls their heart's desire — or any fairy tales at all. Bertha was incapable of concoction, anyway.

146

So that day in the forest, now eager and full of strength, Bertha had tied the basket of mushrooms to the wood on her sledge and dragged both back to Wormhold Tower.

Which was almost deserted. *That,* Adelia thought, *was significant.* Dame Dakers had left for the day to go to a hiring fair in Oxford in order to find a new cook — cooks, it seemed, never endured her strictures for long and were constantly leaving. The other staff, free of the housekeeper's eye, had taken themselves off, leaving Fair Rosamund virtually alone.

So, in an empty kitchen, Bertha had set to work. The amount of fungi had been enough for two meals, and Bertha had divided them, thinking to leave some for tomorrow. She'd put half into a skillet with butter, a pinch of salt, a touch of wild garlic, and a sprinkling of parsley, warmed them over a flame until the juices ran, and then taken the dish up to the solar where Rosamund sat at her table, writing a letter.

"Her could write, you know," Bertha said in wonder.

"And she ate the mushrooms?"

"Gobbled 'em." The girl nodded. "Greedy like."

The magic had worked. Lady Rosamund, most unusually, had smiled on Bertha, thanked her, said she was a good girl.

Later, the convulsions had begun. . . .

Even now, Adelia discovered, Bertha did not suspect the crone in the forest of treachery. "Accident," she said. "Weren't the old un's fault. A wicked mushroom did get into that basket by mistake."

There was no point in arguing, but there had been no mistake. In the selection Bertha had saved and Rowley had shown Adelia, the Death Cap was as numerous as any other species — and carefully mixed in among them.

Bertha, however, refused to believe ill of someone who'd been nice to her. "Weren't her fault, weren't mine. Accident."

Adelia sat back on her stool to consider. Such an undoubted murder, only Bertha could believe it an accident, only Bertha could think that royal servants roamed the forest bestowing gifts of enchanted mushrooms on anyone they met. There had been meticulous planning. The old woman, whoever she was, had spun a web to catch the particular fly that was Bertha on the particular day when Rosamund's dragon, Dakers, had been absent from her mistress's side.

Which argued that the old woman had been privy to the movements of Rosamund's household, or instructed by someone who was.

Rowley's right, Adelia thought, *someone wanted Rosamund dead and the queen implicated.* If Eleanor *had* ordered it done, she'd hardly have chosen an old woman who'd mention her name. No, it hadn't been Eleanor. Whoever had done it had hated the queen even more than Rosamund. Or maybe merely wanted to enrage her husband against her and thereby plunge England into conflict. Which they might.

The shed had become quiet. Bertha's mumbles that it wasn't her fault had faded away, leaving only the sound of cows' chewing and the slither of hay as they pulled more from their mangers.

"For God's sake," Adelia asked Bertha desperately, "didn't you notice *anything* about the old woman?"

Bertha thought, shaking her head. Then she seemed puzzled. "Smelled purty," she said.

"She smelled pretty? In what way pretty?"

"Purty." The girl was crawling forward now, her nose questing like a shrew's. "Like you."

"She smelled like me?"

Bertha nodded.

Soap. Good scented soap, Adelia's one

luxury, used only two hours ago in the allover wash to cleanse her from her travels. Bars of it, made with lye, olive oil, and essence of flowers, were sent to her once a year by her foster mother from Rome — Adelia had complained in one of her letters of the soap in England, where the process was based on beef tallow, making its users smell as if they were ready for the oven.

"Did she smell like flowers?" she asked. "Roses? Lavender? Chamomile?" And she knew it was useless. Even if Bertha was conversant with these plants, she would know them only by local names unfamiliar to Adelia.

It had been a gain, though. No ordinary old woman gathering mushrooms in a forest would smell of perfumed soap, even supposing she used soap at all.

Rising to her feet, Adelia said, "If you smell her scent again on anybody else, will you tell me?"

Bertha nodded. Her eyes were fixed on the cross at Adelia's throat, as if, ignorant of its meaning, it still spoke to her of hope.

And what hope has she, poor thing?

Sighing, Adelia unfastened the chain from her neck and slid it with its cross into Bertha's dirty little hand, closing her fingers over it. "Keep this until I can buy you one of your own," she said.

It cost her to do it, not because of the cross's symbolism — Adelia had been exposed to too many religions to put all her faith in a single one — but because it had been given to her by Margaret, her old nurse, a true Christian, who had died on the journey to England.

But I have known love. I have my child, an occupation, friends.

Bertha, who had none of these things, clasped the cross and, bleating with pleasure, dived back into the straw with it.

As they walked back through the night, Jacques said, "Do you believe that little piggy *can* sniff out your truffle for you, mistress?"

"It's a long shot," Adelia admitted, "but Bertha's nose is probably the best detector we have. If she *should* smell the old woman's scent again, it will be on someone who buys foreign soap and can tell us who their supplier is, who, in turn, could provide us with a list of customers."

"Clever." The messenger's voice was admiring.

After a while, he said, "Do you think the queen *was* involved?"

"Somebody wants us to think so."

FIVE

On the rise above a gentle valley, a dog and four riders from Godstow reined in and considered the building and appurtenances crowning the opposite hill.

After some silence, Adelia said, unwisely, "How on earth do tradesmen penetrate it?"

"Gift of flowers and a nice smile used to do it in my day," the bishop said.

She heard a snort from the two men on either side of her.

"I mean the labyrinth," she said.

Rowley winked. "So do I."

More snorts.

Oh, dear, sexual innuendo. Not that she could blame them. From here, the view of Wormhold Tower and what surrounded it looked, well, *rude*. A very high, thin tower capped by a close-fitting cupola — it even had a tiny walkway around its tip to accentuate the penile resemblance — rose from the ring of a labyrinth that men apparently saw as female pubic hair. It presented an outline that might have been scrawled on the top of its hill by a naughty, adolescent giant. A graffito against the skyline.

The bishop had led them here at a canter, afraid the weather might stop them, but now that the tower was in sight, anxiety had left him relieved and, obviously, with time to enjoy ribaldry.

Actually, it had been an easy journey northward, using the river towpath that ran from Godstow to within a half-mile of the tower. So easy, in fact, that Adelia had been invigorated by it and lost her own fear that the weather would hamper her return to her child.

Such bargemen as they'd encountered had warned them that more snow was on the way, but there was no sign of it. It was a cloudless day, and although the sun hadn't melted the previous night's fall, it had been impossible not to rejoice in a countryside like white washing spread out to dry against a laundered blue sky.

Farther south, on the river they'd just left, Mansur, the bishop's two men-at-arms, and a couple of Godstow's men were bringing up a barge on which to take the body of Rosamund back to the convent — once

Bishop Rowley had retrieved it.

First, though, the labyrinth that surrounded the dead woman's stronghold had to be got through — a prospect that was stimulating the old Adam in Adelia's companions.

"I told you," Rowley said, addressing Adelia but winking at Walt. "Didn't I say it was the biggest chastity belt in Christendom?"

He was trying to provoke her. *Ignore it.* "I hadn't thought it would be quite so large," she said, and then sighed at herself. Another double entendre to make the men snigger.

Well, she hadn't. The labyrinth at Saint Giorgio's in Salerno was considered by the town to be a wonder, supposed to represent in length and complexity the soul's journey through life. But this thing opposite her now was a colossus. It encircled the tower, forming a ring so thick that it took up a wide section of this side of the hill and disappeared behind it. Its outer wall was nine or ten feet high, while, at this distance, its interior seemed to be filled entirely by white wool.

The prioress of Godstow had warned her about it before she set out. "Blackthorn," Sister Havis had told her with disgust. "Can you credit it? Walls of granite with blackthorn planted against them."

What Adelia was looking at was stone and hedge, twisting and turning in frozen undulation.

Not a belt, Adelia thought. *A snake, a huge, constricting serpent.*

Walt said, "Reckon as that's a bugger for its hedgers," nearly causing Rowley to fall off his horse. Jacques was smiling broadly, happy at seeing his bishop unbend.

Sister Havis had said what Adelia could expect. The original labyrinth, she'd said, had been built round his keep by a mad Saxon necromancer and enlarged by his equally mad dispossessor, a Norman, one of the Conqueror's knights, in order to stop his enemies from getting in and his women from getting out.

The Norman's descendants had been dispossessed in their turn by Henry Plantagenet, who'd found it a convenient place in which to install his mistress, abutting, as it did, the forest of Woodstock, where he kept a hunting lodge.

"Architectural vulgarity," Sister Havis had called it, angrily. "An object of male lewdness. Local people are in awe of it, even while they jeer at it. Poor Lady Rosamund. I fear the king found it amusing to put her there."

"He would." Adelia knew Henry Plantagenet's sense of humor.

And Rowley's.

"Of course I can penetrate it," the bishop was saying now, in answer to a question from Jacques. "I've done it. A wiggle to the right, another to the left, and everybody's happy."

Listening to the laughter, Adelia began to be sorry for Rosamund. Had the woman minded living in a place that invited, almost *demanded,* salacious comment from every man who saw it?

Poor lady. Even dead, she was being shown little respect.

With snow resting on the walls and branches of the surrounding labyrinth, the tower looked to be rising from a mass of white fuzz. Adelia was irresistibly reminded of a patient, an elderly male whom her foster father was attending and on whose body he was instructing Adelia how to repair a hernia in the groin. Suddenly, much to his abashed surprise, the patient had sustained an erection.

That's what's scrawled against the sky, she thought, *an old man's last gasp.*

She turned on Rowley. "How. Do. We. Get. In," she said, clearly, "and try to remember there's a dead woman in there."

156

He jerked a thumb. "We ring the bell."

Transfixed by the tower, she hadn't noticed it, though it stood only a few yards away on the hillside, next to a horse trough.

Like everything else belonging to Wormhold, it was extraordinary, an eight-foot-high wooden trapezoid set into the ground, from which hung a bell as massive as any in a cathedral's chimes.

"Go on, Jacques," the bishop said. "Ding-dong."

The messenger dismounted, walked up to the bell, and swung the rope hanging from its clapper.

Adelia clung to her mare as it skittered, and Walt snatched the reins of Jacques's to prevent it from bolting. Birds erupted from the trees, a rookery fell to circling and cawing as the bell's great baritone tolled across the valley. Even Ward, most unresponsive of mongrels, looked up and gave a bark.

The reverberations hung in the air and then settled into a silence.

Rowley swore. "Again," he said. "Where's Dakers? Is she deaf?"

"Must be," Jacques said. "That would waken the dead." He realized what he'd said. "Beg pardon, my lord."

For a second time the great bell tolled, seeming to shake the earth. Again, nothing happened.

"Thought I saw someone," Walt said, squinting against the sun.

So did Adelia — a black smudge on the tower's walkway. But it had disappeared now.

"She'd answer to a bishop, should've worn my episcopal robes," Rowley said. He was in hunting clothes. "Well, there's nothing for it. We can find our own way through — I remember it perfectly."

He set his horse down the hill to the valley, cloak flying. Less precipitately, the others followed.

The entrance in the labyrinth's wall when they reached it sent the men off again. Instead of an arch, two stone ellipses met at top and bottom, forming a ten-foot cleft resembling the female vulva, the inference being emphasized by the stone-carved surround in the shape of snakes coiling into various fruits and out again.

It was difficult to get the horses to enter, though the cleft was big enough; they had to be blindfolded to step through, showing, in Adelia's opinion, more decency than the remarks made by the men tugging at their reins.

Being inside wasn't nice. The way ahead of them was fairly wide, but blackthorn covered it, shutting out the sun to enfold them in the dim, gray light of a tunnel and the smell of dead leaves.

The roof was too low to allow them to remount. They would have to walk the horses through.

"Come on." Rowley was hurrying, leading his horse at a trot.

After a few bends, they could no longer hear birdsong. Then the way divided and they were presented with two tunnels, each as wide as the one by which they'd come, one going left, the other right.

"This way," said the bishop. "We turn northeast toward the tower. Just keep a sense of direction."

The first doubt entered Adelia's mind. They shouldn't have had to choose. "My lord, I'm not sure this is . . ."

But he'd gone ahead.

Well, he'd been here before. Perhaps he did remember. Adelia followed more slowly, her dog pattering after her, Jacques behind him. She heard Walt bringing up the rear, grumbling. "Wormhold. Good name for this snaky bugger."

*Wyrm*hold. *Of course. Wyrm.* In marketplaces, the professional storytellers — that the English still called skalds — frightened their audience with tales of the great snake/

159

dragon that squirmed its way through Saxon legends just as the mimicking tunnels coiled through this labyrinth.

Wistfully, Adelia remembered that Gyltha's Ulf loved those stories and played at being the Saxon warrior — what was his name? — who'd killed one such monster.

I miss Ulf. I miss Allie. I don't want to be in the Wyrm's lair.

Ulf had described it to her with relish. *"Horrible it was, deep in the earth and stunk with the blood of dead men."*

Well, they were spared that stench at least. But there was the smell of earth, and a sense of being underground, pressed in with no way out. *Which is what the Daedalus who concocted this swine intended,* she thought. It explained the blackthorn; without it, they could have climbed a wall, seen where they were heading, and breathed fresh air, but blackthorn had spines that, like the Wyrm, tore flesh to shreds.

It didn't frighten her — she knew how to get out — but she noticed that the men with her weren't laughing now.

The next bend turned south and opened into three more tunnels. Still unhesitating, Rowley took the alley to the right.

After the next bend, the way divided again. Adelia heard Rowley swear. She craned her neck to look past his horse for the cause.

It was a dead end. Rowley had his sword out and was stabbing it into a hedge that blocked the way. The scrape of metal on stone showed that there was a wall behind the foliage. "Goddamn the bastard. We'll have to back out." He raised his voice. "Back out, Walt."

The tunnel wasn't wide enough to turn the horses without scratching them on head and hindquarters, not only injuring them but also making them panic.

Adelia's mare didn't want to back out. It didn't want to go on, either. Sensibly, it wanted to stand still.

Rowley had to squeeze past his own horse to take hers by the bridle in both hands and push until he persuaded the animal to retreat back to the cul-de-sac's entrance, where they could reform their line.

"I *told* you we should keep going northeast," he said to Adelia, as if she had chosen the route.

"Where *is* northeast?"

But, irritated, he'd set off again, and she had to try and drag her reluctant mare into a trot to keep him in sight.

Another tunnel. Another. They might have been wrapped in gray wool that was thickening around them. She'd lost all sense of direction now. So, she suspected, had Rowley.

In the next tunnel, she lost Rowley. She was at a division and couldn't see which branch he'd taken. She looked back at Jacques. "Where's he gone?" And, to the dog, "Where is he, Ward? Where's he gone?"

The messenger's face was grayish, and not just from the light straining through the roof; it looked older. "Are we going to get out, mistress?"

She said soothingly, "Of course we shall." She knew how he felt. The thorned roof rounded them in captivity. They were moles without the mole's means of rising to the surface.

Rowley's voice came, muffled. "Where in hell *are* you?" It was impossible to locate him; the tunnels absorbed and diverted sound.

"Where are *you?*"

"In the name of God, stay *still,* I'm coming back."

They kept shouting in order to guide him. He shouted in his turn, mostly oaths. He was swearing in the Arabic he'd learned on crusade — his choice language when he cursed. Sometimes his voice was so near it made them jump; then it would fade and become hollow, raving against labyrinths in general and this one in particular. Against Dame Dakers and her bloody serpent. Against Eve with *her* bloody serpent. Even, appallingly, after blackthorn tore his cloak, against Rosamund and her bloody mushrooms.

Ward cocked his ears this way and that, as if enjoying the tirade, which, his mistress thought, he probably was, being another male.

It's women to be blamed, always women. He wouldn't curse the man who built this horror, or the king who imprisoned Rosamund in the middle of it.

Then she thought, *They're frightened. Well, Walt may not be, but Rowley is. And Jacques definitely is.*

At last a tall shape loomed out of the shadow ahead, leading a horse and coming toward her. It yelled, "What are you standing there for, woman? Get back. We should have taken the last turning."

Again, it was her fault. Again, the mare wouldn't move until the bishop took its bridle and pushed.

So that he shouldn't be embarrassed in front of the other two men, Adelia lowered her voice. "Rowley, this isn't a labyrinth."

He didn't lower his. "No, it isn't. We're in

the entrails of Grendel's bloody mother, that's what, goddamn her."

It came to her. *Beowulf.* That was the name. Beowulf, Ulf's favorite among all legendary Saxon warriors, killer of the Wyrm, slayer of the half-human monster Grendel and of Grendel's awful avenging mother.

"Waste bitch, boundary walker," Ulf had said of Grendel's mother, meaning she prowled the edge between earth and hell in woman's shape.

Adelia began to get cross. Why was it women who were to blame for everything — *everything,* from the Fall of Man to these blasted hedges?

"We are not in a labyrinth, my lord," she said clearly.

"Where are we, then?"

"It's a maze."

"Same difference." Puffing at the horse: "Get *back,* you great cow."

"No, it isn't. A labyrinth has only one path and you merely have to follow it. It's a symbol of life or, rather, of life and death. Labyrinths twist and turn, but they have a beginning and an end, through darkness into light."

Softening, and hoping that he would, too, she added, "Like Ariadne's. Rather beautiful, really."

"I don't want mythology, mistress, beautiful or not, I want to get to that sodding tower. What's a maze when it's at home?"

"It's a trick. A trick to confuse. To *amaze*."

"And I suppose Mistress Clever-boots knows how to get us out?"

"I do, actually." God's rib, he was sneering at her, *sneering*. She'd a mind to stay where she was and let him sweat.

"Then in the name of Christ, *do* it."

"Stop bellowing at me," she yelled at him. "You're bellowing."

She saw his teeth grit in the pretense of a placatory smile; he always had good teeth. Still did. Between them, he said, "The Bishop of Saint Albans presents his compliments to Mistress Adelia and please to escort him out of this hag's hole, for the love of God. How will you do it?"

"My business." Be damned if she'd tell him. Women were defenseless enough without revealing their secrets. "I'll have to take the lead."

They were forced to back the horses to one of the junctions where there was just enough room to turn each animal round without damage, though not enough to allow one to pass another, so Adelia ended up leading Walt's mount, Walt leading the messenger's behind her, Jacques behind him with hers, Rowley bringing up the rear with his own.

The maneuver was achieved with resentment. Even Jacques, her ally, said, "How are *you* going to get us out, then, mistress?"

"I just can." She paused. "Though it may take some time."

She stumped along in front, holding Walt's mount's reins in her right hand. In the other was her riding crop, which she trailed with apparent casualness so that it brushed against the hedge on her left.

As she went, she chuntered to herself. *Lord, how disregarded I am in this damned country. How disregarded all women are.*

She was back to the reasoning that had made her refuse to marry Rowley. At the time, he'd been expecting the king to offer him a barony, not a bishopric, thus allowing him a wife. Mad for him though she was, acceptance would have meant slipping her wrists into metaphorical golden fetters and watching him lock them on. As his wife, she could never have been herself, a *medica* of Salerno.

Adelia possessed none of the requisite feminine arts: She couldn't dance well, didn't play the lute, had never touched an embroidery frame — her sewing restricted to cobbling back together those cadavers she had dissected. In Salerno, she had been allowed to pursue skills that suited her, but in England there had been no room for them; the Church condemned any woman who did not toe its line — for her own safety, she had been forced to practice as a doctor in secret, letting a man take the credit.

As Baron Rowley's wife she would have been feted, complimented, bowed to, just as long as she denied her true being. And how long could she have done that? *I am who I am.*

Ironically, the lower down the social scale women were, the greater freedom they had; the wives of laborers and craftsmen could work alongside their men — even, sometimes, when they were widowed, take over their husband's trade. Until she'd become Adelia's friend and Allie's nurse, Gyltha had conducted a thriving business in eels and had called no man her master.

Adelia trudged on. *Hag's hole. Grendel's mother's entrails.* Why was this dreadful place feminine to the men lost in it? Because it was tunneled? Womb-like? *Is this woman's magic? The great womb?*

Is that why the Church hates me, hates all women? Because we are the source of all true power? Of life?

She supposed that by leading them out of it, she was only confirming that a woman knew its secrets and they did not.

Great God, she thought, *it isn't a question of hatred. It's fear. They are frightened of us.*

And Adelia laughed quietly, sending a suggestion of sound reverberating backward along the tunnel, as if a small pebble was skipping on water, making each man start when it passed him.

"What in hell was that?"

Walt called back stolidly, "Reckon someone's laughing at us, master."

"Dear God."

Still grinning, Adelia glanced over her shoulder to find Walt looking at her. His gaze was amused, friendlier than it had been. It was directed at her riding crop, still dragging along the left-hand hedge. He winked.

He knows, she thought. She winked back.

Heartened by this new ally, she nevertheless quickened her pace because, when she'd turned, she'd had to squint to make out Walt's expression. His face was indistinct, as if seen through haze.

They were losing the light.

Surely it was still only afternoon outside, but the low winter sun was leaving this side of the labyrinth, whichever side it was, in shadow. She didn't want to imagine what it would be like in blackness.

It was frightful enough anyway. Following the left-hand hedge wherever it went took them into blind alleys time and again so that they became weary with the travail of reversing increasingly restless horses. Each time, she could hear Rowley stamping. "Does the woman know what in hell she's doing?"

She began to doubt it herself. There was one tormenting question: *Are the hedges continuous?* If there was a gap, if one part of this maze was separated from the rest, then they could wander until it suffocated them.

As the tunnels darkened, the shadows conglomerated into a disembodied face ahead of her, malignant, grinning, mouthing impossible things. *You won't get out. I've closed the clefts. You are sewn in. You won't see your baby again.*

The thought made her hands sweat so that the riding crop slipped out of her grasp and, in clutching for it, she bumped into the hedge and set off a small avalanche of frozen snow onto her head and face.

It refreshed her common sense. *Stop it, there's no such thing as magic.* She shut her eyes to the gargoyle and her ears to Rowley's curses — the nudge had set off a shower all along the line — and pressed on.

Walt said, as if passing the time of day, bless him, " 'Tis marvelous to me how they do keep this thorn in trim. Two cuts a year, I reckon. Needs a powerful number of men to do that, mistress. Takes a king to pay them sort of wages."

She supposed it *was* marvelous in its way, and he was right, the maze would require a small army to look after it. "Not only cut it but sweep it," she said. For there were no clippings on the paths. "I wouldn't want my dog to get a thorn in his paw."

Walt considered the animal pattering along behind Adelia, with which he had now been confined at close quarters for some time. "Special breed, is he? Never come across his like afore." Nor, his sniff said, would he rush to do so again.

She shrugged. "I've got used to it. They're bred for the stink. Prior Geoffrey of Cambridge gave me this one's predecessor when I came to England so that I could be traced if I got lost. And then gave me another when the first one . . . died."

Killed and mutilated when she'd tracked down the murderer of Cambridge children to a lair a thousand times more awful than this one. But the scent he'd left to be followed had saved her then, and both the prior and Rowley had ever since insisted that she be accompanied by just such another.

She and Walt continued to chat, their voices absorbing into the network of shrubbery enfolding them. Walt had stopped despising her; it appeared that he was on good terms with women. He had daughters, he told her, and a capable wife who managed their smallholding for him while he was away. "The which I be away a lot, now Bishop Rowley's come. Chose me out of all the cathedral grooms to travel with un, so he did."

"A good choice, too," Adelia told him, and meant it now.

"Reckon 'twas. Others ain't so partial to his lordship. Don't like as he's friend to King Henry, them being for poor Saint Thomas as was massacry-ed at Canterbury."

"I see," she said. She'd known it. Rowley, having been appointed by the king against their wishes, was facing hostility from the officers and servants of his own diocese.

Whether the blame heaped on Henry Plantagenet for the murder of Thomas à Becket on the steps of his own cathedral was justified, she had never been sure, even though, in his temper, the king had called for it while in another country. Had Henry, as he'd screamed for the archbishop's death, been aware that some of his knights, with their own reasons for wanting Becket dead, would gallop off to see it done?

Perhaps. Perhaps not.

But if it hadn't been for King Henry's intervention, the followers of Saint Thomas would have condemned her to the whipping post — and nearly had.

She was on Henry's side. The martyred archbishop had seen no difference between the entities of Church and of God. Both were infallible. The laws of both must be obeyed without question and without alteration as they always had been. Henry, for all his faults the more human man, had wanted changes that would benefit not the Church but his people. Becket had obstructed him at every turn, and was still obstructing him from the grave.

"Me and Oswald and Master Paton and young Jacques, we was all new to our jobs, see," Walt was saying. "We didn't have no grumble with Bishop Rowley, not like the old guard, as was cross with him for being a king's man. Master Paton and Jacques, they joined selfsame day as he was installed."

So with the great divide between king and martyr running through the diocese of Saint Albans, its new bishop had chosen servants as fresh to their roles as he was to his.

Good for you, Rowley. Judging by Walt and Jacques, you've done well.

The messenger, however, was proving less imperturbable than the groom. "Should we shout for help, my lord?" Adelia heard him ask Rowley.

For once, his bishop was gentle with him. "Not long now, my son. We're nearly out."

He couldn't know it, but, in fact, they were. Adelia had just seen proof that they were, though she was afraid the bishop would receive little satisfaction from it.

Walt grunted. He'd seen what she'd seen — ahead in the tunnel was a pile of rounded balls of manure.

"That un dropped that as we was coming in," Walt said quietly, nodding toward the horse Adelia was leading; it had been his own, the last in line when they entered the maze. The four of them would soon be out — but exactly where they had started.

"It was always an even chance." Adelia sighed. "Bugger."

The two men behind hadn't heard the exchange, nor, by the time the hooves of the front two horses had flattened them in

173

passing, did just another lot of equine droppings have any significance for them.

Another bend in the tunnel. Light. An opening.

Dreading the outburst that must follow, Adelia and her horse stepped through the cleft leading out of the Wyrm's maze to be met by clean, scentless cold air and a setting sun illuminating the view of a great bell hanging from a trapezoid set in a hill they had descended more than two hours before.

One by one, the others emerged. There was silence.

"I'm sorry, I'm sorry," Adelia shouted into it. She faced Rowley. "Don't you see, if a maze is continuous, if there aren't any breaks, and *if* all the hedges are connected to each other and you follow one of them and stick rigidly to it wherever it goes, you'll traverse it eventually, you *must,* it's inevitable, only . . ." Her voice diminished into a misery. "I chose the left-hand hedge. It was the wrong one."

More silence. In the dying light, crows flapped joyously over the elm tops, their calls mocking the earthbound idiots below.

"Forgive me," the Bishop of Saint Albans said politely. "Do I understand that if we'd followed the right-hand hedge, we could have eventually reached the destination we wanted in the first bloody place?"

"Yes."

"The right-hand hedge?" the bishop persisted.

"Well . . . obviously, to go back it would be on the left-hand again. . . . *Are* you taking us back in?"

"Yes," the bishop said.

Lord, Lord, he's taking us back in. We'll be here all night. I wonder if Allie's all right.

They rang the great bell again, in case the figure they'd seen on the tower's walkway had relented, but, by the time they'd watered the horses at the trough, it was obvious that he or she had not.

Nobody spoke as loins were girded and a lantern lit. It was going to be very dark in there.

Rowley swept his cap off his head and knelt. "Be with us, Lord, for the sake of Thy dear Son."

Thus, the four reentered the maze. Knowing that it had an end made their minds easier, though the cost of constantly twisting and turning and backing out of the blind alleys was higher now that they were tiring.

"How'd you learn of mazes, mistress?" Walt wanted to know.

"My foster father. He's traveled extensively in the East, where he saw some,

175

though not as big."

"Proper old Wyrm, this, i'n it? Reckon there's a way through as we'm not seeing."

Adelia agreed with him. To be girded to this extent from the outside world would be an intolerable inconvenience; there had to be a straighter route. She suspected that some of the blind ends that appeared to be stone and hedge walls were not lined by masonry at all; they were gates with blackthorn trained over them that could open and shut on a direct path.

No good to her and the others, though. Investigating each one to see if it were movable would take too long and would result only in having to make further choices of tunnels that ended in fixtures.

They were condemned to the long way through.

They made it in silence. Even Walt stopped talking.

Nighttime brought the maze to life. The long-dead trickster who had designed it still tried to frighten them, but they knew him now. Nevertheless, the place had its own means of instilling dread; lantern light lit a thick tube of laced branches as if the men and the woman in it were struggling through an interminable gray stocking infested by creatures that, unseen, rustled out their dry existence in its web.

By the time they emerged, it was too dark to see whether the cleft they stepped through was ornamented like the entrance. They'd lost interest, anyway; amusement had left them.

The tunnels had to some extent protected them from the bitter air that assailed them now. Apart from an owl that, disturbed by their coming, took off from a wall with a slow clap of wings, there was no sound from the tower that faced them across the bailey. It was more massive than it had appeared from a distance, rising sheer and high toward a sky where stars twinkled icily down on it like scattered diamonds.

Jacques produced another lantern and fresh candles from his saddlebag and led them toward a blacker shape in the shadows at the tower's base that indicated the steps to a door.

Nobody had crossed the bailey since the snow fell; nothing human, anyway — there were animal and bird prints aplenty. But the place was an obstacle course. Snowy bumps proved to be abandoned goods: a broken chair, pieces of cloth, a barrel with its staves crushed on one side, battered pans, a ladle. The snow covered a scene of chaos.

Walt, stumbling, revealed a bucket with a dead hen inside. The corpse of a dog, frozen in the act of snarling, lay at the end of its chain.

Rowley gave the bucket a kick that dislodged the hen's carcass. "The disloyal, thieving *bastards.*"

Was that what this was?

It had been said that when William the Norman died, his servants immediately stripped their king's body and ran off with such of his possessions as they could carry, leaving his knights to find the great and terrible Conqueror's corpse naked on the floor of an empty palace room.

Had Rosamund's servants done the same the moment their mistress was dead? Rowley called it disloyalty, but Adelia remembered what she'd thought of Rosamund's neglect of Bertha; loyalty could come only of exchange and mutual regard.

The door to the tower, when the four reached it, was of thick, black oak at the top of a flight of wickedly glistening steps. There was no knocker. They hammered on it but neither dead nor living answered them. The sound echoed as if into an empty cave.

Keeping together — nobody suggested separating — they filed around the tower's base, through arched entrances to courtyards, to where another door proved as immovable as the first. It was, at least, on ground level.

"We'll ram the swine."

First, though, the horses had to be cared for. A path led to a deserted stable yard containing a well that responded with the sound of a splash when Walt dropped a stone down it, allaying his fear that its depths would prove frozen. The stalls had straw in them, if somewhat dirty, and their mangers had been replenished with oats not long before their former occupants had been stolen.

"Reckon as it'll do for now," Walt said grudgingly.

The others left him chipping ice from the well's windlass.

The pillagers had been arbitrary and hurried. An otherwise deserted byre held a cow that had resisted theft by being in the act of delivering its calf. Both were dead, the calf still in its birth sac.

Dodging under a washing line on which hung sheets as stiff as metal, they explored the kitchen buildings. The scullery had been stripped of its sink, the kitchen of everything except a massive table too heavy to lift.

Trying the barn, they found indentations in its earth floor to show where a plow and harrow had once stood. And . . .

"What's this, my lord?"

Jacques was holding up his lantern to a large contraption in a corner by a woodpile.

It was metal. A flanged footplate formed the base of two upright struts attached to it by heavy springs. Both sets of struts ended in a row of triangular iron teeth, shaped to fit into the corresponding row of the other's.

The men paused.

Walt rejoined them, to stare. "Seen 'em as'll take your leg," he said slowly. "Never like this un, though."

"Neither have I," Rowley told him. "God be merciful, somebody's actually oiled it."

"What is it?" Adelia asked.

Without answering, Rowley went up to the contraption and grasped one set of its teeth. Walt took the other and, between them, they pulled the two sets of struts' rows apart until each lay flat on the ground opposite the other, teeth gaping upward. "All right, Walt. Careful now." Rowley bent and, keeping his body well away, extended an arm to fumble underneath the mechanism. "Works by a trigger," he said. Walt nodded.

"What *is* it?" Adelia asked again.

Rowley stood up and picked up a log from the woodpile. He gestured for Adelia to keep her dog away. "Imagine it lying in long grass. Or under snow."

Almost flat, as the thing was now, it would be undetectable.

It's a mantrap. Oh, God help us.

She bent and grasped Ward's collar.

Rowley chucked the log onto the contraption's metal plate.

The thing leaped upward like a snapping shark. The teeth met. The clang seemed to come later.

After a moment, Walt said, "Get you round the whatsis, that would, begging your pardon, mistress. No point in gettin' you out, either."

"The lady didn't care for poachers, it seems," the bishop said. "Damned if I go wandering her woods." He dusted his hands. "Come on, now. This won't beat the Bulgars, as my old granddad used to say. We need a ram."

Adelia stayed where she was, staring at the mantrap. At two and a half feet high, the teeth would engage around the average man's groin, spiking him through. As Walt had said, releasing the victim would make no difference to an agonizing and prolonged death.

The thing was still vibrating, as if it were licking its chops.

The bishop had to come back for her.

"Somebody made it," she said. "Somebody oiled it. For use."

"I know. Come along, now."

"This is an awful place, Rowley."

"I know."

Jacques found a sawing horse in one of the outhouses. Holding it sideways by its legs and running with it, he and Walt managed to break down the tower's back door at the third attempt.

It was nearly as cold inside as out. And more silent.

They were in a round hall that, because of the tower's greater base, was larger than any room they were likely to find upstairs. Not a place for valued visitors to wait; it was more a guardroom. A couple of beautiful watchman's chairs, too heavy to be looted, were its saving grace. For the rest, hard benches and empty weapon racks made up the furniture. Cressets had been torn from the walls, a chandelier from its chain.

Some tapers clipped into their holders were strewn among the rushes of the floor. Lighting them from the lantern, Rowley, Adelia, and Walt took one each and began the ascent of the bare staircase running upward around the wall.

They found the tower to be one circular

room placed on another, like a tube of apothecary's pills wrapped in stiff paper and set upright, the door to each reached by a curving flight and a tiny landing. The second they came to was as utilitarian as the first, its empty racks, some dropped strands of polishing horsetail, and the smell of beeswax suggesting an overlarge cleaning cupboard.

Above that, the maids' room: four wooden beds and little else. All the beds were stripped of palliasse and covering.

Each room was deserted. Each was marginally less uncomfortable than the one below. A sewing room — looted, for the most part, but the bench tables set under each arrow slit to catch the light carried torn strips of material and an errant pincushion. A plaster dummy had been smashed to the floor, and shards of it were seemingly kicked onto the landing.

"They hated her," said Adelia, peering in through the arched doorway.

"Who?"

"The servants."

"Hated who?" The bishop was beginning to puff.

"Rosamund," Adelia told him. "Or Dame Dakers."

"With these stairs? I don't blame 'em."

183

She grinned at his laboring back. "You've been eating too many episcopal dinners."

"As you say, mistress." He was unoffended. It was a rebuff; in the old days, he'd have been indignant.

I must remember, she thought. *We are no longer intimate; we keep our distance.*

The fourth room — or was it the fifth? — had not been looted, though it was starker than any. A truckle bed, its gray, knitted bedspread rigidly tucked in. A deal table on which stood ewer and basin. A stool. A plain chest with a few bits of women's clothing, equally plain and neatly folded.

"Dakers's room," Adelia said. She was beginning to get the feel of the housekeeper, and was daunted by it.

"Nobody's here. Leave it."

But Adelia was interested. Here, the looters had desisted. Here, she was sure, Dragon Dakers had stood on the stairs, as frightening as Bertha described her, and stopped them from going farther.

Rosamund's escutcheon was carved into the eastern section of the west wall above Dakers's bed; it had been painted and gilded so that it dominated the gray room. Raising her candle to look at it, Adelia heard an intake of breath from Rowley in the doorway that wasn't due to exertion.

"God's teeth," he said, "that's madness."

A carved outer shield showed three leopards and the fleur-de-lis, which every man and woman in England now recognized as the arms of their Angevin Plantagenet king. Inside it was a smaller shield, checkered, with one quarter containing a serpent, the other a rose.

Even Adelia's scanty knowledge of heraldry was enough to know that she was looking at the escutcheon of a man and his wife.

The bishop, staring, joined her. "*Henry.* In the name of God, Henry, what were you *doing* to allow this? It's madness."

A motto had been carved into the wall beneath the escutcheon. Like most armorial mottos, it was a pun. *Rosa Mundi.*

Rose of all the world.

"Oh, dear," Adelia said.

"Jesus have mercy," Rowley breathed. "If the queen saw this . . ."

Together, motto and escutcheon made the taunt of all taunts: *He prefers me to you. I am his wife in all but name, the true queen of his heart.*

The bishop's mind was leaping ahead. "Damnation. Whether Eleanor's seen it or not is irrelevant. It's enough for others to assume that she knows of it and had Rosamund killed because of it. It's a reason to kill. It's flaunting usurpation."

"It's a bit of stone with patterns on it put up by a silly woman," Adelia protested. "Does it matter so much?"

Apparently, it did — and would. Pride mattered to a queen. Her enemies knew it; so did the enemies of the king.

"*I'll* kill the bitch if she isn't dead already," said the man of God. "I'll burn the place down, and her in it. This is an invitation to war."

She was puzzled. "You've been here before, I'd expect you to have seen it already."

He shook his head. "We met in the garden; she was taking the air. We gave thanks to God for her recovery, and then Dakers led me back through the Wyrm. Where *is* Dakers?"

He pushed past Jacques and Walt, who stood blinking in the doorway, and attacked the stairs, shouting for the housekeeper. Doors slammed open as he looked into the next room, dismissed it, and raced upward to the next.

They hurried after him, the tower resounding with the crash of boots and the click of a dog's paws on stone.

Now they were climbing past Rosamund's apartments. Dakers, if it *was* Dakers, had been able to preserve them in all their glory. Adelia, trying to keep up, was vouchsafed glimpses of spring and autumn come together. Persian carpets, Venetian goblets, damask divans, gold-rich icons and triptychs, arras, statuary: the spoils of an empire laid at the feet of an emperor's mistress.

Here were glazed windows, not the arrow slits of the rooms below. They were shuttered, but the taper's light as Adelia passed reflected an image of itself in lattices of beautiful and expensive glass.

And through the open doors came perfume, subtle but strong enough to delight a nose deadened by cold and the foul pelt of a dog.

Adelia sniffed. Roses. He even captured roses for her.

Above her, another door was flung against its jamb. A sharp exclamation from the bishop.

"What is it, what is it?" She reached him on the last landing; there were no more stairs. Rowley was standing facing the open door, but the lit candle in his hand was down by his side, dripping wax onto the floor.

"What *is* it?"

"You were wrong," Rowley said.

The cold up here was extraordinary.

"Was I?"

"She's alive. Rosamund. Alive after all."

The relief would have been immeasurable if it hadn't been that he was so strange and there was no light in the room he was facing.

Also, he was making no effort to enter.

"She's sitting there," he said, and made the sign of the cross.

Adelia went in, the dog following her.

No perfume here, the cold obliterated scent. Each window — at least eight of them encircled the room — was open, its glazed lattice and accompanying shutter pushed outward to allow in air icy enough to kill. Adelia felt her face shrivel from it.

Ward went ahead. She could hear him sniffing round the room, giving no sign that he encountered anybody. She went in a little farther.

The glow of the taper fell on a bed against the northerly wall. Exquisite white lace swept from a gilded rondel in the ceiling to part over pillows and fall at either side of a gold-tasseled coverlet. It was a high and magnificent bed, with a tiny ivory set of steps placed so that its owner might be assisted to reach it.

Nobody was in it.

Its owner was sitting at a writing table opposite, facing a window, a pen in her hand.

Adelia, her taper now vibrating a little, saw the glancing facets of a jeweled crown and ash-blond hair curling from it down the writer's back.

Go nearer. You have to. It can't harm you. It can't.

She willed herself forward. As she passed the bed, she stepped on a fold of its lace lying on the floor, and the ice in it crunched under her boot.

"Lady Rosamund?" It seemed polite to say it, even knowing what she knew.

She took off her glove to touch the figure's unexpectedly large shoulder and felt the chill of stone in what had once been flesh. She saw a white, white hand, its wrist braceleted with skin, like a baby's. Thumb and forefinger were supporting a goose quill as if it had only seconds ago drawn the signature on the document on which they rested.

Sighing, Adelia bent to look into the face. Open, blue eyes were slightly cast downward so that they appeared to be rereading what the hand had just written.

But Fair Rosamund was very dead.

And very fat.

Six

"Dakers," Adelia said. "Dakers did this."

Only Dame Dakers could be refusing to let her dead mistress go to her grave.

Rowley was recovering. "We'll never get her in the coffin like that. For the love of God, *do* something. I'm not rowing back to Godstow with her sitting up and looking at me."

"Show some respect, blast you." Banging the last window closed, Adelia turned on him. "You won't be rowing, and she won't be sitting."

Both were compensating in their own way for the impact of a scene that had unmanned him and unnerved her.

Jacques was staring from the doorway, but Walt, having peered in, had retired downstairs in a hurry. Ward, unperturbed, was scratching himself.

Used to dead bodies as she was, Adelia had never feared one — until now. Consequently, she'd become angry. It was the corpse's *employment.* . . . Rosamund hadn't died in that position — if it were the mushrooms that had killed her, the end would have been too violent. No, Dakers had dragged the still-warm carcass onto the Roman chair, arranged it, and then either waited for rigor mortis to set in or, if rigor had already passed, held it in place until the cold coming through the open windows had fixed head, trunk, and limbs as they were now, frozen in the attitude of writing.

Adelia knew this as surely as if she'd seen it happen, but the impression that the dead woman had got up, walked to her table, sat down, and picked up a pen could not be shaken off.

Rowley's peevishness merely disguised the revulsion that had thrown him off balance, and Adelia, who felt the same, responded to it with irritation. "You didn't tell me she was fat."

"Is it relevant?"

No, it wasn't, of course it wasn't, but it was a sort of aftershock. The image Adelia had gained of Fair Rosamund by repute, from meeting Bertha, from tramping through the dreadful maze, from seeing the even more dreadful mantrap, had been of a beautiful woman with the indifference to human suffering of an Olympian goddess: physically lovely, pampered, aloof, cold as a reptile — but slim. Definitely slim.

Instead, the face she'd bent down to peer into had looked back at her with the innocent chubbiness integral to the obese.

It altered things. She wasn't sure why, but it did.

"How long has she been dead?" Rowley demanded.

"What?" Adelia's mind had wandered into inconsequential questioning of the corpse. *Why, with your weight, did you live at the* top *of this tower? How did you get down the stairs to meet Rowley in the garden? How did you get back up?*

"I *said,* how long has she been dead?"

"Oh." It was time to collect her wits and do the job she'd been brought here to do. "Impossible to be exact."

"Was it the mushrooms?"

"How can I tell? Probably yes."

"Can you flatten her?"

God's rib, he was a crude man. "She'll flatten herself," Adelia said, shortly, "just get some heat into this damned room." Then she asked, "Why did Dakers want her to be seen *writing,* do you suppose?"

But the bishop was on the landing, shouting to Walt to bring braziers, kindling, firewood, candles, pushing Jacques into descending and helping the groom, then going down himself on another search for the housekeeper, taking energy with him and leaving the chamber to the quiet of the dead.

Adelia's thoughts rested wistfully on the man whose calm assistance and reassurance had always been her rock during difficult investigations — for never was one likely to be more difficult than this. Mansur, however, was on the barge bringing Rosamund's coffin upriver and, even supposing he had arrived at the landing place that served Wormhold Tower a quarter of a mile away, he, Oswald, and the men with them had been told to stay there until the messenger fetched them.

Which could not be tonight. Nobody was going to face the maze of the Wyrm again tonight.

She had only one light; Rowley had taken his taper with him. She put hers on the writing table as near to the corpse's hand as possible without burning it — a minuscule start to the thawing out of the body that not only would take time but would be messy.

Adelia brought to mind the pigs on which she had studied decomposition at the farm in the hills above Salerno, kept for the purpose by Gordinus, her teacher of the process of mortification. From the various carcasses, her memory went to those frozen in the icehouse he'd had built deep into rock. She calculated weights, times; she envisaged needles of ice crystals solidifying muscle and tissue . . . and the resultant juices as they melted.

Poor Rosamund. She would be exposed to the outrages of corruption when everything in her chamber spoke of a being who'd loved elegance.

Poor Dakers, who had, undoubtedly, loved her mistress to the point of madness.

Who had also put a crown on her mistress's head. A real crown, not a fashionable circlet, not a chaplet, not a coronal, but an ancient thing of thick gold with four prongs that rose in the shape of fleur-de-lis from a jeweled brim — the crown of a royal consort. This, Dakers was saying, is a queen.

Yet the same hand had brushed the lovely hair so that it hung untrammeled over the corpse's shoulders and down its back in the style of a virgin.

Oh, get to it, Adelia told herself. She was not here to be fascinated by the unplumbable depths of human obsession but to find out why someone had found it good that this woman should die and, thereby, who that someone was.

She wished there was some noise from downstairs to ameliorate the deathly quiet of this room. Perhaps it was too high up for sound to reach it.

Adelia turned her attention to the writing table, an eerie business with the shuttered glass on the other side of it acting on it like the silvering of a looking glass, so that she and the corpse were reflected darkly.

A pretty table, highly polished. Near the dead woman's left hand, as if her fingers could dip into it easily, was a bowl of candied plums.

The bowl was a black-and-red pot figured with athletes like the one her foster father had found in Greece, so ancient and precious that he allowed no one to touch it but himself. Rosamund kept sweetmeats in hers.

A glass inkwell encased in gold filigree. A smart leather holder for quills, and a little ivory-and-steel knife to sharpen them. Two pages of the best vellum, both closely written, lying side by side, one under the right hand. A sand shaker, also glass, in gold filigree matching the inkwell, its sand nearly used up. A tiny burner for melting the wax that lay by it in two red sticks, one shorter than the other.

Adelia looked for a seal and found none,

but there was a great gold ring on one of the dead fingers. She picked up the taper and held it close to the ring. Its round face was a matrix that when pressed into softened wax would embed the two letters RR.

Rosamund Regina?

Hmm.

It had mattered to Dakers that Rosamund be recognized as literate — no mean accomplishment in England, even among high-born women. Why else had she been petrified like this? Obviously, she *had* been literate. The table's implements showed heavy use; Rosamund had written a lot.

Was Dakers merely proud that you could *write? Or is there some other significance that I'm not seeing?*

Adelia turned her attention to the two pieces of vellum. She picked up the one directly in front of the corpse — and found it indecipherable in this light; Rosamund's literacy had not extended to good calligraphy — here was a cramped scrawl.

She wondered where Rowley was with more candles, blast him. It was taking the bishop a long time to return. For just a second, Adelia registered the fact, then found that by extending the parchment above her head with one hand, putting the taper dangerously close underneath it with the other, and squinting, it was just possible to make out a superscription. What she held was a letter.

"To the Lady Eleanor, Duchess of Aquitaine and supposed Queen of England, greetings from the true and very Queen of this country, Rosamund the Fair."

Adelia's jaw dropped. So, very nearly, did the letter. This wasn't lèse-majesté, it was outright, combative treason. It was a challenge.

It was *stupid.*

"Were you insane?" The whisper was absorbed by the room's silence.

Rosamund was sending a challenge to Eleanor's authority, and must have known it was one the queen would have to respond to or be forever humiliated.

"You were taking a risk," Adelia whispered. Wormhold Tower might be difficult to seize, but it wasn't impregnable; it couldn't withstand the sort of force that an infuriated queen would send against it.

The deadness of the corpse whispered back, *Ah, but instead did the queen send an old woman with poisoned mushrooms?*

None of the above, Adelia thought to herself, because Eleanor didn't receive the letter. Most likely, Rosamund had never intended to send it; isolated in this awful tower, she'd merely amused herself by scribbling fantasies of queenship onto vellum.

What else had she written?

Adelia replaced the letter on the table and picked up its companion document. In the dimness, she made out another superscription. Another letter, then. Again, it had to be held up so that the taper shone upward onto it. This one was easier to read.

"To the Lady Eleanor, Duchess of Aquitaine and supposed Queen of England, greetings from the true and very Queen of this country, Rosamund the Fair."

The wording was exactly the same. And it was more decipherable only because somebody else had written it. This hand was very different from Rosamund's scrawl; it was the legible, sloping calligraphy of a scholar.

Rosamund had copied her letter from this one.

Ward gave a low growl, but Adelia, caught up in the mystery, paid him no attention.

It's here. I am on the brink of it.

Waving the parchment gently, she thought it out, then saw in the mirror of the window that she was, in fact, tapping Rosamund's head with it.

And stopped, she and the corpse each as rigid as the other. Ward had tried to warn her that someone else had entered the tower room; she'd paid no notice.

Three faces were reflected in the glass, two of them surmounted by crowns. "I am delighted to make your acquaintance, my dear," one of them said — and it wasn't talking to Adelia.

Who, for a moment, stood where she was, staring straight ahead, trying to subdue shivering superstition, gathering all her common sense against belief in the wizardry of conjurement.

Then she turned and bowed. There was no mistaking a real queen.

Eleanor took no notice of her. She walked to one side of the table, bringing with her a scent that subsumed Rosamund's roses in something heavier and more Eastern. Two white, long-fingered hands were placed on the wood as she bent forward to look into the face of the dead woman. "Tut, tut. You *have* let yourself go." A beringed forefinger nudged the Greek pot. "Do I suspect too many sweeties and not enough sallets?"

Her voice belled charmingly across the chamber. "Did you know that poor Rosamund was fat, Lord Montignard? Why was I not told?"

"Cows usually are, lady." A man's voice, coming from a shape lounging in the doorway and holding a lantern. There was an indistinct, taller figure in mail standing behind him.

"So rude," said Eleanor, apologetically, to the body in the chair. "Men are unfair, are they not? And you must have had so many compensating qualities . . . generosity with your favors, things like that."

The cruelty was not only verbal but also accentuated by the two women's physical disparity. Against the tall sweep of the queen's shape, that showed slender even in the fur wrapping it round, Rosamund appeared lumpen, her tumbling hair ridiculous for a mature woman. Compared to the delicate spikes on the white-gold crown Eleanor wore, Rosamund's was an overweight piece of grandiloquence.

The queen had come to the document. "My dear, another of your letters to me? And God froze you to ice in the middle of penning it?"

Adelia opened her mouth and then shut it; she and the men in the doorway were merely sounding boards in the game that Eleanor of Aquitaine was playing with a dead woman.

"I am sorry I was not here at the time," the queen was saying. "I had but landed from France when I received word of your illness, and there were other matters I had

to see to rather than be at your deathbed."
She appeared to sigh. "Always business
before pleasure."

She picked up the letter and held it at
arm's length, unable to read it in the light
but not needing to. "Is this like the others?
*Greetings to the supposed queen from the
true one?* Somewhat repetitious, don't you
think? Not worth keeping, yes?"

She crumpled the parchment and tossed
it onto the floor, grinding it out on the
stones with the twist of an excellent boot.

Slowly, slowly, Adelia bent slightly sideways and down. She slipped the document
she'd been holding into the top of her right
boot and felt her dog lick her hand as she
did it. He was keeping close.

Facing the mirroring window, she looked
to see if the man in the doorway had noticed
the movement. He hadn't. His attention was
on Eleanor; Eleanor's on Rosamund's
corpse.

The queen was cupping her ear as if
listening to a reply. "You don't mind? So
generous, but they say you were always
generous with your favors. Oh, and forgive
me, this bauble is mine." Eleanor had lifted
the crown off the dead woman's head. "It
was made for the wives of the counts of Anjou two centuries ago, and *how dare he give*

it to a stinking great whore like you. . . ."

Control had gone. With a scream, the queen sent the crown spinning away toward the window opposite them both as if she meant to smash the glass with it. Ward barked.

What saved Eleanor's life was that the crown hit the window with the padded underside of its brim. If the glass had shattered, Adelia — dazedly watching the mirroring window shake as the missile bounced off it — would not have seen the reflection of Death slithering toward them. Nor the knife in its hand.

She didn't have time to turn round. It was coming for Eleanor. Instinctively, Adelia flung herself sideways, and her left hand contacted Death's shoulder.

In trying to deflect the knife, she misjudged and had her right palm sliced open by it. But her shove changed the momentum of the attacker, who went tumbling to the floor.

The scene petrified: Rosamund sitting unconcernedly in her chair; Eleanor, just as still, facing the window in which the attack had been reflected; Adelia standing and looking down at the figure lying sprawled facedown at her feet. It was hissing.

The dog approached it, sniffing, and then

backed away.

So for a second. Then Lord Montignard was exclaiming over the queen while the mailed man had his boot on the attacker's back and a sword raised in his two hands, looking at Eleanor for permission to strike.

"No." Adelia thought she'd shrieked it, but shock diminished the word so that it sounded quietly reasonable.

The man paid her no attention. Expressionless, he went on looking at the queen, who had a hand to her head. She seemed to collapse, but it was to kneel. The white hands were steepled, the crowned head bowed, and Eleanor of Aquitaine prayed. "Almighty God," she said, "accept the thanks of this unworthy queen for stretching out Your hand and reducing this, my enemy, to a block of ice. Even in death she did send her creature against me, but You turned the blade so that, innocent and wronged as I am, I live on to serve You, my Lord and Redeemer."

When Montignard helped her to her feet, she was amazingly calm. "I saw it," she said to Adelia. "I saw God choose you as his instrument to save me. Are you the housekeeper? They say this strumpet had a housekeeper."

"No. My name is Adelia. I am Adelia

Aguilar. I assume that is the housekeeper. Her name is Dakers." Pointing to the figure on the floor, her hand dripped blood over it.

Queen Eleanor paid it no attention. "What do you do here, then, girl? How long have you lived here?"

"I don't. I'm a stranger to this place. We arrived an hour or so ago." A lifetime. "I've never been here before. I had only just come up the stairs and discovered . . . this."

"Was this creature with you?" Eleanor dabbled her fingers in the direction of her still-supine attacker.

"No. I hadn't seen her, not until now. She must have hidden herself when she heard us come up the stairs."

Montignard came close to wave the tip of a dagger in her face. "You wretch, it is your queen you talk to. Show respect or I slit your nose." He was a willowy young man, very curly, very brave now.

"My lady," Adelia added dully.

"Stop it, Monty," the queen snapped, and turned to the man in mail. "Is the place secured, Schwyz?"

"Secure?" Still without expression, Schwyz managed to convey his opinion that the tower was about as secure as a slice of carrot. "We took four men in the barge and

204

three downstairs." He didn't address the queen by her title, either, but Adelia noticed that Montignard didn't threaten to slit Schwyz's nose for it; the man stood square on thick legs, more like a foot soldier than a knight, and nobody was in any doubt that if Eleanor had given the nod, he'd have skewered the housekeeper like a flapping fish. And Montignard, for that matter.

A mercenary, Adelia decided.

"Did these three men downstairs bring you with them?" the queen asked.

"Yes." Dear Lord, she was tired. "My lady," she added.

"Why?"

"Because the Bishop of Saint Albans asked me to accompany him." Rowley could answer the questions; he was good at that.

"Rowley?" The queen's voice had altered. "*Rowley's* here?" She turned to Schwyz. "Why was I not told?"

"Four men in the boat and three downstairs," Schwyz repeated stolidly. His accent was London with a trace of something more foreign. "If a bishop is among them, I don't know it." He didn't care, either. "We stay the night here?"

"Until the Young King and the Abbot of Eynsham arrive."

Schwyz shrugged.

Eleanor cocked her head at Adelia. "And why has his lordship of Saint Albans brought one of his women to Wormhold Tower?"

"I can't say." At that moment, she didn't have the energy to recount the train of events, and certainly not to make them comprehensible. She was too tired, too shocked, too struck down by horrors even to refute the imputation of being "one of his women," though not to wonder how many he was known to have.

"We shall ask him," Eleanor said brightly. She looked down at the writhing shape on the floor. "Raise her."

The courtier Montignard pushed forward and made a fuss of kicking the would-be assassin's knife across the floor. Hauling her upright from under Schwyz's boot, he maintained her with one arm round the chest and put the point of his dagger to her neck with the other.

It *was* Death, a better facsimile than any in the marketplace mystery plays. The hood of a black cloak had wrinkled back to disclose the prominent cheekbones and teeth of a skull with pale skin so tight that the only indication, in this bad light, to show that the face had any at all was a large and sprouting mole on the upper lip. The eyes were set deep; they might have been holes. All it lacked was the scythe.

It was still hissing sporadically, the words mixed with spittle. ". . . dare to touch the true queen, you dissembler . . . my Master, my most northerly Lord . . . burn your soul . . . cast you . . . utmost obscenity."

Eleanor leaned forward, cupping her ear again, then stood back. "Demons? *Belial?*" She turned to her audience. "The woman threaten me with Belial. My dear, I married him."

"Only let me strangle her, lady. Let me cauterize this pus," Montignard said. A pearl of blood appeared from where the tip of the dagger pierced the woman's skin.

"Leave her alone," Adelia managed a shout now. "She's mad, and she's half dead already, leave her alone." Instinctively, she'd put her fingers round the woman's wrist, feeling a hideously slow pulse among bones almost as cold as Rosamund's. Dear God, how long had she been hiding in this ice chamber?

"She needs warmth," Adelia said to Eleanor. "We must warm her."

The queen looked at Adelia's dripping hand held out to her in appeal, then at the housekeeper. She shrugged. "We are informed the creature needs warming, Monty.

I imagine that does not entail putting it into the fire. Take it downstairs, Schwyz, and see to it. Gently, now. We shall question it later."

Scowling, the courtier handed his captive over to Schwyz, who took her to the door, gave an order to one of his men, saw her taken away, and came back. "Madam, we should leave. I cannot defend this place."

"Not yet, Master Schwyz. Go about your duties."

Schwyz stumped off, not a happy man.

The queen smiled at Adelia. "You see? You ask for the woman's life, I give it. Noblesse oblige. Such a gracious monarch am I."

She was impressive; Adelia gave her that. The prickling weakness of shock that threatened to collapse Adelia's legs left this woman seemingly untouched, as if attempted assassination was the everyday round of royalty. Perhaps it was.

Montignard hesitated. He nodded toward Adelia. "Leave you alone with this wench, lady? I shall not. Does she wish you harm? I do not know."

"My lord." Eleanor had a metaphorical whip in her boot. "Whoever she may be, she saved my life. Which" — the whip cracked — "*you* were too slow to do. Now go attend to that eyesore. Also, we could profit from some warmth ourselves. See to it. And bring me the Bishop of Saint Albans."

Self-preservation helped Adelia to mumble, "And some brandy. Send up brandy." She'd just properly seen the wound in her hand; it went deep and, goddamn all assassins, she needed her right hand.

The queen nodded her permission. She showed no sign of leaving the chamber and descending to another. While Adelia considered that perverse, not to say unhallowed, considering the poor body occupying it, she was grateful to be spared the stairs. Sidling out of the royal sight, she sank down onto the floor by the side of the bed and stayed there.

People came and went, things were done, the bed stripped and its covers and mattress sent downstairs to be burned — the queen was insistent about that.

A beautiful young woman, presumably one of Eleanor's attendants, came in, fluttered at the sight of Rosamund, fainted prettily, and had to be taken out again. Maids, manservants — how many had she brought with her? — carried in braziers, candles enough to light the Vatican, incense and oil burners, lamps, flambeaux. Adelia, who'd thought she'd never be warm again, began to think kindly and soporifically of the cold. She closed her eyes. . . .

". . . in hell are you doing here? If he's coming, he'll come straight for this tower." It was Rowley's voice, very loud, very angry.

Adelia woke up. She was still on the floor by the bed. The chamber was hotter; there were more people in it. Rosamund's body, ignored, sat at its table, though some merciful soul had covered the head and shoulders with a cloak.

"You dare address my glorious lady like that? She goes where she please." This was Montignard.

"I'm talking to the queen, you bastard. Keep your snout out of . . . *it.*" He jerked the last word — somebody had punched him.

Peering under the bed, Adelia saw the bottom half of the queen and all of Rowley kneeling in front of her. His hands were tied. Mailed legs — she recognized one pair as Schwyz's — stood behind him and, to the side, Montignard's fine leather boots, one of them raised for another kick.

"Leave him, my lord," Eleanor said icily. "This is the language I have come to expect from the Bishop of Saint Albans."

"It's called truth, lady," Rowley said.

"When did you ever hear anything else from me?"

"Is it? Then the question is not what *I* do here, but what *you* do."

It'll come in a minute, Adelia thought. The appalling coincidence of this forgathering must seem sinister to a queen who'd just been attacked.

Cautiously, she began undoing the strings of the purse hanging from her belt and feeling for the small roll of velvet containing the surgical instruments she always carried when traveling.

"I told you. I came on your behalf." Rowley jerked his head in the direction of the writing table. "My lady, rumor is already blaming you for Rosamund's death. . . ."

"*Me?* Almighty God killed her."

"He had help. Let me find out whose — it's why I came, to find out . . ."

"In the dark? This night of nights?" Montignard interrupting again. "You come and same time a demon rush out of the wall to stab the queen?"

Here it was. Adelia's hand found the tiny, lethally sharp knife in the roll and loosened it so that its handle protruded. What to do with it she wasn't sure, but if they hurt him . . .

"*What?* What demon?" Rowley asked.

Eleanor nodded. "The housekeeper, Dampers. Did you hire her to kill me, Saint Albans?"

"Elean-oor." It was the protesting growl of one old friend to another; everybody else in the chamber was diminished by the claim of a hundred shared memories. It made the queen go back in her tracks.

"Well, well," she said, more gently, "I suppose you must be absolved, since it was your leman who pushed aside the blade."

Adelia's hand relaxed.

"My leman?"

"I forgot you have so many. The one with the foreign name and no manners."

"Ah," the bishop said. "*That* leman. Where is she?"

Using her one good hand, Adelia pulled herself up by the bed frame and stood where everybody could see her. She felt afraid and rather foolish.

Awkwardly, Rowley looked round. He had blood on his mouth.

Their eyes met.

"I rejoice that she served such a mighty purpose, madam," the Bishop of Saint Albans said slowly. He looked back at the queen. "Keep her if you will, she's of no use to me — as you say, she has no manners."

Eleanor shook her head at Adelia. "See

how easily he discards you? All men are knaves, king or bishop."

Adelia began to panic. *He's abandoning me to her. He can't. There's Allie. I must get back to Godstow.*

Rowley was answering another question. "Yes, I have. Twice. The first time I came was when she was taken ill — Wormhold is part of my diocese; it was my duty. And tonight when I heard of her death. That's not the point. . . ." Being bound and on his knees wasn't going to stop the bishop from lecturing the queen. "In the name of God, Eleanor, why didn't you make for Aquitaine? It's madness for you to be here. Get away. I beg you."

" *'That's not the point'?"* Eleanor had heard only what was important to her. Her cloak swished across the floor as she retrieved Rosamund's letter from it. "This is the point. This, *this*. I have received ten such." She smoothed the letter out and held it out. "You and the whore were in league with Henry to set her up as queen."

There was a moment's quiet as Rowley read.

"God strike me, I knew nothing of it," he said — and Adelia thought that even Eleanor must hear that he was appalled. "Nor does the king, I swear. The woman was

213

insane."

"*Evil.* She was *evil.* She shall burn in this world as in the next — her and all that is hers. The brushwood is being put in place, ready for the flame. A fitting end for a harlot. No Christian burial for her."

"Jesus." Adelia saw Rowley blanch and then gather himself. Suddenly, the tone of his voice changed to one that was wrenchingly familiar; it had got her into his bed. "Eleanor," he said gently, "you are the greatest of queens, you brought beauty and courtesy and music and refinement to a realm of savages, you civilized us."

"Did I?" Very soft, all at once girlish.

"You know you did. Who taught us chivalry toward women? Who in hell taught me to say please?" He followed up the advantage of her laugh. "Do not, I beg you, commit an act of vandalism that will resound against you. No need to burn this tower; let it stand in its filth. Retire to Aquitaine, just for a while, give me time to find out who actually killed Rosamund so that I can treat with the king. For the sake of Christ crucified, lady, until then *don't antagonize him.*"

It was the wrong note.

"Antagonize him?" Eleanor said sweetly. "He had me imprisoned at Chinon, Bishop. Nor did I hear your voice amongst those

214

raised against it."

She signaled to the men behind Rowley, and they began dragging him out.

As they reached the doorway, she said clearly, "You are Henry Plantagenet's man, Saint Albans. Always were, always will be."

"And yours, lady," he shouted back. "And God's."

They heard him swearing at his captors bumping him down the stairs. The sound became fainter. There was a silence like the dust-settling quiet that comes after a building has crashed to the ground.

Schwyz had stayed behind. "The *schweinhund* is right that we should leave, lady."

The queen ignored him; she was circling, agitated, muttering to herself. Shrugging resignation, Schwyz went away.

"He'd never hurt you, lady," Adelia said. "Don't hurt him."

"Don't love him," the queen snapped back.

I don't, I won't. *Just don't hurt him.*

"Let me take out his eyes, my queen." Montignard was breathing hard. "He would assassinate you with that demon."

"Of course he wouldn't," Eleanor said — and Adelia let out a breath of relief. "Rowley told the truth. That woman, Dampers . . . I had inquiries made, and it is well

215

known she was mad for her mistress, *ugh*. Even now, she would kill me ten times over."

"Really?" Montignard was intrigued. "They were Sapphos?"

The queen continued to circle. "Am I a killer of whores, Monty? What can they accuse me of next?"

The courtier bent and picked up the hem of her cloak to kiss it. "You are the blessed Angel of Peace come to Bethlehem again."

It made her smile. "Well, well, we can do nothing more until the Young King and the abbot arrive." From downstairs came the sound of furniture being overturned and the slamming of shutters. "What is Schwyz *doing* down there?"

"He puts archers at each window ready to defend. He is afraid the king will come."

The queen shook her head indulgently, as if at overenthusiastic children. "Even Henry can't travel fast through in this weather. God kept the snow off for me, now he sends it to impede the king. Well then, I shall stay here in this chamber until my son comes." She looked toward Adelia. "You too, yes?"

"Madam, with your permission I shall join the —"

"No, no. God has sent you to me as a talisman." Eleanor smiled quite beautifully. "You will stay here with me and" — she

216

walked over to the body and snatched off its covering cloak — "together we shall watch Fair Rosamund rot."

So they did.

What Adelia remembered of that night afterward were the hour-long silences when she and the queen were alone — apart from Montignard, who fell asleep — and during which Eleanor of Aquitaine sat, untiring, her back straight as a plumb line, eyes directed at the body of the woman her husband had loved.

She also remembered, though with disbelief, that at one point a young courtier with a lute came in and strolled about the chamber, singing winsomely in the langue d'oc, and that, after receiving no response from his queen and even less from the corpse, he wandered out again.

And the heat. Adelia remembered the heat of the braziers and a hundred candle flames. At one point, she begged for relief. "May we not open a window for a minute, madam?" It was like being in a pottery kiln.

"No."

So Adelia, the lucky charm, privileged by her status as God-sent savior to royalty, sat in its presence, crouching on the floor with her cloak under her while the queen, still in her furs, sat and watched a corpse.

Eleanor's eyes left it only when they brought the brandy, and Adelia, instead of drinking the spirit, tipped it over the cut in her hand and took a needle and silk thread from the traveling pack of instruments in her pocket.

"Who taught you to cleanse with brandy?" Eleanor wanted to know. "I use twice-distilled Bordeaux myself. . . . Oh, here, I shall do it."

Tutting at Adelia's attempt to stitch the wound together with her left hand, she took the needle and thread and did it instead, putting in seven ligatures where Adelia herself would have used only five, thus making a neater, if more painful, job of it. "We who went on Crusade had to learn to treat the wounded, there were so many," she said briskly.

Most of them caused by the ineptitude of the King of France, its leader, according to Rowley, after his own, much later, time in the Holy Land.

Not that the Church had condemned Louis for it, preferring instead to dwell on the scandal Eleanor, then his queen, had caused by insisting on going with him and taking with her a train of similarly adventurous females.

"Born to trouble as the sparks fly upwards, that lady," Rowley had said of her, not without admiration. "Her and her Amazons. And an affair with Uncle Raymond of Toulouse when she arrived in Antioch. What a woman."

Something of that daring remained; her very presence here showed as much, but time, thought Adelia, had twisted it into desperation.

"Is that . . . *urgh.*" Adelia wished to be brave, but the queen was plying the needle with more skill than gentleness. "Was that where you learned . . . how to thread a maze? In the . . . *oofff* . . . East?" For there was no sign that Eleanor had spent as much time blundering around Wormhold's hedges as she and the others had.

"My lady," insisted the queen.

"My lady."

"It was, yes. The Saracen is skilled in such devices, as in so much else. I have no doubt your bishop also learned the trick of it from the East. Rowley went there on my orders . . . a long time ago." Her voice had softened. "He took the sword of my dead little son to Jerusalem and laid it on Christ's own altar."

Adelia was comforted; the bond between Eleanor and Rowley made by that vicarious crusade went deep. It might be stretched to its limit in present circumstances, but it still held. The queen had taken him prisoner; she wouldn't allow him to be killed.

She's a mother, Adelia thought. *She'll let me go back to my baby.* There would be an opportunity to ask for that when she and the queen were better acquainted. In the meantime, she still had to learn all she could about Rosamund's murder. *Eleanor hadn't ordered it. Who had?*

Taper light had been kinder to the queen than the blazing illumination around them now. Elegance was there and always would be, so was the lovely, pale skin that went with auburn hair, now hidden, but wrinkles were puckering at her mouth and the tight, gauze wimple around her face did not quite hide the beginning of sagging flesh under the chin. Slender, yes, fine bones, yes. Yet there was another sag above the point where a jeweled belt encircled her hips.

No wonder, either. Two daughters by her first husband, Louis of France, and, since their divorce, eight more children from her marriage to Henry Plantagenet, five of them sons.

Ten babies. Adelia thought of what carrying Allie had done to her own waistline. She's a marvel to look as she does.

There wouldn't be any more, though; even if king and queen had not been estranged, Eleanor must now be, what, fifty years old?

And Henry probably not yet forty.

"There," the queen said, and bit through the needle end of the silk now holding Adelia's palm together. Producing an effusion of lace that served her as a handkerchief, she bound it efficiently round Adelia's hand and tied it with a last, painful tug.

"I am grateful, my lady," Adelia said in earnest.

But Eleanor had returned to her watch, her eyes on the corpse.

Why? Adelia wondered. *Why this profane vigil? It's beneath you.*

The woman had escaped from a castle in the Loire Valley, had traveled through her husband's hostile territory gathering followers and soldiers as she went, had crossed the Channel and slipped into southern England. All this to get to an isolated tower in Oxfordshire. And in winter. True, most of the journey had obviously been made before the roads became as impassable as they now were — to arrive at the tower, she must have been camped not far away. Nevertheless, it was a titanic journey that had tired out everybody but Eleanor herself. *For what? To gloat over her rival?*

But, Adelia thought, *the enemy is vanquished, petrified into a winter version of Sodom and Gomorrah's block of salt. An assassination has been thwarted by me and an Eleanor-preserving God. Rosamund turns out to have been fat. All this is sufficient, surely, to satisfy any lust for revenge.*

But not the queen's, obviously; she must sit here and enjoy the vanquished one's decomposition. *Why?*

It wasn't because she'd envied the younger mistress the ability to still bear children. Rosamund hadn't had any.

Nor was it as if Rosamund had been the only royal paramour. Henry swived more women than most men had hot dinners. "Literally, a father to his people," Rowley had said of him once, with pride.

It was what kings did, almost an obligation, a duty — in Henry's case, a pleasure — to his realm's fertility.

To make the damn crops grow, Adelia thought sourly.

Yet Eleanor's own ducal ancestors themselves had encouraged the growth of acres of Aquitanian crops in their time; she'd been brought up not to expect marital fidelity. Indeed, when she'd had it, wedded to the praying, monkish King Louis, she'd been so bored she'd petitioned for divorce.

222

And hadn't she obliged Henry by taking one of his bastards into her household and rearing him? Young Geoffrey, born of a London prostitute, was proving devoted and useful to his father; Rowley had a greater regard for him than for any of the king's four remaining legitimate sons.

Rosamund, only Rosamund, had inspired a hatred that raised the heat of this awful room, as if Eleanor's body was pumping it across the chamber so that the flesh of the woman opposite would putrefy quicker.

Was it that Rosamund had lasted longer than the others, that the king had shown her more favor, a deeper love?

No, Adelia said to herself. *It was the letters.* Menopausal as Eleanor was, she'd believed their message: Another woman was being groomed to take her place; in both love and status, she was being overthrown.

If it *had* been Eleanor who'd poisoned Rosamund, it was tit for tat. In her own way, Rosamund had poisoned Eleanor.

Yet Rowley had been right: This queen hadn't murdered anybody.

There was no proof of it, of course. Nothing that would absolve her. The killing had been plotted at long range; people would say she had ordered it while she was still in France. There was nothing to scotch the

223

rumor — apart from Eleanor's own word.

But it wasn't her style. Rowley had said so, and Adelia now agreed with him. If Eleanor had engineered it, she would have wanted to be present when it happened. This curiously naïve, horrible overseeing of her rival's disintegration was to compensate her for not having been there to enjoy the last throes.

But damn it, I don't have to witness it with you. All at once, Adelia was overwhelmed by the obscenity of the situation. She was tired, and her hand stung like fire; she wanted her child. Allie would be missing her.

She stood up. "Lady, it is not healthy for you to be here. Let us go downstairs."

The queen looked past her.

"Then I will," Adelia said.

She walked to the door, skirting Montignard, who was snoring on the floor. Two spears clashed as they crossed, blocking the doorway in front of her; the first man-at-arms had been reinforced by another.

"Let me by," she said.

"You want to piss, use a pot," one of the men said, grinning.

Adelia returned to Eleanor. "I am not your subject, lady. My king is William of Sicily."

The queen's eyes remained on Rosamund.

Adelia gritted her teeth, fighting desperation. *This is not the way. If I'm to see Allie again, I must be calm, make this woman trust me.*

After a while, followed by her dog, Adelia began circling the chamber, not looking for a way out — there was none — but using this trapped time to find out where Dakers had hidden herself.

It couldn't have been under the bed or Ward would have sniffed her out; he didn't have the finest nose in the world, it being somewhat overwhelmed by his own scent, but he wouldn't have missed that.

Apart from the bed, the room contained a prie-dieu, smaller than the one in the bishop's room at Saint Albans but as richly carved. Three enormous chests were stuffed with clothes.

A small table held a tray that had been brought in for the queen's supper: a chicken, veal pie, a cheese, a loaf — somewhat mildewed — dried figs, a jug of ale, and a stoppered bottle of wine. Eleanor hadn't touched it. Adelia, who'd last eaten at the nunnery, sliced heavily into the chicken and gave some to Ward. She drank the ale to satisfy her thirst and took a glass of wine with her to sip as she explored.

An aumbry contained pretty bottles and

phials with labels: *Rose oyl. Swete violet. Rasberrie vinigar for to whiten teeth. Oyle of walnut to smooth the hands.* Nearly all were similarly cosmetic, though Adelia noted that Rosamund had suffered from breathing problems — *I'm not surprised, with your weight* — and had taken elecampane for it.

The bed took up more of the center of the room than was necessary by standing a foot or so out from the wall. Behind it was a tapestry depicting the Garden of Eden — obviously a favorite subject, because there was another, a better one, on the same theme on the easterly wall between two of the windows.

Going closer, so that she stood between the bed and the hanging, Adelia felt a blessed coolness.

The tapestry was old and heavy; the considerable draft emerging from underneath it did not cause it to shift. Where in the one on the other wall Adam and Eve sported in joyful movement, here cruder needlework stood them opposite each other amid unlikely trees, as frozen as poor Rosamund herself. The only depiction of liveliness was in the coiling green toils of the serpent — and even that was moth-eaten.

Adelia went closer; the chill increased.

There was a small gap in the canvas where the snake's eye should have been — and it wasn't the moth that had caused it. It had been deliberately made; there was buttonhole stitching round its edges.

A spy hole.

She had to exert some strength to push the hanging aside. Icy air came rushing out at her, and a stale smell. What she saw was a tiny room, corbeled into the tower's wall. Rosamund hadn't had to use chamber pots; hers was the luxury of a garderobe. Set into a curved bench of polished wood was a bottom-shaped, velvet-lined hole over a drop to the ground some hundred feet below. Soap in the shape of a rose lay in a holder next to a little golden ewer. A bowl within hand's reach contained substantial wipes of lamb's wool.

Good for Rosamund. Adelia approved of garderobes, as long as the pit beneath them was dug out regularly; they saved maidservants having to go up and downstairs carrying, and often slopping, noisome containers.

She was not so enamored of the mural painted on the plastered walls; its eroticism being more suited to a bordello than to a privy, but perhaps Rosamund had enjoyed looking at it while she sat there, and undoubtedly Henry Plantagenet would have. Although, come to think of it, had even he been aware of the existence of the garde-robe and its spy hole?

Adelia moved behind the tapestry so that she could apply her eye to the hole — and found that she could see right down the bed to the writing desk and the window beyond.

Here, then, was where Dakers had con-cealed herself and — unpleasant thought — had watched her, Adelia, at her investiga-tions. What patience and what stamina to endure the cold; only fury inspired at seeing Eleanor snatch the crown off her mistress's head had impelled her out of it.

But the careful stitching around the peep-hole indicated that tonight wasn't the only time somebody had employed their time looking through it.

It would have been invited guests who'd ventured up to this floor — it was an English custom for the higher classes to entertain in their bedrooms. If Dakers had spied on them, she would have to have taken up position in the garderobe — with Rosa-mund's permission and knowledge.

To watch the guests? The king? The bed and its activities?

Speculation opened an avenue that Adelia did not want to explore, still less the relationship between mistress and housekeeper.

To hell with the queen's permission; she needed to breathe clean air. She slid herself out from under the hanging. Eleanor appeared not to have noticed. Adelia went to the nearest window, lifted the lattices' catch, pulled it inward, and pushed the shutters open. Kicking a footstool into position, she stood on it and leaned out.

The bitter night sky crackled with stars. Peering downward to the ground, she saw scattered watch fires with armed men moving around them.

Oh, God, if they're putting brushwood around the tower's base . . . if a breeze comes up and blows a spark from one of the fires . . .

She and Eleanor were at the top of a chimney.

That was enough fresh air. Shivering, not merely from the cold, Adelia closed the shutters. In doing so, she put too much weight on one side of the footstool and returned to the floor in a noisy scramble.

Glancing at the queen, expecting a rebuke, she wondered if Eleanor was in a trance; the queen's eyes had not shifted from Rosamund. From his position on the floor, Montignard kicked out, muttered, and then continued to snore.

Adelia bent down to replace the footstool

and saw that its marquetry top had come adrift, revealing that it was, in fact, the lid of a box on legs. There were documents inside. She scooped them out and returned to her former place on the floor at the other side of the bed to read them.

Letters again, half a dozen or more, all of them addressed to Eleanor, all purporting to have been written by Rosamund, yet in the same hand as the one Adelia had put into her boot.

Each had the same jeering superscription and, in this light, she was able to read what followed; it was not always the same in every letter, but the inherent message was repeated over and over.

"Today did my lord king sport with me and tell me of his adoration . . ." "My lord king has this moment left my bed . . ." "He speaks of his divorce from you with longing . . ." ". . . the Pope will look kindly on divorce on the grounds of your treachery to my lord king in that you do inflame his sons against him." ". . . the arrangements for my coronation at Winchester and Rouen." ". . . my lord king will announce to the English who is their true queen."

Poison in ink, drip, drip.

And the writer had penned them for Rosamund to duplicate in her own hand. He or she — more likely he — had even attached notes for her instruction.

"Be more legible, for the queen did scoff at your lettering and call you ignoramus."

"Write quickly that this may reach the queen on her anniversary as she does set much store by that date and will be the more affected."

"Hurry, for my messenger must come to Chinon, where the queen is kept, before the king moves her elsewhere."

And most telling of all: *"We win, lady. You shall be queen before summer comes again."*

At no point did the instructor name himself. But, thought Adelia, he was someone who'd been near enough to Eleanor to know that she had ridiculed Rosamund's writing.

And a fool. If his hope was to engineer a divorce between Henry and Eleanor and set Rosamund up as queen, he was lacking the most fundamental political sense. Henry would never divorce Eleanor. For one thing, even if wifely treason was grounds for divorce — and Adelia didn't think it was — Henry had caused too much offense to the Church over the death of Becket and had suffered for it; he dare not offend again. For another, he had a regard for the order of things. Even more important to him was the fact that by losing Eleanor, he would

231

lose her great Duchy of Aquitaine, and Henry, though a beast, was a beast that never gave up land.

In any case, the easygoing English might wink at their king's mistress, but not a mistress imposed on them as queen; it would be an insult.

I *know that, and I'm a foreigner.*

And yet these letters had been good enough to inspire a stupid, ambitious woman to copy and send them, good enough to inflame a queen into escaping and urging war by her sons against their father.

Rowley could be right; the person who had written these things had done so to create war.

There was a loud sniff from the other side of the room. Eleanor spoke in triumph. "She is going. She has begun to stink."

That was quicker than expected. Surprised, Adelia looked up to where Rosamund was still stiffly inclined over her work.

She looked round further and saw that, in search of comfort, Ward had settled himself on the trailing end of the queen's ermine cloak. "I'm afraid that's merely my dog," she said.

"*Merely?* Get him off. What does he do here?"

One of the men-at-arms who'd been nodding in the doorway roused himself and came in to deposit Ward on the landing outside, then, at a nod from his queen, returned to his post.

Eleanor shifted; she'd become restive. "Saint Eulalie grant me patience. How long will this take?" The vigil was becoming tiresome.

Adelia nearly said, "A while yet," and then didn't. Until she knew more about the situation, she had better stay in the role of a woman whom the queen accepted as a somewhat soiled part of Rowley's baggage train but who'd nevertheless been chosen by God to save the royal life and was being kept close to the royal side as a reward.

But you should *know more about me,* Adelia thought, irritated. *I am dying with curiosity; so should you be. You should know more about everything: how Rosamund died, why she wrote the letters, who dictated them . . . you should have had the room searched and found these exemplars before I did. It's not enough to be a queen; you should ask questions. Your husband does.*

Henry Plantagenet was a ferret and an employer of ferrets. He'd nosed out Adelia's profession in a second and penned her up in England, like one of the rarer animals in his menagerie, until he found a use for her. He knew exactly how things stood between her and his bishop; he'd known when their baby was born — and its sex, which was more than the child's father had known. A few days afterward, to prove that he knew, a royal messenger in plain clothes had delivered a gloriously lacy christening gown to Adelia's fenland door with a note: "Call her what you will, she shall always be Rowley-Powley to me."

Compared to the king, Eleanor walked within a circle of vision encompassing only her personal welfare and the certainty that God was most closely concerned with it. The questions she'd asked in this chamber had related solely to herself.

Adelia wondered whether she should enlighten her. Rowley and the queen must have corresponded in the past; she would know his writing. Showing her these documents would at least prove that he hadn't written them for Rosamund to copy. She might even recognize the penmanship and know who had.

Wait, though. There were two crimes here.

If Mansur or her foster father had been watching Adelia at that moment, they would have seen her adopt what they called her "dissecting face," the mouth tightened into a line, eyes furious with concentration, as they always were when her knife followed the link of muscle to sinew, pursued a vein, probed, and cut effect in order to find cause.

What made her a brilliant anatomist, Dr. Gershom had once told her, was instinct. She'd been offended. "Logic and training, Father." He'd smiled. "Man provided logic and training, maybe, but the Lord gave you instinct, and you should bless him for it."

Two crimes.

One, Rosamund had copied inflammatory letters. Two, Rosamund had been murdered.

Discovering whom it was who had urged Rosamund to write her letters was one thing. Discovering her murderer was another. And both solutions were contradictory, as far as Eleanor of Aquitaine and the Bishop of Saint Albans were concerned.

For the queen, the letter writer would be the villain and must be eliminated. Eleanor didn't give a damn who'd killed Rosamund — would, if she learned who it was, probably reward him.

But for Rowley, the murderer was endangering the peace of the kingdom and must be eliminated. And his claim was the greater, because murder was the more terrible crime.

It would be better, at this stage, to give

Rowley open ground for *his* investigation rather than complicating it by allowing the queen to pursue *hers*.

Hmm.

Adelia gathered up the documents on her lap, put them back in the footstool box, and replaced its lid. She would do nothing about them until she could consult Rowley.

Eleanor continued to fidget. "Has this benighted tower no place of easement?"

Adelia ushered her toward the garderobe.

"Light." The queen held out her hand for a candle, and Adelia put one into it — reluctantly. She would see the naughty paintings.

If Adelia could have been any sorrier for the woman, it was then. When you came down to it, Eleanor was consumed by sexual jealousy as raging as that of any fishwife catching her husband in flagrante, and was being stabbed by reminders of it at every turn.

Adelia tensed herself for a storm, but when the queen emerged from under the hanging she looked tired and old, and was silent.

"You should rest, madam," Adelia said, concerned. "Let us go down . . ."

There was noise from the stairs, and the two guards in the doorway uncrossed their spears and stood at attention.

A great hill of a man entered, sparkling with energy and frost and dwarfing Schwyz, who followed him in. He was enormous; kneeling to kiss the queen's hand only put his head on a level with hers.

"If I'd been here, my dear, 'twouldn't have happened," he said, still kneeling. He pressed Eleanor's hand to his neck with both of his, closing his eyes and rocking with the comfort of it.

"I know." She smiled fondly at him. "My dear, dear abbot. You'd have put your big body in the way of the knife, wouldn't you?"

"And gone rejoicing to Paradise." He sighed and stood up, looking down at her. "You going to burn 'em both?"

The queen shook her head. "I have been persuaded that Dampers is mad. We will not execute the insane."

"Who? Oh, Dakers. She's mad, sure enough, I told you she was. Let the flame have her, I say. And her bloody mistress with her. Where is the whore?"

He strode across the room to the table and poked the corpse's shoulder. "Like they said, cold as a witch's tit. Bit of fire'd warm they both up, get 'em ready for hell." He turned to wag his finger at Eleanor. "I'm a simple Gloucestershire man, as you know, and, Sweet Mary save me, a sinner, too, but I love my God, and I love my queen with all my soul, and I'm for putting their enemies to the torch." He spat on Rosamund's hair. "That's the Abbot of Eynsham's opinion of *you,* madam."

The visitor had caused Montignard to stand up. He was busily and jealously — and uselessly — trying to gain the queen's attention by urging her to eat. Eynsham, a man built more for tossing bales of hay than for shepherding monastic sheep, dominated the room, taking the breath out of it with the power of his body and voice, filling it with West Country earthiness and accent.

Bucolic he might have been, but everything he wore was of expensive and exquisite clerical taste, though the pectoral cross that had swung from his neck as he bent to the queen was overdone — a chunk of dull gold that could have battered a door in.

He'd taken years off Eleanor; she was loving it. Apart from the egregious Montignard, her courtiers had been too weary from traveling to make much fuss over her escape from death.

Or my part in it, Adelia thought, suddenly sour. Her hand was hurting.

"Bad news, though, my glory," the abbot said.

Eleanor's face changed. "It's Young Henry. Where is he?"

"Oh, he's right enough. But the chase was snappin' at our heels all the way from Chinon, so the Young King, well, he decides to make for Paris 'stead of yere."

Suddenly blind, the queen fumbled for the arm of her chair and sank into it.

"Now, now, it's not as bad as that," the abbot said, his voice deep, "but you know your lad, he never did take to England — said the wine was piss."

"What are we to do? What are we to do?" Eleanor's eyes were wide and pleading. "The cause is lost. Almighty God, what are we to do now?"

"There, there." The abbot knelt beside her, taking her hands in his. "Nothing's lost. And Schwyz here, we've been speaking together, and he reckons it's all to the good. Don't ee, Schwyz?"

At his urging, Schwyz nodded.

"See? And Schwyz do know what he's about. Not much to look at, I grant, but a fine tactician. For here's the good news." Eleanor's hands were lifted and hammered against her knees. "You hear me, my glory? Listen to me. Hear what our commander Jesus have done for us — He've brought the King of France onto our side. Joined un to

239

Young Henry, yes he has."

Eleanor's head came up. "*He has?* Oh, at last. God be praised."

"King Louis as ever is. He'll bring his army into the field to fight alongside the son against the father."

"God be praised," Eleanor said again. "*Now* we have an army."

The abbot nodded his great head as if watching a child open a present. "A saintly king. Weedy husband he was to you, I'll grant, but we ain't marrying him, and God'll look kindly on his valor now." He hammered Eleanor's knees again. "D'you see, woman? Young Henry and Louis'll raise their banner in France, we'll raise ours here in England, and together we'll squeeze Old Henry into submission. Light will prevail against Dark. Twixt us, we'll net the old eagle and bring un down."

He was forcing life into Eleanor; her color had come back. "Yes," she said, "yes. A pronged attack. But have we the men? Here in England, I mean? Schwyz has so few with him."

"Wolvercote, my beauty. Lord Wolvercote's camped at Oxford awaiting us with a force a thousand strong."

"Wolvercote," repeated Eleanor. "Yes, of course." Despondency began to leave her as she climbed the ladder of hope the abbot held for her.

"Of *course* of course. A thousand men. And with you at their head, another ten thousand to join us. All them as the Plantagenet has trampled and beggered, they'll come flocking from the Midlands. Then we march, and oh what joy in Heaven."

"Got to get to fuck Oxford first," Schwyz said, "and quick, for fuck's sake. It's going to snow, and we'll be stuck in this fuck tower like fuck Aunt Sallies. At Woodstock, I told the stupid bitch it couldn't be defended. Let's go straight to Oxford, I said. I can defend you there. But *she* knew better." His voice rose from basso to falsetto. *"Oh, no, Schwyz, the roads are too bad for pursuit, Henry can't follow us here."* The tone reverted. "Henry fuck can, I know the bastard."

In a way, it was the strangest moment of the night. Eleanor's expression, something between doubt and exaltation, didn't change. Still kneeling by her side, the abbot did not turn round.

Didn't they hear him?

Did I?

For Adelia had been taken back to the lower Alps of the Graubünden, to which, every year, she and her foster parents had

241

made the long but beautiful journey in order to avoid the heat of a Salerno summer. There, in a villa lent to them by the Bishop of Chur, a grateful patient of Dr. Gershom's, little Adelia had gone picking herbs and wildflowers with the goatherd's flaxen-haired children, listening to their chat and that of the adults — all of them unaware that little Adelia could absorb languages like blotting paper.

A strange language it had been, a guttural mixture of Latin and the dialect of the Germanic tribes from which those alpine people were descended.

She'd just heard it again.

Schwyz had spoken in Romansh.

Without looking round, the abbot was giving the queen a loose translation. "Schwyz is saying as how, with your favor on our sleeve, this is a war we'll win. When he do speak from his heart, he reverts to his own patter, but old Schwyz is your man to his soul."

"I know he is." Eleanor smiled at Schwyz. Schwyz nodded back.

"Only he can smell snow, he says, and wants to be at Oxford. An' I'll be happier in my bowels to have Wolvercote's men around us. Can ee manage the journey, sweeting? Not too tired? Then let you go down to the kitchens with Monty and get some hot grub inside ee. It'll be a cold going."

"My dear, dear abbot," Eleanor said fondly, rising, "how we needed your presence. You help us to remember God's plain goodness; you bring with you the scent of fields and all natural things. You bring us courage."

"I hope I do, my dear. I hope I do." As the queen and Montignard disappeared down the stairs, he turned and looked at Adelia, who knew, without knowing how she knew, that he had been aware of her all along. "Who's this, then?"

Schwyz said, "Some drab of Saint Albans's. He brought her with him. She was in the room when the madwoman attacked Nelly and managed to trip her up. Nelly thinks she saved her life." He shrugged. "Maybe she did."

"Did she now?" Two strides brought the abbot close to Adelia. A surprisingly well-manicured hand went under her chin to tip her head back. "A queen owes you her life, does she, girl?"

Adelia kept her face blank, as blank as the abbot's, staring into it.

"Lucky, then, aren't you?" he said.

He took his hand away and turned to leave. "Come on, my lad, let us get this *festa stultorum* on its way."

"What about her?" Schywz jerked a thumb toward the writing table.

"Leave her to burn."

"And *her?*" The thumb indicated Adelia.

The abbot's shrug suggested that Adelia could leave or burn as she pleased.

She was left alone in the room. Ward, seeing his chance, came back in and directed his nose at the tray with its unfinished veal pie.

Adelia was listening to Rowley's voice in her mind. *"Civil war . . . Stephen and Matilda will be nothing to it . . . the Horsemen of the Apocalypse . . . I can hear the sound of their hooves."*

They've come, Rowley. They're here. I've just seen three of them.

From the writing table came a soft sound as Rosamund's melting body slithered forward onto it.

SEVEN

By going against the advice of its commander and dragging her small force with her to Wormhold Tower, Eleanor had delayed its objective — which was to join up with the greater rebel army awaiting her at Oxford.

Now, with the weather worsening, Schwyz was frantic to get the queen to the meeting place — armies tended to disperse when kept idle too long, especially in the cold — and there was only one sure route that would take her there quickly: the river. The Thames ran more or less directly north to south through the seven or so miles of countryside that lay between Wormhold and Oxford.

Since the queen and her servants had ridden from their last encampment, accompanied by Schwyz and his men on foot, boats must be found. And had been. A few. Of a sort. Enough to transport the most important members of the royal party and a contingent of Schwyz's men but not all of either. The lesser servants and most of the soldiers were going to have to journey to Oxford via the towpath — a considerably slower and more difficult journey than by boat. Also, to do so, they were going to have to use the horses and mules that the royal party had brought with them.

All this Adelia gathered as she emerged into the tower's bottom room, where shouted commands and explanations were compounding chaos.

A soldier was pouring oil onto a great pile of broken furniture while servants, rushing around, screamed at him to wait before applying the flame as they removed chests, packing cases, and boxes that had been carried into the guardroom only hours before. Eleanor traveled heavy.

Schwyz was yelling at them to leave everything; neither those who were to be accommodated in the few boats nor those who would make the trek overland to Oxford could be allowed to carry baggage with them.

Either they didn't hear him or he was ignored. He was being maddened further by Eleanor's insistence that she could not proceed without this servant or that and, even when agreement was reached, by the favored ones' refusal to stand still and be counted. Part of the trouble seemed to be that the Aquitanians doubted the honesty of their military allies; Eleanor's personal maid shrieked that the royal wardrobe could not be entrusted to "sales mercenaries," and a man declaring himself to be the sergeant cook was refusing to leave a single pan behind for the soldiers to steal. So outside the tower, soldiers struggled with frozen harnesses to ready the horses and mules, and the queen's Aquitanians argued and ran back and forth to fetch more baggage, none of which could be accommodated.

There and then Adelia decided that whatever else happened, she herself would make for the towpath if she could — and quickly. Among this amount of disorganization, nobody would see her go and, with luck and the Lord's good grace, she could walk to the nunnery.

First, though, she had to find Rowley, Jacques, and Walt.

She stood on the stairs looking for them in the confusion before her; they weren't there, they must have been taken outside. What she did see, though, was a black shape that kept to the shadow of the walls as it made its way toward the stairs, jumping awkwardly like a frog because its feet were hobbled. The rope that had been put round its neck flapped as it came.

Adelia drew back into the dark of the staircase, and as the creature hopped up the first rise, caught it by its arm. "No," she said.

The housekeeper's hands and feet had been tied tightly enough to restrain a normal woman, but whoever had done it hadn't reckoned with the abnormal: Dakers had hopped from wherever her guards had left her in order to try and join her mistress at the top of the tower.

And still would if she could. As Adelia grabbed her, Dakers threw her thin body to shake her off. Unseen by anyone else, the two women struggled.

"You'll *burn*," hissed Adelia. "For God's sake, do you want to burn with her?"

"Yes-s-s."

"I won't let you."

The housekeeper was the weaker of the two. Giving up, she turned to face Adelia. She had been roughly treated; her nose was bleeding, and one of her eyes was closed and puffy. "Let me go, let me go. I'll be with her. I *got* to be with her."

How insane. How sad. A soldier was readying the tower's destruction; servants were oblivious to all but their own concerns. Nobody cared if the queen's would-be assassin died in the flames, might even prefer it if she did.

They can't do that. She's mad. One of the reasons Adelia loved England was that if Dakers were brought to trial for her attempt on the queen's life, no court in the country, seeing what she was, would sentence her to death. Eleanor herself had held to it. Restrain the woman with imprisonment, yes, but the reasonable, ancient dictum of *"furiosus furore solum punitur"* (the madness of the insane is punishment enough) meant that anyone who'd once possessed reason but by disease, grief, or other accident had lost the use of his or her understanding must be excused the guilt of his or her crime.

It was a ruling that agreed with everything Adelia believed in, and she wasn't going to see it bypassed, even if Dakers herself was a willing accessory and preferred to die, burning, alongside Rosamund's body. Life was sacred; nobody knew that better than a doctor who dealt with its absence.

The woman was pulling away from her again. Adelia tightened her grip, feeling a physical revulsion; she, who was never nauseated by corpses, was repelled by this living body she had to clutch so closely to her, by its thinness — it was like hugging a bundle of sticks — by its passion for death.

"Don't you want to avenge her?" She said it because it was all she could think of to keep the woman still, but, after a minute, a measure of sanity came into the eyes glaring into hers.

The mouth stopped hissing. "Who did it?"

"I don't know yet. I'll tell you this much, it wasn't the queen."

Another hiss. Dakers didn't believe her. "She paid so's it could be done."

"No." Adelia added, "It wasn't Bertha, either."

"I know that." Contemptuously.

There was a sudden, curious intimacy. Adelia felt herself sucked into whatever understanding the woman possessed, saw her own worth as an ally calculated, dismissed — and then retrieved. She was, after all, the *only* ally.

"I find things out. It's what I do," Adelia said, slackening her grip a little. Suppressing distaste, she added, "Come along with me and we'll find things out together."

Once more she was weighed, found wanting, weighed again, and adjudged as possibly useful.

Dakers nodded.

Adelia fumbled in her pocket for her knife and cut the rope round the housekeeper's ankles and took the noose from round the neck over her head. She paused, unsure whether to free her hands as well. "You promise?"

The only good eye squinted at her. "You'll find out?"

"I'll try. It's why the Bishop of Saint Albans brought me here." Not very reassuring, she thought, considering that the Bishop of Saint Albans was leaving the place as a prisoner and Armageddon was about to break out.

Dakers held out her skinny wrists.

Schwyz had left the guardroom in order to gain control of the situation in the bailey outside. Some of the servants had gone with him; the few that remained were still gathering their goods and didn't notice the two women sidling out.

There was equal confusion in the bailey. Adelia covered Dakers's head with the hood of her cloak and then put up her own so that they would be just two more anonymous figures in the scurry.

A rising wind added to the noise as it whirled little showers of snowflakes that were slow to melt. Moonlight came and went like a guttering candle.

Disregarded, still clutching Dakers, Adelia moved through the chaos with Ward at her heels, looking for Rowley. She glimpsed him on the far side of the bailey, and it was a relief to see that Jacques and Walt were with him, all three roped together. Nearby, the Abbot of Eynsham was arguing over them with Schwyz, his voice dominating the noise made by the wind and bustle. ". . . I don't care, you tyrant, I need to know what they know. They come with us." Schwyz's retort was whirled away, but Eynsham had won. The three prisoners were prodded toward the crowd at the gateway, where Eleanor was getting up on a horse.

Damn, damn *it.* She *must* talk to Rowley before they were separated. Whether she could do it unnoticed . . . and with a failed assassin in tow . . . yet she dared not let go of Dakers's hand.

And Dakers was laughing, or, at least, a low cackle was emerging from the hood round her face. "What is it?" Adelia asked, and found that in taking her eyes off Rowley and the others she had lost sight of them. "Oh, be *quiet.*"

Agonized with indecision, she towed the woman toward the archway that led to the outer bailey and the entrance to the maze. The wind blew the servants' cloaks open and closed as they milled about so that the golden lion of Aquitaine on their tabards flickered in the light of the torches. Soldiers, tidy in their padded jackets, tried to impose order, snatching unnecessary and weighty items away from clutching arms and restraining their owners from snatching them back. Only Eleanor was calm, controlling her horse with one hand and shielding her eyes with the other in order to watch what was being done, looking for something.

She saw Ward, like a small, black sheep against the snow, and pointed the animal out to Schwyz with a gloved finger as she gave an order. Schwyz looked round and pointed in his turn. "That one, Cross," he shouted at one of his men. "Bring her. That one with the dog."

Adelia found herself seized and hoisted onto a mule. She struggled, refusing to let go of Dakers's hand.

The man called Cross took the line of least resistance; he lifted Dakers as well so that she clung on to Adelia's back. "And bloody stay there," he yelled at them. With one hand on the mule's bridle and his body pinning Adelia's leg, he took his charges through the archway and into the outer bailey, holding back until the rest of the cavalcade joined them.

Eleanor rode to the front, Eynsham just behind her. The open gates of the maze yawned like a black hole before them.

"Go straight through, Queen of my heart," the abbot called to her joyfully. "Straight as my old daddy's plow."

"Straight?" The queen shouted back.

He spread his arms. "Didn't you order I to learn the whore's mysteries? Diddun I do it for ee?"

"There's a direct way through?" Eleanor was laughing. "Abbot, my abbot. *'And the crooked shall be made straight. . . .' "*

"*'. . . and the rough places plain,' "* he finished for her. "That old Isaiah, he knew a thing or two. I am but his servant, and yours. Go, my queen, and the Lord's path shall lead you through the whore's thicket."

Preceded by some of her men, one holding a lantern, Eleanor entered the maze, still laughing. The cavalcade followed her.

Behind them, Schwyz gave another order and a lit torch arched through the air onto the piled tinder in the guardroom. . . .

The abbot was right; the way through the maze had been made straight. Alleys were direct passageways into the next. Blocking hedges revealed themselves as disguised, now open, doors.

Mystery had gone. The wind took away

the maze's silence; the hedges around them bent and shivered like ordinary storm-tossed avenues. Some insidious essence had been withdrawn; Adelia couldn't be sorry. What she found extraordinary was that if the strange abbot who declared himself a devotee of the queen could be believed, Rosamund herself had shown him the secret of the way through.

"You know that man?" she asked over her shoulder. Flinching, she felt Dakers's thin chest heave up and down against her back as the housekeeper began cackling again.

"Ain't he the clever one." It wasn't so much a reply as Dakers's commentary to herself. "Thinks he's bested our wyrm, so he do, but that's still got its fangs." Perhaps it was part of her madness, Adelia thought, that there was no animosity in her voice toward a man who, self-confessed, had visited Rosamund in her tower in order to betray her to the queen.

They were through the maze within minutes. Swearing horribly at the mule, Cross urged it into a trot so that Adelia and Dakers were cruelly bumped up and down on its saddleless spine as it charged the hill.

The wind strengthened and drove snow before it in sporadic horizontal bursts that shut out the moon before letting it ride the sky again. As they crested the hill it slammed, shrieking, into their faces.

Adelia looked back and saw Rowley, Jacques, and Walt being prodded out of the maze by the spears of the men behind them.

There was a howl of triumph from Dakers; her head was turned to the tower — a black, erect, and unperturbed outline against the moon.

"That's right, that's right," Dakers screamed, "our lord Satan did hear me, my darling. I'll be back for ee, my dear. Wait for me."

The tower wasn't burning. It should have been a furnace by now, but despite broken furniture, oil, a draft, and a torch, the bonfire hadn't caught. Something, some *thing,* had put out the fire.

Its door faced the wind, Adelia told herself. The wind carried snow and extinguished the flames.

But what couldn't be extinguished was the image of Rosamund, diabolically preserved, waiting in that cold upper chamber for her servant to return to her. . . .

It was a sad little flotilla at the river: rowing boats, punts, an old wherry, all found moored along the banks and commandeered by Schwyz's soldiers. The only vessel of any substance was the barge that Mansur and

Oswald and the Godstow men had brought upriver to collect Rosamund's body. Adelia looked for Mansur and, when she didn't see him, became frightened that the soldiers had killed him. These were crude men; they reminded her of the followers of Crusade armies passing through Salerno who'd been prepared to slaughter anybody with an appearance different from their own. There *was* a tall figure standing in the barge's prow, but the man was cloaked and hooded like everybody else and the snow hindered identification. It could be Mansur, it could be a soldier.

She tried reassuring herself with the fact that Schwyz and his men were mercenaries and more interested in utility than the slaughter of Saracens; they would surely see the need to keep alive every skilled boatman they had to take them to Oxford.

The chaos that had reigned in Wormhold's bailey was now redoubled as Eleanor's people fought to accompany their queen on the Godstow barge — the only one with a cabin. If there was someone managing the embarkation, he was overwhelmed.

The mercenary Cross, in charge of Adelia and Dakers, waited too long for orders; by the time he realized there weren't going to be any, the barge was dangerously overladen with the queen's servants and baggage. He and the two women were waved away from it.

Cursing, he hauled them both along to the next vessel in line and almost threw them into its stern. Ward made a leap and joined them.

It was a rowing boat. An *open* rowing boat tied by a hawser onto the stern of the Godstow barge. Adelia shrieked at the soldier, "You can't put us here. We'll freeze." Exposed to the lacerating wind in this thing, they'd be dead long before they reached Oxford, two corpses as rigid as Rosamund's.

The boat shuddered as three more people were forced into it by another guard, who clambered in after them. A voice deeper than Adelia's and more used to carrying overrode the wind: "In the name of God, man, do you want to kill us? Get us under cover. Ask the queen, that lady there saved her life." The Bishop of Saint Albans had joined her, and her protest. Still roped to Jacques and Walt and at a spear's end, he nevertheless carried authority.

"I'm getting it, aren't I?" Cross shouted back. "Shut your squalling. Sit there. In front of the women."

Once everybody was settled to his satisfaction, he produced a large bundle that turned out to be an old sail and called to his companion, addressing him as Giorgio, to help him spread it.

Whatever their manners, he and his companion were efficient. The wind tried to whip the canvas away from them, but Dakers and Adelia were made to sit on one end of it before it was looped back and up, bringing it forward so that it covered them as well as the three prisoners and, finally, the two soldiers themselves, who took their seat in the prow. Their efforts had been self-preservation; they were coming, too. With deliberate significance, Giorgio placed a stabbing sword across his knees.

The sail was dirty and smelly, and rested heavily on the top of everybody's head, not quite wide enough for its purpose, so that covering themselves fully against the slanting wind on one side left a gap on the other. Ice formed over it immediately, rendering it stiff but also making a protective layer. It was shelter of a sort.

The river was being whipped into a fury that slopped wavelets of icy water over the gunwales. Adelia heaved Ward onto her lap, covered him with her cloak, and put her feet up against Rowley's back to keep them out of the wet — he was on the thwart immediately in front of her on the starboard side where the gap was. Jacques sat between him and Walt.

"Are you all right?" She had to shout against the shriek of the wind.

"Are you?" he asked.

"Splendid."

The messenger was also trying to be brave. Adelia heard him say, "Boat trip — makes a nice change."

"It'll come out of your wages," the bishop told him. Walt grunted.

There was no time for more. The two soldiers were yelling at them to bail "before this bloody scow goes under," and were handing out receptacles with which to do it. The three prisoners were given proper bailers while two jugs were passed to the women. "And put your bloody backs to it."

Adelia began bailing — if the boat sank beneath them, they'd be dead before they could scramble to the bank. As fast as she could, she chucked icy water out into the river. The river chucked it back.

Seen through the gap in the sail, the scudding snow was vaguely illuminated by the lamp on the stern of the barge ahead and the prow of whatever vessel was behind them, providing just enough light for Adelia to recognize the pitifully inadequate jug with which she was bailing. It was of silver and had lately stood on the tray on which a servant had brought food and drink to Eleanor in Rosamund's chamber. The Aquitanians had been right; the mercenaries — the two in this boat, at any rate — were thieves.

Adelia experienced a sudden fury that centered on the stolen jug but had more to do with being cold, tired, wet, in extreme discomfort, and frightened for her life. She turned on Dakers, who was doing nothing. "Bail, blast you."

The woman remained motionless, her head lolling. *Probably dead,* Adelia thought.

Anger had afflicted Rowley as well. He was shouting at his captor to free their hands so he and Jacques and Walt could bail faster — they were being slowed by having to scoop the water up and out in awkward unison.

He was again told to shut his squalling, but after a minute Adelia felt the boat rock even more heavily and then heard the three men in front of her swearing. She gathered from their abuse that they'd been cut free of one another but the separate pieces of rope that bound each pair of wrists were still in place.

Still, the three could now bail quicker — and did. Adelia transferred her fury to Dakers for dying after all she, Adelia Aguilar, had done for her. "Sheer ingratitude," she snapped, and grabbed the woman's wrist. For the second time that night, she felt a weak pulse.

Leaning forward so that she nearly squashed the dog on her lap, she jerked Dakers's feet out of the bilge and, to warm them, pushed one between the bodies of Rowley and Jacques and the other between Jacques and Walt.

"How long are we going to sit here?" she screamed over their heads at the soldiers. "God's rib, when are we going to *move?*"

But the wind screamed louder than she could; the men didn't hear her. Rowley, though, nodded his head in the direction of the gap.

She peered out at the whirling curtain of snow. They *were* moving, had been moving for some time, and had reached a bend in the river where a high bank of trees must have been sheltering them a little.

Whether the barge in front, to which they were attached, was being poled by men or pulled by a horse, she didn't know — a dreadful task for either. It was probably being poled; they seemed to be going faster than walking pace. The wind at their backs and the flow of the river was helping them along, sometimes too much — the prow of their boat bumped into the stern of the barge, and the soldiers were having to take turns to struggle out from under the sail cover to fend off with an oar.

How far Oxford was she didn't know, either, but at this rate of progress, Godstow could only be an hour or so away — and there, somehow, she must get ashore.

With this determined, Adelia felt calmer, a doctor again — and one with an ailing patient on her hands. Part of her extreme irritation had been because she was hungry. It came to her that Dakers was probably even hungrier than she was, faint from it — there'd been no sign of food in the Wormhold kitchen when they'd investigated it.

Adelia, though she might condemn the thieving mercenaries, hadn't come empty-handed out of Rosamund's chamber, either; there'd been food left on the queen's tray, and hard times had taught her the value of foraging.

Well, Rosamund wasn't going to eat it.

She delved into her pocket and brought out a lumpy napkin, unfolded it, broke off a large piece from the remains of Eleanor's veal pie, and waved it under Dakers's nose. The smell of it acted as a restorative; it was snatched from her fingers.

Making sure the soldiers couldn't see her — she could barely see them in the darkness under the sail — she leaned forward again and slid the cheese she'd also filched between Jacques and Rowley until she felt the roped hand of one of them investigate it, grasp it, and squeeze her own hand in acknowledgment. There came a pause in the three men's bailing, during which, she guessed, the cheese was being secretly portioned, causing the soldiers to shout at them again.

The remains of the veal pie she divided between herself and Ward.

After that there was little to be done but endure and bail. Every so often, the sail drooped so heavily between them that one of the men had to punch it from underneath in order to rid it of the snow weighting it.

The level of water slopping below her raised legs refused to go down, however much she threw over the side; each breath she expelled wetted the cloak muffling her mouth, freezing immediately so that her lips became raw. The sailcloth scraped against her head as she bent and came up again. But if she stopped, the cold would congeal the blood in her veins. Keep on bailing, stay alive, live to see Allie again.

Rowley's elbow jerked into her knees. She

went on bailing, lean, dip, toss, lean, dip, toss; she'd been doing it forever, would continue forever. Rowley had to nudge her again before she realized she could stop. There was no water coming in.

The wind had lessened. They were in a muffled silence, and light of a sort — was it day? — came through the window of the sail's gap, beyond which snow was falling so thickly it confused the eye into giving the impression that the boat was progressing through air filled with swansdown.

The cold also coming in through the gap had numbed her right side and shoulder. She leaned forward and pressed against Rowley's back to preserve some warmth for the two of them, pulling Dakers with her so that the housekeeper's body was against Jacques's.

Rowley turned his head slightly, and she felt his breath on her forehead. "Well?"

Adelia shifted higher to peer over his shoulder. Despite the fall in the wind, the swollen river was running faster than ever and putting the rowing boat in danger of crashing into the barge or veering against a bank.

One of the soldiers — she thought it was Cross, the younger of the two — was fending off, having abandoned the shelter of the sail so that it drooped over his companion, who was hunched over the prow thwart, exhausted or asleep, or both.

There was no movement, either, from Walt or Jacques. Dakers was still slumped against Jacques's back.

Adelia nosed Rowley's hood away from his ear and put her lips against it: "They're going to raise Eleanor's standard at Oxford. They think the Midlands will rise up and join her rebellion."

"How many men? At Oxford, how many men?"

"A thousand, I think."

"Did I see Eynsham back there?"

"Yes. Who is he?"

"Bastard. Clever. Got the ear of the Pope. Don't trust him."

"Schwyz?" she asked.

"Bastard mercenary. First-class soldier."

"Somebody called Wolvercote is in charge of the army at Oxford."

"A bastard."

That disposed of the main players, then. She rested her face against his cheek in momentary contentment.

"Got your knife?" he asked.

"Yes."

"Cut this bloody rope." He jiggled his bound hands.

She took another look at the soldier crouching the prow; his eyes were closed.

"Come on." Rowley's mouth barely moved. "I'll be getting off in a minute." They might have been journeying luxuriously together and he'd remembered a prior destination to hers.

"No." She put her arms round him.

"Don't," he said. "I've *got* to find Henry. Warn him."

"No." In this blizzard, nobody would find anybody. He'd die. The fen people told tales about this sort of snowstorm, of unwary cottagers, having ventured out in it to lock up their poultry or bring in the cow, unable to find their way back through a freezing, whirling thickness that took away sight and sense of direction so that they ended up stiff and dead only yards from their own front doors. "No," she said again.

"Cut this bloody rope."

The soldier in the prow stirred and muttered. "What you doing?"

They waited until he settled again.

"Do you want me to go with my hands tied?" Rowley breathed.

Christ *God,* how she loathed him. And loathed Henry Plantagenet. The king, always the king if it costs my life, yours, our child's, all happiness.

She delved into her pocket, gripped the knife, and seriously considered sticking it into his leg. He couldn't then go wandering about in a circle and end up as a mound of ice in some field.

"I hate you," she told him. Tears were freezing on her eyelashes.

"I know. Cut the bloody rope."

Holding the knife, she slid her right arm farther around him, all the time watching the man in the prow, wondering why she didn't alert him so that Rowley would be restrained. . . .

She couldn't. She didn't know what fate Eleanor intended for her prisoner or, even it was a benign one, what Eynsham or Schwyz might do.

Her fingers found his hands and walked their way to the rope round his wrists. She began cutting, carefully — the knife was so sharp that a wrong move could open one of his veins.

One strand severed, another. As she worked, she hissed bile. "Your leman, am I? No use to you, am I? I hope you freeze in hell — and Henry with you."

The last strand went, and she felt him flex his hands to get their circulation back.

He turned his head so that he could kiss her. His chin scraped her cheek.

"No use at all," he said, "except to make the sun come up."

And he was gone.

Jacques took charge. Adelia heard him put a sob into his voice, telling the furious Cross that the collision with the bank had caused the bishop to fall overboard.

She heard the mercenary's reply: "He's dead meat, then."

Jacques burst into a loud wail but smoothly took Ward off Adelia's lap, shifted her so that she sat between him and Walt with the sleeping Dakers resting on her back, and returned the dog to its place under her cloak.

She was barely aware of the change. *Except to make the sun come up.*

I'll make the sun come up if I see him again. I'll kill him. Dear Lord, keep him safe.

The snow stopped, and the heavy clouds that carried it rolled away westward. The sun came out and Cross rolled back the sail, thinking there was warmth to be had.

Adelia took no notice of that, either, until Walt nudged her. "What's up with he, mistress?"

She raised her head. The two mercenaries were sitting on the prow thwart opposite. The one called Cross was trying to rouse his companion. "Come on, Giorgio, upsy-daisy. Weren't your fault we lost the bloody bishop. Come on, now."

"He's dead," Adelia told him. The man's boots were fixed in the solidified bilge water. Just another frozen corpse to add to the night's list.

"Can't be. *Can't* be. I kept him in the warm, well, warm as I could." Cross's bad-tempered face was agonized.

Lord, this death is important to this man. It should be important to me.

For the look of the thing, Adelia stretched so that her hand rested against the dead man's neck where a pulse should be. He was rigid. She shook her head. He'd been considerably older than his friend.

Jacques and Walt genuflected. She took the living soldier's hand in one of hers. "I'm sorry, Master Cross." She spoke the end words: "May God have mercy on his soul."

"He was bloody sitting here, keeping warm, I thought."

"I know. You did your best for him."

"Why ain't you lot dead, then?" Anger was returning. "You was sitting same as him."

Useless to say that they had been bailing and therefore moving, just as Cross himself, who, even though exposed to the wind, had been active in preventing collision. And poor Giorgio had been alone, with no human warmth next to him.

"I'm sorry," she said again. "He was old, the cold was too much for him."

Cross said, "Taught me soldiering, he did. We been through three campaigns together. Sicilian, he was."

"So am I."

"Oh."

"Don't move him," she said sharply.

Cross was trying to gather the body up so as to lay it along the thwart. Like Rosamund's, its rigor would persist until it encountered heat — there was none in this sun — and the sight of it on its back with knees and hands curved like a dog's was not one its friend would want to see.

Walt said, "By Gor, ain't that Godstow by there?"

Allie.

She realized that she was surrounded by a glittering, diamond-hard landscape that she had to shade her eyes to look at. Trees had been upended, their roots like ghastly, desperate, twiggy fingers frozen in the act of appeal. For the rest, the countryside appeared flattened by the monstrous weight of snow fallen on it so that what had been dips in the ground were merely smooth shallows

271

among the rises they interspersed. Straight threads of smoke rising against a cornflower-blue sky showed that the lumps scattered on the rise above the bank were half-buried houses.

There was a small, humped bridge in the distance, white as marble; she and Rowley had stood on it one night in another century. Beyond that — she had to squeeze her eyes nearly shut to see — many threads of smoke and, where the bridge ended, a wood and the suggestion of gates.

She was opposite the village of Wolvercote. Over there, though she couldn't see it, stood the nunnery of Godstow. Where Allie was.

Adelia stood, slipped, and rocked the boat in her scramble to get up again. "Put us ashore," she told Cross, but he didn't seem to hear her. Walt and Jacques pulled her down.

The galloper said, "No good, mistress, even supposing . . ."

"Look at the bank, mistress," Walt told her.

She looked at it — a small cliff where flat pasture should have been. Farther in, what appeared to be enormous frozen bushes were, in fact, the spread branches of mature oak trees standing in drifts that must be —

Adelia estimated — fifteen feet or more deep.

"We'd never get through," Jacques was saying.

She pleaded, begged, while knowing it was true; perhaps when the inhabitants disinterred themselves, they would dig tunnels through the snow to reach the river, but until then, or until it thawed, she was separated from the convent as if by a mountain barrier. She would have to sit in this boat and be swept away past Allie, only God knowing how or when, or *if,* she could get back to her.

They'd passed the village now. They were nearly at the bridge that crossed the tributary serving the mill. The Thames was widening into the great sweep that would take it around the convent's meadows.

And something was happening to it. . . .

The barge had slowed. Its sides were too high to see what was occurring on its deck, but there was activity and a lot of swearing.

"What's the matter?"

Walt picked up one of the bailers, dipped it over the side, brought it back, and stirred his finger in it. "Look at this."

They looked. The cupped water was gray and granulated, as if somebody had poured salt into it. "What is it?"

"It's ice," Walt said softly. "It's bloody ice." He looked around. "Must be shallower here. It's ice, that's what it is. The river's freezing up."

Adelia stared at it, then up at Walt, then back to the river. She sat down suddenly and gave thanks for a miracle as wonderful as any in the Bible; liquid was turning solid, one element changing into another. They would *have* to stop. They could walk ashore and, many as they were, they could dig their way through to the convent.

She looked back to count the boats behind them.

There were no boats. As far as the eye could see, the river was empty, graying along this stretch but gaining a blueness as it twisted away into a dazzling, silent distance.

Blinking, she searched for a sight of the contingent that should have been accompanying them along the towpath.

But there was no towpath — of course there wasn't. Instead, where it had been, was a wavy, continuous bank of frozen snow, taller than two men in some places, with its side edge formed by wind and water as neatly as if some titanic pastry cook with a knife had sheared off the ragged bits of icing round the top of a cake.

For a second, because her mind was directed only at reaching her daughter, Adelia thought, *It doesn't matter, there are enough of us to dig a path. . . .*

And then, "Dear Lord, where are they?" she said. "All those people?"

The sun went on shining beautifully, unfairly, pitilessly, on an empty river where, perhaps, in its upper reaches men and women sat in their boats as unmoving as Giorgio sat in this one, where, perhaps, corpses rolled in sparkling water.

And what of the riders? Where were they, God help them? Where was Rowley?

The answering silence was terrible because it was the only answer. It trapped the oaths and grunts of effort from the barge as if in a bell jar, so that they echoed back in an otherwise soundless air.

The men on board it labored on, plunging poles through the shallow, thickening water until they found purchase on the river bottom and could push the barge another yard, another . . .

After a while, the bell jar filled with sounds like the cracks of whips — they were encountering surface sheet ice and having to break through it.

They inched past the point of the river where it divided and a stream turned off toward the mill and the bridge. There was no noise from the millrace, where a fall of water hung in shining stillness.

And, oh, God Almighty save our souls, in all this wonder, somebody had used the bridge as a gibbet; two glistening, distorted figures hung from it by the neck — Adelia, looking up, glimpsed two dead faces looking quizzically sideways and down at her, saw two pairs of pointing feet, as if their owners had been frozen in a neat little dancing jump.

Nobody else seemed to notice, or care. Walt and Jacques were using the oars to pole the rowing boat along so that it didn't drag on the barge. Dakers sat next to her now, her hood over her face; somebody had placed the sail around the two of them to keep them warm.

They inched past the bridge and into an even wider bend where the Thames ran along a Godstow meadow — which, astonishingly, still *was* a meadow. Some freak of the wind had scoured it of snow so that a great expanse of frosted grass and earth provided the only color in a white world.

And here the barge stopped because the ice had become too thick to proceed farther. It didn't matter, *it didn't matter* — there was a scar leading down the rise from the convent to the shore and, at the bottom of it, convent men with shovels were shouting and waving, and everybody in the two boats was shouting and waving back as if it were they who were marooned and had glimpsed a rescuing sail coming toward them. . . .

Only then did Adelia realize that she had been sustained through the night on borrowed energy and it was now being debited out of her body so quickly that she was close to the languor that comes with death. It had been a very near thing.

They had to disembark onto ice and cross it to reach land. Ward's paws slipped and he went down, sliding, until he could scrabble resentfully up again. An arm went round Adelia's waist to help her along and she looked up into the face of Mansur. "Allah is merciful," he said.

"Somebody is," she said. "I was so frightened for you. Mansur, we've lost Rowley."

Half-carried, she stumbled across the ice beside him and then across the flattened grass of the meadow.

Among the small crowd ahead, she glimpsed Eleanor's upright figure before it disappeared into the tunnel that led up to the convent gates, a steep, thin pathway with walls twice head height on either side. It had been dug to take Rosamund's coffin; instead, it received a litter made out of oars and wrapped around with sailcloth, under which rested the contorted body of a mercenary soldier.

A beautiful tunnel, though. At its top stood an elderly woman, her studied impassivity displaying her relief. "You took your time."

As Adelia fell, babbling, into her arms, Gyltha said, "A'course she's well. Fat and fit as a flea. Think as I can't look after her? Gor dang, girl, you only left her yesterday."

EIGHT

If her heart sank at the prospect of feeding and housing the forty or so exhausted, bedraggled, frostbitten men, women, and dogs shambling through her gates, Mother Edyve gave no sign of it, though it must have sunk further when she saw that they included the Queen of England and the Abbot of Eynsham, neither of them friends to Godstow, to say nothing of a troop of mercenary soldiers.

It didn't occur to her that she was welcoming a force of occupation.

She ordered hot possets for her guests. She surrendered her house to Queen Eleanor and her maids, lodged the abbot and Montignard in the men's guesthouse with their and the queen's male servants, and quartered Schwyz on the gatekeeper. She put the queen's dogs and hawks in her own kennels and mews, distributing the other mercenaries as widely as she could, billeting one on the smith, another in the bakery, and the rest among individual — and aged — retainers and pensioners in the houses that formed a small village within the convent walls.

"So's they'm split up and not one of 'em where there's girls," Gyltha said approvingly. "She's a wily one, that Ma Edyve."

It was Gyltha who had carried the report of the events at Wormhold to the abbess. Adelia was too tired and, anyway, hadn't been able to face telling her of Rowley's death.

"She don't believe it," Gyltha said on her return. "No more don't I. Now, then, let's be seeing to you two."

Mansur hated fuss and kept declaring that he was well, but he had been exposed to the open cold while poling the barge as Adelia, Jacques, and Walt had not, and she and Gyltha were worried about him.

"Look what you done to your hands, you great gawk," Gyltha said — her disquiet always took the form of anger. Mansur's palms were bleeding where his mittens, and then his skin, had worn through against the wood of the pole.

Adelia was concerned more for his fingers, which were white and shiny where they emerged from the wrecked mittens. "Frostbite."

"They cause me no pain," Mansur said stolidly.

"They will in a minute," Adelia promised.

Gyltha ran to Mansur's lodging to get him a dry gown and cloak, and brought back with her a bucket of hot water from the kitchen and would have plunged her lover's hands into it, but Adelia stopped her. "Wait til it cools a little."

She also prevented Gyltha from hooking the brazier nearer to him. The condition of frostbite had interested her foster father after he'd seen the effects of it during their holidays in the Alps — he had actually braved a winter there to study it — and his conclusion had been that the warming must be gradual.

Young Allie, always deprived of burning herself on the brazier — it was kept within a guard — turned her attention to trying to pull the bucket over her head. Adelia would have enjoyed watching the resulting tussle between Gyltha and that remarkable child if her own toes hadn't ached agonizingly with the return of blood to frozen muscle and bone.

She estimated the worth of dosing herself and Mansur with willow-bark decoction for the pain and then rejected it; each of them was a stoic, and the fact that her toes and his fingers were turning red without blistering indicated that the affliction was mild — better to keep the drug for those in whom it might be worse.

She crawled onto the bed to suffer in comfort. Ward leaped on after her, and she had neither the energy nor will to turn him off. The dog had shared his body heat with her on the boat — what were a few fleas if she shared hers with him?

"What did you do with Dakers?" she asked.

"Oh, her." Gyltha had not taken to the walking skeleton that Adelia had dragged, unaware that she *was* dragging it, through the convent gates, but had seen, *because* Adelia was dragging it, that there was a necessity to keep it alive. "I give her to Sister Havis, and she give her to Sister Jennet in the infirmary. She's all right, ugly thing."

"Well done." Adelia closed her eyes.

"Don't you want to know who's turned up here since you been away?"

"No."

When she woke up, it was afternoon. Mansur had gone back to the men's guesthouse to rest. Gyltha was sitting beside the bed, knitting — a skill she'd picked up from one of her Scandinavian customers during her eel-selling days.

Adelia's eyes rested on the chubby little figure of Allie as it hitched itself around the floor on its bottom, chasing the dog and grimacing to show the one tiny tooth that had manifested itself in her lower gum since her mother had last seen her. "I swear I'll never leave you again," she told her.

Gyltha snorted. "I keep telling you, 'twas only thirty hours."

But Adelia knew the separation had been longer than that. "It was nearly permanent," she'd said, and added painfully, "For Rowley, it has been."

Gyltha wouldn't countenance it. "He'll be back, large as life and twice as natural. Take more than a bit of old snow to finish off that lad." To Gyltha, the Right Reverend Lord Bishop of Saint Albans would always be "that lad."

"He can stay away for me," Adelia said. She clung on to her grievance against him like a raft to keep her from being subsumed in grief. "He didn't care, Gyltha, not for his life, not Allie's, not mine."

"Except to make the sun come up."

"A'course he didn't, he's out to stop a war as'll take more lives than yours. God's work that is, and the Lord'll watch over un according."

Adelia clung to that, too, but she had been deeply frightened. "I don't care, if it's God's work, let Him do it. We are leaving. As soon as the snow clears, we're all slipping away back to the fens."

"Oh, ar?" Gyltha said.

"It's not *'oh, ar.'* I mean it." In the fens, her life had been acceptable, regulated, useful. She'd been ripped away from it, subjected to, and then abandoned in, physical and mental turmoil by the man *at whose request* she had become embroiled in it in the first place. Almost worse than anything, he had revived in her an emotion that she'd thought to be dead, that was better dead.

"Except to make the sun come up."

Damn him, don't think of it.

Gaining anger, she said, "It's all high politics, anyway. That's what Rosamund's killing was, as far as I can see — an assassination to do with queens and kings and political advantage. It's outside my scope. Was it the mushrooms? Yes, it probably was. Do I know who sent them? No, I don't, and there's an end to it. I'm a doctor, I won't be drawn into their wars. God's rib, Gyltha, Eleanor abducted me, *abducted* me — I nearly ended up joining her damned army."

"Shouldn't have saved her life, then, should you?"

"What was I to do? Dakers was coming at her with a knife."

"You sure you don't want to know who else's turned up?"

"No. I only want to know whether anybody's likely to stop us going."

But it appeared that in the physical collapse affecting all the travelers, even Eleanor, on their arrival at the convent, nobody had spared a thought for the woman who had saved the queen's life — or, for that matter, the woman who had nearly taken it. The priority had been a place to get warm and to sleep.

Perhaps, Adelia thought, the queen had forgotten Dakers and herself altogether and, when the roads were open again, would proceed to Oxford without attending to either. By which time Adelia would be beyond reach, taking Gyltha, Mansur, and Allie with her and leaving Dame Dakers to her own hideous devices — she no longer cared what they were.

Gyltha went to fetch their supper from the kitchen.

Adelia leaned down from the bed, picked up her daughter, pressing her nose against the warm satin of the child's cheek, and propped her up against her own knees so that they faced each other.

"We're going home, aren't we, mistress? Yes, we are. We won't get involved in their old wars, will we? No, we won't. We'll go far off, we'll go back to Salerno, we don't care what that nasty old King Henry says, do we? We'll find the money from somewhere. It's no good making faces. . . ." For Allie was extending her lower lip and showing her new tooth in an expression reminiscent of the camel in Salerno's menagerie. "You'll like Salerno, it's warm. We'll take Mansur and Gyltha and Ulf, yes, we will. You miss Ulf, don't you? So do I."

On an investigation like this — *had* she been going to proceed with it — Gyltha's grandson would have been her eyes and ears, able to go about unremarked as only an eleven-year-old urchin could, his plain, very plain, features giving the lie to his extreme intelligence.

Nevertheless, Adelia thanked her God that Ulf, at least, was out of harm's way. She found herself wondering, though, what the boy would have said about the situation. . . .

Allie started wriggling, wanting to continue with her persecution of Ward, so Adelia set her down absently, listening to a harsh little voice in her head that asked questions like an insistent crow.

Two murders, ain't there? Rosamund's and

286

the fella on the bridge? You think they're con-
nected?

"I don't know. It doesn't matter," she answered out loud.

It was goin' to depend on who turned up, weren't it? Somebody was, to see why there hadn't been no fuss about the dead un on the bridge? Whoever done it wanted him dead, din't they? An' wanted a hullabaloo about it, din't they?

"Such was my assumption. But there hasn't been time, the snow would have delayed them."

Somebody's come.

"I don't care. I'm going home, I'm frightened."

Leavin' the poor bugger in the icehouse, is that it? Very godly, I'm sure.

"Oh, shut up."

Adelia liked order; in a sense, it was what her profession was about — and you could say this for the dead, they didn't make unexpected moves or threaten you with a knife. To be out of control and at the whim of others, especially the malignantly inclined, as she had been at Wormhold and on the river, had discomposed her very being.

The convent enfolded her; the long, low, plain room spoke soothingly of proportion.

It was dark outside now, and the glow of the brazier gave a shadow to each of the beams in the ceiling, making a pleasingly uniform pattern of dark and not-so-dark stripes against white plaster. Even muffled by the wool that Gyltha had stuffed in the cracks of the shutters to keep out the cold, the distant sound of the nuns singing Vespers was a reassurance of a thousand years of disciplined routine.

And all of it an illusion, because a corpse lay in its icehouse and, seven miles away, a dead woman sat at a writing table, both of them waiting . . . for what?

Resolution.

Adelia pleaded with them: *I can't give it to you, I'm frightened, I want to go home.*

But jagged, almost forgotten images kept nudging at her mind: snowy footprints on a bridge, a letter crumpled in a saddlebag, other letters, copied letters, Bertha's piglike nose snuffling at a scent. . . .

Gyltha returned carrying a large pot of mutton and vegetables in broth, some spoons, a loaf tucked under one arm, and a leather bottle of ale under the other. She poured some of the broth into Allie's bowl and began mashing it to a pulp, putting the pieces of meat into her mouth and chewing them with her big, strong teeth until they, too, were pulp, then returning them to the bowl. "Turnip and barley," she said. "I'll say this much for the sisters, they do a fair supper. And good, warm milk from the cow with little un's porridge this morning."

Reluctantly, because to mention one of the convent's problems was somehow to solidify it, Adelia asked, "Is Bertha still in the cowshed?"

"Won't come out, poor soul. That old Dakers still want to scrag her?"

"I don't think so, no."

Feeding Allie, who was making spirited attempts to feed herself, took concentration that allowed no thought for anything else.

When they'd wiped food off her hair as well as off their own, the child was put down to sleep and the two women ate their supper in silence, their feet stretched out to the brazier, passing the ale bottle back and forth between them.

Warm, the pain beginning to lessen, Adelia thought that such security as there was in her world rested at this moment in the gaunt old woman on the stool opposite hers. A day didn't go by without a reminder of the gratitude she owed to Prior Geoffrey for their introduction, nor a strike of fear that Gyltha might leave her, nor, for that matter, puzzlement at why she stayed.

Adelia said, "Do you mind being here, Gyltha?"

"Ain't got no choice, girl. We'm snowed up. Been snowing again, if you'd notice. Path down to the river's gone and blocked itself again."

"I mean, galloping across country to get here, away from home, murder . . . everything. You never complain."

Gyltha picked a strand of mutton from her teeth, considered it, and popped it back into her mouth. "Somewhere to see, I suppose," she said.

Perhaps that was it. Women generally had to stay where they were put, which in Gyltha's case had been Cambridgeshire fenland, a place that Adelia found endlessly exotic but that was undoubtedly very flat. Why should not Gyltha's heart drum to adventure in foreign places like any crusader's? Or long to see God's peace retained in her country as much as Rowley did? Or require, despite the risk, to see God's justice done on those who killed?

Adelia shook her head at her. "What would I do without you?"

Gyltha poured the remnants of the broth from Adelia's bowl into hers and put it down on the floor for Ward. "For a start, you wouldn't have no time to find out who done in that poor lad, nor who it was done for Rosamund," she said.

"Oh," Adelia said, sighing. "Very well, tell me."

"Tell ee what?" But Gyltha was smirking a satisfied smirk.

"You know very well. Who's arrived? Who's been asking questions about the boy in the icehouse? Somebody wanted him found and, sure as taxes, that somebody is going to question why he hasn't been. Who is it?"

It was more than one. As if blown ahead of the snow that had now encased them, four people had arrived at Godstow during Adelia's absence.

"Master and Mistress Bloat of Abingdon, they're ma and pa to that young Emma as you took to. Come to see her married."

"What are they like?"

"Big." Gyltha spread her arms as if to encompass tree trunks. "Big bellies, big words, big voices — he has, anyhow, bellows like a bull as how he ships more wine from foreign parts than anybody else, sells more'n anybody else — for a nicer price than anybody else, I wouldn't be surprised. Hog on a high horse, he is."

By which Adelia gathered that Master Bloat reveled in a position he'd not been born to. "And his wife?"

In answer, Gyltha arranged her mouth into a ferocious simper, picked up the ale bottle, and ostentatiously prinked her little finger as she pretended to drink from it. She hadn't taken to the Bloats.

"Unlikely murderers, though," Adelia said. "Who else?"

"Their son-in-law-as-will-be."

Another person with a valid reason for coming to Godstow. *"Aaaah."* So the beautiful, gallant writer of poetry had come to take his bride. How nice for that wild, charming girl, how nice that love would lighten the winter darkness for a while at least. "How did he get here?"

Gyltha shrugged. "Arrived from Oxford afore the blizzard set in, like the others. Seems he's lord of the manor over the bridge, though he don't spend much time there. Run-down old ruin, Polly says it is." Gyltha had made friends in the kitchen. "His pa as took Stephen's side in the war had a castle further upriver during the war, the which King Henry made un pull it down."

"Is he as handsome as Emma thinks he is?"

But Adelia saw that here was another that hadn't been taken to — this time, in depth.

"Handsome is as handsome does," Gyltha said. "Older'n I expected, and a proper lord, too, from his way of ordering people about. Been married before, but her died. The Bloats is lickin' his boots for the favor of him making their girl a noblewoman." Gyltha leaned forward slightly. "And him kindly accepting two hundred marks in gold as comes with her for a dowry."

"Two hundred marks?" An immense sum.

"So Polly says. In gold." Gyltha nodded. "Ain't short of a shilling or two, our Master Bloat."

"He can't be. Still, if he's prepared to purchase his daughter's happiness . . ." She paused. "*Is* she happy?"

Gyltha shrugged. "Ain't seen her. She's kept to the cloisters. I'da thought she'd come rushing to see this Lord Wolvercote. . . ."

"Wolvercote?"

"That's his lordship's name. Suits him, an' all; he do look proper wolfish."

"Gyltha . . . Wolvercote, that's the man . . . he's the one who's raised an army for the queen. He's supposed to be at Oxford, waiting for Eleanor to join him."

"Well, he ain't, he's here."

"*Is* he now? But . . ." Adelia was determined to follow the gleam of romance where it led. "He's not a likely murderer, either. It speaks well for him if he's prepared to delay a war because he can't wait to marry young Emma."

"He's delayin' it," Gyltha pointed out, "for young Emma plus two hundred marks. *In* gold." She leaned forward, pointing with her knitting needle. "You know the first thing he do when he got back to the village? Finds a couple of rogues robbin' his manor and hangs 'em quicker'n buttered lightning."

"The two on the bridge? I wondered about them."

"Sister Havis ain't happy. She made a right to-do about it, according to Polly. See, it's the abbey's bridge, and the sisters don't like it being decorated with corpses. 'You take 'em down now,' she told his lordship. But he says as it's *his* bridge, so he won't. And he ain't."

"Oh, dear." So much for romance. "Well, who's the fourth arrival?"

"Lawyer. Name of Warin. Now he *has* been asking questions. Very worried about his young cousin, seemingly, as was last seen riding upriver."

"Warin, Warin. He wrote the letter the boy carried." It was as if an ice barrier was melting and allowing everything to flood back into her memory. *Your affct cousin, Wlm Warin, gentleman-at-law, who hereby sends: two silvr marks as an earnest of your inheritance, the rest to be Claimed when we do meet.*

Letters, always letters. A letter in the dead man's saddlebag. A letter on Rosamund's table. Did they connect the two murders? Not necessarily. People wrote letters when they could write at all. On the other hand . . .

"When did Master Warin arrive seeking his cousin?"

"Late last night, afore the blizzard. And he's a weeper. Crying fit to bust for worry as his cousin might've got caught in the snow, or been waylaid for his purse. Wanted to cross the bridge and ask at the village, but the snow started blowing, so he couldn't."

Adelia worked it out. "He was quick off the mark to know the boy was missing, then. Talbot of Kidlington — it must be him in the icehouse — was only killed the night before."

"Is that a clue?" The gleam in Gyltha's eye was predatory.

"I don't know. Probably not. Oh, dear *God,* what now?"

The church bell across the way had begun

to toll, shivering the ewer in its bowl, sending vibrations through the bed. Allie's mouth opened to yell, and Adelia scrambled to get to her and cover her ears. "What is it? What is it?" This was no call to worship.

Gyltha had her ear to the shutters, trying to listen to shouts in the alley below. "Everybody to the church."

"Is it fire?"

"Dunno. Summoning bell, more like." Gyltha ran to the line of pegs where their cloaks hung. Adelia began wrapping Allie in her furs.

Outside, groups of people hurried from both ends of the alley and joined the congestion in the noisy church porch, where those pausing to let others go in chattered in alarm, asking one another questions and receiving no answers. They took noise in with them . . . and quieted.

Though it was crowded, the church was silent and mostly dark, all light concentrated on the chancel, where men sat in the choir stalls, *men,* some of them in mail. The bishop's throne had been placed in front of the altar for Queen Eleanor to sit in; she wore her crown, but the enormous chair dwarfed her.

Beside her stood a knight, helmeted, his cloak flung back to show the scarlet-and-black blazon of a wolf's head on the chest of his tabard. A gauntleted hand rested on his sword's hilt. He was so still he might have been a painted sculpture, but his was the figure that drew the eye.

The trickle of sound that came in with newcomers dried up. Godstow's entire population was here now, all those who could walk, at least. Adelia, fearing that the child in her arms might be crushed, looked round for space and was helped up onto a tomb by people already standing on it. Gyltha and Ward joined her.

The bell stopped tolling; it had been mere background to what was developing and only became noticeable now by its cessation.

The knight nodded, and a liveried man behind the choir stalls turned and opened the vestry door, which was the entrance used by the religious.

Mother Edyve came in, leaning on her cane, followed by the nuns of Godstow. She paused as she reached the chancel and regarded the men who occupied the places reserved for her and the sisters. The Abbot of Eynsham sat there, so did Schwyz, Montignard, others. None of them moved.

There was a hiss of appalled breath from the congregation, but Mother Edyve merely cocked her head and limped past them, a finger raised to beckon at her flock as she went down the steps to stand with the congregation.

Adelia peered round the nave, looking for Mansur. She couldn't see him; instead, she found herself looking at mailed men with drawn swords standing at intervals along the walls, as if the ancient stones had sprung rivets of steel and iron.

Warders.

She turned back. The knight in the chancel had begun speaking.

"You all know me. I am the Lord of Wolvercote, and from this moment I claim this precinct of Godstow in the name of our Lord Savior and my gracious liege lady, Queen Eleanor of England, to be held against the queen's enemies until such time as her cause prevails throughout this land."

It was a surprisingly high, weak voice from such a tall man, but in that silence it didn't need strength.

There was a murmur of disbelief. Behind Adelia, somebody said, "What do he mean?"

Somebody else muttered, "Gor bugger, is he tellin' us we're at war?"

There was a shout from the nave: "What enemies is that, then? We ain't got no enemies, we'm all snowed up." It sounded

298

to Adelia like the voice of the miller who had questioned Bishop Rowley. There was a general, nervous snigger.

Immediately, two of the men-at-arms against the southern wall barged forward, hitting people aside with the flat of their swords until they reached the interrupter. Seizing his arms, they pulled him through the crowd to the main doors.

It *was* the miller. Adelia got a glimpse of a round face, its mouth open in shock. The men dragging him wore the wolf's head blazon. A boy ran after them. "Pa. Leave my pa alone." She couldn't see what happened after that, but the doors slammed shut and silence descended again.

"There will be no disobedience," said the high voice. "This abbey is now under military rule, and you people are subject to martial law. A curfew will be imposed. . . ."

Adelia struggled with disbelief. The most shocking thing about what was happening was its stupidity. Wolvercote was alienating the very people he needed as friends while the snow lasted. *Needlessly.* As the miller said, there was no enemy. The last she'd heard, the nearest military force was at nearby Oxford — and that was Wolvercote's own.

Oh, God, a stupid man — the most dangerous animal of them all.

In the choir stalls, Montignard was smiling at the queen. Most of the others were watching the crowd in the nave, but the Abbot of Eynsham was examining his fingernails while the scowl on Schwyz's face was that of a man forced to watch a monkey wearing his clothes.

He wouldn't have done this, Adelia thought. *He's a professional. I wouldn't have done it, and I don't know anything about warfare.*

". . . the holy women will keep to their cloister, rationing will be introduced while the snow lasts, and one meal a day shall be eaten communally — gentles in the refectory, villeins in the barn. Apart from church services, there shall be no other gatherings. Any group of more than five people is forbidden."

"That's done for his bloody meals, then," Gyltha breathed.

Adelia grinned. Here was stupidity in extremis; the kitchen staff alone numbered twenty; if they couldn't congregate, there would be no cooking.

Whatever that man is up to, she thought, *this is not the way to do it.*

Then she thought, *But he doesn't know any other. This is a man for whom frightened people are obedient people.*

And we are *frightened.* She could feel it, collective memory like a chill lancing through body heat in the church. An old helplessness. The Horsemen were with them, introduced into their peace by a stupid, stupid swine.

For what?

Adelia looked to where Schwyz and Abbot Eynsham sat, radiating discomposure. If this is the queen's war, they are all on the same side. Is Wolvercote establishing himself over his allies before he can be challenged? Grabbing authority *now?* Not the Abbot of Eynsham, not Schwyz, nor any other to win the glory, if glory was to be won. Wolvercote had arrived to find the queen of England at hand and must establish himself as her savior before anyone else could. If she succeeded under his generalship, Wolvercote might even be the true regent of England.

I'm watching a man throw dice.

He'd come to the end of his orders. He was turning, kneeling to Eleanor, his sword proffered, hilt first, for her to touch. "Always your servant, lady. To you and God in majesty, I swear my fealty."

And Eleanor was touching the hilt. Standing up. Skirting him to get to the chancel steps. Raising her small fist. Looking beautiful.

"I, Eleanor, Queen of England, Duchess of Aquitaine, do swear that you are my people and that I shall love and serve you as I love and serve my gracious Lord, Jesus Christ."

If she expected applause, she didn't get any. But she smiled; she was sure of her charm. "My good and faithful vassal, Lord Wolvercote, is a man of war, yet he is also a man of love, as shall be witnessed by his marriage to one of your own within a day or two, a celebration to which everyone here shall be invited."

That didn't get any applause, either, but from somewhere deep within the congregation, somebody farted. Loudly.

The men-at-arms turned their heads this way and that, looking for the culprit, but, though a shiver swept through the crowd, every face remained stolid.

How I love the English, Adelia thought.

The Abbot of Eynsham was on his feet, retrieving the situation by administering a blessing. At the "go in peace," the doors opened and they were allowed to file out between a phalanx of armed men who directed them to go home without talking.

Back in their room, Gyltha tore off her cloak. "Are they all gone daft, or is it me?"

"They have." She put Allie onto the bed; the child had been bored by the proceedings and had fallen asleep.

"What's to be gained by it?"

"Infighting," Adelia said. "He's making sure he's queen's champion before she can get another. Did you see Schwyz's face? Oh, poor Emma."

" 'Queen's champion'?" scoffed Gyltha. "If Godstow wasn't for Henry Plantagenet before, it bloody is now — that's what the queen's champion's gone and done."

There was a knock on the door.

It was the mercenary, Cross, truculent as ever. He addressed Gyltha but pointed his chin at Adelia. "She's got to come along of me."

"And who are you? Here, you're one of them." Angrily, Gyltha pushed the man out onto the steps. "She ain't going anywhere with you, you pirate, and you can tell that bloody Wolvercote I told you so."

The mercenary staggered under the assault as he held it off. "I ain't Wolvercote's, I'm Schwyz's." He appealed to Adelia. "Tell her."

Gyltha kept pushing. "You're a bastard Fleming, whoever you be. Get away."

"Sister Jennet sent me." It was another appeal to Adelia; Sister Jennet was Godstow's infirmarian. "The doctor wants you for summat. Urgent."

Gyltha ceased her assault. "What doctor?"

"The darky. Thought he was a bargee, but turns out he's a doctor."

"A patient," Adelia said, relieved. Here was something she could deal with. She bent down to kiss Allie and went to get her bag. "Who is it? What's the trouble?"

Cross said, "It's Poyns, ain't it?" as if she should know. "His arm's bad."

"In what way bad?"

"Gone sort of green."

"Hmmm." Adelia added her bundle of knives to the bag's equipment.

Even as they left, accompanied by Ward, Gyltha was giving the mercenary little shoves. "An' you bring her back as good as she goes, you scavengin' bugger, or it's me you'll answer to. And what about your bloody curfew?"

"Ain't my curfew," Cross shouted back. " 'S Wolvercote's."

It was in operation already. Ward gave a grunt in reply to the bark of a fox somewhere out in the fields, but apart from that, the abbey was quiet. As they skirted the church and turned up by the barn, a sentry stepped out of the doorway of the little, round pepper pot of a building that served as the convent's lockup.

The flambeau above the doorway shone on his helmet. He had a pike in his hand. "Who goes there?"

"Infirmary, mate," Cross told him. "This here's a nurse. Pal of mine's poorly."

"Give the password."

"What bloody password? I'm a queen's soldier, same as you."

"In the name of Lord Wolvercote, give us the password, see, or I'll run you through."

"Listen here, friend . . ." Avoiding the pike, Cross shambled up to the sentry, apparently to explain, and hit him on the jaw.

He was a short man, Cross, but the taller sentry went down as if poleaxed.

Cross didn't even look at him. He gestured to Adelia. "Come *on,* will you?"

Before obeying, she stooped to make sure the sentry was breathing. He was, and beginning to groan.

Oh, well, it had been a password of sorts. "I'm coming."

Sister Jennet was imperiling her immortal soul by bringing in on one of her cases a man she thought to be a heathen doctor. Nor was she doing it any good, either, by acquiescing to the presence of his "assistant," a woman whose relationship with

305

the bishop had caused speculation among the sisterhood.

Yet that same bishop during his visit had spoken of the skill and scope of Arab medicine in general and of this practitioner in particular, and if she was religious, Sister Jennet was also a doctor manqué; it was against every instinct of her nature to watch one of her patients die from a condition about which she could do nothing but a Saracen could.

The tug and counter-tug of the battle within her was apparent in the anger with which she greeted Adelia. "You took your time, mistress. And leave this dog outside. It's bad enough that I have to countenance mercenaries in the ward." The infirmaress glared at Cross, who cowered.

Adelia had seen infirmaries where Ward's presence would have improved the smell. But not here. She looked around her; the long ward was as clean as any she'd encountered. Fresh straw on its boards, the scent of burning herbs from the braziers, white sheets, every patient's head cropped close against lice, and the ordered bustle of the attendant nuns suggesting that here was efficient care for the sick.

She shut Ward outside. "Perhaps you would tell me what I can do."

Sister Jennet was taken aback; Adelia's manner and plainness of dress were unexpected in a bishop's moll. Somewhat mollified, the infirmaress explained what she required of Dr. Mansur. ". . . but we are both imprisoned in the damned Tower of Babel."

"I see," Adelia said. "You can't understand him." Mansur probably understood quite well but could not move without her.

"Nor he me. It is why I sent for you. You speak his tongue, I understand." She paused. "Is he as skilled as Bishop Rowley declared him to be?" At the mention of the name, her eyes flickered to Adelia's face and away.

"You will not be disappointed," Adelia promised her.

"Well, anything is better than the village barber. Don't stand there. Come along." She glared again at the mercenary. "You, too, I suppose."

The patient was at the far end of the ward. They'd put woven screens of withies round the bed, but the smell coming from beyond confirmed the reason for Sister Jennet's need of unchristian help.

He was a young man, his terror at his surroundings enhanced by the tall, white-robed, dark-faced figure looming over him.

"It don't hurt," he kept saying. "It don't hurt."

Mansur spoke in Arabic. "Where have you been?"

Adelia replied in the same tongue. "Summoned to church. We're under military rule."

"Who are we fighting?"

"God knows. Snowmen. What have we got here?"

Mansur leaned forward and gently lifted a covering of lint from the boy's left arm.

"No time to waste, I think."

There wasn't. The mangled lower arm was black and discharging stinking, yellow pus.

"How did it happen?" Adelia demanded in English — and added, as she so often had to, "The doctor wants to know."

Cross spoke up. "Caught it under a cartwheel on the march to the tower, clumsy young bugger. Put some ointment on it, can't you?"

"Can you leave him his elbow?" Mansur asked.

"No." The telltale signs of necrosis were already racing upward beyond the joint.

"We'll be lucky if we can save his life."

"Why did the little woman not do it herself earlier?"

308

"She can't. She's not allowed to shed blood."

The Church's proscription against surgery was absolute. Sister Jennet could not disobey it.

Mansur's hawklike nose wrinkled. "They would leave him to die?"

"They were going to send for the Wolvercote barber." The horror of it overcame her. "A *barber,* dear God."

"A barber who sheds blood? He need not shave me, Imshallah."

Even had he been called in, the barber would have had to do his work in the kitchen to avoid offending God's nose with bloodshed in the area of the sacred cloister. Now, so would Adelia. This added tussle of medicine versus her religion caused such turbulence in Sister Jennet that she made arrangements for the operation in a rap of furious orders, and watched Mansur carry her patient out of the ward as if she hated them both. "And you," she shouted at the despised Cross, "you crawl back to your kennel. They don't want you."

"We do," Adelia told her. "He . . . er, he knows the password."

However, the procession of doctor, patient, doctor's assistant, her dog, mercenary, and two nuns bearing clean linen and palliasse went unchallenged as it emerged via the door from the infirmary chapel and turned left toward the kitchen.

Adelia let the others go in first and caught Cross by the front of his jerkin before he could enter. She was going to need him; the patient would be less frightened if Cross, his friend, were present. She didn't like Cross much — well, he didn't like her — but she thought she could trust him to keep silent. "Listen to me, that boy's arm has to come off, and I . . ."

"What you mean 'come off'?"

She kept it simple. "There's poison spreading up your friend's arm. If it gets to his heart, he will die."

"Ain't the darky going to say magic words over it or summat?"

"No, he's going to amputate, cut it off. Or rather, I am going to do it for him but . . ."

"Can't. You're a woman."

Adelia shook him; there wasn't time for this. "Have you seen the state of the doctor's hands? They're in bandages. You will hear him talk and see me work but . . ."

"He's going to tell you what to do, is that it?" Cross was slightly reassured. "Here, though, what's my lad going to do without his bloody arm?"

"What's he going to do without his bloody

life?" Adelia shook the man again. "The point is . . . you must swear never to tell anybody, *anybody,* what you see tonight. Do you understand?"

Cross's unlovely, troubled face cleared. "*Is* magic, ain't it? The darky's going to do sorcery, that's why the nuns ain't allowed to see."

"Who's your patron saint?"

"Saint Acacias, a'course. He always done well by me."

"Swear on him that you will not tell."

Cross swore.

The kitchen was deserted for the night. The nuns prepared its enormous chopping block with the palliasse and clean sheets for the patient to lie on, then bowed and left.

Young Poyns's eyes were goggling in his head and his breathing was fast; he was feverish and very frightened. "It don't hurt. It don't hurt at all."

Adelia smiled at him. "No, it wouldn't. And it won't, you're going to go to sleep." She got the opium bottle and a clean cloth out of her bag. Mansur was already lowering her net of knives into the bubbling pot of water hanging from a jack over the fire; hot steel cut better than cold.

The light in the kitchen, however, was insufficient. "You," she said to Cross. "Two candles. One in each hand. Hold them where I tell you, but don't let them drip."

Cross was watching Mansur raise the knives from the pot and take them out of the net with his bandaged hands. "You sure he knows what he's doing?"

"Candles," Adelia hissed at him. "Help or get out."

He helped; at least, he held the candles, but as she put the opium-soaked cloth over the patient's face, he tried to intervene. "You're smotherin' him, you bitch." Mansur held him back.

She had a few seconds; the boy must not breathe the opium too long. "This arm has to come off. You know that really, don't you? He may die anyway, but he can't live if I don't operate right away."

"He's telling you what to do, though?" Cross had begun to be overawed by Mansur, who, with his strength, his robe, and kaffiyeh, was impressive. "He's a sorcerer, ain't he? That's why he talks funny."

"You'll have to appear to be instructing me," Adelia said in Arabic.

Mansur began gabbling in Arabic.

She had to work fast, thanking God that opium grew plentifully in the Cambridgeshire fens and she had brought a good supply but measuring its benignity against its danger.

The world shrank to a tabletop.

Since he had to keep talking, Mansur chose as his theme *Kit b'Alf Layla wa-Layla,* also known as *The Book of a Thousand Nights.* So an Oxfordshire convent kitchen rang with the high-pitched voice of a castrato recounting in Arabic the stories that the Persian Scheherazade had concocted for her sultan husband three hundred years earlier in order to delay her execution. He'd told them to Adelia as a child and she had loved them. Now she heard them no more than she heard the pop and crackle of the fire.

Had Rowley, saved from the cold waters, entered the kitchen, Adelia wouldn't have looked up, nor recognized him if she had. The mention of her child's name would have brought the response "Who?" There was only the patient — not even him, really, just his arm. Fold back the flaps of skin.

"Suturae."

Mansur slapped a threaded needle into her outstretched hand and began mopping blood.

Arteries, veins.

Saw the bone or cleave it? How the patient might manage his life with only a shoulder stump was not her concern; her thinking could only advance at the speed of the operation.

A heavy object thumped into the kitchen waste pail.

More stitches. Ointment, lint, bandage.

At last she wiped her forearm across her forehead. Slowly, her vision expanded to take in the beams and pots and a roaring fire.

Somebody was bothering her. "What's he say? Will he be all right?"

"I don't know."

"That was wunnerrful, though, weren't it?" Cross was shaking Mansur warmly by the hand. "Tell him he's a marvel."

"You're a marvel," Adelia said in Arabic.

"I know."

"How are your hands, my dear?" she asked. "Can you carry him back to the infirmary?"

"I can."

"Then wrap him up warm and be quick before the soporific wears off. Careful of his shoulder. Tell Sister Jennet he's likely to vomit when he comes round. I'll be along in a minute."

"He'll live now, won't he? Going to be all right, the lad, ain't he?"

She turned on the botherer. She was always bad-tempered at this point; it had

314

been a race and, like a runner, she needed time to recover and — Cross, was it? — wasn't giving her any.

"The doctor doesn't *know*," she said — to hell with the bedside manner; it wasn't as if this man had been nice to her on the boat. "Your friend has youth on his side, but his injury was poisoned for too long and" — she leaned in to the attack — "*should have been treated before this.* Now go away and leave me alone."

She watched him slouch off after the laden Mansur, then sat herself by the fire, making lists in her head. There was plenty of willow bark, thanks be; the patient would need it for the pain. If he lived.

The stink of decomposition coming from the kitchen pail was a worry to her; after all, this was the kitchen that served their food. A rat appeared from behind a cupboard, its whiskers twitching in the direction of the pail. Adelia reached for the woodpile and threw a log at it.

What to do with severed limbs? In Salerno, she'd had other people to dispose of them. She'd always suspected they mixed them with the pigs' swill; it was one of the reasons she had been wary of eating pork.

Wrapping herself in her cloak and carrying the bucket, she went out into the alley to find some place of disposal. It was shockingly cold after the kitchen's heat, and very dark.

Farther down the alley someone began screaming. Went on screaming.

"I can't," Adelia said out loud. "I just can't." But she began blundering toward the sound, hoping somebody else would get there first and deal with whatever it was.

A lantern came bobbing out of the darkness with the sound of running. "Who's that?" It was the messenger, Jacques. "Oh, it's you, mistress."

"Yes. What is that?"

"I don't know."

They trotted toward it, being joined as they went by other lanterns that gave glimpses of alarmed faces and slippered feet.

Past the laundry, past the smithy, past the stables — all of it déjà vu, and horrible because Adelia now knew where the screams were coming from.

The cowshed doors were open, with people clustering around outside them, some trying to comfort a hysterical milkmaid, though most were transfixed and gaping, holding their lanterns high so that light shone on the dangling figure of Bertha.

A strap round her neck hung her from a hook in a beam. Her bare toes pointed downward toward a milking stool where it lay on its side among the straw.

The nuns lamented over the dead girl. What, they asked, could have possessed her to commit suicide, that so very grievous sin? Had she not known that God was the owner of her life and, consequently, that she had committed an unlawful act against God's own dominion, forbidden by Scripture and Church?

No, Adelia thought angrily, *Bertha hadn't known that; nobody would have taught her.*

Guilt, the sisters said. Hers was the hand that had given poisoned mushrooms to Rosamund; remorse had overcome her.

But they were good and charitable women, and though Bertha would have to be interred in unconsecrated ground outside their convent walls, they took the body to their own chapel to keep a vigil over it in the meantime. They chanted prayers for the dead as they went. The crowd from the cowshed followed them.

Bertha had never had so much attention. Death in such a small community, after all, was always an event; felo-de-se was unheard of and worthy of much attention.

As she followed the procession through the dark alleys, Adelia stayed angry, thinking how wrong it was that a creature who had been denied so much in her short life must now be denied even a Christian burial.

Jacques, walking beside her, shook his head. "Terrible thing this is, mistress. To hang herself, poor soul. Felt herself responsible for Lady Rosamund's death, I reckon."

"She didn't, though, Jacques. You were there. *'Not my fault, not my fault.'* She said it over and over." It was one thing Bertha had been clear about.

"Well, then, she was mortal afraid of Dame Dakers. Couldn't face her, I reckon."

Yes, she had been afraid of Dakers. That would be the verdict. Either Bertha had suffered intolerable remorse for the death of her mistress or she had been so terrified of what Dakers would do to her that she had preferred to take her own life.

"It's wrong," Adelia said.

"A sin," Jacques agreed. "God have mercy on her soul all the same."

But it was wrong, everything was *wrong*. The scene of Bertha hanging from the hook had been wrong.

They were approaching the chapel. Such laypeople as had been accompanying the body stopped. This was the nuns' territory; they must stay outside. Even if she could have gone on, Adelia couldn't bear it anymore, not Jacques and his gloomy chatter, not the accompanying, expostulating men and women, not the nuns' chanting. "Where's the guesthouse from here?"

Jacques showed her the way back. "A good night's sleep, mistress. That's what you need."

"Yes." But it wasn't fatigue, though she *was* very tired, it was the wrongness of everything. It hammered at her mind like something wanting to come in.

The messenger lighted her up the steps and then went off, muttering and shaking his head.

Gyltha had heard the screaming even from their room and had called out the window to find its cause. "Bad business," she said. "They're saying sorrow made her do it, poor mite."

"Or perhaps she was frightened that Dame Dakers would turn her into a mouse and give her to the cat, yes, I know."

Gyltha looked up from her knitting, alerted. "Oh, ar? What's this?"

"It's wrong." Adelia fondled Ward's ears, then pushed the dog away.

Gyltha's eyes narrowed, but she said nothing more on the subject. "How's the Fleming?"

"I don't think he'll survive." Adelia wandered to their communal bed and soothed back her sleeping daughter's hair.

"Serve un right." Gyltha didn't hold with mercenaries, whose extensive use during the Stephen and Matilda war had made them universally loathed. Whether they came from Flanders or not — and most of them did — the name "Fleming" had become a euphemism for rape, pillage, and cruelty. "One thing about the king," she said, "he got rid of all they bastards, and now Eleanor's bringing 'em back."

"Hmmm."

Gyltha raised her eyebrows. She'd prepared a hot posset — the room smelled deliciously of hot milk and rum. She handed a beaker to Adelia. "You know what time it is?" She pointed to the hour marks on the candle by the bed. "Time you was in bed. Nearly morning. They'll be singing Matins soon."

"It's all wrong, Gyltha."

Gyltha sighed; she knew the signs. "It'll keep til morning."

"No, it won't." Adelia roused herself and refastened her cloak. "A measure, I need a measure. Have we any string?"

There was cord that they used to bind their traveling packs. "And I want that back," Gyltha said. "Good cord that is.

Where you going?"

"I left the medicine bag in the kitchen. I'd better go and get it."

"You stay there," Gyltha told her sharply. "You ain't going nowhere without that old Arab goes, too."

But Adelia had gone, taking the cord and a lantern with her. Not to the kitchen. She made her way to the nuns' chapel. It was dawn.

They had laid Bertha's body on a catafalque in the little nave. The sheet they'd covered it with dragged all the vague light from the high windows to its own oblong whiteness, condemning the rest of the space to a misty dust.

Adelia strode up the nave, the shushing of her feet in the rushes disturbing the quiet so that the nun on her knees at the foot of the catafalque turned to see who it was.

Adelia paid her no attention. She put the lantern on the floor while she turned back the sheet.

Bertha's face had a bluish tint; the tip of her tongue was just visible where it stuck out of the side of her mouth. This, with her tiny nose, gave her a look of impudence, like some fairy child.

The nun — she was one Adelia didn't know — hissed her concern as Adelia picked up the lantern and, with the other hand, pulled back Bertha's lids to expose the eyes.

There were flecks of blood in their whites. Only to be expected.

Getting onto her knees, Adelia held the lantern as close as she could to the neck. There were lines from the edges of the strap that the girl had hung by, but there were other marks — gouges that traveled down the throat.

And running horizontally around the skin of the neck beneath the strap bruises was a line of tiny circular indentations.

The nun was on her feet, trying to flap Adelia away from the body. "What are you doing? You are disturbing the dead."

Adelia ignored her, didn't even hear her. She re-covered Bertha's face with the sheet and turned it back at the other end, lifting the girl's skirts to expose the lower body.

The nun ran from the chapel.

The vagina showed no sign of tearing or, as far as it was possible to see, any trace of semen.

Adelia replaced the sheet.

Damn. There *was* a way of knowing. Her old tutor, Gordinus, had shown her by opening the necks of prisoners who'd been hanged and comparing their hyoid bones with bones of those who'd been garroted —

a form of execution peculiar to a district of Pavia, which had inherited it from the Romans. *"See, my dear? The bone is rarely broken in garroting, whereas it is, almost invariably, in hanging. Thus, if we are suspicious in a case of strangulation, we may distinguish whether it was self-inflicted or the result of an attack by another. Also, in the case of hanged suicides, there is seldom bleeding into the neck muscles, whereas if we find it in a corpse supposed to have hanged itself, we have cause to be suspicious that we are looking at a case of murder."*

A dissection . . . if she could just do a dissection . . . oh, well, she'd have to rely on measurements . . .

"And what is this?" The deep voice rang through the chapel, dispelling its quiet, seeming to disturb the dust motes and bring in a sharper light.

The nun was gabbling. "Do you see her, my lord? This woman . . ."

"I see her." He turned on Adelia, who had run the cord from the top of Bertha's head to her bare toes. "Are you mad? Why do you dishonor the dead, mistress? Even one such as this?"

"Hmmm." Having made a knot in it, Adelia wound the cord around her hand and began vaguely wandering toward the door.

Splendid in breadth and height and color, the abbot blocked her way. "I *asked,* mistress, why you interfere with the poor soul lying there?" The West Country accent had gone, replaced by schooled vowels.

Adelia moved past him. *The strap,* she thought, *perhaps it's still in the cowshed. And my chain.*

The abbot watched her go and then, with a sweep of his arms, sent the nun back to her vigil.

Outside, despite a suicide, the presence of a queen, occupation by her mercenaries, and the terrible cold, the wheel of the abbey's day was being sent spinning. Slipping on dirty, nobbling ice, Godstow's people hurried past her to reawaken damped-down fires and start their work.

Jacques caught up with Adelia as she passed the stables. "I waited, mistress. What's to be done with this?" He was carrying a bucket and swung it in front of her so that she had to stop. It contained an arm; Adelia stared at it for a moment before remembering that, in what seemed like another epoch, she had performed an amputation.

"I don't know. Bury it somewhere, I suppose." She pressed on.

"Bury it," Jacques said, looking after her.

"And the ground like bloody iron."

The cowshed in daylight. Warm, despite the open doors. Sun shining onto its bespattered floor, quiet except for a rhythmic swish from one of the stalls, where a young woman was milking. The stool she sat on was the one that had been kicked over underneath Bertha's hanging body.

Her name, she said, was Peg, and it was she who, entering the shed early to begin the morning's milking, had discovered Bertha. The sight had sent her into screams, and she'd had to run back home for a drop of her mother's soothing cordial before she could face returning to the scene and start work.

" 'Tis why I'm so late today. These poor beasts've been lowing for me to come and relieve 'em but 'twas the shock, d'ye see. Opened the doors and there she was. Never get over it, I won't. This old shed, 'twill never be the same again, not to me it won't."

Adelia knew how she felt; the comforting smell of animal flatulence and straw, the innocent homeliness of the place had been invaded. An ancient beam from which a body had hung was now a gibbet. She wouldn't get over it, either. Bertha had died here, and of all the deaths, Bertha's cried out the loudest.

"Can I help ye, mistress?" Peg wanted to know, carrying on milking.

"I'm looking for a necklet, a cross and chain. I gave it to Bertha. She isn't wearing it now, and I'd like to put it in her grave with her."

Peg's cap went askew as she shook her head without it losing contact with the cow's ribs. "Never seen un."

In her mind's eye, Adelia resurrected the scene of an hour or so ago. A man — she thought it was Fitchet the gatekeeper — had run forward, righted the stool that lay below Bertha's feet, stood on it, and lifted the body so that the strap it hung by came free of the beam's hook.

What, then? That's right, that's right, other men had helped him lay the body down. Somebody had undone the strap and tossed it away. The people clustering around, hopelessly trying to revive the dead girl, had hindered Adelia from seeing whether her cross and chain was on Bertha's neck. If it had been, the strap had covered it and pressed it tightly against the girl's skin as she hanged, forcing its links into her flesh and causing those indentations.

But if she *hadn't* been wearing it . . .

Adelia began looking around.

In a cobwebby corner, she found the strap. It was a belt, an old one. A worn rivet showed where the owner had been wont to fasten it, but at the far end of the leather, another rivet had been badly contorted where it had been slipped over the hook on the beam and taken the weight of Bertha's body.

"Where did she get a belt from, I wonder?" Adelia asked herself out loud, putting it over her shoulder.

"Dunno, she never had no belt," Peg said.

That's right. She hadn't. Adelia walked slowly to the far end of the cowshed, kicking up wisps of hay as she went to see if they hid anything.

Behind her came the swish of milk as it went into the pail and Peg's reflective voice: "Poor thing, I can't think what come to her. 'Course, she were a bit of a looby, but even so . . ."

"Did she say anything to you?"

"Said a lot, always muttering away up the other end there, enough to give you goose bumps, but I paid her no mind."

Adelia reached the stall that Bertha had occupied. It was dark here. She balanced the lantern on top of a partition and went down on her knees to start sifting the straw, feeling through it to the hard-packed earth underneath.

She heard Peg address her cow, "You're done then, madam," and the friendly slap on its rump as the milkmaid left it to go on to the next, and the sound of footfalls as some new person entered the shed, and Peg's voice again: "And a good morning to you, Master Jacques."

"Good morning to *you*, Mistress Peg."

There was flirtation in both voices that brought a lightness to the day. Jacques, Adelia thought, despite his sticking-out ears and breathy overeagerness, had made a conquest.

He came hurrying up the aisle and paused to watch Adelia as she scrabbled. "I buried it, mistress."

"What? Oh, good."

"Can I help whatever it is you're doing, mistress?" He was becoming used to her eccentricities.

"No."

Because she'd found it. Her fingers had encountered the harsh thread of metal, little and broken — the cross was held by the fastening, but farther along, the links had snapped.

God help us all. This, then, was where it had happened. In this dark stall, Bertha had torn at her own neck in an attempt to

328

dislodge the necklet with which strong hands were strangling her.

Oh, the poor child.

Adelia again saw Bertha crawling toward her, sniffing, telling her what the old woman in the forest, who had given her the mushrooms for Rosamund, had smelled like.

"Purty. Like you."

The memory was unbearable. The short, sad little life ending in violence . . . *Why? Who?*

"Mistress?" Jacques was becoming troubled by her stillness.

Adelia picked herself up. Gripping the necklet, she walked with the messenger down to where Peg was pouring her full pail of foaming milk into a bigger bucket, her backside giving a provocative wiggle at Jacques's approach.

The milking stool. She knew now that Bertha had been murdered, but there was just one more proof. . . .

As Peg went to collect the stool to take it to the next cow, Adelia was ahead of her. "May I have this for a moment?"

Peg and Jacques stared as she took the stool and placed it directly under the hook in the beam. She unwound the length of cord from her hand and pushed it toward Jacques. "Measure me."

"Measure you, mistress?"

"*Yes.*" She was becoming irritable. "From my crown to my feet."

Shrugging, he held one end of the cord to the top of Adelia's head and let it drop. He stooped and pinched the place where it touched the ground. "There. You're not very tall, mistress."

She tried to smile at him — his own lack of height bothered him; without his raised boots, he wouldn't be much higher than she was. Looking at the cord where he held it, she saw that it extended a little way from the knot she had made when she'd measured the corpse on the catafalque. She was nearly two inches taller than Bertha had been.

Now to see.

Peg said, "She got excited yesterday, round about evening milkin', now I come to think on it."

"Who did? Bertha?"

"Said she'd got summat to tell the lady with the cross and went rushin' out. That's what she'd call a nun, I suppose, on account of she didn't know better."

No, Adelia thought, *it was me. I was the lady with the cross.* "Where did she go?"

"Can't have been far," Peg said, "for she were soon back and takin' on like she'd seen the devil stinkin' of sulphur. Summat about acres."

"Dakers?" Jacques asked.

"Could've been."

"Must've seen Dame Dakers," Jacques said. "She was mortal afraid of that woman."

Adelia asked, "She didn't say what it was she wanted to tell the nun?"

"Kept mutterin' something about wasn't her, 'twas him."

Adelia steadied herself against a stall's stanchion, grasping it hard. "Could it have been: *'It wasn't a her, it was a him'*?"

"Could've been."

"Hmmm." She wanted to think about it, but the cows farther up the line were lowing with discomfort, and Peg was becoming restive at the annexation of her milking stool.

Adelia slipped the belt into its buckle and put it round her neck, pulling it close. Stepping up on the stool, she tried extending the free piece of the belt to the hook, managing only to make the end of the leather touch it, leaving a gap between hook and rivet. She stood on tiptoe; rivet and hook still didn't meet — and she was taller than Bertha had been.

"It's too short," she said. "The belt's too short."

That was what had bothered her. The sight of the dangling body had been too shocking to take in at the time, but her mind had registered it — *Bertha's feet could not have reached the stool to kick it away.*

She began choking, struggling to get the buckle undone before unseen arms could lift her up and attach the belt to the hook; she couldn't breathe.

Jacques's hands fumbled at her neck and she fought them, as Bertha had fought those of her killer. "All right, mistress," he said. "Steady. Steady now." When he'd got the belt off, he held her arm and stroked her back as if soothing a frightened cat. "Steady now. Steady."

Peg was watching them as if at the capering insane. Jacques nodded at her, indicating the stool, and with relief she took it up and went back to her cows.

Adelia stood where she was, listening as Peg's capable, cold-chapped hands squeezed and relaxed on the cow's teats, sending milk into the pail with the regularity of a soft drumbeat.

"It wasn't a her, it was a him."

Jacques's eyes questioned her; he, at least, had understood what she'd been about.

"Well," Adelia said, "at least now Bertha can be buried in consecrated ground."

"Not suicide?"

"No. She was murdered."

She saw again how his young face could age.

"Dakers," he said.

NINE

The nuns thought the same.

"Let me understand you," Mother Edyve said. "You are saying that Dame Dakers hanged that poor child?"

They were in the chapter house; the abbess was in conclave with her senior nuns.

They had not welcomed Adelia. After all, they had serious matters to mull over: Their abbey had been as good as invaded; dangerous mercenaries occupied it; there were bodies hanging from their bridge; if the snow continued, they would soon run out of supplies. They did not want to listen to the outlandish, unsettling report of a murder — *murder?* — in their midst.

However, Adelia had done one thing right; she had brought Mansur along. Gyltha had persuaded her. "They won't pay *you* no mind," she'd said, "but they might attend to that old Arab." And after a few hours' sleep, Adelia had decided she was right. Mansur had been recommended to the nuns by their bishop, he looked impressive, he stood high in the estimation of their infirmaress; above all, he was a man, and as such, even though a foreigner, he carried more weight than she did.

It had been difficult to get a hearing until the chapter meeting was over, but Adelia had refused to wait. "This is the king's business," she'd said. For so it was; murder, wherever it occurred, came under royal jurisdiction. The lord Mansur, she told them, was skilled in uncovering crimes, had originally been called to England by Henry II's warrant to look into the deaths of some Cambridgeshire children — well, so he had, in a way — and the killer had been found.

Apologizing for Mansur's insufficiency in their language, she had pretended to interpret for him. She'd begged them to examine for themselves the marks on Bertha's neck, had shown them the evidence by which she proved murder . . . and heard her voice scrabbling at them as uselessly as Bertha's fingers had scrabbled at the necklet strangling her.

She answered Mother Edyve, "The lord Mansur is not accusing Dame Dakers. He is saying that *somebody* hanged Bertha. She did not hang herself."

It was too gruesome for them. Here, in their familiar, wooden-crucked English chapter house, stood a towering figure in outlandish clothing — a heathen, king's warrant or not — telling them what they did not want to hear through the medium of a woman with a dubious reputation.

They didn't have investigative minds. It seemed as if none of them, not even their canny old abbess, possessed the ferocious curiosity that drove Adelia herself, nor any curiosity at all. All questions had been answered for them by the resurrection of Jesus Christ and the rule instituted by Saint Benedict.

Nor were they too concerned with earthly justice. The murderer, if a murderer there was, would be sentenced more terribly when he faced the Great Judge, to whom all sins were known, than by any human court.

The belt, the broken chain, and the measuring cord lay snaked on the table before them, but they kept their eyes away.

Well, yes, they said, but was the lack of distance between Bertha's feet and the milking stool significant? Surely that poor misguided girl could have somehow climbed onto one of the cowshed stalls with the belt round her neck and jumped? Who knew what strength was given to the desperate?

Certainly, Bertha had been in fear of what Dame Dakers might do to her, but did not that in itself argue felo-de-se?

Rowley, if only you were here . . .

"It was murder," Adelia insisted. "Lord Mansur has proved it was murder."

Mother Edyve considered the matter. "I would not have credited Dakers with the strength."

Adelia despaired. It was like being on a toasting fork — whichever side was presented, it was flipped over so that the other faced the fire. If Bertha had been murdered, then Dakers, revenging Rosamund's death, had been the murderer — who else could it have been? If Dakers wasn't the murderer, then Bertha had not been murdered.

"Perhaps one of the Flemings did it, Wolvercote's or Schwyz's," Sister Bullard, the cellaress, said. "They are lustful, violent men, especially in liquor. Which reminds me, Mother, we must set a guard on the cellars. They are already stealing our wine."

That opened a floodgate of complaint: "Mother, how are we to feed them all?"

"Mother, the mercenaries . . . I fear for our young women."

"And our people — look how they beat the poor miller."

"The courtiers are worse, Mother. The

337

lewd songs they sing . . ."

Adelia was sorry for them. On top of their worries, here were two strange persons, who had arrived at Godstow in company with a murdered body from the bridge, now suggesting that another killer was at large within the abbey's very walls.

The sisters did not — indeed, *could* not — blame them for either death, but Adelia knew from some sideways looks from under the nuns' veils that she and Mansur had acquired the taint of carrion.

"Even if what Lord Mansur says is true, Mother," said Sister Gregoria, the almoner, "what can be done about it? We are snowed up; we cannot send for the sheriff's coroner until the thaw."

"And while the snow lasts, King Henry cannot rescue us," Sister Bullard pointed out. "Until he can, our abbey, our very existence, is in peril."

That was what mattered to them. Their abbey had survived one conflict between warring monarchs; it might not survive another. If the queen should oust the king, she would necessarily reward the blackguard Wolvercote, who had secured her victory — and Lord Wolvercote had long desired Godstow and its lands. The nuns could envisage a future in which they begged for their bread in the streets.

"Allow Lord Mansur to continue his inquiries," Adelia pleaded. "At least do not bury Bertha in unconsecrated ground until all the facts are known."

Mother Edyve nodded. "Please tell Lord Mansur we are grateful for his interest," she said in her fluting, emotionless voice. "You may leave us to question Dame Dakers. After that, we shall pray for guidance in the matter."

It was a dismissal. Mansur and Adelia had to bow and leave.

Discussion broke out behind them almost before they'd reached the door — but it was not about Bertha. "Yes, but where *is* the king? How may he come to our aid if he doesn't even know we are in need of it? We cannot trust that Bishop Rowley reached him — I fear for his death."

As the two went out of the chapter house door, Mansur said, "The women are frightened. They will not help us search for the killer."

"I haven't even persuaded them there *is* a killer," Adelia said.

They were skirting the infirmary when, behind them, a voice called Adelia's name. It was the prioress. She came up, puffing. "A word, if I may, mistress." Adelia nodded, bowed a farewell to Mansur, and turned back.

For a while, the two women went in silence.

Sister Havis, Adelia realized, had not spoken a word during the discussion in the chapter house. She was aware, too, that the nun did not like her. To walk with her was like accompanying the apotheosis of the cold that gripped the abbey, a figure denuded of warmth, as frozen as the icicles spiking the edge of every roof.

Outside the nuns' chapel, the prioress stopped. She kept her face averted from Adelia, and her voice was hard. "I cannot approve of you," she said. "I did not approve of Rosamund. The tolerance that Mother Abbess extends to sins of the flesh is not mine."

"If that's all you have to say . . ." Adelia said, walking away.

Sister Havis strode after her. "It is not, but it has to be spoken." She withdrew a mittened hand from under her scapular and held it out to bar Adelia's progress. In it were the broken necklet, the measuring cord, and the belt. She said, "I intend to use these objects as you have done, in investigation. I shall go to the cowshed. Whatever your weaknesses, mistress, I recognize an analytical soul."

Adelia stopped.

The prioress kept her thin face turned away. "I travel," she said. "Mine is the work to administer our lands around the country, in consequence of which I see more of the dung heap of humanity than do my sisters. I see it in its iniquity and error, its disregard for the flames of hell which await it."

Adelia was still. This was not just a lecture on sin; Sister Havis had something to tell her.

"Yet," the prioress went on, "there is greater evil. I was present at Rosamund Clifford's bedside; I witnessed her terrible end. For all that she was adulterous, the woman should not have died as she did."

Adelia went on waiting.

"Our bishop had visited her a day or two before; he questioned her servants and went away again. Rosamund was still well then, but he believed from what he'd been told that there had been a deliberate attempt to poison her, which, as you and I know, subsequently succeeded." Suddenly, the prioress's head turned and she was glaring into Adelia's eyes. "Is that what he told you?"

"Yes," Adelia said. "It was why he brought us here. He knew the blame would fall on the queen. He wanted to uncover the real killer and avert a war."

"He set great store by you, then, mistress." It was a sneer.

"Yes, he did," Adelia hissed back at her. Her feet were numb with standing, and her grief for Rowley was undoing her. "Tell me whatever you want to tell me, or let me go. In God's name, are we discussing Rosamund, Bertha, or the bishop?"

The prioress blinked; she had not expected anger.

"Bertha," she said, with something like conciliation. "We are discussing Bertha. It may interest you to know, mistress, that I took charge of Dame Dakers yesterday. The female is deranged, and I did not want her roaming the abbey. Just before Vespers I locked her in the warming room for the night."

Adelia's head went up. "What time is evening milking?"

"*After* Vespers."

They had begun walking in step. "Bertha was still alive then," Adelia said. "The milkmaid saw her."

"Yes, I have talked to Peg."

"I *knew* it wasn't Dakers."

The prioress nodded. "Not unless the wretched female can walk through a thick and bolted door. Which, I may say, most of my sisters are prepared to believe that she can."

"You may say, you may say." Adelia stopped, furious. "Why didn't you say all this in chapter?"

The prioress faced her. "You were making yourself busy proving to us that Bertha was murdered. I happened to know Dakers could not have killed her. The question then arose, who did? And why? It was not a wolf I wanted to loose amongst sisters who are troubled and frightened enough already."

Ah. At last, Adelia thought, *a logical mind. Hostile, cold as winter to me, but brave.* Here, beside her, was a woman prepared to follow terrible events to their terrible conclusion.

She said, "Bertha had some knowledge about the person who gave her the mushrooms in the forest. She didn't know she had it. It came to her yesterday, and I think, I *think,* that she left the cowshed to come and tell me. Something, or perhaps it was someone, stopped her, and she went back again. To be strangled and then hanged."

"Not a random killing?"

"I don't believe so. Nor was there any sexual interference, as far as I can tell. It wasn't robbery, either; the chain was not stolen."

Unconsciously, they had begun pacing up and down together outside the chapel. Adelia said, "What she told Peg was that it wasn't a her, it was a him."

"Meaning the person in the forest?"

"I think so. I think, I *think*, Bertha remembered something, something about the old woman who gave her the mushrooms for Rosamund. I think it came to her that it wasn't an old woman at all — her description always sounded . . . I don't know, odd."

"Old women peddling poisoned mushrooms aren't odd?"

Adelia smiled. "Overdone, then. Playacting. I think that's what Bertha wanted to tell me. *Not a her but a him.*"

"A man? Dressed as a woman?"

"I think so."

The prioress crossed herself. "The inference being that Bertha could have told us who it was that killed Rosamund . . ."

"Yes."

". . . but was strangled before she could tell us . . . *by that same person.*"

"I think so."

"I was afraid of it. The Devil stalks secretly amongst us."

"In human form, yes."

" 'I shall not fear,' " quoted Sister Havis. " 'I shall not fear for the arrow that flieth by day, for the matter that walketh in darkness, nor for the Devil that is in the noonday.' " She looked at Adelia. "Yet I do."

"So do I." Oddly, though, not as much as she had; there was a tiny comfort in having passed on what she knew to authority, and here, though personally hostile, was almost the only authority the convent could offer.

After a while, Sister Havis said, "We have had to take the body from the bridge out of the icehouse. A man came asking for him, a cousin, he said — a Master Warin, a lawyer from Oxford. We laid out the body in the church for its vigil and so that he might identify it. Apparently, it is that of a young man called Talbot of Kidlington. Is he another of this devil's victims?"

"I don't know." She realized she had been saying "I" all this time. "I shall consult with the Lord Mansur. He will investigate."

The slightest flicker of amusement crossed the prioress's face; she knew who the investigator was. "Pray do," she said.

From the cloister ahead of them came the sound of laughter and singing. It had, Adelia realized, been going on for some time. Music, happiness, still existed, then.

Automatically, the prioress began walking toward it. Adelia went with her.

A couple of the younger nuns were

screaming joyously in the garth as they dodged snowballs being pelted at them by a scarlet-clad youth. Another young man was strumming a viol and singing, his head upraised to an upper window of the abbess's house, at which Eleanor stood laughing at the antics.

This, in the sanctum. Where no layman should set foot. Probably never had until now.

From Eleanor's window came a trail of perfume, elusive as a mirage, shimmering with sensuality, a siren scent beckoning toward palm-fringed islands, a smell so lovely that Adelia's nose, even while it analyzed — bergamot, sandalwood, roses — sought longingly after its luxury before the icy air took it away from her.

Oh, Lord, I am so tired of death and cold.

Sister Havis stood beside her, rigid with disapproval, saying nothing. But in a minute the players saw her. The scene froze instantly; the troubadour's song stopped in his throat, snow dropped harmlessly from the hand of his companion, and the young nuns assumed attitudes of outraged piety and continued their walk as if they had never broken stride. The snowballer swept his hat from his head and held it to his chest in parodied remorse.

346

Eleanor waved from her window. "Sorry," she called, and closed the shutters.

So I am not the only taint, Adelia thought, amused. The queen and her people were bringing the rich colors of worldliness into the convent's black-and-white domain; the presence of Eleanor, which had undermined an entire Crusade, threatened Godstow's foundations as even Wolvercote and his mercenaries did not.

Then the amusement went. *Did she bring a killer with her?*

Adelia was too tired to do much for the rest of the morning except look after Allie while Gyltha went off to meet friends in the kitchen. It was where she picked up a good deal of information and gossip.

On her return, she said, "They're busy cooking for young Emma's wedding now that Old Wolfie's turned up. Poor soul, I wouldn't fancy marryin' that viper. They're wondering if she's having second thoughts — she's keeping to the cloister and ain't spoke a word to him, so they say."

"It's bad luck to see your bridegroom before the wedding," Adelia said vaguely.

"I wouldn't want to see *him* after," Gyltha said. "Oh, and later on the sisters is going to see about them hangin' off the bridge.

Abbess says it's time they was buried." She took off her cloak. "Should be interestin'. Old Wolfie, he'll be the sort as likes corpses decoratin' the place." There was gleam in her eye. "Maybe as there'll be a battle atwixt 'em. Oh, Lord, where you going *now?*"

"The infirmary." Adelia had remembered her patient.

Sister Jennet greeted her warmly. "Perhaps you can convey my gratitude to the Lord Mansur. Such a neat, clean stump, and the patient is progressing well." She looked wistful. "How I should have liked to witness the operation."

It was the instinct of a doctor, and Adelia thought of the women lost to her own profession, as this one was, and thanked her god for the privilege that had been Salerno.

She was escorted down the ward. All the patients were men — "women mainly treat themselves" — most of them suffering from congestion of the lungs caused, the infirmaress said, by living on low-lying ground subject to unhealthy vapors from the river.

Three were elderly, from Wolvercote. "These are malnourished," the infirmaress said of them, not bothering to lower her voice. "Lord Wolvercote neglects his villagers shamefully; they haven't so much as a church to pray in, not since it fell down. It is God's grace to them that we are nearby."

She passed on to another bed where a nun was applying warm water to a patient's ear. "Frostnip," she said.

With a pang of guilt, Adelia recognized Oswald, Rowley's man-at-arms. She'd forgotten him, yet he had been one of those, along with Mansur, poling the barge that the convent had sent to Wormhold.

Walt was sitting at his bedside. He knuckled his forehead as Adelia came up.

"I'm sorry," she told Oswald. "Is it bad?"

It looked bad. Dark blisters had formed on the outer curve of the ear so that the man appeared to have a fungus attached to his head. He glowered at her.

"Shoulda kept his hood pulled down," Walt said, cheerfully. "We did, didn't we, mistress?" The mutual suffering on the boat had become a bond.

Adelia smiled at him. "We were fortunate."

"We're keeping an eye on the ear," Sister Jennet said, equally cheerful. "As I tell him, it will either stay on or fall off. Come along."

There were still screens round young Poyns's bed — not so much, Sister Jennet explained, to provide privacy for him as to prevent his evil mercenary ways from infecting the rest of the ward.

"Though I must say he has not uttered a

single oath since he's been here, which is unusual in a Fleming." She pulled the screen aside, still talking. "I can't say the same for his friend." She shook a finger at Cross, who, like Walt, was visiting.

"We ain't bloody Flemings," Cross said wearily.

Adelia was not allowed to look at the wound. Dr. Mansur, apparently, had already done so and declared himself satisfied.

The stump was well bandaged and — Adelia sniffed it — had no smell of corruption. Mansur, having attended so many operations with her, would have been able to tell if there was any sign of mortification.

Poyns himself was pale but without fever and taking food. For a moment, Adelia allowed herself to glory in him, orgulous as a peacock at her achievement, even while she marveled at the hardihood of the human frame.

She inquired after Dame Dakers; here was another she had neglected, and for whom she felt a responsibility.

"We keep her in the warming room," Sister Jennet said, as of an exhibit. "Once she was recovered, I couldn't let her stay here — she frightened my patients."

In a monastery, the warming room would

have been the scriptorium where such monks as had the skill spent their days copying manuscripts while carefully guarded braziers saved their poor fingers from cramping with cold.

Here were only Sister Lancelyne and Father Paton — he came as a surprise; Adelia had forgotten the existence of Rowley's secretary. Both were writing, though not books.

Thin winter sun shone on their bent heads and on the documents with large seals attached to them by ribbon covering the table at which they sat.

Adelia introduced herself. Father Paton screwed up his eyes and then nodded; he'd forgotten her also.

Sister Lancelyne was delighted to make her acquaintance. She was the sort of person to whom gossip was without interest unless it was literary. Nor did she seem to know that Rowley was lost. "Of course, you came with the bishop's party, did you not? Please extend to his lordship my gratitude for Father Paton; *what* I would do without this gentleman . . . I had vowed to arrange our cartulary and register in some sort of order, a task that proved beyond me until his lordship sent this Hercules into my Augean stables."

Father Paton as Hercules was something to savor; so was Sister Lancelyne herself, an old, small, gnomelike woman with the bright, jewellike eyes of a toad; so was the room, shelved from floor to ceiling, each shelf stacked with rolls of deeds and charters showing their untidy, sealed ends.

"Alphabetical order, you see," chanted Sister Lancelyne. "That is what we have to achieve, and a calendar showing which tithe is due to us on what day, what rent . . . but I see you are looking at our book."

It was the *only* book, a slim volume bound in calfskin; it had a small shelf to itself that had been lined with velvet like a jewel box. "We have a Testament, of course," Sister Lancelyne said, apologizing for the lack of library, "and a breviary, both are in the chapel, but . . . oh, dear." For Adelia had advanced on the book. As she took its spine between finger and thumb to remove it, there was a gasp of relief from the nun. "I see you care for books; so many drag at its top with a forefinger and break . . ."

"Boethius," Adelia said with pleasure. " *'O happy race of men if love that rules the stars may also rule your hearts.'* "

" *'To acquire divinity, become gods,'* " exulted Sister Lancelyne. " *'Omnis igitur bea-*

tus deus . . . by participation.' They imprisoned him for it."

"And killed him. I know, but as my foster father says, if he hadn't been in prison, he would never have written *The Consolation of Philosophy.*"

"We only have the *Fides and Ratio,*" said Sister Lancelyne. "I long for . . . no, mea culpa, I *covet* the rest as King David lusted on Bathsheba. They have an entire *Consolation* in the library at Eynsham, and I ventured to beg the abbot if I might borrow it to copy, but he wrote back to say it was too precious to send. He does not credit women with scholarship and, of course, you can't blame him."

Adelia was not a scholar herself — too much of her reading had largely and necessarily been expended on medical treatises — but she possessed a high regard for those who were; the talk of her foster father and her tutor, Gordinus, had opened a door to the literature of the mind so that she'd glimpsed a shining path to the stars, which, she promised herself, she would investigate one day. In the meantime, it was nice to discover it here among shelves and the smell of vellum and this little old woman's unextinguished desire for knowledge.

Carefully, she replaced the book. "I was

hoping to find Dame Dakers with you."

"Another great help," Sister Lancelyne said happily, pointing to a hooded figure squatting on the floor, half-hidden by the shelves.

They'd given Rosamund's housekeeper a knife with which to sharpen their quills. Goose feathers lay beside her, and she held one in her hand, the shreds of its calamus scattered on her lap. A harmless occupation, and one she must have engaged in a hundred times for Rosamund, yet Adelia was irresistibly reminded of something being dismembered.

She went to squat beside the woman. The two scribes had gone back to their work. "Do you remember me, mistress?"

"I remember you." Dakers went on shaving the quill end, making quick movements with the knife.

She had been fed and rested; she looked less bleached, but no amount of well-being was ever going to plump the skin over Dakers's skeleton, nor was it going to distract her hatred. The eyes bent on her work still glowed with it. "Found my darling's killer yet?" she asked.

"Not yet. Did you hear of Bertha's death?"

Dakers's mouth stretched, showing her teeth. She had — and happily. "I summoned my master to punish her, and he's a'done it."

"What master?"

Dakers turned her head so that Adelia stared full into her face; it was like looking into a charnel pit. "There is only The One."

Cross was waiting for her outside, and loped truculently alongside as she walked. "Here," he said, "what they goin' to do with Giorgio?"

"Who? Oh, Giorgio. Well, I suppose the sisters will bury him." The corpses were piling up at Godstow.

"Where, though? I want him planted proper. He was a Christian, was Giorgio."

And a mercenary, thought Adelia, which might, in Godstow's eyes, put him in the same category as others who'd relinquished their right to a Christian grave. She said, "Have you asked the nuns?"

"Can't talk to 'em." Cross found the holy sisters intimidating. "*You* ask 'em."

"Why should I?" The sheer gracelessness of this little man . . .

"You're a Sicilian, ain't you? Like Giorgio. You said you was, so you got to see him planted proper, with a priest and the blessing of . . . what was that saint had her tits cut off?"

"I suppose you mean Saint Agnes," Adelia said coldly.

"Yeah, her." Cross's unlovely features creased into a salacious grin. "They still carry her tits around on festival days?"

"I'm afraid so." She had always considered it an unfortunate custom, but the particularly horrible martyrdom of poor Saint Agnes was still commemorated in Palermo by a procession bearing the replicas of two severed breasts on a tray, like little nippled cakes.

"He thought a lot of Saint Agnes, Giorgio did. So you tell 'em."

Adelia opened her mouth to tell *him* something, then saw the mercenary's eyes and stopped. The man agonized for his dead friend, as he had agonized for the injured Poyns; there was a soul here, however ungainly.

"I'll try," she said.

"See you do."

In the large open area beyond the grain barn, one of Wolvercote's liveried men was walking up and down outside the pepper pot lockup, though what he might be guarding Adelia couldn't imagine.

Farther along, the convent smith was pounding at the ice on the pond to crack a hole through which some aggrieved-looking ducks might have access to water. Children — presumably his — were skimming around the edges of the pond with bone skates strapped to their boots.

Wistfully, Adelia paused to watch. The joy of skating had come to her late — not until she'd spent a winter in the fens, where iced rivers made causeways and playgrounds. Ulf had taught her. Fen people were wonderful skaters.

To skim away from here, free, letting the dead bury the dead. But even if it were possible, she could not leave while the person was at liberty who had hung Bertha up on a hook like a side of meat. . . .

"You skate?" Cross asked, watching her.

"I do, but we have no skates," she said.

As they approached the church, a dozen or so nuns, led by their prioress, came marching out of its doors like a line of disciplined, determined jackdaws.

They were heading for the convent gates and the bridge beyond, one of them pushing a two-wheeled cart. A sizable number of Godstow's lay residents scurried behind them expectantly. Adelia saw Walt and Jacques among the followers and joined them; Cross went with her. As they passed the guesthouse, Gyltha came down its steps with Mansur, Allie cocooned in her arms.

"Don't want to miss this," she said.

At the gates, Sister Havis's voice came clear. "Open up, Fitchet, and bring me a knife."

Outside, a path had been dug through the snow on the bridge to facilitate traffic between village and convent. Why, since it led to nowhere else, Lord Wolvercote had thought it necessary to put a sentry on it was anybody's guess. But he had — and one who, facing a gaggle of black-clad, veiled women, each with a cross hanging on her chest, still found it necessary to ask, "Who goes there?"

Sister Havis advanced on him, as had Cross upon his fellow the night before. Adelia almost expected her to knock him out; she looked capable of it. Instead, the prioress pushed aside the leveled pike with the back of her hand and marched on.

"I wouldn't arse about, friend," Fitchet advised the sentry, almost sympathetically. "Not when they're on God's business."

When she'd glimpsed the bodies from the boat, Adelia had been too cold, too scared, too occupied to consider the manner in which they'd been hanged — only the image of their dangling feet had stayed in her memory.

Now she saw it. The two men, their arms

tied, had been stood on the bridge while one end of a rope was attached round each neck and the other to one of the bridge's stanchions. Then they'd been thrown over the balustrade.

Bridges were communication between man and man, too sacred to be used as gallows. Adelia wished that Gyltha hadn't brought Allie; this was not going to be a scene she wanted her daughter to watch. On the other hand, her child was looking around in a concentration of pleasure; the surrounding scenery was a change, a lovely change, from the alleys of the convent where she was taken for her daily outings in fresh air. The bridge formed part of a white tableau, its reflection in the sheeted river below was absolute, and the waterfall on its mill side had frozen in sculptured pillars.

The mill wheel beyond was motionless and glistened with icicles as if from a thousand stalactites. It was an obscenity for distorted death to decorate it. "Don't let her see the bodies," she told Gyltha.

"Get her used to it," Gyltha said. "Her'll see plenty of hangings as she grows. My pa took me to my first when I were three year old. Enjoyed it, too, I did."

"I don't want her to enjoy it."

Getting the bodies up wasn't going to be

easy; they were weighted by accumulated ice, and the rope holding them was stretched so tightly over the balustrade that it had frozen to it.

Walt joined Adelia. "Prioress says we ain't to help; they got to do it theyselves, seemingly."

Sister Havis considered for a moment and then gave her orders. While one used Fitchet's knife to scrape the ice from the ropes, the tallest of the nuns, the cellaress, leaned over, stretching her arm to grasp the hair of one of the hanging men. She lifted, giving the rope some slack.

A seagull that had been pecking at the man's eyes flew off, yelping, into the clear sky. Allie watched it go.

"Haul, my sisters." The prioress's voice rang after it. "Haul for the mercy of Mary."

A row of black backsides bent over the balustrade. They hauled, their breath streaming upward like smoke.

"What in hell are you women doing?"

Lord Wolvercote was on the bridge, to be no more regarded by the sisters than the seagull. He stepped forward, hand on his sword. Fitchet and Walt and some other men rolled up their sleeves. Wolvercote looked round. His sentry's helpless shrug told him he would get no help against God's female battalion. He was outnumbered. He shouted instead, "Leave them. This is *my* land, *my* half of the bridge, and villains shall hang from it as and when I *see fit*."

"It's our bridge, my lord, as you well know." This was Fitchet, loud but weary with the repetition of an old argument. "And Mother Abbess don't want it decorated with no corpses."

One body was up now, too stiff to bend, so the sisters were having to lift it vertically over the balustrade, its cocked head angled inquiringly toward the man who had sentenced it to death.

The nuns laid him on the cart, then returned to the balustrade to raise his fellow.

The dispute had brought the miller's family to their windows, and faces lined the sills to watch the puffs of air issuing like dragons' breath from the two arguing men.

"They were *rogues*, you dolt. Thieves. In possession of stolen property, and I made an example of them, as I have a right to do by infangthief. Leave them *alone*."

He was tall, dark-complexioned, age about thirty or so, and would have been handsome if his thin face hadn't settled into lines of contempt that at the moment were emphasized by fury. Emma had talked joyously of her future husband's poetry, but Adelia saw no poetry here. Only stupidity. He had made an example of the two thieves; they'd been hanging here for two days, and the river's lack of traffic meant that anybody who was going to see them had already done it. A more sensible man would have bowed to the inevitable, given his blessing, and walked away.

Wolvercote can't, Adelia thought. He sees the sisters as undermining his authority, and it frightens him; he must be cock of the heap or he is nothing.

Infangthief. She searched her memory — one of the English customary laws; Rowley had once mentioned it, told her, *"Infangthief? Well, it's a sort of legal franchise that certain lords of the manor hold by ancient right to pass the death penalty on thieves caught on their property. The king hates it. He says it means the buggers can hang anybody they've a mind to."*

"Why doesn't he get rid of it, then?"

But ancient rights, apparently, were not to be discarded without resentment, even rebellion, by those who held them. *"He will — in time."*

The second corpse had been retrieved, and sacking was laid over both. The nuns were beginning to push their loaded cart back across the bridge, their feet slipping on the ice.

"See, my duck," Gyltha said to Allie. "That were fun, weren't it?"

Sister Havis stopped as they passed Wolvercote, and her voice was colder than the dead men. "What were their names?"

"Names? What do you want their names for?"

"For their graves."

"They didn't have names, for God's sake. They'd have gone on to take the chalice off your own damned altar if I hadn't stopped them. They were *thieves,* woman."

"So were the two crucified with Our Lord; I don't remember Him withholding mercy from them." The prioress turned and followed her sisters.

He couldn't leave it. He called after her, "You're an interfering old bitch, Havis. No wonder you never got a man."

She didn't look back.

"They're going to bury them," Adelia said. "Oh, dear."

Jacques, nearby, grinned at her. "It's a fairly usual custom with the dead," he said.

"Yes, but I didn't look at their boots. And you," she said to Gyltha. "Take that child home." She hurried after the nuns and delayed the cart by standing in front of it.

"Would you mind? Just a minute?"

She knelt down in the snow so that her eyes were on a level with the legs of the corpses and raised the sacking.

She was transferred to the bridge when she had first seen it, at nighttime, when the awful burden it carried and the footprints in its snow had told her the sequence of murder as clearly as if the two killers had confessed to it.

She heard her own voice speaking to Rowley: *"See? One wears hobnails, the other's boots have bars across the soles, maybe clogs bound with strips. They arrived here on horseback and took their horses into those trees. . . . They ate as they waited. . . ."*

Facing her was a pair of stout hobnailed boots. The other corpse had lost the footwear from its right foot, but the clog on its left had been retained by the tight bands of leather passing under the sole and crossgartered around the lower leg.

Carefully, she replaced the sacking and stood up. "Thank you."

Nonplussed, the nuns with the cart continued on their way. Sister Havis's eyes met Adelia's for a moment. "Were they the ones?"

"Yes."

Walt overheard. "Here, is these the buggers as done for that poor horse?"

Adelia smiled at him. "And the traveler. Yes, I think so." She turned and found that Wolvercote had approached to see what she'd been up to. The crowd of abbey people waited to hear the exchange.

"Do you know where they came from?" she asked him.

"What do you care where they came from? I found them robbing my house; they had a silver cup, *my* silver cup, and that's all I needed to know." He turned to the porter. "Who is this female? What's she doing here?"

"Came with the bishop," Fitchet told him shortly.

Walt piped up, proprietorially: "She's with the darky doctor. She can tell things, she can. Looks at things and knows what happened."

It was badly phrased. Adelia hunched as she waited for the inevitable.

Wolvercote looked at her. "A witch, then," he said.

The word dropped into the air like ink into pristine water, discoloring it, webbing it with black, spiky traces before graying it forever.

Just as the allusion to Havis as a frustrated virgin would be a label that stuck to her, so the surrounding people hearing the name "witch" applied to Adelia would always remember it. The word that had stoned and set fire to women. There was no appeal against it. It tinged the faces of the men and women listening. Even Jacques's and Walt's showed a new doubt.

She castigated herself. *Lord, what a fool; why didn't I* wait? She could have found some other opportunity to look at the men's boots before they were buried. But no, she'd had to make sure immediately. Thoughtless, *thoughtless.*

"Damn it," she said. *"Damn."* She looked back. Lord Wolvercote had gone, but everybody else was looking in her direction; she could hear the murmurs. The damage had been done.

Breathily, Jacques came loping up to her. "I don't think you're a witch, mistress. Just stay in your room, eh? Out of sight, out of mind. Like Saint Matthew says: *'Sufficient unto the day is the evil thereof.'*"

But the day was not gone yet. As they passed through the gates of the convent, a fat man, wild-eyed, emerged out of the church door farther along. He gestured at Jacques. "You," he shouted, "fetch the infirmaress."

The messenger went running. The fat man

turned and rushed back into the church.

Adelia teetered outside. *'Sufficient unto the day . . .' There's been enough evil, and you've brought some of it on yourself. Whatever this is, it is not for you.*

But the sounds coming from inside the building were of distress.

She went in.

The sunshine was managing poorly within the large church, where, by day, candles were unlit. Glacial shafts of sun were lancing into the dark interior from the high, narrow windows above the clerestory, splashing a pillar here and there and cutting across the nave in thin stripes that avoided the middle, where the distress was centered.

Until her eyes adjusted to the contrast, Adelia couldn't make out what was happening. Slowly, it took shape. There was a catafalque, and two burly figures, a male and a female, were trying to drag something off it.

The something — she could see it now — was young Emma, very still, but her hands were gripping the far side of the catafalque so that her body could not be shifted away from the body that lay beneath her.

"Leave un, girl. Come on up now. 'Tis shameful, this. Gor dang it, what be it with her?" The fat man's voice.

367

The woman's was kinder but no less disturbed. "Yere, yere, don't take on like this, my duck, you'm upsetting your pa. What's this dead un to you? Come on up now."

The fat man looked around in desperation and caught sight of Adelia standing in the doorway, illuminated by the sun behind her. "Here, you, come and give us a hand. Reckon our girl's fainted."

Adelia moved closer. Emma hadn't fainted; her eyes were wide and stared at nothing. She had thrown herself so that she lay arched over the corpse under her. The knuckles of her gripping hands were like tiny white pebbles against the black wood of the catafalque beneath it.

Going closer still, Adelia peered down.

The nuns had put coins over the eyes, but the face was the face of the dead young man on the bridge, whom she and Rowley had lowered into the icehouse. This was Master Talbot of Kidlington. Only minutes before, she had been examining the boots of his murderers.

She became aware that the fat man was blustering — though not at her. "Fine convent this is, leaving dead people round the place. It's right upset our girl, and I don't wonder. Is this what we pay our tithes for?"

The infirmaress had come into the church, Jacques with her. Exclamation and exhortation created a hubbub that had an echo, Sister Jennet's crisp pipe — "Now, now, child, this will not do" — interspersed with the bellows of the father, who was becoming outraged and looking for someone to blame, while the mother's anxiety made a softer counterpoint to them both.

Adelia touched Emma's clawed hand, gently. The girl raised her head, but what she saw with those tormented eyes Adelia couldn't tell. "Do you see what they've done? To him, to *him*?"

The father and Sister Jennet were standing away now, openly quarreling. The mother had stopped attending to her daughter in order to join in.

"Control yourself, Master Bloat. Where else should we have lain a body but in a church?" Sister Jennet did not add that as far as Godstow and bodies were concerned, they were running out of space.

"Not where a man can fall over it; that's not what we pay our tithes for."

"That's right, Father, that's right. . . ." This was Mistress Bloat. "We was just being shown round, wasn't us? Our girl was showing us round."

Emma's eyes still stared into Adelia's as if into the Pit. "Do you see, oh, God, do you see?"

"I see," Adelia told her.

And she did, wondering how she could have been so blind not to see it before. So *that* was why Talbot of Kidlington had been murdered.

TEN

"Where were you going to elope *to?*"

"Wales."

The girl sat on a stool in the corner of Adelia and Gyltha's room. She'd torn the veil off her head, and long, white-blond hair swayed over her face as she rocked back and forth. Allie, upset by the manifestations of such grief, had begun to bawl and was being jiggled quiet again in her mother's arms. Ward, also showing an unexpected commiseration, lay with his head on Emma's boots.

She'd fought to be there, literally. When at last they'd been able to prise her away from the body, she'd stretched her arms toward Adelia, saying, "I'll go with her, *her.* She understands, *she knows.*"

"Dang sight more'n I do," Master Bloat had said, and Adelia had rather sympathized with him — until, that is, he'd tried to drag his daughter off, putting a hand over her mouth so that her noise would attract no more attention than it had.

Emma had been his match, twisting and shrieking to beat him off. At last Sister Jennet had advised compliance. "Let her go with this lady for now. She has some medical knowledge and may be able to calm her."

They could do nothing else, but from the looks Master and Mistress Bloat gave her as she helped their daughter toward the guesthouse, Adelia was aware that she'd added two more to her growing list of enemies.

She managed to persuade the girl to drink an infusion of lady's slipper, and it calmed her enough that she could answer questions, though Gyltha, who was gently rubbing the back of Emma's neck with rose oil, frowned at Adelia every time she asked one. A silent argument was going on between them.

Leave the poor soul alone, for pity's sake.

I can't.

She's breaking her heart.

It'll mend. Talbot's won't.

Gyltha might sorrow for the stricken one, but Adelia's duty as she saw it was to Talbot of Kidlington, who had loved Emma Bloat and had ridden to the convent through snow to take her away and marry her, an elopement so financially disastrous to a third party — Adelia's thoughts rested on the Lord of Wolvercote — that it had ordered his killing.

Master Hobnails and Master Clogs hadn't been waiting on an isolated bridge on a snowy night for any old traveler to come along; common scoundrels though they undoubtedly were, they weren't brainless. They knew, because somebody had told them, that at a certain hour a certain man would ride up to the convent gates. . . . Kill him.

They *had* killed him, and then they'd fled over the bridge to the village — to be killed themselves.

By the very man who'd employed them in the first place?

Oh, yes, Wolvercote fitted that particular bill nicely.

Though perhaps not entirely. Adelia still puzzled over the lengths someone had gone to in order to make sure that the corpse was identified as Talbot's. She supposed, if it *was* Wolvercote, he'd wanted Emma to know of her lover's death as soon as possible, and that her hand — and her fortune — was now his again.

Yes, but presumably, when Talbot didn't turn up, that way would have been made open. Why did the corpse have to be put under her nose, as it were, right away? And why in circumstances that pointed the accusing finger so directly at Wolvercote himself?

Do you see what they've done?

Who were the "they" that Emma thought had done it?

Adelia put Allie on the floor, gave her the teething ring that Mansur had carved for the child out of bone, and sat herself by Emma, smoothing back the long hair and mouthing "I have to" over her head at Gyltha.

The girl was almost apathetic with shock. "Let me stay here with you." She said it over and over. "I don't want to see them, any of them. I can't. You've loved a man, you had his child. You understand. They don't."

" 'Course you can stay," Gyltha told her.

"My love is dead."

So is mine, Adelia thought. The girl's grief was her own. She forced it away. There'd been murder done, and death was her business. "You were going to Wales?" she asked, "In *winter?*"

"We'd had to wait, you see. Until he was twenty-one. To get his inheritance." The sentences came in pieces with an abstracted dullness.

To Talbot of Kidlington, That the Lord and

*His angels bless you on this Day that Enters
you into Man's estate.*

And on that day Talbot of Kidlington had
set out to carry off Emma Bloat with, if
Adelia remembered aright, the two silver
marks that had been enclosed in Master
Warin's letter.

"His inheritance was two silver marks?"
Then she recalled that Emma didn't know
about the marks because she didn't know
about the letter.

The girl barely noticed the interjection.
"The land in Wales. His mother left it to
him, Felin Fach. . . ." She said the name
softly, as if it had been spoken often, a sweet
thing held out to her in her lover's voice.
" *'Felin Fach,'* he used to say. *'The vale of the
Aêron, where salmon leap up to meet the rod
and the very earth yields gold.'* "

"Gold?" Adelia looked a question at
Gyltha. *Is there gold in Wales?*

Gyltha shrugged.

"He was going to take possession as soon
as he gained his majority. It was part of his
inheritance, you see. We were going there.
Father Gwilym was waiting to marry us.
'Funny little man, not a word of English . . .' "
She was quoting again, almost smiling. " *'Yet
in Welsh he can tie as tight a marriage knot
as any priest in the Vatican.'* "

This was dreadful; Gyltha was wiping her eyes. Adelia, too, was sorry, so sorry. To watch suffering like this was to be in pain oneself, but she had to have answers.

"Emma, who knew you were going to elope?"

"Nobody." Now she did actually smile. " *'No cloak, or they'll guess. I'll have one for you. Fitchet will open the gate. . . .'* "

"Fitchet?"

"Well, of course Fitchet knew about us; Talbot paid him."

Apparently, the gatekeeper counted as nobody in Emma's reckoning.

The girl's face withered. "But he didn't come. I waited in the gatehouse . . . I waited . . . I thought . . . I thought . . . oh, Sweet Jesus, show mercy to me, I *blamed* him. . . ." She began clawing the air. "Why did they kill him? Couldn't they just take his purse? Why kill him?"

Adelia met Gyltha's eyes again. That was all right, then; Emma put her lover's killing down to robbers — as, at this stage, it was probably better that she should. There was no point in inflaming her against Wolvercote until there was proof of his culpability. Indeed, he might be innocent. If he hadn't known of the elopement . . . But Fitchet had known.

"So it was a secret, was it?"

"Little Priscilla knew, she guessed." Again, that entrancement at being taken back to the past; the subterfuge had been thrilling. "And Fitchet, he smuggled our letters in and out. And Master Warin, of course, because he had to write the letter to Felin Fach so that Talbot could take seisin of it, but they were all sworn not to tell." Suddenly, she gripped Adelia's arm. "Fitchet. He wouldn't have told the robbers, would he? He *couldn't.*"

Adelia gave a reassurance she didn't feel; the number of nobodies who'd known about the elopement was accumulating. "No, no. I'm sure not. Who is Master Warin?"

"Were they waiting for him?" She had her nails into Adelia's skin. "Did they know he was carrying money? *Did they know?*"

Gyltha intervened. "A'course they didn't." She pulled Emma's hand off Adelia's arm and enfolded it in her own. "Just scum, they was. Roads ain't safe for anybody."

Emma looked wide-eyed at Adelia. "Did he suffer?"

Here, at least, was firm ground. "No. It was a bolt to the chest. He'd have been thinking of you, and then . . . nothing."

"Yes." The girl sank back. "Yes."

"Who is Master Warin?" Adelia asked again.

"But how can I go on without him?"

We do, Adelia thought. *We have to.*

Allie had hitched herself over to replace Ward by pushing him off and settling her bottom on Emma's boots. She put a pudgy hand on the girl's knee. Emma stared down at her. "Children," she said. "We were going to have lots of children." The desolation was so palpable that for the other two women the firelit room became a leafless winter plain stretching into eternity.

She's young, Adelia thought. *Spring will come to her again one day perhaps, but never with the same freshness.* "Who is Master Warin?"

Gyltha tutted at her; the girl had begun to shake. *Stop it now.*

I can't. "Emma, who is Master Warin?"

"Talbot's cousin. They were very attached to each other." The poor lips stretched again. " *'My wait-and-see Warin. A careful man, Emma, but never did a ward have such a careful guardian.' "*

"He was Talbot's guardian? He handled his business affairs?"

"Oh, don't worry him with them now. He will be so . . . I must see him. No, I can't. . . . I can't face his grief. . . . I can't face

378

anything."

Emma's eyelids were half down with the fatigue of agony.

Gyltha wrapped a blanket round her, led her to the bed, sat her down, and lifted her legs so that she fell back on it. "Go to sleep now." She returned to Adelia. "And you come wi' me."

They went to the other side of the room to whisper.

"You reckon Wolvercote done in that girl's fella?"

"Possibly, though I'm beginning to think the cousin-cum-guardian had a lot to lose when Talbot came into his estates. If he's been handling Talbot's affairs . . . It's starting to look like a conspiracy."

"No, it ain't. It was robbery pure and simple, and the boy got killed in the course of it."

"He didn't. The robbers *knew*."

"No, they bloody didn't."

"Why?" She'd never seen Gyltha like this.

"A'cause that poor girl's going to have to marry Old Wolfie now whether she likes it or don't, and better if she don't think it was him as done for her sweetheart."

"Of course she won't have to . . ." Adelia squinted at the older woman. "*Will* she?"

Gyltha nodded. "More'n like. Them Bloats

is set on it. *He's* set on it. That's why her wanted to elope, so's they couldn't force her."

"They can't force her. Oh, Gyltha, they *can't*."

"You watch 'em. She's a high-up, and it happens to high-ups." Gyltha looked toward Heaven and gave thanks that she was common. "Nobody didn't want me for my money. Never bloody had any."

It did happen. Because it hadn't happened to Adelia, she hadn't thought of it. Her foster parents, that liberal couple, had allowed her to pursue her profession, but around her in Salerno, young, well-born female acquaintances had been married off to their father's choice though they cried against it, part of a parental plan for the family's advancement. It was that or continual beating. Or the streets. Or a convent.

"She could choose to become a nun, I suppose."

"She's their only child," Gyltha said. "Master Bloat don't want a nun, he wants a lady in the family — better for business." She sighed. "My auntie was cook to the De Pringhams and their poor little Alys was married off screamin' to Baron Coton, bald old bugger that he was."

"You have to say yes. The Church says it's

not legal otherwise."

"*Hunh.* I never heard as little Alys said yes."

"But Wolvercote's a bully and an idiot. You know he is."

"So?"

Adelia stared into Emma's future. "She could appeal to the queen. Eleanor knows what it is to have an unhappy marriage; she managed to get a divorce from Louis."

"Oh, yes," Gyltha said, raising her eyes. "The queen's sure to go against the fella as is fighting her battle for her. Sure to." She patted Adelia's shoulder. "It won't be so bad for young Em, really. . . ."

"Not bad?"

"She'll have babies, that's what she wants, ain't it? Anyways, I don't reckon she'll have to put up with un for long. Not when King Henry gets hold of un. Wolvercote's a traitor, and Henry'll have his tripes." Gyltha inclined her head to consider the case. "Might not be bad at all, really."

"I thought you were sorry for her."

"I am, but I'm facing what she's facing. Bit o' luck she'll be widowed afore the year's out, then she'll have his baby and his lands . . . yes, I reckon it might turn out roses."

"*Gyltha.*" Adelia drew back from a practicality unsuspected even of this practical woman. "That's foul."

"That's business," Gyltha said. "That's what high-ups' marriage is, ain't it?"

Jacques was kept busy that day, bringing messages to the women in the guesthouse. The first was from the prioress: "To Mistress Adelia, greetings from Sister Havis, and to say that the girl Bertha will be interred in the nuns' own graveyard."

"Christian burial. Thought you'd be pleased," Gyltha said, watching Adelia's reaction. "What you wanted, ain't it?"

"It is. I'm glad." The prioress had ended her investigation and managed to persuade the abbess that Bertha had not died by her own hand.

But Jacques hadn't finished. He said dutifully, "And I was to warn you, mistress, you're to remember the Devil walks the abbey."

There lay the sting. The nuns' agreement that a killer was loose in Godstow made his presence more real and added to its darkness.

Later still that morning, the messenger turned up again. "To Mistress Adelia, greetings from Mother Edyve, and will she return Mistress Emma to the cloister? To keep the peace, she says."

"Whose peace?" Gyltha demanded. "I suppose them Bloats is complaining."

"So is the Lord Wolvercote," said Jacques. He grimaced, wrinkling his eyes and showing his teeth as one reluctant to deliver more bad news. "He's saying . . . well, he's saying . . ."

"What?"

The messenger blew out his breath. "It's being said as how Mistress Adelia has put a spell on Mistress Emma and is turning her against her lawful husband-to-be."

Gyltha stepped in. "You can tell that godless arse-headed bastard from me . . ."

A hand on her shoulder stopped her. Emma was already wrapping herself in her cloak. "There's been trouble enough," she said.

And was gone down the steps before any of them could move.

Inside the abbey, the various factions trapped within its walls fractured like frozen glass. A darkness fell over Godstow that had nothing to do with the dimming winter light.

In protest against its occupation, the nuns disappeared into their own quadrangles, taking their meals from the infirmary kitchen, their exercise in the cloister.

The presence of two bands of mercenaries began to cause trouble. Schwyz's were the more experienced, a cohesive group that had fought in wars all over Europe and considered Wolvercote's men mere country ruffians hired for the rebellion — as, indeed, many of them were.

But the Wolvercoters had smarter livery, better arms, and a leader who was in charge — anyway, there were more of them; they bowed to nobody.

Schwyz's men set up a still in the forge and got drunk; Wolvercote's raided the convent cellar and got drunk. Afterward, inevitably, they fought one another.

The nights became dreadful. Godstow's people and guests cowered in their rooms, listening to the fighting in the alleys, dreading a crashed-in door and the entry of liquored mercenaries with robbery or rape on their minds.

In an effort to protect their property and women, they formed a militia of their own. Mansur, Walt, Oswald, and Jacques, like dutiful men, joined it in patrolling — but the result was that, more often than not, the nightly brawls became tripartite affairs.

An attempt by the chaplain, Father Egbert, to minister to the flock the nuns had deserted ended when, during Sunday-evening communion, Schwyz shouted at Wolvercote, "Are you going to discipline your men, or do I do it for you?" and a fight broke out between their adherents that spread even to the Lady Chapel, smashing lamps, a lectern, and several heads. One of Wolvercote's men lost an eye.

It was as if the world had frozen and would not turn, allowing no other weather to reach a beleaguered Oxfordshire than a bright sun by day and stars that filled the sky at night, neither bringing any relief from the cold.

Every morning, Adelia pushed open the shutters briefly to allow air into their room and searched the view for . . . what? Henry Plantagenet and his army? Rowley?

But Rowley was dead.

There had been more snow. It was impossible to distinguish river from land. There was no human life out there, hardly any animal life.

Crisscross patterns like stitching showed that birds, frantic with thirst, had hopped around in the early dawn to fill their beaks with snow, but where were they? Sheltering in the trees that stood like iron sentinels across the river, perhaps. Could they withstand this assault? Where were the deer? Did fish swim beneath that ice?

Watching a solitary crow flap its way across the blue sky, Adelia wondered whether it saw a dead, pristine world in which Godstow was the only circle of life. As she stared at it, the crow folded its wings and fell to earth, a small, untidy black casualty in the whiteness.

If the nights weren't bad enough, Godstow's days became morbid with the *hit-hit* of picks hacking out graves in the frozen earth while the church bell tolled and tolled for the dead as if it had lost the capacity to ring for anything else.

Adelia was keeping to the guesthouse as much as possible; the looks from people she encountered if she went out and their tendency to cross themselves and make the sign of the evil eye as they passed her were intimidating. But there were some funerals she had to attend.

Talbot of Kidlington's, for one. The nuns reappeared for that. A little man at the front of the congregation, who Adelia supposed was the cousin, Master Warin, wept all through it, but Adelia, skulking at the back, saw only Emma, white and dry-eyed, in the choir, her hand clasped tightly in little Sister Priscilla's.

A funeral for Bertha. This was held at

night and in the privacy of the abbess's chapel, attended by the convent chapter, the milkmaid, Jacques, and Adelia, who'd folded Bertha's hands around a broken chain and a silver cross before the plain, pine coffin was interred in the nuns' own graveyard.

A funeral for Giorgio, the Sicilian. No nuns this time, but most of the Schwyz mercenaries were there, and Schwyz himself. Mansur, Walt, and Jacques came, as they had to Talbot's. So did Adelia. She'd begged a reluctant Sister Havis for Giorgio to be treated as a Christian, arguing that they knew no harm of him apart from his profession. Due to her, the Sicilian was lowered into a cold Christian grave with the blessing of Saint Agnes.

There was no word of thanks from his friend Cross. He left the graveyard after the interment without speaking, though later three pairs of beautifully fashioned bone skates complete with straps were left outside Adelia's door.

A funeral for two Wolvercote villagers who'd succumbed to pneumonia. Sister Jennet and her nurses attended, though Lord Wolvercote did not.

A funeral for the two hanged men. Nobody except the officiating priest was present, though those bodies, too, each went into a churchyard grave.

His duty done, Father Egbert closed the church and, like the nuns, retired to an inner sanctum. He would not, he said, hold regular services when any mercenary was likely to be in the congregation; the advent of Christ's birth was not to be despoiled by a load of feuding heathens who wouldn't recognize the Dove of Peace if it shat on their heads. Which he hoped it would.

It was a sentence on the whole community. No *Christmas?*

A shriek went up, loudest of all from the Bloats; they'd come to see their girl married at the Yule feast. And their girl, thanks to malefic influence from a woman no better than she should be, was now saying she didn't want to marry at all. This wasn't what they paid their tithes for.

One voice, however, was raised above theirs. With more effect. Sister Bullard, the cellaress, was, materially, the most important person in the abbey and the one who'd become the most sorely tried. Even with the convent's new militia trying to protect it, her great barn of a cellar suffered nightly raids on its ale tuns, wine vats, and foodstuff.

Worried that the entire convent would

soon be unable to feed itself, she turned to the only earthly authority left to her — the Queen of England.

Eleanor had been staying to her own apartments, paying little attention to anything except the effort to keep herself amused. Finding the rest of the abbey tedious, she had ignored its troubles. However, marooned as she was on the island of Godstow for the duration of the snow, she had to listen to Sister Bullard telling her that she faced discord and starvation.

The queen woke up.

Lord Wolvercote and Master Schwyz were summoned to her rooms in the abbess's house, where it was pointed out to them that only under her banner could they attract allies — and she had no intention of leading rabble, which, at the moment, was what they and their men were becoming.

Rules were laid down. Church services would resume — to be attended only by the sober. Wolvercote's men must cross the bridge each night to sleep at their lord's manor in the village, leaving only six of their number behind to join Schwyz's men in enforcing the curfew.

No more raids on the cellar by either side — any mercenary doing so, or found fighting, was to be publicly flogged.

Of the two culprits, Lord Wolvercote should have come out of the meeting better; Schwyz, after all, was being paid for his services, whereas Wolvercote was rendering his for free. But the Abbot of Eynsham was also present, and, as well as being a friend to Schwyz, he had the cleverer and more persuasive tongue.

It was noted by those who saw Lord Wolvercote emerge from the queen's presence that he was snarling. "A'cause he don't get young Emma, neither," Gyltha reported. "Not yet, at any rate."

"Are you sure?"

"Certain sure," Gyltha said. "The girl's been pleading with Mother Edyve, and she's asked for Eleanor's protection. The which the queen says old Wolfie ought to wait."

Again, this had come from the convent kitchen, where Gyltha's friend Polly had helped the royal servants carry refreshment to the meeting between the queen and the mercenary leaders. Polly had learned many things, one of them being that the queen had complied with Mother Edyve's request for Emma's marriage to Wolvercote to be delayed indefinitely, "until the young woman has recovered from the affliction to her spirits that now attends them."

Polly reported that "his Wolfie lordship

weren't best pleased."

Adelia, relieved, didn't think the Bloats would be, either. But by now, everybody knew what the affliction was that attended Emma's spirits and, according to Gyltha, there was general sympathy for her, much of which sprang from the equally general dislike for Wolvercote.

There was more good news from the kitchen. With order restored, Eleanor had, apparently, announced that the church was to be reopened, services resumed, and, when it came, Christ's Mass to be celebrated with a feast.

"Proper old English one, too," Gyltha said, a pagan gleam in her eye. "Caroling, feastin', mummers, Yule log, and all the trimmin's. They're killin' the geese and hangin' them this very minute."

It was typical of Eleanor, Adelia thought, that having saved the convent's store of food and drink, she now imperiled it. Feasting the entire community would be an enormous and expensive undertaking. On the other hand, the queen's orders had been necessary and perceptive; they might well defuse a situation that was becoming intolerable. And if a feast could introduce gaiety into Godstow, by God, it needed it.

With the resurgence of Eleanor's energy came an invitation. "To Mistress Adelia, a summons from her gracious lady, Queen Eleanor." Jacques brought it.

"You running errands for royalty now?" Gyltha asked at the door. The messenger had found brighter clothes from somewhere, curled hair hid his ears, and his perfume reached Adelia, who was across the room.

He'd also found a new dignity. "Mistress, I am so favored. And now I must go to the Lord Mansur. He, too, is summoned."

Gyltha watched him go. "Aping they courtiers," she said with disapproval. "Our Rowley'll kick his arse for him when he comes back."

"Rowley's not coming back," Adelia said.

When Mansur strode into the royal chamber, one of the courtiers muttered audibly, "And now we entertain heathens." And as Adelia followed behind with Ward ambling at her heels, "Oh, Lord, *look* at that cap. And the *dog,* my dear."

Eleanor, however, was all kindness. She came sweeping forward, offering her hand to be kissed. "My Lord Mansur, how pleased we are to see you." To Adelia: "My dear child, we have been remiss. We have been kept busy with matters of state, of course, but even so I fear we have neglected one with whom I fought against the devil's spawn."

The long upper room had been the abbess's, but now it was definitely Eleanor's. For surely Mother Edyve had not scented it with the richness of the heathen East nor filled it with artifacts so colorful — shawls, cushions, a gloriously autumnal triptych — that they eliminated the naïve, biblical pastels on her walls. Mother Edyve had never knelt at a prie-dieu made from gold, nor would her bedposts have roared with carved lions, nor had gossamer, floating like cobwebs, descended from the bed's tester over her pillow, nor male courtiers like adoring statuary, nor a beautiful minstrel to fill the abbatial air with a love song.

Yet, Adelia thought, still astonished by the bed — how had they got the thing on the boat? — the effect was not sexual. Sensual certainly, but this was not the room of a houri, it was merely . . . Eleanor.

It had certainly drawn Jacques into its spell. Lounging in a corner, he bowed to her, beaming and waggling his fingers. So here he was, and — to judge from the joy exuding from him, his even higher boots, and a new style of hair that hid his wide ears — in Aquitanian fashion paradise.

The queen was plying Mansur with dried dates and almond-paste sweetmeats. "We who have been to Outremer know better than to offer you wine, my lord, but" — a click of elegant royal fingers toward a page — "our cook magicks a tolerable sherbet."

Mansur kept his face stolidly blank.

"Oh, dear," Eleanor said. "Does the doctor not understand me?"

"I fear not, lady," Adelia said. "I translate for him." Mansur was fairly fluent in Norman French, which was being spoken here, but the pretense that he was restricted to Arabic had served the two of them well, and probably would again; it was surprising what he learned when among those who believed him not to understand. And if Bertha's killer was somewhere among this company . . .

What could be wanted of him? He was being treated with honor for someone whose race the queen had gone on Crusade to defeat.

Ah, Eleanor was asking her to pass on praise to Mansur for his medical skill in saving the life of "one of dear Schwyz's mercenaries"; Sister Jennet had sung *so* highly of him.

That was it, then. A good physician was always worth having. Christian disdain for Arab and Jew did not extend to their doctors, whose cures among their own people — partly brought about, Adelia believed, by their religions' strict dietary laws — gave them a high reputation.

So she herself was here merely as an interpreter.

But no, apparently she was a witness to Eleanor's courage; history was being changed.

Propelling her around by a hand on her shoulder, the queen told the story of what had happened in the upper room of Wormhold Tower, where, in the presence of a rotting corpse, a sword-wielding demon had appeared.

Eleanor, it seemed, had held up a calm hand to it. "Thou art a Plantagenet fiend, for that race is descended from demons. In the name of Our Savior, go back to thy master."

And lo, the fiend had dropped its sword and slunk back whence it had come.

What did I do? Adelia wondered.

". . . and this little person here, my own Mistress Athalia, then picked up the sword the fiend had dropped, though it was still very hot and stank of sulphur, and threw it out of the casement."

Glad I could help. Adelia speculated on whether the queen believed her own nonsense and decided she didn't. Perhaps Dakers's attack had shocked and embarrassed her so that she must now present it to her advantage. Or perhaps she was playing games. She was bored; all these people were bored.

Having *ooh*ed and *aah*ed throughout the recital, the courtiers applauded — except Montignard, who, with a dirty look at Adelia, burst out with, "But it was I who ministered to you afterwards, lady, did I not?" though the list of the things he had done was overlaid by a slow hand clap from the Abbot of Eynsham leaning against one of the bedposts.

Eleanor turned on him, sharp. "Our neglect is actually yours, my lord. We charged you to look after our brave Mistress Amelia, did we not?"

The abbot surveyed Adelia from the tips of her snow-rimed boots to the unattractive cap with its earflaps on her head and down again until his eyes met hers. "Lady, I thought I had," he said.

The queen was still talking. Shocked,

Adelia didn't hear her. The man wished her harm, had tried to procure it. At the same time, she felt his regard, like that of a swordsman saluting another. In a way she had not yet fathomed, she, Vesuvia Adelia Rachel Ortese Aguilar, known only in this place as the Bishop of Saint Albans's fancy and a useful picker up of demonic swords, mattered to Lord Abbot of Eynsham. He'd just told her so.

The queen's hands were spread out in a question, and she was smiling. The courtiers were laughing. One of them said, "The poor thing's overwhelmed."

Adelia blinked. "I beg your pardon, lady."

"I *said*, dear, that you must join us here; we cannot have our little helpmeet living in whatever hole the abbey provides. You shall move in with my waiting women, I am sure they have room, and you shall take part in our sport. You must be so bored out there."

You *are*, Adelia thought again. Eleanor probably *did* secretly feel she had a debt for having her life saved, but even more, she needed a new pet to play with. Ennui was everywhere, in the screech of female bickering coming from the next room where the waiting women waited, in the pettish laughter directed at herself, the sense that they had run out of butts for their wit and required another.

This, after all, was a company and queen that left one castle once it had begun to stink and moved on to the next, hunting, entertaining, and being entertained, kept clean and fed by an army of cooks, fullers, laundresses, and servants, many of whom had been left behind on the trail to war that Eleanor had taken, and even more subsequently lost to the snow. Without these resources, they festered.

One of the courtiers was ostentatiously holding his nose over Ward, though the young man's own person, let alone his linen, was hardly more delectable.

Move in with them all? Lord, help me. She wasn't going to accept an invitation to step into an overcrowded hell, even when extended by a queen.

On the other hand, if one of these was Bertha's killer, how better to sniff him out than by asking questions and, hopefully, receiving answers? *Move in with them?* No, but if, by day, she could have access to the royal chambers . . .

Adelia bowed. "Lady, you are all goodness. As long as my baby would not disturb your nights . . ."

"A child?" The queen was intrigued. "Why didn't they tell me? A little boy?"

"A girl," Adelia told her. "She is teething and therefore wakeful . . ."

There was a light scream from Montignard. *"Teething?"*

"A synonym for screaming, so I do understand," Eynsham said.

"Our two lords do not like babies," Eleanor confided to Adelia.

"I do, sweet lady." This was the abbot again. "So I do. Lightly broiled with parsley, I find them right toothsome."

Adelia pressed on. "Also, I must assist my master, Dr. Mansur here, when he is called to the infirmary at night as he so often is. I keep his potions."

"A synonym for stinks and rattling pots," the abbot said.

Montignard was clasping his hands beseechingly. "Lady, you'll not have a wink of rest. If that bell tolling the hours and the sisters singing them were not enough, we'll have the screech of babies and Lord knows what devilry . . . you'll be exhausted."

Bless him, Adelia thought.

Eleanor smiled. "Such a hedonist you are, my swain." She reflected, "I *do* need my sleep, yet I am reluctant not to reward the girl."

"Oh, let her come and go," Eynsham said wearily, "though *not* in them clothes."

"Of course, of *course*. We shall dress her."

It was a new thing, it would pass the time.

It was also Adelia's passport — though she had to pay for it. She was carried through to the women's room, its door not quite closed, so that male heads poking round it added a chorus of comment to the humiliation of being stripped to her chemise while swathes of material were held against her skin and capless head to be pronounced too this, too that, not *mauve,* my dear, not with that complexion — *so* corpselike. Where *had* she found such fine white linen for her chemise? Was she Saxon that she was so fair? No, no, Saxons had blue eyes, probably a Wend.

She wasn't even asked whether she wanted a new gown. She didn't; she dressed to disappear. Adelia was an observer. The only impact she ever wished to make was on her patients, and then not as a woman. Well . . . she'd wished to make an impact on Rowley, but she'd done that without any clothes on at all. . . .

The poor seamstresses among the queen's ladies weren't consulted, either, though the necessary needlework to transform whatever material was decided on into a bliaut for her — very tight at the top, very full in the skirt, sleeves narrow to the elbow, then widening almost to the ground — would be onerous, especially as Eleanor was demanding that it should have filigree embroidery at the neck and armholes, and be finished for the Christmas feast.

Adelia wondered at seamstresses being taken to war and at anyone who required a military transport to contain presses full of dazzlingly colored brocades, silks, linens, and samite.

In the end, Eleanor decided on velvet of a dark, dark blue that had, as she said, "the bloom of the Aquitanian grape."

When the queen did something, she did it wholeheartedly: a flimsy veil — she herself demonstrated how it should be attached to the barbette — a thin, gold circlet, a tapestried belt, embroidered slippers, a cope and hood of wool fine enough to draw through a ring, all these things were Adelia's.

"Only your due, my dear," Eleanor said, patting her head. "It was a very nasty demon." She turned to Eynsham. "We're safe from it now, aren't we, Abbot? You said you'd disposed of it, did you not?"

Dakers. What had they done to Dakers?

"Couldn't have it wandering around loose to attack my heart's lady again, could I?" The abbot was jovial. "I found un hiding among the convent books and, doubting it could read, would have hanged it there and then. But there was an outcry from the good sisters so, *pendent opera interrupta,* I had it put in the convent lockup instead. We'll take it with us when we go and hang it then" — he winked — "if it ain't frozen to death in the meantime."

There was appreciative laughter in which Eleanor joined, though she protested, "No, no, my lord, the female is possessed, we cannot execute the insane."

"Possessed by the evil of her mistress. Better dead, lady, better dead. Like Rosamund."

It was a long night. Nobody could retire until the queen gave her permission, and Eleanor was inexhaustible. There were games, board games, fox and geese, Alquerque, dice. Everybody was required to sing, even Adelia, who had no voice to speak of and was laughed at for it.

When it was Mansur's turn, Eleanor was enraptured and curious. "Beautiful, beautiful. Is that not a castrato?"

Adelia, sitting on a stool at the queen's feet, admitted it was.

"How interesting. I have heard them in Outremer but never in England. They can pleasure a woman, I believe, but must remain childless, is that true?"

"I don't know, lady." It was, but Adelia wasn't prepared to discuss it in this company.

The room became hot. More games, more singing.

Adelia began to nod, jerked awake each time by a draft from the door as people came and went.

Jacques was gone — no, there he was, bringing more food from the kitchen. Montignard was gone, and Mansur, no, they had come back from wherever they'd been. The abbot was gone, reappearing with string to satisfy Eleanor's sudden desire to play cat's cradle. There he was again, this time with Mansur, a table between them, their heads bent over a chessboard. A courtier entered, clutching snow to cool the wine . . . another young man, the one who'd thrown snowballs at the nuns, was singing to a lute. . . .

Adelia forced herself to her feet. Crossing to the chess table, she surveyed the board. "You're losing," she said in Arabic.

Mansur didn't look up. "He is the better player, Allah curse him."

"Say something more."

He grunted. "What do you want me to say? I am tired of these people. When do we go?"

Adelia addressed Eynsham. "My lord

403

Mansur instructs me to ask you, my lord, what you can tell him about the death of the woman, Rosamund Clifford."

The abbot raised his head to look at her and, again, there was that piercing connection. "Does he? Does he indeed? And why should my lord Mansur want to inquire of it?"

"He is a doctor; he has an interest in poison."

Eleanor had heard Rosamund's name. She called across the room. "What is that? What are you saying?"

Immediately, the abbot was another man, bucolic, convivial. "The good doctor do want to know about bitch Rosamund's death. Wasn't I with you when we heard of it, my sweeting? Didn't they tell us as we was landing, having crossed from Normandy? Didn't I fall to my knees and give thanks to the Great Revenger of all sin?"

Eleanor held out her hands to him. "You did, Abbot, you did."

"But you knew Rosamund before that," Adelia said. "You said so when we were at Wormhold."

"Did I know Rosamund? Oh, I knew her. Could I allow vileness unchecked in my own county? My old daddy would have been ashamed. How many days did I spend in that Jezebel's lair, a Daniel exhorting her to fornicate no more?" He was playing to the queen, but his eyes never left Adelia's.

More songs, more games, until even Eleanor was tired. "To bed, good people. Go to bed."

As he escorted Adelia home, Mansur was broody, chafed by his defeat at chess, of which he was himself a skilled exponent. "He is a fine player, that priest. I do not like him."

"He had a hand in Rosamund's death," Adelia said, "I know it; he was taunting me with it."

"He was not there."

True, Eynsham had been across the Channel when Rosamund died. But there was *something.* . . .

"Who was the fat one with the pox?" Mansur asked. "He took me outside to show me. He wants a salve."

"Montignard? Montignard has the pox? Serve him right." Adelia was irritable with fatigue. It was nearly dawn. A Matins antiphon from the direction of the chapel accompanied them as they trudged.

Mansur raised the lantern to light her up the guesthouse steps. "Has the woman left the door unbarred for you?"

"I expect so."

"She should not. It is not safe."

"Then I'll have to wake her, won't I?" Adelia said, going up. "And her name's Gyltha. Why don't you ever say it?" *Damn it,* she thought, *they're as good as married.*

She stumbled over something large that rested on the top step, nearly sending it over the edge and down to the alley. "Oh, dear God. Mansur. *Mansur.*"

Together, they carried the cradle into the room; the child in it was still asleep and wrapped in her blankets. She seemed to have taken no harm from being left in the cold.

The candle had gone out. Gyltha sat unmoving in the chair on which she had been waiting for Adelia to come back. For an appalling moment, Adelia thought she'd been murdered — the woman's hand was dangling over the place where the cradle always lay.

A snore reassured her.

The three of them sat in a huddled group around the cradle, watching Allie sleep, as if afraid she would evaporate.

"Someone come in here and stole her? Put her on the step?" Gyltha couldn't get over it.

"Yes," Adelia told her. One inch farther on the step, just one inch . . . In her mind she kept seeing the cradle turn in midair as it fell into the alley some twenty feet below.

"Someone come in here? And I never heard un? Put her out on the step?"

"Yes, *yes.*"

"Where's the sense in it?"

"I don't know." But she did.

Mansur voiced it: "He is warning you."

"I know."

"You ask too many questions."

"I know."

"What questions?" Gyltha, in her panic, wasn't keeping up. "*Who* don't want you asking questions?"

"I don't know." If she had, she would have groveled to him, squirmed at his feet in supplication. *You've won. You're cleverer than I am. Go free, I won't interfere. But leave me Allie.*

ELEVEN

The instinct was to hide with Allie in the metaphorical long grass, like a hare and leveret in their form.

When the queen sent Jacques to inquire for her, Adelia sent back that she was ill and could not come.

The killer conversed with her in her head.

How submissive are you now?

Submissive, my lord. Totally submissive. I shall do nothing to displease you, just don't hurt Allie.

She knew him now, not *who* he was but *what* he was. Even as he'd plucked Allie's cradle from under the sleeping Gyltha's hand and put it on the steps, he'd revealed himself.

Such a simple expedient to reduce his opponent to impotence. If she didn't fear him so much, she could admire it — the audacity, the economy, the *imagination* of it.

And it had told her for which killings he

had been responsible.

There had been two lots of murder, she knew that now, neither one having anything to do with the other; only the fact that she'd witnessed the corpses of both within a short time had given them a seeming relationship.

Talbot of Kidlington's death was the most straightforward, because it had been for the oldest of reasons: gain.

Wolvercote had good reason to kill the boy; the elopement with Emma would have deprived him of a valuable bride.

Or the inheritance Talbot had gained on his twenty-first birthday would have deprived his guardian of an income, for Master Warin could have been defrauding the boy — it wasn't unknown for an heir to come into his estates only to find that they'd gone.

Or, and this was a possibility Emma herself had raised while not believing it, Fitchet had alerted two friends to the fact that a young man would be arriving at the convent by night with money in his purse. After all, the gatekeeper had been acting as go-between for the two lovers — presumably for a fee — which indicated he was corruptible.

Or — the least likely — the Bloats had discovered their daughter's plan and had hired killers to prevent it.

Such was Talbot's murder.

Yet not one on the list of his likely killers fitted the character of the man who'd crept into the guesthouse and put Allie's cradle on the steps outside. The smell of him was different, it had none of the direct brutality with which Talbot had been eliminated.

No, this man was . . . what? Sophisticated? Professional? *I do not kill unless I must. I have given you a warning. I trust you will heed it.*

He was the murderer of Rosamund and Bertha.

There was more snow. The sides of the track that had been dug down to the Thames fell in under it.

It was left to Gyltha to fetch their meals from the kitchen, to empty their chamber pots in the latrine, and to gather firing from the woodpile.

"Ain't we ever a'going to take that poor baby for some air?" she wanted to know.

"No."

I am outside, watching. How submissive are you?

Totally submissive, my lord. Don't hurt my child.

"Nobody can't snatch her, not with that old Arab along of us."

"No."

"We stay here, then, with the door barred?"

"Yes."

But of course, they couldn't. . . .

The first alarm came at night. Somewhere a handbell was ringing and people were shouting.

Gyltha leaned out of the window to the alley. "They're yellin' fire," she said. "I can smell smoke. Oh, dear Lord, preserve us."

Bundling Allie into her furs, they dressed themselves, snatching up what belongings they could before carrying her down the steps.

Fire, that greatest of threats, had brought out everybody on this side of the abbey. Fitchet came running from the gates carrying two buckets; men were emerging out of the guesthouse: Mansur, Master Warin.

"Where is it? Where is it?"

The ringing and hubbub was coming from the direction of the pond.

"Barn?"

"Lockup, sounds like."

"Oh, God," Adelia said. *Dakers.* She handed Allie to Gyltha and began running.

Between the pond and the lockup, Peg was swinging a bell as if she were thwacking an unruly cow with it. She'd seen the flames on her way to the milking. "Up there." She pointed with the bell toward the narrow slit that allowed air into the little beehive building of stone that was the convent lockup.

Volunteers, already forming a line, shouted to hasten the smith as he hammered an iron spar into the pond to gain water for their pails.

Mansur came up beside Adelia. "I smell no fire."

"Neither do I." There was a slight smitch in the air, nothing more, and no flames apparent in the lockup's slit.

"Well, there damn was," Peg said.

The door to the lockup opened and a bad-tempered sentry came out. "Oh, get on home," he shouted. "No need for this rumpus. Straw caught fire, is all. I stamped it out." It was Cross. He locked the door behind him and gestured at the crowd with his spear. "Go on. Get off with you."

Relieved, grumbling, people began to disperse.

Adelia stayed where she was.

"What is it?" Mansur asked.

"I don't know."

Cross leveled his spear at her as she came up to him from the shadows. "Get back there, nothing to see. Go home . . . oh, it's you, is it?"

"Is she all right?"

"Old Mother Midnight? She's all right. Hollered a bit, but she's dandy in there now, bloody sight dandier than it is out here. Warm. Gets her meals regular. What about the poor buggers got to guard her, that's what I say."

"What started the fire?"

Cross looked shifty. "Reckon as she kicked the brazier over."

"I want to see her."

"That you don't. Captain Schwyz told me: 'No bugger talks to her. No bugger to go near 'cept to bring her meals. And keep the bloody door locked.' "

"And who told Schwyz? The abbot?"

Cross shrugged.

"I want to see her," Adelia said again.

Mansur reached out and took the spear from the mercenary's hand with the ease of pulling up a weed.

Blowing out his cheeks, Cross unlatched an enormous key from his belt and put it in the lock. "Just a peep, mind. Captain's bound to be here in a minute; he'll have heard the rumpus. Bloody peasants, bloody rumpus."

It *was* only a peep. Mansur had to lift Adelia up so that she could see over the mercenary's shoulder as he blocked the

413

door to stop them from going in.

What light there was inside came from burning logs in a brazier. Except for an ashy patch on one side, a deep ring of straw circled the curve of the stone walls. Something moved in it.

Adelia was reminded of Bertha. For a moment, a pair of eyes in the straw reflected the glow from the brazier and then disappeared.

Boots could be heard crunching the ice as their owner came toward them. Cross tore his spear away from Mansur. "Captain's coming. Get away, for God's sake."

They got away.

"Yes?" Mansur asked as they walked.

"Somebody tried to burn her to death," Adelia said. "The slit's up on the back wall, on the opposite side from the entrance. I think somebody tossed a lighted rag through it. If Cross was guarding the door, he wouldn't have seen who it was. But he knows it happened."

"The Fleming said the brazier tipped over."

"No. It's bolted to the floor. There was no sign that a brand fell out of it. Somebody wanted to kill her, and it wasn't Cross."

"She is a sad, mad *bint*. Perhaps she tried to burn herself."

"No." It was a natural progression. Rosamund, Bertha, Dakers. All three had known — in Dakers's case, still did — something they should not.

If it hadn't been for Cross's quick reaction in putting the fire out, the last of them would have been silenced.

Early the next morning, armed mercenaries broke into the chapel where the nuns were at prayer and carried off Emma Bloat.

Adelia, sleeping in, heard of it when Gyltha came scurrying back from the kitchen where she'd been to fetch their breakfast. "Poor thing, poor thing. Terrible to-do 'twas. Prioress tried to stop 'em and they knocked her down. In her own chapel. *Knocked her down.*"

Adelia was already dressing. "Where did they take Emma?"

"Village. Wolvercote it was, and his bloody Flemings. Carried her to his manor. Screaming, so they said, poor thing, poor thing."

"Can't they get her back?"

"The nuns is gone after her, but what can they do?"

By the time Adelia reached the gates, the rescue party of nuns was returning across the bridge, empty-handed.

"Can nothing be done?" Adelia asked as

they went by.

Sister Havis was white-faced and had a cut below her eye. "We were turned back at spearpoint. One of his men laughed at us. He said it was legal because they had a priest." She shook her head. "What sort of priest I don't know."

Adelia went to the queen.

Eleanor had just been acquainted with the news herself and was raging at her courtiers. "Do I command savages? The girl was under my protection. Did I or did I not tell Wolvercote to give her time?"

"You did, lady."

"She must be fetched back. Tell Schwyz — where is Schwyz? — tell him to gather his men. . . ." She looked around. Nobody had moved. *Well?*

"Lady, I fear the . . . *um* . . . damage is done." This was the Abbot of Eynsham. "It appears that Wolvercote keeps a hedge priest in the village. The words were said."

"Not by the girl, I'll warrant, not under those circumstances. Were her parents present?"

"Apparently not."

"Then it is abduction." Eleanor's voice was shrill with the desperation of a ruler losing control of the ruled. "Are my orders to be ignored in such a fashion? Are we living in the caves of brute beasts?"

Apart from Adelia's, the queen's was the only anger in the room. Others, the men, anyway, were disturbed, displeased, but also faintly, very faintly, amused. A woman, as long as it wasn't their own, carried off and bedded was broad comedy.

There was an embryonic wink in the abbot's eye as he said, "I fear our lord Wolvercote has taken the Roman attitude towards our poor Sabine."

There was nothing to be done. Words had been said by a priest; Emma Bloat was married. Like it or not, she had been deflowered and — as it was in every male mind — probably enjoyed it.

Helpless, Adelia left the room, unable to bear its company.

In the cloister walk, one of Eleanor's young men, lost to everything about him, was blocking the way as he walked up and down, strumming a viol and trying out a new song.

Adelia gave him a push that sent him staggering. The door of the abbey chapel at the end of the cloister beckoned to her, and she marched in, only knowing, on finding it blessedly empty, that she was wild for a solace that — and she knew this, too — could not be granted.

She went to her knees in the nave.

Dear Mother of God, protect and comfort her.

The icy, incense-laden air held only the reply: *She is cattle as you are cattle. Put up with it.*

Adelia pummeled the stones and made her accusation out loud. "Rosamund dead, Bertha dead. Emma raped. Why do You allow it?"

The reply came: "There will be medicine for our complaint eventually, my child. You of all people, with your mastery of healing, should know that."

The voice was a real one, dry and seemingly without human propulsion, as if it rustled out of the mouth on its own wings to flutter down from the tiny choir to the nave.

Mother Edyve was so small, she was almost hidden in the stall in which she sat, her hands folded on her walking stick, her chin on her hands.

Adelia got up. She said, "I have intruded, Mother. I'll go."

The voice alighted on her as she made for the door. "Emma was nine years old when she came to Godstow, bringing joy to us all."

Adelia turned back. "No joy now, not for

418

her, not for you," she said.

Unexpectedly, Mother Edyve asked, "How is Queen Eleanor taking the news?"

"With fury." Because she was sour with a fury of her own, Adelia said, "Angry because Wolvercote has flaunted her, I suppose."

"Yes." Mother Edyve rubbed her chin against her folded hands. "You are unjust, I think."

"To Eleanor? What can she do except rant? What can any of us do? Your joyful child's enslaved for life to a pig, and even the Queen of England is helpless."

"I have been listening to the songs they sing to her, to the queen," Mother Edyve said. "The viol and the young men's voices — I have been sitting here and thinking about them."

Adelia raised her eyebrows.

"What is it they sing of?" Mother Edyve asked. *"Cortez amors?"*

"Courtly love. A Provençal phrase. Provençal fawning and sentimental rubbish."

"Courtly love, yes. A serenade to the unattainable lady. It is most interesting — earthly love as ennoblement. We could say, could we not, that what those young men yearn for is a reflected essence of the Holy Mary."

Silly old soul, thought Adelia, savagely. "What those young men yearn for, Abbess, is not holiness. This song will end in a high-flown description of the secret arcade. It's their name for the vagina."

"Sex, of course," said the abbess, amazingly, "but with a gentler longing than I have ever heard ascribed to it. Oh, yes, basically, they are singing to more than they know; they sing to God the Mother."

"God the *Mother?*"

"God is both our father and our mother. How could it be otherwise? To create two sexes yet favor only one would be lopsided parentage, though Father Egbert chides me for saying so."

No wonder Father Egbert chided; it was a wonder he didn't excommunicate. God masculine and feminine?

Adelia, who considered herself a modern thinker, was confounded by a perception of an Almighty who, in every religion she knew of, had created weak and sinful woman for man's pleasure, human ovens in which to bake his seed. A devout Jew thanked God daily that he had not been born female. Yet this little nun was plucking the beard from God's chin and providing Him not only with the breasts but also with the mind of a female.

420

It was a philosophy of most profound rebellion. But now that Adelia came to consider her, Mother Edyve *was* a rebel, or she would not have been prepared to flout the Church by giving space in her graveyard to the body of a king's whore. Only independence of mind could at the same time be extending charitable thought to a queen who had brought nothing but turbulence into the abbey with her.

"Yes," the birdlike voice went on, "we grieve for the lopsidedness of the world as the Almighty Feminine must grieve for it. Yet God's time is not our time, we are told; an age is but a blink of an eye to one who is Alpha and Omega."

"Ye-es." Frowning, Adelia moved nearer and sat sideways on the chancel steps, hugging her knees, staring at the still figure in the stall.

"I have been thinking that in Eleanor we are witnessing a blink," it said.

"Eh?"

"Yes, for the first time to my knowledge, we have a queen who has raised her voice for the dignity of women."

"Eh?"

"Listen," the abbess said.

The trouvère in the cloister had finished composing his song. Now he was singing it, the lovely tenor of his voice flowing into the gray chapel like honey. *"Las! einssi ay de ma mort exemplaire, mais la doleur qu'il me convendra traire, douce seroit, se un tel espoir avoie . . ."*

If the singer was dying of love, he'd chosen to set his pain to a melody as pretty as springtime. Despite herself, Adelia smiled; the combination ought to win him his lady, all right.

". . . Dame, et se ja mes cuers riens entreprent, don't mes corps ait honneur n'avancement, De vous venracom loneins que vos soie . . ."

So if his heart ever undertook anything that would bring him honor, it would come from the beloved, however far away she was.

The music that attended Eleanor wherever she went had, to Adelia's indiscriminatory ear, been another of her affectations, the incipient background of a woman with every frailty ascribed to the feminine nature: vain, jealous, flighty, one who, in order to assert herself, had chosen to go to war to challenge a man greater than she was.

Yet the abbess was attending to it as if to holy script.

Attending to it with her, Adelia reconsidered. She'd dismissed the elaborate, sighing poetry of the male courtiers, their interest in dress, their perfumed curls, because she judged them by the standard of rough masculinity set by a rough male world. *Was regard for gentleness and beauty decadent? Rowley,* she thought, with a tearing rush of fondness, *would say that it was* — he loathed femininity in men; he equated his messenger's liking for scent with the worst excesses of the Emperor Caligula.

Eleanor's version, though, could hardly be decadence, because it was new. Adelia sat up. *By God, it was* new. The abbess was right; deliberately or not, the queen was carrying into the uncultured farmyard of her domains an image of women demanding respect, people to be considered and cherished for their personal value rather than as marketable goods. It demanded that men *deserve* women.

For a moment back there in the queen's apartment, Eleanor had held Wolvercote up to her courtiers, not as a powerful male gaining what was his but as a brute beast dragging its prey into the forest to be gnawed.

"I suppose you're right," she said, almost reluctantly.

"*. . . vous que j'aim tres loyaument . . . Ne sans amours, emprendre nel saroie.*"

"But it's a pretense, it's artificial," Adelia

423

protested. "Love, honor, respect. When are they ever extended to everyday women? I doubt if that boy actually practices what he's singing. It's . . . it's a pleasant hypocrisy."

"Oh, I have a high regard for hypocrisy," the little nun said. "It pays lip service to an ideal which must, therefore, exist. It recognizes that there is a Good. In its own way, it is a token of civilization. You don't find hypocrisy among the beasts of the field. Nor in Lord Wolvercote."

"What good does the Good do if it is not adhered to?"

"That is what I have been wondering," Mother Edyve said calmly. "And I have come to the conclusion that perhaps the early Christians wondered it, too, and perhaps that Eleanor, in her fashion, has made a start by setting a brick in a foundation on which, with God's help, our daughters' daughters can begin to build a new and better Jerusalem."

"Not in time for Emma," Adelia said.

"No."

Perhaps, Adelia thought drearily, *it was only a very old woman who could look hopefully on a single brick laid in a wasteland.*

They sat a while longer, listening. The singer had changed his tune and his theme.

"I would hold thee naked in my arms at eve, that we might be in ecstasy, my head against thy breast. . . ."

"That, too, is love of a sort, nevertheless," Mother Edyve said, "and perhaps all one to our Great Parent, who made our bodies as they are."

Adelia smiled at her, thinking of being in bed with Rowley. "I have been convinced that it is."

"So have I, which speaks well for the men we have loved." There was a reflective sigh. "But don't tell Father Egbert."

The abbess got up with difficulty and tested her legs.

Warmed, Adelia went to help her settle her cloak. "Mother," she said on impulse, "I am afraid for Dame Dakers's safety."

A heavily veined little hand flapped her away; Mother Edyve had become impatient to go. "You are a busy soul, child, and I am grateful for it, but you may leave Dakers's safety to me."

As she hobbled out, she said something else, but the words were indistinct, something like, "After all, I have the keys to the lockup."

By the end of that day, Adelia had changed. Perhaps it was anger at Emma Bloat's rape.

Perhaps it was anger at the attempt on Dakers's life. Perhaps it was the courage inspired by Mother Edyve.

Whatever it was, she knew she couldn't cower in the guesthouse anymore while murderers and abductors went unchecked.

In essence, the killer of Rosamund and Bertha had made a contract with her: *Leave me alone and your child is safe.*

A shameful contract. Nevertheless, she would have abided by it, taking it as a given that he would not kill again.

But he'd tossed a burning rag through an aperture as if the living woman inside was rubbish.

I can't allow that, she told him.

She was afraid, very afraid indeed; her baby would have to be protected as no child ever had been, but she, Adelia, could not live, *her daughter* could not live, at the cost of other people's deaths.

"Where you going?" Gyltha called after her.

"I'm going to ask questions."

She found Jacques in the cloister, being taught how to play the viol by one of the troubadours. The courtiers were colonizing the place. *And the nuns,* she thought, *are now too intimidated by everything that has*

426

happened to stop them.

She dragged the unwilling messenger away toward the almonry and sat him and herself down on a mounting block.

"Yes, mistress?"

"I want you to help me find out who ordered the killing of Talbot of Kidlington."

He was set aback. "I don't know as I'm up to that, mistress."

She ignored him and recounted the list of those she suspected: "Wolvercote, Master Warin, the gatekeeper, and the Bloats." She went into detail.

He rubbed his chin; it was closely shaved now, like all the young men's at Eleanor's court.

"I can tell you one thing, if it helps," he said. "Lawyer Warin made a to-do when he was introduced to my lord Wolvercote in church. *'So honored to make your acquaintance, my lord. We have not met, but I have long wished to know . . .'* He made a point of it — I was there and heard him. If he mentioned that they had not encountered each other before, he must have said it three or four times."

"How did Wolvercote greet Master Warin?"

"Like he treats everybody, as if he'd been squirted out of a backside." He grimaced, afraid of having offended her. "Sorry, mistress."

"But you believe Warin was insisting they hadn't met before when, really, they had?"

Jacques thought about it. "Yes, I do."

Adelia was shivering. Ward had crept under her skirts and was pressing against her knees for warmth. A gargoyle on the gutter of the abbess's house opposite gaped at her, its chin bearded with icicles.

I am watching you.

She said, "Emma thought kindly of Master Warin, which means that Talbot did, too, which also means the boy trusted him. . . ."

"And confided his intention to elope?" The messenger was becoming interested.

"I know he did," she said. "Emma told me so. The boy told Warin he was choosing his birthday as the day for the elopement so that he could take possession of his inheritance. . . ."

"Which, unbeknownst, Master Warin had squandered . . ." This was exciting.

Adelia nodded. "Which, indeed, Master Warin may have squandered, thereby necessitating his young cousin's removal . . ."

". . . and it dawns on Master Warin that he has an ally in Lord Wolvercote. Old Wolfie will be deprived of a bride and a fortune if the elopement goes ahead."

"Yes. So he approaches Lord Wolvercote and suggests Talbot should die."

They sat back to think it through.

"Why was it so urgent that Talbot's body be identified right away?" Adelia wondered.

"That's easy, mistress. Lawyer Warin may be pressed for money — he looks a man who likes to live well. If he's Talbot's heir, it would take too long to prove to a coroner that the estate of the anonymous corpse was his. That takes a long time. Courts are slow. His creditors would come in before he inherited."

"And it would suit Wolvercote for Emma to realize that her lover was dead. Yes, it's all of a piece," she said. "It was Wolvercote who provided the killers. Warin probably didn't know any."

"And got rid of them once they'd done the deed. It could be so, mistress."

Talking it over had hardened the case for Adelia, turning theory to reality. Two men had conspired to blot out a young life. Wickedness was discussed in lawyers' offices as business, considered in manor houses over a flagon of wine; men were instructed in it. Normality, goodness were commodities to be traded for greed. Innocence was helpless against it. *She* was helpless against it. It gibbered at her from

429

the rooftops.

"How to prove it, though?" Jacques asked.

"Plotters distrust one another," she said. "I think it can be done, but I shall need you to help me."

She let him go then, and hurried back to the guesthouse, unable to shake off her fear for Allie.

"Right as a shilling," Gyltha said. "Look at her."

But Adelia knew that Gyltha, too, was afraid, because she'd told Mansur to move in with them, day and night.

"Anyone as doesn't like it can go and . . . well, you know what," she said. "So you do what you got to do. Mansur's on guard."

But so was the killer . . .

Now she had to go and see Father Paton.

This time she did it carefully, waiting until night, watching for watchers, slipping from shadow to shadow until she was protected by the narrow walk that led to the warming room stairs.

Sister Lancelyne was at Vespers, and the little priest was alone, poring over the cartulary by candlelight, none too pleased to be interrupted.

Adelia told him everything, *everything*, beginning with finding Talbot's body on the bridge — the little priest might have missed it while he'd been keeping warm in the cart — proceeding to the happenings at Wormhold, to the return to Godstow and the death of Bertha, her suspicions of who did what, the threat to Allie, the threat to Dame Dakers.

He didn't want to hear it. He kept shifting and glancing longingly at the documents open in front of him. This was a tale reeking of the cardinal sins, and Father Paton preferred humanity in the abstract. "Are you certain?" he kept asking. "Surely not. How dare you reckon such things?"

Adelia persisted, skewering him with logic like a pin through a butterfly. She didn't like him much; he didn't like her at all, but he was separated from the battle in which she was engaged, and his mind was like one of his own ledgers; she needed it as a register.

"You must keep it all very, very secret," she told him. "Mention it to nobody except the king." This bloodless little man had to be the repository of her knowledge so that, in the event of her death, he could pass it on to Henry Plantagenet. "When the king comes, he will know what to do."

"But I do not."

"Yes, you do." And she told him what it

was that he must look for.

"This is impudence." He was shocked. "In any case, I doubt that, even if it is extant, it will prove your case."

Adelia doubted it, too, but it was all she had in her armory. She attempted an encouragement that she didn't feel. "The king *will* come," she said, "and he *will* prevail in the end." That was her only certainty. Eleanor might be extraordinary, but she had pitted herself against one who straddled his kingdom like a colossus; she could not win.

There Father Paton agreed with her. "Yes, yes," he said, "a queen is only a woman, unable to fight any cause successfully, let alone her own. All she may expect is God's punishment for rebelling against her rightful lord."

He turned on Adelia. "You, too, mistress, are a mere woman, sinful, impertinent, and right or wrong, you should not be questioning your betters."

She held her temper and instead dangled a carrot. "When the king *does* come," she said, "he'll want to know who murdered Rosamund. There will be advancement for the man that can tell him who it was."

She watched the priest's mouth purse as he entered possible promotion to an abbacy, even a bishopric, into a mental balance sheet against the risk and lèse-majesté of what he was being asked to do.

"I suppose I shall be serving God, who is all truth," he said slowly.

"You will," she said, and left him to get on with it.

And then it was Christmas.

The church was so packed with bodies for Angel Mass that it was actually hot, and the smell of humanity threatened to overwhelm the fresh, bitter scent of holly and ivy garlands.

Adelia almost sweltered in her beaver cloak. She kept it on because, underneath, she was wearing the bliaut that Eleanor's seamstresses had finished just in time and knew that she looked so nice in it, with all the other trimmings the queen had given her, that she felt she would attract attention.

"You show yourself," Gyltha had protested. "You don't look half bad." Which, from her, was praise.

But the instinct to keep out of the killer's eye was still strong. Perhaps she would take off her cloak at the coming feast; perhaps she wouldn't.

The choir stalls, once more reserved for the nuns, provided a black-and-white edging to the embroidered, bedecked altar with its blaze of candles and the robes of the abbot and two priests as they moved through the litany like glowing chess pieces.

The magic was infallible.

The queue for Communion included murderous men, hostile factions, every gamut of human weakness and sorrow, yet, as it moved quietly forward, it was gripped by the same awe. At the rail, the miller knelt beside one of the men who had belabored him. Adelia received the host from the Abbot of Eynsham, whose hands rested for a second in blessing on the head of Baby Allie. The cup passed from a Wolvercote mercenary to one of Schwyz's before each lumbered back to his place, chewing and exalted.

There was common and growing breathlessness as Mary labored in her stable a few yards away. The running footfalls of the shepherds came nearer and nearer. Angels chanted above the starlit, snow-stacked church roof.

When the abbot, raising his arms, announced a deep-throated "The Child is born," his exhortation to go in peace was lost in a great shout of congratulation, several of the women yelling advice on breast-feeding to the invisible but present

Mary and prompting her to "make sure and wrap that baby up warm now."

Bethlehem was here. It was now.

As Adelia filed into the great barn, Jacques pushed through the crowd to touch her shoulder. "The queen's greeting, mistress, and she will be disappointed if you are not wearing the gifts she gave you."

Reluctantly, Adelia took off her cloak with its hood, revealing the bliaut and the barbette, and felt naked. Walt, who was beside her, looked at her and stared. "Wondered who this stranger was," he said. She supposed that, too, was a compliment. And indeed, she received a lot of surprised looks — most of them friendly. For this was another gift Eleanor had, unconsciously, given her; by showing her favor, the queen had cleansed her of the taint of witchcraft.

Though Eleanor and her court had made plans for its entertainments, the feast in the barn was expropriated by the English.

Expropriated? It was run away with.

Charming Aquitanian carols were drowned in roaring wassails as the flaming Yule log, dragged in on the end of a harness by an ox, was set on a hearth in the middle of the great square formed by the tables in the barn. A minstrel in the gallery — actually, the hayloft — tried singing to the diners, but since, it turned out, all the convent's people and most of the village had been invited and were making too much noise to hear him, he gave up and descended to eat with the rest.

It was a Viking meal. Meat and more meat. The icehouse had yielded its best. Eleanor's cook had, literally, battled for his art in the kitchen, but his winter sallats and frumenty, his pretty painted pastry castles and delicate flower-water jellies had been so overwhelmed and dripped on by lard and blood-gravy that he'd been taken poorly and now sat staring into space as his apprentice popped comforting little squares of roast pork into his mouth.

There were no courses, either. The convent servants had coped for too long with Godstow's overflowing and demanding guests, and the advent of Christmas had worked them even harder. They'd spent the last few days in the scorching heat of cooking fires and in decorating the barn until it resembled a glade in a forest; they weren't bloody going to miss the feast for which they'd sweated by running back and forth to the kitchens. Everything they'd cooked — savory, sweet, sauced, plain, breads and pudding — was dumped on the tables in one glorious heap while they clambered onto the benches nearest the barn doors to enjoy it.

This was a good thing; there was so much carving to be done at once, so much handing of dishes up and down the tables, so many shouts back and forth for "some of that stuffing for my lady," "a slice off the gander, if you please," "pass up the turnip mash, there" that a camaraderie of gustation grew between high and low, though it did not extend to the dogs waiting under the tables for scraps and squabbling when one fell their way.

Ward kept close to Adelia's knees, where he was fed royally — his mistress was a small eater and, in order not to offend Mansur, who was sitting beside her and kept heaping her platter, she secretly slipped hunks of meat to her dog.

Eleanor, Adelia saw, was taking it all well. With good humor, the queen had put on the monstrous crown of ivy and bay leaves presented to her by the smith's wife, thereby ruining her own simple headdress and adding to the growing paganism of the night by her sudden resemblance to an earth goddess.

Apart from the royal cook, the only person to take no part in the jollity was Emma, a glacial, unmoving figure sitting next to her husband, who ignored her. Adelia tried to catch her eye, and then didn't; the girl looked at nothing.

How were Master and Mistress Bloat going to deal with the situation? Adelia wondered. Were they condemning the abduction of their daughter?

No, they'd decided to overlook it. They'd placed themselves on the inner side of one of the tables opposite the abductor, though Wolvercote was rebuffing most of their attempts to engage him in conversation.

Master Bloat even tried to stand up and make a toast to the happy couple, but the volume of noise increased alarmingly as he did so, and Emma, coming to life for the first time, regarded her father with a look so bitter that the man's words withered in his mouth and he sat down again.

With Mansur on her left and Allie tied firmly in a sling to her hip — there was to be no more abduction of daughters — Adelia turned her attention to the man on her right. She had taken pains to get a seat next to him.

Master Warin had kept to himself until now, and the fact that he had to ask her, politely, who she was and did not react unfavorably when she told him her name showed that he had been isolated from convent gossip.

He had a nervous habit of licking his lips and had none of the smooth superiority of most lawyers, an unremarkable person who'd softened but did not try to hide a strong Gloucestershire accent. Adelia got the impression that gaining legal qualification had been hard for him, both financially and intellectually, and that he confined himself to *consilio et auxilio,* advising on wills, assarts, boundary disputes, contracts of service, all the minutiae of everyday law, though important enough to those involved with them.

When she commiserated with him on the death of his young cousin, he wet his lips again and real tears came into his short-sighted eyes: The murder had bereft him of family, he told her, since he had no wife as yet. "How I envy you this bonny little girl, mistress. I would dearly like children."

Adelia had built a case against the lawyer. She had to keep reminding herself that *somebody* had passed on the information that led to killers waiting on the bridge for Talbot of Kidlington, and none was more likely than this little man, who said of Talbot, "We were closer than cousins. He was my younger brother after his parents died. I looked after him in everything."

But while it was modest, his clothing was of a quality not to be expected of a family lawyer, and the large seal ring on his finger was entirely of gold; Master Warin did himself well. Also, his taste did not run to mead and ale; his grabs at the wine jug as it was passed round were frequent.

Adelia applied the spur. "Your cousin didn't confide to you his intention to run away with Mistress Bloat, then?" she asked.

"Of course not." Master Warin's voice became sharp. "A lunatic idea. I would have dissuaded him from it. Lord Wolvercote is an important man. I would not have him shamed by one of my family."

He was lying. Emma had said he'd been part of the elopement conspiracy.

"Did you know him, then? Wolvercote?"

"I did not." Master Warin's tongue wriggled around his lips. "We met in church the other night for the first time."

Lying again. This was her man.

"I'd only wondered if you knew what your cousin was planning, because people are saying that you came here hot on his heels. . . ."

"Who says that?"

"You arrived at the abbey so soon after . . ."

"That is a calumny. I was worried for my cousin traveling in the snow. Who are these slanderers? Who are *you?* I don't need to sit here. . . ." His tongue flickering like a snake's, Master Warin grabbed his wine cup and moved away to find a seat farther down the table.

Mansur turned his head to watch the lawyer's agitated progress. "Did he kill the boy?" he asked in Arabic.

"In a way. He told Wolvercote so that Wolvercote could kill him."

"As guilty, then."

"As if he shot the bolt himself, yes. He could have said he knew about the elopement and turned up at the abbey in order to stop it, thus explaining why he was so prompt on the scene. But he wouldn't say that — I gave him the opportunity — because people would think he was in Wolvercote's pocket, and he insists they never met. Actually, it wouldn't condemn him if he said they had, but they conspired together to kill the boy, you see, and it's warping his judgment. Guilt is making him distance himself from Wolvercote when he doesn't need to."

"He betrayed his own kin, Allah spit on him. Can we prove it?"

"We'll try." Adelia took Allie out of the

sling and rubbed her cheek against her daughter's downy head. How much more depressing was the banal ordinariness of a murderer like little Lawyer Warin than the brutality of a Wolvercote.

There was a sudden push, and she was shoved to one side by Cross taking the place that Warin had left and bringing with him the chill of outside. "Move up there." The mercenary began reaching for dishes like a starving man.

"What have you been up to?" she asked.

"What you think I been up to? Marching up and down outside that bloody lockup. And a waste of bloody time *that* was. She's gone."

"Who's gone?"

"The demon. Abbot hisself told me she was a demon. Who'd you think?"

"Dakers? Dakers has gone?" She was on her feet, startling Allie, who'd been sucking the marrow of a beef bone. "Oh, dear God, they've taken her."

Cross looked up at her, gravy dripping from his mouth. "What you on about? Nobody ain't taken her. She's vanished. That's what demons do, they vanish."

Adelia sat down. "Tell me."

How it had been done, or even when, Cross couldn't tell her, because he didn't know; nobody knew. It hadn't been discovered until a short while ago when, on instructions from the cellaress, a kitchen servant had brought a tray of Christmas food for its prisoner and Cross had used his key to open the lockup's door.

" 'S on a ring, the key is, see," he said. "Each guard passes it on to the next one as takes over. Oswald passed it to me when I went on duty, an' Walt'd passed it to him when *he* went on duty, and they both swears they never opened that bloody door, an' I know I didn't, not til I unlocked it just now. . . ."

There was a pause while he scooped beef into his mouth.

"And?" Adelia asked, impatient.

"An' so I fits the key in the lock, turns it, opens the door, and the boy goes in with the basket, and there she was . . . gone. Place as bare as a baby's arse."

"Somebody must have let her out." Adelia was still worried.

"No, they bloody ain't," Cross said. "I tell you, nobody din't open the bloody door til then. She's vanished. 'S what demons do. Turned herself into a puff a smoke and out through one of the slits, that's what she done."

He'd called for Schwyz to come to the

443

lockup, he said, nodding toward the empty space on the upper table where the mercenary leader had been sitting. Sister Havis, too, had been summoned.

"But, like I told 'em, you won't find her a'cause she's vanished, gone back to hell where she come from. What else you expect from a demon? Here he comes, look, shittin' hisself six ways from Sunday."

A scowling Schwyz had entered the barn and was striding up to the table where the Abbot of Eynsham sat next to the queen. All the diners were too busy carousing and eating to pay him any attention, except those to whom he had to deliver the news. Adelia saw that Eleanor merely raised her eyebrows, but the abbot immediately got to his feet; he seemed to be shouting, though the noise in the barn was too great for Adelia to hear him.

"He's wanting the abbey searched," Cross said, interpreting. "No bloody chance of that, though. Nobody ain't leaving Yule food to go huntin' a demon in the dark. I ain't, I know that."

So much was obvious. The abbot was talking urgently to Lord Wolvercote, who was shrugging him off like a man who didn't care. Now he was appealing to the abbess, whose response, while more courteous, showed a similar refusal to be of help.

As she spread her hands to indicate the uselessness of interrupting the diners, Mother Edyve's eyes rested for a moment without expression on Adelia's across the room.

After all, I have the keys to the lockup.

"What you laughing at?" Cross asked.

"At a man hoist with his own petard."

However the abbess had managed the escape, whichever of Dakers's guards had been commanded to turn a blind eye, the Abbot of Eynsham could neither accuse nor punish. He was the one who, in locking her up, had demonized Rosamund's housekeeper; he could not now complain if, as Cross said, she had done what demons did.

Still grinning, Adelia leaned forward to tell Gyltha, who was on the Arab's other side, what had happened.

"Good luck to the old gargoyle." Gyltha took another swig from her beaker; she'd been imbibing with energy for some time.

Mansur said in Arabic, "Convent men have been digging a path through the snow down to the river. The abbess ordered it. I overheard the man Fitchet say it was so that the queen could go skating on the ice. Now I think that they have been making an escapeway for Rosamund's woman."

"They've let her leave? In this weather?" It wasn't funny anymore. "I thought they'd hide her somewhere in the abbey."

Mansur shook his head. "It is too crowded, she would be found. She will survive if Allah wills it. It is not far to Oxford."

"She won't go to Oxford."

There was only one place Dame Dakers would be making for.

For the rest of the meal and as the tables were put aside to clear the barn for dancing, Adelia thought of the river and the woman who would be following its course northward. Would the ice hold her? Could she survive the cold? Had the abbot, who would know where she was heading, sent men and dogs after her?

Mansur, looking at her, said, "Allah protects the insane. He will decide whether the woman lives or dies."

But it was because Dakers was insane *and* friendless *and* knew too much that Adelia's shoulders were bowed by responsibility for her.

Allah, God, whoever You are, look out for her.

However, in seeing to young Allie, who, having fed and slept and now woken up again, needing to be wiped top and bottom

446

and to have her clouts changed, and demanding entertainment, Adelia was forced to dwell on what was immediate.

There was entertainment in plenty. The troubadours had gathered in the hayloft and were now playing with a force and rhythm that couldn't be denied; the queen and her court danced to the music with toe-pointing, hand-arching elegance at one end of the barn while, at the other, the English jounced in swinging, noisy rings.

A convent pensioner was juggling apples with a dexterity that belied his years, and the smith, against the advice of his wife, was swallowing a sword.

Activity and grunts from under the hayloft eventually produced a wild assortment of figures that proceeded to put on an impromptu and scatological version of Noah's flood so exuberantly that the dancers paused to become its audience.

Adelia, sitting on the ground with a crowing, pointing Allie against her knees, found herself enjoying it. It was doubtful if Noah would have recognized the species capering up this invisible gangplank into an invisible ark. The only real animal, the convent donkey, outperformed the rest of the cast by dropping a pungent criticism of their performance on the foot of a unicorn, played by Fitchet, making Gyltha laugh so hard that Mansur had to drag her away until she recovered.

For all their sophistication, Eleanor's party couldn't resist the applause accorded to such vulgarism. They joined in, dropping refinement and showing themselves to be clowns manqués as they appeared in startling wigs and skirts, faces painted with flour and madder.

What was it about some men that they must ape women, Adelia thought, even as she booed an irascible Mrs. Noah, played with brio by Montignard, belaboring Noah for being drunk.

Was that Jacques under the warts, straw hair, and extended bosom of Japhet's wife? Surely that wasn't the Abbot of Eynsham black-faced and whirling so fast on his toes that his petticoat flared in a blur?

Allie, still clutching her marrow bone, had fallen asleep again. It was time to go to bed before the manic hilarity of the night descended into brawling, as it almost inevitably would. Already Schwyz's men and Wolvercote's had separated into drunken coteries and were focusing blearily on one another in a way suggesting that the spirit of Christmas was on its last legs.

Wolvercote himself had already gone, taking Emma with him. The queen was thanking the abbess before departing, and Mother Edyve was signaling to her nuns. Master Warin had disappeared. The smith, clutching his throat, was being led away by his wife.

Adelia looked around for Gyltha and Mansur. Oh, dear, her beloved Arab — possibly the only sober person in the barn apart from herself — had been inveigled into doing his sword dance for the delight of some convent servants, and Gyltha was gyrating round him like an inebriated stoat. Not a drinker usually, Gyltha, but she could never resist alcohol when it was free.

Yawning, Adelia picked up Allie and took her to the corner in which they'd left the cradle, put the child in it, took away the marrow bone, gave it to Ward, covered up her daughter, and raised the cradle's little leather hood, then settled down beside it to wait.

And fell asleep to dream a frenetic, rowdy dream that turned hideous when a bear picked her up and, clutching her to its pelt, began dragging her away into the forest. She heard growling as Ward attacked the bear and then a yelp as it kicked him away.

Struggling, almost smothered, her legs trailing, Adelia woke up fully. She was being pulled into the darkest corner under the hayloft in the arms of the Abbot of Eynsham. He slammed her so hard against the outer wall that bits of lathe and plaster showered them both, pushing his great body against her.

He was very, very drunk and whispering. "You're his spy, you bitch. The bishop. I know you . . . pretending to be prim with me, you whore, I know . . . what you got up to. How's he do it? Up the arse? In your mouth?"

Brandy fumes enveloped her as his blackened face came down onto hers.

She jerked her head away and brought up her knee as sharply as she could, but the ridiculous skirt he was wearing gave him protection and, though he grunted, his weight stayed on her.

The whispering went on and on. ". . . think you're so clever . . . see it in your eyes, but you're a stinking strumpet. A spy. I'm better than Saint Albans. . . . I'm *better*. . . ." His hand had found her breast and was squeezing it. "Look at me, I can do it . . . Love me, you bitch, love *me*. . . ." He was licking her face.

Outside the suffocating cubicle she was trapped in, somebody was intervening, trying to pull the heaving, hissing awfulness off her. "Leave her, Rob, she's not worth it." It was Schwyz's voice.

"Yes, she is. She looks at me like I'm shit . . . like she knows."

There was the sound of a loud smack, then air and space. Relieved of weight, Adelia slid down the wall, gasping.

The abbot lay on the ground, onto which Mansur had flattened him. He was weeping. Beside him, Schwyz was on his knees, giving comfort like a mother. "Just a whore, Robert, you don't want that."

Mansur stood over them both, sucking his knuckles but impassive as ever. He turned and held out his hand to Adelia. She took it and got to her feet.

Together, they walked back to the cradle. Before they reached it, Adelia paused, wiping her face, smoothing her clothes. Even then, she couldn't look down at her child. How impure they made you feel.

Behind her, Schwyz's soothing went on, but the wail of the abbot rose high above it. "Why Saint Albans? *Why not me?*"

With Mansur carrying the cradle, they collected a staggering, singing Gyltha and walked back to the guesthouse through the welcome cold of the night.

Adelia was too deep in shock to be angry, though she knew she would be; after all, she had more regard for herself than women who, miserably, expected assault as the price for being women. But even while her body was shaking, her mind was trying to fathom the reason for what had happened. "I don't understand," she said, wailing. "I thought he was a different sort of enemy."

"Allah punish him, but he would not have hurt you, I think," Mansur said.

"What are you talking about? He *did* hurt me. He tried to rape me."

"He is incapable, I think," Mansur said. His own condition had made a judge of such things; he found the sexuality of so-called normal men interesting. Though castrated, unable to have children, he himself could still have sex with a woman, and there was lofty pity in his voice for one who could not.

"He seemed capable enough to me." Sobbing, Adelia stopped and scooped up snow to rub over her face. "Why are you so tolerant?"

"He wants, but he cannot have. I think so. He is a talker, not a doer."

Was that it? Inadequacy? Among all the filth, there had been a despairing appeal for love, sex, *something.*

Rowley had said of him, *"Bastard. Clever. Got the ear of the Pope."*

452

And with all the cleverness, this friend of popes must, when drunk, plead for a despised woman's regard like a child for somebody else's toy.

Because *she* despised *him?*

And I do, she thought. If there was vulnerability, it made the abbot the more loathsome to her. Adelia preferred her enemies straightforwardly and wholeheartedly without humanity.

"I hate him," she said — and *now* she was angry. "Mansur, I'm going to bring that man down."

The Arab bent his head. "Let us pray that Allah wills it."

"He'd better."

Fury was cleansing to the mind. Nevertheless, as Mansur persuaded Gyltha to stop kissing him and go to sleep, Adelia washed herself all over in a bowl of icy water from the ewer. And felt better.

"I'll bring him down," she said again, "somehow."

For a minute, which was all that could be borne of the cold, she opened one of the shutters to look out on the geometric shadows that the pitches of the abbey's roofs were throwing onto the stretch of snow beyond its walls.

A blacker runnel scarred the moonlit

whiteness where a new track had been dug to the river. They were linked now, the abbey and the Thames. For the first time, there was an escape route from this seething, overfilled cauldron of humanity where paragons and monsters fought the ultimate, yet never-ending, battle in suffocating collision.

At least one soul had taken it. Somewhere in that metallic wilderness, Dakers was risking her life not, Adelia knew, in order to disappear from her captors but to reach the thing she loved, though it was dead.

TWELVE

When, early next morning, Adelia opened the shutters on Saint Stephen's Day, it was to find that something had happened to the view from the guesthouse. Yes, of course, a new path was leading down to the bank — they'd cut rough steps in it — but it was more than that; the sense of isolation was gone, and expectation had taken its place.

It was difficult to see why; dawn was blessing the deserted countryside with its usual ephemeral touch of apricot. The snow was as solid as it had been and contained no human footprints as far as the eye stretched.

Yet the white forest across the river was, somehow, less rigid. . . .

"They're here."

Mansur joined her at the window. "I see nothing."

"I thought I saw something in those trees."

They stood looking. Adelia's excitement trickled away; the expectation was in her, not in the view.

"Wolves, most like," said Gyltha, who was skulking at the rear of the room, avoiding the light. "I heard them last night, horrid close they was."

"Was that when you were vomiting into the chamber pot?" Adelia asked interestedly.

Gyltha ignored her. "Right up to the walls, they were. I reckon they found young Talbot's horse as was left in the woods."

Adelia hadn't heard them — it had been bears that prowled her sleep. But Gyltha was probably right; it would be wolves among the trees — less frightening than those inside the walls.

Yet the leap of hope that Rowley was alive and had brought the king and his men to them had been so volcanic that she couldn't relinquish it altogether. "There *could* be an army hiding out there," she said. "It wouldn't attack without knowing the strength of the force inside the abbey — the sisters might get hurt. He'd wait, Henry would wait."

"What for?" Mansur asked.

"Yes what for?" Gyltha was being determinedly talkative to show that she wasn't suffering. "He wouldn't need an army to take this place — me and little Allie could storm it by ourselves. And how'd the king get here? No, old Wolf knows he's safe til the snow melts. He ain't even posted lookouts."

"He has now," Mansur said.

Adelia leaned out. Gyltha joined her. Immediately below, a man in Wolvercote scarlet and black was patrolling the walkway running along the hopelessly inadequate castellations of the convent wall, his morning shadow falling rhythmically on the merlons as he passed and disappearing at each crenel. He had a pike in one hand and a rattle in the other.

"What's he guarding us from?" Gyltha asked. "Magpies? There ain't no army out there. Nobody don't fight in winter."

"Henry does," Adelia said. She was hearing Rowley's voice, vibrating from the near-incredulous pleasure with which he'd spoken of his king's exploits, recounting the tale of the young Plantagenet when, fighting for his mother's right to the throne of England against his uncle Stephen, he'd crossed the Channel with a small army in a bitter Christmas gale, catching his enemies hibernating — and beating them.

Until now, Wolvercote had been relying on an English winter to keep his enemy as powerless to move as he was. But whether it was because the umbilical path through the snow now connected the convent to the outside world, or whether there was something in the air today, Saint Stephen's day, he had set a guard. . . .

"He's afraid." Adelia's own voice vibrated. "He thinks Henry's coming. And he could, Mansur, the king *could* — his men could skate upriver and get here." She had another thought: "I suppose Wolvercote could even skate his men down to Oxford and join the other rebels. Why hasn't he?"

"The man Schwyz thought of it. He is the better tactician," Mansur said. "He asked Fitchet if it could be done. But further down, the Thames is deeper and has more tributaries, its ice does not hold and cannot be risked. Nobody can go or come that way." Mansur spread his hands in apology to Adelia for disappointing her. "Local knowledge. No one moves until the snow melts."

"And close them bloody shutters," Gyltha said. "You want this baby to freeze?" Suddenly gentle, she added, "Nobody in the outside world don't know we're here, my duck."

"The woman is right," Mansur said.

They've lost hope, she thought. *They've given Rowley up for dead at last.* Godstow

458

festered like an unsuspected bubo in the world's white flesh, waiting to spread its poison. Only the birds overhead could know that it flew the pennant of a rebel queen — and birds weren't likely to tell anybody.

But today, against all evidence, hope told Adelia that there was something beyond these shutters. At least there were steps leading to the river, and the river, however treacherous, led to the outside world. It was sunny, and there was an indefinable feeling in the air.

She'd been afraid too long, besieged too long, threatened too long, shut in dark rooms during daylight like a hostage — they all had.

Hearing talk and laughter, she gave the shutters a push that threw them back against the wall and leaned out again.

Farther along, the convent gates were opening and a crowd of chattering men and women were assembling outside them. In their center was a slim, elegant figure dressed in furs with a sheen that glowed in the sun.

"The queen's going skating," Adelia said. She turned round. "And so are we. All of us. Allie, too."

Everybody did. It was, after all, Saint Stephen's Day, which, by tradition, belonged to the servants, whom, since they could not go home to their villages, had to enjoy it in situ. Tonight it would be their privilege to have their own private feast on last night's leftovers.

Almost every worker in the abbey tumbled out onto the ice, some without skates but all carrying the traditional clay box that they rattled invitingly under the noses of the guests.

Having made her contribution, Adelia turned to delighting her daughter by attaching her belt to the cradle and skimming the child in it over the ice as she skated. Others on skates similarly obliged those who had none, so that the wide sweep of the Thames became a whirl of sledges and trays, of puffed jokes and pink cheeks, through which a smiling queen sailed, swanlike, with her courtiers gaggling after her.

The nuns joined them after Lauds, the younger ones shrieking happily and vying with Sister Havis, who, while making it seem stately, outraced them all.

A brazier was placed on the ice near the bank and a chair carried to it so that Mother Edyve could sit by its warmth in company with the walking wounded that Sister Jennet had brought from the infirmary. Ward, whose attempts to scrabble along behind

Adelia kept ending with his legs splaying into a quadrant, gave up the battle and settled down to sulk on the piece of carpet under the abbess's chair.

Adelia saw her patient and skated over to him, dragging the cradle behind her. "Are you progressing well?"

Poyns's young face was abeam. "Right nicely, mistress, I thank ee. And the abbess is giving me a job, assistant gatekeeper to Master Fitchet. Don't need two arms in gatekeepin'."

Adelia smiled back at him. *What* a nice abbey this was.

"And thank Master Man . . . Manum . . . thank the doctor for me; God and the saints bless him."

"I will."

Tables appeared bearing some remnants of the Christmas feast.

Sitting on somebody's homemade sledge on the far bank where Ward joined them, Adelia and Gyltha masticated Allie's dinner for her and ate their own, ignoring the child's persistent "Bor, bor," asking to be taken onto the ice again.

"She means 'more,'" Adelia said proudly. "That's her first word."

"Them's her first orders," Gyltha said. "Who's a little tyrant, then?" She abandoned her lamb chop to Ward, picked up the belt, and skated off with the cradle, throwing up a spray of ice behind her.

Adelia and her dog sat on. From here she had a panorama of the convent walls. There were now two of Wolvercote's men patrolling, both of them keeping their eyes on the trees behind her. A figure stood at one of the windows in the men's guesthouse — she thought it was Master Warin.

No sign of the abbot, thanks be to God; he'd become dreadful to her, as, with her rejection, she must have become dreadful to him — and would be punished for it.

The bridge had been closed; she could tell that because some Wolvercote villagers were crowding the far side of it, wistfully watching the merrymakers on ice. Others were digging their own path down to the river.

Behind her, in the forest that she'd hoped would be hiding Henry Plantagenet and his army, she could hear the shouts of the younger convent men as, careless of wolves, they scoured the undergrowth in the hunt for a wren, their noise indicating that they were not encountering anything larger.

She looked back to see their figures running through the trees, faces blackened with soot, as tradition demanded they should be.

Why it was necessary to catch a wren at all on Saint Stephen's Day she did not understand; she could never fathom English customs. Pagan, most of them.

She returned to watching the scene on the ice.

Wolvercote was talking to Eleanor at the food table. Where was Emma?

Adelia wondered what it was that had stirred the man into setting a watch now, when he had neglected any precaution for so long. Perhaps he'd sensed the same alertness in the air that so invigorated herself — or had just glimpsed another opportunity to assert his control. Either way, he was a fool as well as a brute; what point was there in guarding the abbey and, apparently, readying it in case of siege when nearly all its occupants were capering outside its walls, any one of whom could carry news of his presence in it to his enemy?

She was glad of it — the liberation. If it hadn't meant leaving her nearest and dearest behind, she'd have been tempted to skate off and find Henry for herself.

But Schywz had just come out of the abbey gates and was viewing the indisciplined joyousness below him like a man who could organize things better. And, damn him, he was *going* to organize them better. Descending the steps, approaching Wolvercote, berating . . .

Within minutes he'd stationed his mercenaries at each end of the river's bend. Nobody would get away now. He was actually scolding Eleanor, pointing her toward the convent gate. . . . She was shaking her head, having too much fun, skating away from him.

They'd have to go in soon; the sun was getting low, withdrawing brightness and such warmth as it had bestowed. At last, Eleanor's clear diction was heard thanking Mother Edyve for the entertainment. "So refreshing . . ." People were beginning to climb the steps of the track.

"Mistress," said a crisp voice behind Adelia. It was Father Paton.

Rowley's little secretary looked incongruous on skates, but he balanced on them neatly, his mittened, inky hands crossed on his chest as if protecting himself from the unworthy. "I have it," he said.

She stared at him. "You . . . *found* it? I can't believe . . . it was such a long shot." She had to pull herself together. "And is it the same?"

"Yes," he said, "I regret to say that the similarity with the one you gave me is undeniable."

"It would stand up in a court of law?"

"Yes. There are peculiarities common to each that even the illiterate would recognize. I have it here, I have them both. . . ." He began unbuckling the large scrip hanging from his belt.

Adelia stopped him. "No, no, I don't want them. You keep them, and my affidavit. Keep them very safe until the time comes . . . and in the name of Jesus, tell nobody you have them."

Father Paton pursed his lips. "I have written my own account of this affair, explaining to whomsoever it may concern that I have done what I have done because I believe it to be the will of my master, the late Bishop of Saint Albans. . . ."

There was a swirl of ice as the bishop's messenger encircled them and came to a sliding stop.

Jacques's face was ruddy with exercise; he looked almost handsome, though his bishop would not have approved of the elaborate, hand-twirling, very Aquitanian bow he gave Adelia. "It's done, mistress. With good fortune, they're meeting in the church at Vespers. You and this gentleman should take your positions early."

"What nonsense is this?" Father Paton disapproved of Jacques only slightly less

465

than he did of Adelia.

"Jacques has been delivering two invitations that I've written, Father," she told him. "We are going to eavesdrop; we are going to prove who contrived the death of Talbot of Kidlington."

"I will have nothing to do with all your supposed killings. You expect me to eavesdrop? Preposterous, I refuse."

"What supposed killings?" Jacques asked, puzzled.

"We shall *be* there," Adelia told the priest. She cut off his protests. "Yes, you shall. We need an independent witness. God in Heaven, Father, a young man was put to death."

A rough figure with an even rougher voice had come up to them. "Get inside, you lot, and quick about it." Cross had his arms held wide to scoop the three of them toward the steps.

Glad to go, Father Paton skated off.

"*Can* he help us with Bertha's death?" Jacques asked.

"I'm not telling you again," Cross said. "The chief says inside, so get bloody inside."

Jacques obeyed. Adelia lingered.

"Come on, now, missis. 'S getting chilly." The mercenary took her arm, not unkindly. "See, you're shaking."

"I don't want to go in," she said. The convent walls would imprison her and the killer together again; she was being dragged back into a cage that held a monster with blood on its fangs.

"You ain't staying here all night." As he pulled her over the ice, Cross shouted over his shoulder at the wren hunters in the trees. "Time to go in, lads."

When they reached the steps, he had to haul Adelia up them like an executioner assisting a prisoner to the gallows.

Behind them, a crowd of men emerged from the trees of the far bank, shouting in triumph over a small cage twisted from withies in which fluttered a frightened wren. They were hooded, covered in snow, their black faces rendering them unrecognizable.

And if, whooping and capering with the rest, there was one more figure going in through the convent gates than had left them, nobody noticed it.

The convent carpenter had laid boards across the end rafters of the church's Saint Mary side chapel in order to facilitate the removal and replacement of struts that showed signs of rotting, creating a temporary and partial little loft in which the two people now hiding in it could listen but not

467

see. Adelia and Father Paton were, quite literally, eavesdroppers.

It had taken considerable urging to get the priest to accompany her into the rafters. He'd protested at the subterfuge, the risk, the indignity.

Adelia hadn't liked it, either. This wasn't her way of doing things, it was arbitrary, unscientific. Worse, the fear she felt at being once more in the abbey sapped her energy, leaving her with a deadening feeling of futility.

But coming in through the chapel's door, a draft had wavered the candles burning on the Virgin's altar, one of them lit by Emma for Talbot of Kidlington, and so she had bullied, shamed, and cajoled. "We have a duty to the dead, Father." It was the bedrock of her faith, as fundamental to her as the Athanasian Creed to Western liturgy, and perhaps the priest had recognized its virtue, for he had stopped arguing and climbed the ladder Jacques set for them.

Now Vespers had chimed, the faint chanting from the cloisters had stopped. The church was empty — ever since the mercenaries had proved troublesome, the nuns had transferred the vigil for their dead to their own chapel.

Somewhere a dog barked. Fitchet's mongrel, probably — a bristled terror at whose every approach Ward, not renowned for his courage, lay down and rolled over.

They were too far back in the loft to see anything below. Only a glow from the altar candles in the church proper reached them so that they could, at least, make out the wagon roof above them. It gave Adelia the impression that she and the priest were lying on the thwarts of an upended boat. Uncomfortably.

Fierce little beads that were the eyes of the bats hanging from the lathes overhead glared down at her.

A scamper nearby caused Father Paton to squeak. "I abhor rats."

"Be quiet," she told him.

"This is foolishness."

Perhaps it was, but they couldn't alter it now — Jacques had taken the ladder away, replacing it in the bell tower next door from whence it had come, perching himself in the shadows at the tower's top.

A latch clicked. The unoiled hinges of the chapel's side door protested with a screech. Somebody hissed at the noise. The door closed. Silence.

Warin. It would be the lawyer; Wolvercote wouldn't creep as this one crept.

Adelia felt a curious despair. It was one

thing to theorize about a man's guilt, another to have it confirmed. Somewhere below her stood a creature who'd betrayed the only relative he had, a boy in his care, a boy who'd trusted him and had been sent to his death.

A rasp of hinges again, this time accompanied by the stamp of boots. There was a vibration of energy.

"Did you send me this?" Wolvercote's voice. Furious. If Master Warin protested, the listeners did not hear him because Wolvercote continued without pause. "Yes you did, you whoreson, you puling pot of pus, you stinking spittle, you'll not tax me for more, you crapulous bit of crud. . . ."

The tirade, its wonderful alliteration unsuspected from such a source, was accompanied by slaps, presumably across Master Warin's face, that resounded against the walls like whip cracks — each one making Father Paton jump so that Adelia, lying beside him in the rafters, flinched in unison.

The lawyer was keeping his head, though it had to be buzzing. "Look, look, my lord. In the name of Christ, *look*." The onslaught stopped.

He's showing *his* letter.

Apart from giving the time and place of the suggested meeting, the message she'd written to each man had been short: *We are discovered.*

There was a long pause while Wolvercote — not a reading man — deciphered the note sent to Warin. The lawyer said quietly, "It's a trap. Somebody's here."

There were hurried, soft footfalls as Warin searched, the opening of cupboards — a thump of hassocks falling to the floor as they were dislodged. "Somebody's *here.*"

"*Who's* here? *What* trap?" Wolvercote was staying where he was, shouting after Warin as the little man went into the body of the church to search that, too. "Didn't *you* send me this?"

"What's up there?" Master Warin had come back. "We should look up there."

He's looking upward. The impression that the man's eyes could see through the boards tensed Adelia's muscles. Father Paton didn't move.

"Nobody's up there. How could anybody get up there? *What* trap?"

"My lord, somebody knows." Master Warin had calmed himself a little. "My lord, you shouldn't have hanged the knaves. It looked badly. I'd promised them money to leave the country."

So you *supplied the killers.*

"Of course I hanged the dogs." Wolvercote was still shouting. "Who knew if they would keep their mouths shut. God curse you, Warin, if this is a ploy for more payment. . . ."

"It is not, my lord, though Sweet Mary knows it was a great service I rendered you. . . ."

"Yes." Wolvercote's tone had become quieter, more considering. "I am beginning to wonder why."

"I told you, my lord. I would not have you wronged by one of my own family; when I heard what the boy intended . . ."

"And no benefit to you? Then why in hell did you come here? What brought you galloping to the abbey to see if he was dead?"

They were moving off into the nave of the church, their voices trailing into unintelligible exchanges of animosity and complaint.

After a long time, they came back, only footsteps giving an indication of their return. The door scraped open. Boots stamped through it as loudly as they had come.

Father Paton shifted, but Adelia clamped his arm. *Wait.* They won't want to be seen together. Wolvercote has left first.

Silence again. A quiet little man, the lawyer.

Now he was going. She waited until she heard the fall of the latch, then wriggled forward to peer over the boards.

The chapel was empty.

"Respectable men, a baron of the realm, ogres, ogres." Father Paton's horror was tinged with excitement. "The sheriff shall be told, I must write it down, yes, write it down. I am witness to conspiracy and murder. The sheriff will need a full affidavit. I am an important deponent, yes, I would not have believed . . . a baron of the realm."

He could hardly wait for Jacques to bring the ladder. Even as he descended it, he was questioning the messenger on what had been said in the church.

For a moment, Adelia lay where she was, immobile. It didn't matter what else had been said; two murderers condemned themselves out of their own mouths, as careless of the life they had conspired to take as of a piece of grass.

Oh, Emma.

She thought of the bolt buried in the young man's chest, stopping that most wonderful organ, the heart, from beating, the indifference of the bowman who'd loosed it into the infinite complexity of vein and muscle, as indifferent as the cousin who had ordered it to be loosed, as the lord who'd paid him to do it.

Emma, Emma.

Father Paton scuttled back to the warming room — he wanted to write out his deposition right away.

There was a bright, cold moon, no necessity for a lantern. As Jacques escorted her home, he told her what he'd managed to hear in the church. Mostly it had been repetition of the exchanges in the chapel. "By the time they left," he said, "they were deciding it was a trick played on them. Lord Wolvercote did, anyway, he suspects his mercenaries. Lawyer Warin was still atremble, I'll wager he leaves the country if he can."

They said good-bye at the foot of the guesthouse steps.

Unbelievably tired, Adelia dragged herself up, taking the last rise gingerly as she always did, now with the memory of an event that hadn't happened but in which, constantly, she watched a cradle tumble over the edge.

She stopped. The door was slightly open, and it was dark inside. Even if her little household had gone to sleep, a taper was always left burning for her — and the door was never left open.

She was reassured by Ward coming to

greet her, the energetic wag of his tail releasing more odor than usual. She went in.

The door was shut behind her. An arm encircled her chest, a hand clamped itself across her mouth. "Quietly now," somebody whispered. "Guess who."

She didn't need to guess. Frantically, she wriggled around in the imprisoning arms until she faced the man, the only man.

"You *bastard*," she said.

"True, to an extent," he said, picking her up. He chucked her onto the nearest bed and planted himself on top of her. "Ma and pa married eventually, I remember exactly, I was there."

There wasn't time to laugh — though, with his mouth clamped onto hers, she did.

Not dead — deliciously living, the smell of him so right, he was rightness, *everything* was right now that he was here. He moved her to the very soul and very, *very* much to her innards, which turned liquid at his touch. She'd been parched for too long.

Their bodies pumping like huge wings took them higher and higher on a flight into cataclysmic air and then folded into the long, pulsing drop to a truckle bed in a dark, cold room.

When the earth stopped rocking and settled, she wriggled from underneath him and sat up.

"I knew you were nearby," she said. "Somehow, I knew."

He grunted.

She was energized, as if he had been a marvelous infusion bringing her body back to life.

She wondered if there would be another baby, and the thought made her happy.

Her lover had relapsed into postcoital inertia. She jabbed a finger into his back. "Where's Allie? Where are Gyltha and Mansur?"

"I sent them to the kitchens, the servants are having a revel." He sighed. "I shouldn't have done that."

So that she could look at him, she got up and stumbled for the table, felt around, pinched some tinder out of its box, struck a flint, and lit a taper at its flame.

He was thin, oh, bless him, but beautiful. In trousers — now down around his hocks — like a peasant, his face smeared with what looked like tree bark.

"A wren hunter," she said, delighted. "You came in with the wren hunters. Has Henry come?"

"Had to get in somehow. Thank God it's Saint Stephen's Day, or I'd have had to climb the bloody wall."

"How did you know we'd be at God-stow?"

"With the river freezing? Where else would you be?"

He wasn't responding properly. "We could be dead," she pointed out. "We nearly were."

He sat up. "I was in the trees," he said, "watched you skating. Very graceful, a little shaky on the turns, perhaps . . . By the saints, that's a bonny baby, isn't she?"

Our baby, Adelia thought. *She's* our *bonny baby.*

She punched his shoulder, not altogether playfully. "Damn you, Rowley. I suffered, I thought you were dead."

"I knew that bit of the Thames," he said, "that's why I got off, belongs to Henry, part of Woodstock forest; there's a river keeper close by — I'd baptized his child for him. I made for his cottage, wasn't easy but I got there." He sat up, suddenly. "Now then . . . what's to do here?"

"Rowley, I *suffered.*"

"No need. The keeper took me to Oxford — we used snow shoes. Bloody place was teeming with rebels, every bastard that had fought for Stephen and suffered for it was in arms and flying Eleanor's standard or Young Henry's. We had to bypass the town and make for Wallingford instead. Always a royal stronghold, Wallingford. The Fitz-Counts held it for the empress during the war. I knew the king'd go there first." He wiped his forehead with the back of his hand. "Jesus save me, but it was hard going."

"Serve you right," she said. "Did you find the king? Is he here?"

"More that he found me, really. I was laid up at Wallingford with a rheum in the chest, I damn near died. What I needed was a doctor."

"I'm sorry I couldn't attend," she said tartly.

"Yes, well, at least I could keep an eye on the river from there. And sure enough, he came, and a fleet of boats with him." Rowley shook his head in wonder. "He was in Touraine, putting down Young Henry's rebellion, when he heard about Rosamund. God punish that boy, now he's joined with Louis of France against his own father. *Louis,* I ask you." Rowley's fists went to the sides of his head in disbelief. "We all knew he was an idiot, but who'd have dreamed the treacherous little whelp would go to his father's greatest enemy for aid?"

He leaned forward. "And Eleanor had urged him to do it. Do you know that? Our spies told us. Urged their son against

478

his father."

"I don't care," she told him. "I don't care what they do. What is happening *now?*"

But she couldn't shift him. He was still with Henry Plantagenet, who had captured two Touranian castles from the Young King's supporters before making tracks for England with a small army in the heaviest winter in years.

"How he did it I don't know. But here he comes, up the Thames, trailing boats full of men behind him. Did I tell you he was *rowing?* The barge crew weren't going fast enough for the bugger, and there he was, pulling at an oar like a pirate and swearing the sky black."

"Where is he now?"

"On his way." There was a pause. "He wants to see you."

"Does he?"

"Sent me to fetch you. Wants to know if it was Eleanor that did for Rosamund. I said you'd be able to tell him yea or nay."

"Great God," she said. "Is that why you've come?"

"I'd have come anyway. I was worried about leaving you . . . but I should've known you were safe enough." He cocked his head, sucking his teeth as if in admiration at her capacity for survival. "God kept you in His hand. I asked Him to.”

" 'Safe enough'?" It was a screech. “You left me to die in an open boat.” He had to hush her. She went on more quietly. " 'Safe enough'? We’ve been cooped up with killers, your daughter, all of us. There’s been murder done here, betrayal . . . weeks, *weeks* I’ve been afraid . . . for Allie, for all of us . . . weeks.” She scrubbed the tears off her cheeks with her fists.

“Ten days, it was,” he said gently. “I left you ten days ago.” He was on his feet, pulling up his trousers, adjusting his shirt. “Get dressed and we’ll go.”

“Go where?”

“To Henry. I said he wants to see you.”

“Without Allie? Without Gyltha and Mansur?”

“We can hardly take them with us; I’ve found a path through the snow, but it’ll be rough traveling, even on horses, and I only brought two.”

“No.”

“Yes.” It was a sigh. “I was afraid of this. I told the king. ‘She won’t come without the child,’ I said.” He made it sound like a whim.

She’d had enough. “Will you tell me? *Where is Henry?*”

“Oxford, at least that’s where he was

heading."

"Why isn't he here?"

"Look," he said, reasonably, "Godstow's a side issue. The important thing is Oxford. Henry's sending young Geoffrey Fitzroy up here with a small force, it shouldn't need more — Mansur says Wolvercote and Schwyz have few men. Henry's not arriving in person. . . ." She saw the flash of a grin. "I don't think our good king trusts himself to meet Eleanor face-to-face; he might run her through. Anyway, it's somewhat embarrassing to arrest one's own wife."

"When? When will this Geoffrey come?"

"Tomorrow. That's if I can get back to guide him and tell him the placements here — make sure he doesn't kill the wrong people."

He will do it, she thought. *He will track back through this dreadful countryside, disgruntled because I won't leave our daughter behind but assured that she and I will be safe enough. He is all maleness and bravery, like his damn king, and we understand each other not at all.*

Well, she thought, *he is what he is, and I love him.*

But a chill was growing; there was new strangeness; she'd thought it was the old Rowley back — and for a while, gloriously, it had been, but there was constraint. He

481

talked with the remembered insouciance yet didn't look at her. He'd put out a hand to wipe the tears from her face, then withdrawn it.

She said, because she was impelled to, "Do you love me?"

"Too much, God help me," he said. "Too much for my soul. I shouldn't have done it."

"Done what?"

"Almighty God forgive me. I promised, I swore an oath that if He kept you safe, I would abstain from you, I would not lead you to sin again. It was touching you that did it. I want you too much. Feeling you was . . . too much."

"What am I? Something to be given up for Lent?"

"In a way." His voice had become measured, a bishop's. "My dear, every Sunday I have to preach against fornication in one church or another, hearing my own exhortation mingling with God's whisper, 'You are a hypocrite, you lust for her, you are damned and she is damned.' "

"Much to be said for hypocrisy," she said dully. She began dragging on her clothes.

"You must see. I can't have you punished for my sin. I left you to God. I made a bargain with Him. 'While she is safe, Lord,

I am Your servant in all things.' I swore the oath in the king's presence, to seal it." He sighed. "And now look what I've gone and done."

She said, "I don't care if it is sin."

"I do," he said heavily. "I'd have married you, but no, you would keep your independence. So Henry had his bishop. But a bishop, don't you see? A keeper of other people's souls. His own, yours . . ."

Now he looked at her. "Adelia, it matters. I thought it would not, but it does. Beyond the panoply and the choirs — you wouldn't believe the singing that goes on — there is a still, small voice . . . nagging. Say you understand."

She didn't. In a world of hatred and killing, she did not understand a God who regarded love as a sin. Nor a man who obeyed that deity.

He was raising his hand as if about to make the sign of the cross over her. She hit it. "Don't you dare," she said. "Don't you dare bless me."

"All right." He began struggling into his clothes. "Listen to me, though. When Geoffrey attacks, *before* he attacks, you're to go to the cloister — he'll keep the fighting away from there. Take Allie and the others. I've told Walt to make sure you get there. . . .

'She's important to the king,' I said."

She didn't listen. She'd never been able to compete with Henry Plantagenet; for sure she wouldn't be able to outrival God. It was winter, after all. To an extent, for her now, it always would be.

Like a fishhook in the mind, something dragged her attention away from despair. She said, "You told Walt?"

"Mansur fetched him here while I was waiting. . . . Where have you been, by the way?"

"You told Walt," she said.

"And Oswald — they didn't know where Jacques was, nor Paton, but I told them to spread the word, I want all my men ready — they'll need to get to the gates and open them to Geoffrey. . . ."

"Dear Christ," she said.

Ward was snarling softly.

She almost tripped as she made for the door so that she slammed against it. She slid the bolt across, then put her ear to the wood and listened. They wouldn't have long, only the grace of God had allowed the two of them this long. "How were you going to get out?"

"Cross the gatekeeper's palm with silver. What is it?"

"Shssh."

The sound of boots running through the slush of the alley. "They're coming for you. Oh, God. Oh, God."

"Window," he said. He crossed the floor and jerked the shutters open so that moonlight lit the chamber.

Window, yes.

They dragged blankets off the bed and knotted them together. As they slung them out of the window, the assault on the door began. "Open. Open up." Ward hurled himself at it, barking.

Rowley tied the blanket rope round the mullion and heaved back on it to test it. "After you, mistress."

She was always to remember the polite quirk of his hand as at an invitation to dance. "I can't," she said. "They won't hurt me. It's you."

He glanced down and then back at her. "I *have* to go. I've got to guide them in."

"I know." The door was being assaulted; it wasn't a strong door, it would give any minute. "Do it, then," she hissed.

He grinned, took a falchion from his belt, and gave it to her. "See you tomorrow."

As he reached the parapet, she tried to undo the knot around the mullion and then, because it was too tight, began sawing at it with the blade, glancing out every other second. She saw him make for the nearest crenel and jump, cloak flying. It was deep snow, a soft enough landing for him. But could he get to the steps?

He had. As, behind her, the door splintered and a dreadful yelp came out of Ward's throat, she saw her man skidding across the ice like a boy.

She was thrown to one side. Schwyz roared, "There he is. Opposite bank. Loso. Johannes."

Two men leaped for the door. Another took Schwyz's place at the window, frantically winding a crossbow, his foot in its stirrup. He aimed, loosed. *"Ach, scheiss."* He looked at Schwyz. *"Nein."*

Adelia closed her eyes, then opened them. There was another step on the outside landing.

A giant figure bowed its head to get through the door and looked calmly around. "Perhaps it would be better if we relieved Mistress Adelia of her dagger."

She wouldn't have used it on a human being in any case. She handed it over, hilt first, to the Abbot of Eynsham, who had written the letters for Rosamund to copy and send to the queen, and then had her killed.

He thanked her, and she went down on her knees to attend to Ward, where he had crawled under one of the beds. As she felt the kicked and broken rib, he looked at her with self-pitying eyes. She patted him. "You'll live," she said. "Good dog. Stay here."

Politely, the abbot held her cloak for her while she put it on, then her hands were tied behind her back and a gag put in her mouth.

They took her to the gatekeeper's lodge.

There was nobody else about; the abbey had gone to bed. Even if she'd been able to shout for help, nobody at this end of the convent would have heard her — or come to her rescue if they had. Master and Mistress Bloat were not on her side. Lawyer Warin most definitely was not. There was no sign of Wolvercote's men, but they wouldn't have helped her, either.

The great gates were open, but all activity was centered in the lodge chamber that led off the porch, where Schwyz's men hurried to and fro.

They pushed Adelia inside. Fitchet was dead on the floor, his throat cut. Father Paton lay alongside him, coughing out some of his teeth.

She slid to kneel beside the priest. Beneath the bruises, his face showed indignation. "Kep' hi'n me," he said. "Too le'ers." He tried harder. "Took the lett-ers."

Men were fastening hoods and cloaks, collecting weapons into bundles, emptying Fitchet's food cupboard, and rounding up some frightened hens into a crate.

"Did our worthy gatekeeper possess such a thing as wine?" The abbot asked. "No? Tut, tut, how I *loathe* ale." He sat on a stool, watching the bustle, fingering the huge cross on his chest.

The two mercenaries who had chased after Rowley came in, panting. "He had horses."

"*Siech.* That ends it, then. We go." Schwyz took hold of the pinion round Adelia's hands and jerked her to her feet with an upward pull that nearly displaced her shoulders. He dragged her over to the abbot. "We don't need her, let me kill the whore."

"Schwyz, my dear, good Schwyz." Eynsham shook his great head. "It seems to have escaped your notice that at this moment, Mistress Adelia is the most valuable object in the convent, the king's desire for her company being such that he sends a bishop to collect her — whether for her sexual prowess or such information as she may possess is yet to be determined. She is our trump card, my dear, the Atalantean golden apple that we may have to throw behind us to delay pursuit. . . ." He reflected. "We might even appease the king by handing her back to him, should he catch up with us . . . yes . . . that is a possibility."

Schwyz had no time for this. "Do we take her or not?"

"We do."

"And the priest?"

"Well, there I fear we must be less forgiving. Master Paton's possession of the letters is unfortunate. He has evidence I would not wish king or queen to hear, even supposing he could voice it, which —"

"Christ's eyes, do I *finish* him?"

"You do."

"Nnnnnn." Adelia threw herself forward. Schwyz pulled her back.

"I know, I know." The abbot nodded. "These things are upsetting, but I have no wish to lose the queen's esteem, and I fear Father Paton could disabuse her of it. Did you provide him with my text on which dear Rosamund based her letters? Of course you did. What an enterprising little soul you are."

He was talking. He'd condemned the priest to death and he was talking, amused.

"Since I stand in high regard with our blessed Eleanor, it would be — what is the word? — *inconvenient* if she knew I was the goad that pricked her into further rebellion. In view of my desertion, she might tell Henry. As it is, she will be informed of a murderous intruder to the abbey, d'ye see, and that we, the good Schwyz and myself, are in brave pursuit to stop him before he reaches the king's lines. In fact, of course, we are leaving the lady to her inevitable fate; the snow has proved too much for us, the amiable Lord Wolvercote too little. . . . As Master Schwyz says of that gentleman in his rough way — he couldn't fight a sack of shit."

Schwyz had let go of her and was walking toward Father Paton.

Adelia closed her eyes. *God, I beg you.*

A whimper from Father Paton, a hot smell. A hush, as if even this company was awed by the passage of a soul to its maker.

Then somebody said something, somebody else laughed. Men began carrying bundles and crates out to the porch and down to the river.

The abbot's finger went under Adelia's chin and tilted her head.

"You interest me, madam, you always have. How does a foreign slut like yourself command the attention not only of a bishop but a king? And you, forgive me, without an apparent grace to bless yourself with."

Keeping her eyes closed, she jerked away from him, but he grasped her face and angled it back and forth. "Do you satisfy them both? At the same time? Are you a mistress of threesomes? Do you excel at *lit à trois?* Cock below and behind? Arsehole and *pudendum muliebre?* What my father in his elegant way used to call a bum-*and*-belly?"

There would be a lot of this before the end, she thought.

She looked straight into his eyes.

Great God, he's a virgin.

How she knew it in that extremity . . . but she knew it.

The face above hers diminished into an agonized, pleading vulnerability — *Don't know me, don't know me* — before it resumed the trompe l'oeil that was the Abbot of Eynsham.

Schwyz had been shouting at them both; now he came and hauled Adelia upright. "She better be no trouble," he said. "We got enough to carry."

"I am *sure* she won't be." The abbot smiled on Adelia. "We could send to the kitchen for the baby if you prefer and take it with us, though whether it would survive the journey . . ."

She shook her head.

Eynsham, still smiling, gestured toward

the door. "After you, mistress."

She went through it and down the ice steps like a lamb.

THIRTEEN

The moon had edged a little toward the west, so that two more cloaked mercenaries cast long, sharp, stunted shadows on the ice as they loaded a large sledge with the packages the others were bringing down. One of them picked up Adelia and slung her on top of the bundles, hurting her arms as she landed on them. Somebody else slung a tarpaulin over her, and she had to toss her head round until a fold fell back and she could see.

Go south, she thought. *Make them go south, Henry's there. Lord, make them go south.*

The abbot, Schwyz, and some of the other men were clustered around her, balancing against the sides of the sledge as they put on skates, intent, not talking.

They have *to go south — they don't know the king's attacking Oxford.*

Oh, but of course they did. They knew

everything — Rowley had inadvertently told them.

Lord, send them south.

The abbot made experimental pirouettes on the ice, admiring his shadow in the steel mirror of the river. "Yes, yes," he said. "One never forgets."

He paid no attention to Adelia — she was luggage now. He nodded at Schwyz, who nodded at his men. Two mercenaries picked up trails of harness leading from the sledge and heaved themselves into the straps. Somebody else mounted the sledge's running board behind Adelia and grasped the guiding struts.

The abbot looked up at the convent walls lowering above him. "Queen Eleanor, sweet broken reed, farewell. *Veni, vidi, vadi,*" then raised his eyes to the star-sprinkled sky. "Well, well, on to better things. Let us go."

"And quiet about it," Schwyz said.

The sledge hissed as it moved.

They headed north.

Adelia retched into her gag. Nothing to stop him from killing her now.

For a while, she was so afraid that she could hardly see. He was going to kill her. *Had* to kill her.

Appalling sadness overtook her. Images of Allie missing her, growing up without her,

494

small, needy. *I'll die loving you. Know it, little one, I never stopped loving you.*

Then the guilt. *My fault, darling; a better mother would have passed it by, let them all slaughter one another — no matter, as long as you and I weren't wrenched apart. My fault, my grievous fault.*

On and on, grief and fear, fear and grief, as the untidy, white-edged banks slid by and the sledge whispered and grated and the men pulling it grunted with effort, their breath puffing wisps of smoke into the moonlight, taking her further and further into hell.

Discomfort forced itself on her attention — the bundle beneath her had spears in it. Also, the gag tasted abominable and her arms and wrists hurt.

Suddenly irritable, she shifted, sat up, and began to take notice.

Two mercenaries were pulling the sledge. Another was behind. Four skated on either side, Schwyz and the abbot ahead. Nine in all. None of them her friend Cross — she hadn't been able to make out the faces of the two mercenaries packing the sledge, but both were thinner than Cross.

No help, then. Wherever they were headed, Schwyz was taking only his most trusted soldiers; he'd abandoned the others.

Where are *we going? The Midlands?* There was still smoldering discontent against Henry Plantagenet in the Midlands.

Adelia shifted and began investigating the sacking with her wrists, tracing the spears in it along the shafts to their blades. *There.*

She pressed down and felt a point prick into her right palm. She began trying to rub the rope against the side of the blade but kept missing it and encountering the spear point instead so that it went uselessly into the rope's fibers and out again, an exercise that might eventually unpick them if she had a week or two to spare . . .

It was something to do, though, to fight off the inertia of despair. Of course Eynsham would have her killed. Her use to him as a bargaining counter would last only until he could be sure Henry wasn't pursuing him — and the chance of that receded with every mile they went north. Most of all, he would kill her because she'd seen the worm wriggling in that brilliant, many-faceted, empty carapace, and he had seen her see it.

Her arms were becoming tired. . . .

Tears still wet on her face, Adelia dozed.

It was heavy going for the men pulling the sledge, and even for those merely skating. Afraid of pursuit, they hadn't lit torches, and though the moon was bright, the ice gave a deceptive, smooth sheen to branches and other detritus that had been frozen into it so that the mercenaries fell frequently or had to make detours round obstructions — occasionally heaving the sledge over them.

In her sleep, Adelia was vaguely aware of being rolled around during the portages and of muffled swearing, aware, too, that men were taking rests on the sledge, crawling under the tarpaulin with her to get their strength back before giving up their place to the next. There was nothing sexual in it — they were too exhausted — and she refused to wake up. Sleep was oblivion. . . .

Another passenger came aboard, exhaling with the relief at being off the ice. Fingers fumbled at the back of her head and undid the gag. "No need for this now, mistress. Nor this." Gently, somebody pushed her forward and a knife sawed at the rope round her wrists. "There. More comfy?"

There was a waft of sweet, familiar scent. Licking her mouth, Adelia flexed her shoulders and hands. They hurt. They were still traveling, and it was still very cold, but the stars had dulled a little; the moon shone through a light veil of mist.

"You didn't need to kill Bertha," she said.

There was a pause.

"I rather think I did," Jacques said reasonably. "Her nose would have betrayed me sooner or later. I'm afraid the poor soul literally sniffed me out."

Yes. Yes, she had.

Bertha crawling forward in the cowshed, snuffling, using the keenest sense she had to try and describe the old woman in the forest who'd given her the mushrooms for Rosamund.

"Smelled purty . . . like you."

It wasn't me, Bertha. It was the man standing behind me. "A him. Not a her."

The girl had been sniffing the messenger's scent — the perfume that was a feature of him even when he dressed up as an old woman picking mushrooms.

"Do you mind?" he asked now. It was solicitous, hoping she wasn't upset. "She wasn't much of a loss, really, was she?"

Adelia kept her eyes on the two mercenaries dragging the sledge.

Jacques tucked the tarpaulin round her and sat sideways to peer into her face, reasonable, explaining, no longer the wide-eyed young man with big ears, much older, at ease. She supposed that's what he was, a shape-changer; he could be what he wanted when circumstances demanded.

He'd taken Allie in her cradle and put her on the step.

"Ordinarily, you see, there is no need for what I call auxiliary action, as there was in Bertha's case," he said. "Usually, one fulfills one's contract and moves on. All very tidy. But this particular employment has been complicated — interesting, I don't deny, but complicated." He sighed. "Snowed up in a convent, not only with one's employer but, as it turns out, a *witness* is not an experience one wants repeated."

A killer. *The* killer.

"Yes, I see," Adelia said.

After all, she'd lived with revulsion ever since she'd become aware that he'd poisoned Rosamund. To use him in the necessary business of getting Wolvercote and Warin to convict themselves in the church had been an exercise in terror, but she'd been unable to think of any other stratagem to placate him. By then she'd sniffed the mind that permeated the abbey with a greater menace than Wolvercote because it was free of limitation, a happy mind. Kill this one, spare that, remain guiltless.

It had been necessary to amuse it, like a wriggling mouse enthralling the cat. To gain time, she'd let it watch her play at solving the one murder of which it was innocent. To keep the cat's teeth out of the neck of a mouse that asked questions.

She asked, "Did Eynsham order you to kill her?"

"Bertha? Lord, no." He was indignant. "I do have initiative, you know. Mind you" — an elbow nudged Adelia's ribs — "he'll have to pay for her. She'll go on his account."

"His account," she said, nodding.

"Indeed. I am not the abbot's vassal, mistress. I really must make that clear; I am independent; I travel Christendom providing a service — not everybody approves of it, I know, but it is nevertheless a service."

"An assassin."

He considered. "I suppose so. I prefer to think of it as a profession like any other. Let's face it, Doctor, your own business is termed witchcraft by those who don't understand it, but we are both professionals pursuing a trade that neither of us can lay public claim to. We both deal in life and death." But she'd touched his pride. "How did I give myself away? I did try to warn you against too much curiosity."

His visits to Bertha, his constant proximity, the indefinable sense of menace that lurked in the cowshed when he was there. The scent that Bertha had recognized. A freedom to roam the abbey, unnoticed, that no one else possessed. In the end, he was the only one it could have been.

"The Christmas feast," she said.

She'd known for sure then. In the capering, warty old woman of Noah's ark, she'd recognized a grotesque of the crone that Bertha had seen in the forest.

"Ah," he said. "I really should avoid dressing up, shouldn't I? I have a weakness for it, I'm afraid."

She asked, "When did Eynsham hire you to kill Rosamund?"

"Oh, ages ago," he said. "I'd only recently come to England to pick up commissions. Well, I'll tell you when it was; I'd just become the bishop's messenger — in my line of work, it's always useful to have a reason to travel the countryside. Incidentally, mistress, I hope I gave the bishop good service. . . ." He was in earnest. "I like to think I'm an excellent servant, no matter what the work."

Yes, excellent. When Rowley had crept into the abbey and alerted his men, it hadn't occurred to him that his messenger should not be informed of the coming attack along with the rest — not the irritating, willing Jacques, one of his own people.

"In fact, I shall miss working for Saint Albans," he was saying now, "but as soon as Walt told me the king was coming, I had to inform Eynsham. I couldn't let Master Abbot be taken, could I? He owes me money."

"Is that how it goes?" she asked. "The word is spread? Assassin for hire?"

"Virtually, yes. I haven't lacked employment so far. The contractor never likes to reveal himself, of course, but do you know how I found out this one was our abbot?"

The joy of it raised his voice, launching an owl off its tree and making Schwyz, up ahead, turn and swear at him. "Do you know how I recognized him? Guess."

She shook her head.

"His boots. Master Abbot wears exceptionally fine boots, as I do. Oh, yes, and he addressed his servant as 'my son,' and I said to myself, *By the saints, here is a churchman, a rich churchman.* All I had to do was ask around Oxford's best bootmakers. The problem, you see, is to get the other half of the fee, isn't it?" He was sharing their occupational troubles. "So much as down payment, so much when the job's done. They never like to pay the second installment, don't you find that?"

She didn't say anything.

"Well, I do. Getting the other half of the fee is why I've had to attach myself to my lord Eynsham like fish glue. Actually, in this instance, it isn't his fault; circumstances have been against him: the retreat from

Wormhold, the snow . . . but apparently we're calling in at his abbey on the way north — that's where he keeps the gold, in his abbey."

"He'll kill you," she said. It was an observation to keep him talking; she didn't mind one way or the other. "He'll get Schwyz to cut your throat."

"*Aren't* they an interesting couple? *Doesn't* Schwyz adore him? They met in the Alps, apparently. I have wondered whether they were . . . well, *you* know . . . but I think not, don't you? I'd welcome your medical opinion. . . ."

One of the mercenaries in harness was slowing down, wheeling his arm for the messenger to take his place.

The voice in Adelia's ear became a confidential whisper, changing from a gossip's to an assassin's. "Don't worry for me, mistress. Our abbot has too many enemies that need to be silenced *in* silence. Schwyz leaves a butcher's trail behind. I don't. No, no, my services will always be in demand. Worry for yourself."

He threw back the tarpaulin in order to get off the sledge.

"Will it be you who kills me, Jacques?" she asked.

"I do hope not, mistress," he said politely.

"That would be a shame."

And he was gone, refusing to take his place in the harness. "My good fellow, I am not an ox."

Not human, either, she thought, a *lusus naturae,* a tool, no more culpable for what it did than an artifact, as blameless as a weapon stuck on a wall and admired by the owner for its beautiful functionality.

The lingering trail of his perfume was obliterated by a smell of sweat and damp dirt from the next man who crawled under the tarpaulin to fall asleep and snore.

The abbot had taken position on the step behind her, but instead of helping to propel the sledge along, he became a passenger, his weight slowing the men pulling it to a stumping crawl that threatened their balance. They were complaining. At an order from Schwyz, they removed their skates and, to give them better purchase, continued in their boots.

Which, Adelia saw, were splashing. The sledge had begun to send up spray as it traveled. There were no stars now, and the vague moon had an even more vague penumbra. Schwyz had lit a torch and was holding it high as he skated.

It was thawing.

From over her head came a fruity boom:

"I don't wish to complain, my dear Schwyz, but any more of this and we'll be marching on the river bottom. How much further?"

"Not far now."

Not far to where? Having been asleep and not knowing for how long, she couldn't estimate how far they'd come. The banks were still their featureless, untidy conglomeration of reed and snow.

It was even colder now; the chill of increasing damp had something to do with it, but so had fear. Eynsham would be reassured by their unpursued and uninterrupted passage up the river. Once he was in safe territory, he could rid himself of the burden he'd carried to it.

"Up ahead," Schwyz called.

There was nothing up ahead except a dim twinkle in the eastern sky like a lone star bright enough to penetrate the mist that hid the others. A castle showing only one light? A turret?

Now they were approaching a landing stage, white edged and familiar.

Then she knew.

Rosamund had been waiting for her.

Adelia had remembered Wormhold as a place of jagged, shocking flashes of color where men and women walked and talked in madness.

Now, through the dawn mist, the tower returned to what it was — a mausoleum. Architectural innuendo had gone. And the maze, for those who dragged the sledge through slush into it, was merely a straight and dreary tunnel of gray bushes leading to a monument like a giant's tombstone against a drearier sky.

The door above its steps stood open, sagging now. The unlit bonfire remained untouched in the hall where a mound of broken furniture, like the walls, shone with gathering damp in Schwyz's torchlight.

As they went in, a scuttle from escaping rats accentuated the hall's silence, as did the abbot's attempt to raise the housekeeper. "Dakers. Where are you, little dear? 'Tis your old friend come to call. Robert of Eynsham."

He turned to Schwyz as the echo faded. "She doesn't know it was me as had her locked up, does she?"

Schwyz shook his head. "We fooled her, Rob."

"Good, then I'm still her ally. Where *is* the old crow? We need our dinner. *Dakers.*"

Schwyz said, "We can't stay long, Rob. That bastard'll be after us."

"My dear, stop attributing the powers of

Darkness to him, we've outmaneuvered the bugger." He grimaced. "I suppose I'd better go up and search for my letters. If our Fair Rosamund kept one, she might have kept others. I *told* the fat bitch to burn them, but did she? Women are *so* unreliable." He pointed at the bonfire. "Get that alight when the time comes. Some food first, I think, a nap, and then, when our amiable king arrives, we'll be long gone, leaving a nice warm fire to greet him. *Dakers.*"

He must know where she is, Adelia thought. The only life here is in the top room with the dead.

"Up you go, then." Schwyz turned away to give orders to his men, and then turned back. "What do you want done with the trollop?"

"*This* trollop?" The abbot looked down at Adelia. "We'll hang on to her until the last minute, I think, just in case. She can come up and help me look for the letters."

"Why? She'll be better down here." Schwyz was jealous.

The abbot was patient with him. "Because I didn't see any letters lying around when we were here last, but little Mistress Big Eyes had one, hadn't you, my dear? If she found one, she can find the others. Bind her hands, if you like, but in front this time

507

and not too tight; she's looking wan."

Adelia's hands were pinioned again — not gently, either.

"Up, up." The abbot pointed her toward the stairs. "Up, up, up." To the mercenary, he said, "Tell the men to put their minds to my dinner. And Schwyz . . ." The tone had changed.

"What?"

"Set a damn good watch on that river."

He's frightened, Adelia thought suddenly. *He, too, credits Henry with supernatural powers. Oh, dear God, let him be right.*

Going up the tiny, wedge-shaped, slippery, winding steps without the balancing use of hands was not easy, but Adelia did better than the abbot, who was grunting with effort before they reached the second landing. That was the stage where the tower cut them off from the noise at its base, imposing a silence in which the echo of their footsteps troubled the ears as if they disobeyed an ordinance from the dead. *Go back. This is a tomb.*

Light that was hardly light at all came, sluggish, through the arrow slits onto the same broken mess that had littered the landings when she'd climbed up here with Rowley. Nobody had swept it away, nobody ever would.

Up and up, past Rosamund's apartments, empty of their carpets and gold ornaments now, looted by mercenaries, maybe even the Aquitanians, while Eleanor had kept her vigil over a corpse. Much good it had done them; loot and looters had gone to the bottom of the Thames.

They were getting close to the top now.

I don't want to go in there. Why doesn't it stop? It's impossible I should die here. Why doesn't somebody stop this?

The last landing, the door a crack open but with its ornate key in the lock.

Adelia stood back. "I'm not going in."

Gripping her shoulder, the abbot pushed her in front of him. "Dakers, my dame. Here's the Abbot of Eynsham, your old friend, come to pay his respects to your mistress."

A smell like a blast of wind teetered him on the threshold.

The room was furnished as Adelia had last seen it. No looting here — there hadn't been time.

Rosamund no longer sat at the writing table, but something lay on the bed with the frail curtains framing it and a cloak covering its upper half.

There was no sign of Dakers, but, if she had wanted to preserve her mistress still, she had made the mistake of closing the windows and lighting funerary candles.

"Dear God." With a handkerchief to his nose, the abbot hurried around the room, blowing out candles and opening the windows. "Dear God, the whore *stinks.* Dear God."

Moist, gray air refreshed the chamber slightly.

Eynsham came back to the bed, his eyes fascinated.

"Leave her," Adelia advised him.

He whipped the cloak off the body and let it fall to the floor. *"Aach."*

Her lovely hair fanned out from the decomposing face onto a pillow, with another pillow propping her crown near the top of her head. The crossed hands on her breast were mercifully hidden by a prayer book. Feet bulged wetly out of the tiny gold slippers that peeped from under the graceful, carefully arranged folds of a gown as blue as a spring sky. Patches of ooze were staining its silk.

"My, my," said the abbot, softly. *"Sic transit Rosa Mundi.* So the rose of all the world rots like any other . . . Rosamund the Foul . . ."

"Don't you dare," Adelia shouted at him. If she'd had her hands free, she'd have hit

him. "Don't you *dare* mock her. You brought her to this, and, by God, this is what you'll come to — your soul with it."

"Oof." He stepped back like a child faced by a furious parent. "Well, it's a horror . . . admit it's a horror."

"I don't care. You treat her with respect."

For a moment he was wrong-footed by his own lapse in taste. Tentatively, standing well back from the bed, his hand traced a blessing in the air toward it. *"Requiescat in pace."* After a moment, he said, "What *is* that white stuff growing out of her face?"

"Grave wax," Adelia told him. Actually, it was very interesting; she'd not seen it on a human flesh before, only on that of a sow at the death farm.

For a moment she was a mistress in the art of death again, aware only of the phenomenon in front of her, vaguely irritated that lack of time and means were preventing her from examining it.

It's because she was fat, she thought. The sow in Salerno had been fat, and Gordinus had kept it in an airtight tin chest away from flies. *"You see, my child? Bereft of insects, this white grease — I call it* corpus adipatus*— will accrete on plumper areas, cheeks, breasts, buttocks, et cetera, and hold back putrefaction, yes, actually delay it. Though*

511

whether it causes the delay or the delay causes it is yet to be determined."

Bless him, Gordinus had called it a marvel, which it was, and *damn it* that she was seeing it manifest on a human corpse only now.

It was especially interesting that the room's new warmth was, to judge from what was seeping through Rosamund's gown, bringing on putrefaction at the selfsame time. That couldn't be caused by flies — could it? — there were none at this time of year . . . blast it, if her hands were free, she could find out what was breeding under the material. . . .

"Oh, what?" she asked, crossly. The abbot was pulling at her.

"Where does she keep the letters?"

"What letters?" This opportunity to advance knowledge might never come again. If it wasn't flies . . .

He swung her round to face him. "Let me explain the position to you, my dear. In all this I have only been pursuing my Christian duty to bring down a king who had the good Saint Thomas murdered on the steps of his own cathedral. I intended a civil war that our gracious queen would win. Since that outcome now seems unlikely, I need to retrieve my position because, if Henry finds my letters, Henry will send them to the

Pope. And will the Holy Father sanction what I have done to punish the wicked? Will he say, 'Well done, thou good and faithful Robert of Eynsham, you have advanced our great cause'? He will not. He must pretend outrage, because a worthless whore was poisoned in the process. He will wash his Pilate's hands. Will there be oak leaves? Reward? Ah, no."

He stopped savoring the sound of his own voice. "Find those letters for me, mistress, or when Henry comes he will discover in the ashes of his bordello the bones of not just one of his harlots but two." He was diverted by a happy thought. "Together, in each other's arms, perhaps. Yes, perhaps . . ."

He mustn't see that she was afraid; he *mustn't* see that she was afraid. "In that case, the letters will be burned, too," she said.

"Not if the bitch kept them in a metal box. Where are they? You had one, mistress, and were quick enough to show it around. *Where did she keep the letters?*"

"On the table, I took it from the table."

"If she kept one, she kept more." He shouted for the housekeeper again. "*Dakers.* She'll know. Where is the hellhag?"

And then Adelia knew where Dakers was.

All the visits he'd made to this room, and he'd never known he was observed from a garderobe with a spy hole. He didn't know now.

Eynsham was examining the table, sweeping its writing implements aside, sending the ancient bowl in which Rosamund had kept sweetmeats onto the floor, where it broke. He bent to look under the table. There was a grunt of satisfaction. He came up holding a crumpled piece of vellum. "Is this all there was?"

"How could I know?" It was the letter Rosamund had been writing to the queen, that Eleanor in her fury had thrown to the floor. Adelia had given the abbot's template to poor Father Paton and, if she died for it, she wasn't going to tell this man that there were others hidden in a box stool only inches from his right boot.

Let him doubt, let there be a worm of worry for as long as he lives.

Great God, he's reading it.

The abbot had lumbered to the open window and was holding the parchment to the light. "Such an appalling hand the trollop had," he said. "Still, it's amazing she could write at all."

And let Dakers doubt *him.* No wonder the housekeeper had laughed as they were taken to the boats that night; she'd seen Eynsham, who had always been Rosamund's friend and, therefore, would be a friend to her.

If she was listening now, if she could be got to switch sides . . .

Adelia raised her voice. "Why did you make Rosamund write letters to Eleanor?"

The abbot lowered the parchment, partly exasperated, partly amused. "Listen to the creature. Why does she ask a question when her brain cannot possibly encompass the answer? What use to tell you? How can you even approach in understanding the exigencies that we, God's agents, are put to in order to keep His world on its course, the descent we must make into the scum, the instruments we must use — harlots like that one on the bed, cutthroats, all the sweepings of the cesspit, to achieve a sacred aim."

He was telling her anyway. A wordy man. A man needing the reassurance of his own voice and, even more, the sanctification of what he had done.

And still hopeful. It surprised her. That he was having to abandon his great game as a lost cause and desert his championship of Eleanor was stimulating him, as if certain he could retrieve the situation with charm, tactics, a murder here or there, using the false urbanity, his common-man-with-learning, all the air in the balloon that had bounced him into the halls of popes and royalty. . . .

A mountebank, really, Adelia thought.

Also a virgin. Mansur had seen it, told her, but Mansur, with the superiority of a man who could hold an erection, had discounted the agony of supposed failure turned to malevolence. Another churchman might bless a condition that ensured his chastity, but not this one; he wanted, lusted after, that most natural and commonplace gift that he was denied.

Perhaps he was making the world pay for it, meddling with brilliance in high politics, pushing men and women round his chess board, discarding this one, moving that one, compensating himself for the appalling curiosity that kept him outside their Garden of Eden as he jumped up and down in an effort to see inside it.

"To stimulate war, my dear," he was saying. "Can you understand that? Of course you can't — you are the clay from which you were made and the clay to which you will return. A war to cleanse the land of a barbarous and unclean king. To avenge poor Becket. To return England to God's writ."

"Rosamund's letters would do all that?" she asked.

He looked up. "Yes, as a matter of fact. A wronged and vengeful woman, and believe me, nobody is more vengeful than our gracious Eleanor, will escape any bonds, climb any mountains, cross all oceans to wreak havoc on the wrongdoer. And thus she did."

"Then why did you have Rosamund poisoned?"

"Who says I did?" Very sharp.

"Your assassin."

"The merry Jacques has been chattering, has he? I must set Schwyz onto that young man."

"People will think the queen did it."

"The king does, as was intended," he said vaguely. "Barbarians, my dear, are easily manipulated." He turned back to the letter and continued to read. "Excellent, oh excellent," he said. "I'd forgotten . . . To the *'supposed Queen of England . . . from the true and very Queen of this country, Rosamund the Fair.'* What I had to endure to persuade that tedious wench to this . . . Robert, Robert, such a subtle fellow you are. . . ."

A draft twitched at Adelia's cloak. The hanging behind Rosamund's bed had lifted. As air came up the corbel of the hidden garderobe and into the room, it brought a different, a commoner stench to counter that of the poor corpse on the bed. It was cut off as the hanging dropped back.

Adelia walked across to the window. The

abbot was still holding the letter to the light, reading it. She took up a position where, if he looked up, he would see her and not the figure creeping down the side of the bed. It had no knife in its hand, but it was still death — this time, its own.

Dakers was dying; Adelia had seen that yellowish skin and receded eyes too often not to know what they meant. The fact that the woman was walking at all was a miracle, but she was. And silently.

Help me, Adelia willed her. *Do something.* Without moving, she used her eyes in appeal. *Help me.*

But Dakers didn't look at her, nor at the abbot. All her energy was bent on reaching the staircase.

Adelia watched the woman slip between the partially open door and its frame without touching either and disappear. She felt a tearing resentment. *You could have hit him with something.*

The abbot had sat himself in Rosamund's chair as he read, still muttering bits of the letter out loud. " '. . . *and I did please the king in bed as you never did, so he told me . . .*' I'll wager you did, girl. Sucking and licking, I'll wager you did. '. . . *he did moan with delight . . .*' I'll wager he did, you filthy trollop. . . ."

518

He's exciting himself with his own words.

As Adelia thought it, he glanced up — into her eyes. His face gorged. "What are you looking at?"

"Nothing," she told him. "I am looking at you and seeing nothing."

Schwyz was calling from the stairs, but his voice was drowned in Eynsham's scream: "You judge *me? You,* a whore . . . judge *me?"*

He got up, a gigantic wave rising, and engulfed her. He clutched her to his chest and carried her so that her feet trailed between his knees. Blinded, she thought he was going to drop her out of the window, but he turned her round, holding her high by the scruff of the neck and her belt. For a second, she glimpsed the bed, heard the grunt as she was thrown down onto what lay on it.

As Adelia's body landed on the corpse, its belly expelled its gases with a whistle.

The abbot was screaming. "Kiss her. Kiss, kiss, kiss . . . suck, lick, you bitches." He pushed her face into Rosamund's. He was twisting Adelia's head like a piece of fruit, pressing it down into the grease. "Sniff, suck, lick . . ."

She was suffocating in decomposing flesh. "Rob. Rob."

The pressure on her head lessened slightly, and she managed to turn her smeared face sideways and breathe.

"Rob. *Rob.* There's a horse in the stable."

It stopped. It had stopped.

"No rider," Schwyz said. "Can't find a rider, but there's somebody here."

"What sort of horse?"

"Destrier. A good one."

"Is it his? He can't be here. Jesus save us, is he *here?*"

The slam of the door cut off their voices.

Adelia rolled off the bed and groped her way across the floor to one of the windows, her tied hands searching outside the sill for its remnant of snow. She found some and shoved it into her mouth. Another window, more snow into the mouth, scrubbing her teeth with it, spitting. More, for the face, nostrils, eyes, hair.

She went from window to window. There wasn't enough snow in the world, not enough clean, numbing ice. . . .

Drenched, shaking, she slumped into Rosamund's chair, and with her pinioned hands still scrubbing at her neck, she laid her head on the table and gave herself up to heaving, gasping sobs. Uninhibited, like a baby, she wept for herself, for Rosamund, Eleanor, Emma, Allie, all women everywhere and what was done to them.

"What are you bawling for?" a male voice said, aggrieved. "You think that's bad? Try spending time cooped up in a shithole with Dakers for company."

A knife ripped the rope away from round her hands. A handkerchief was pushed against her cheek. It smelled of horse liniment. It smelled beautiful.

With infinite care, she turned her head so that her cheek rested on the handkerchief and she could squint at him.

"Have you been in there all the time?" she asked.

"All the time," the king told her.

Still with her head on the table, she watched him walk over to the bed, pick up his cloak, and replace it carefully over the corpse. He went to the door to try its latch. It didn't move. He bent down to peer through the keyhole.

"Locked," he said, as if it was a comfort.

The ruler of an empire that stretched from the border of Scotland to the Pyrenees was in worn hunting leathers — she'd never seen him in anything else; few people did. He walked with the rolling bandiness of a man who spent more time in the saddle than out of it. Not tall, not handsome, nothing to distinguish him except an energy that drew the eye. When Henry Plantagenet was in the room, nobody looked anywhere else.

Deeper lines ran from his nose to the corners of his mouth than had when she'd last seen him, there was a new dullness in his eyes, and his red hair was dimmer; something had gone out of him and not been replaced.

Relief brought a manic tendency to giggle. Adelia began rubbing her wrists. "Where are your men, my lord?"

"Ah, well there . . ." Grimacing, he came back from the door and edged round the table to peer cautiously out. "They're on their way, only a few, mind, but picked men, fine men. I had a look at the situation in Oxford and left young Geoffrey to take it before he moves on to Godstow."

"But . . . did Rowley find you? You know the queen is at Godstow?"

"That's why Geoffrey'll take it next," he said irritably. "He won't have any trouble in either place. The rebels, God rot 'em, I'll eat them alive, were practically running up the white flag at Oxford already, so . . ."

"My daughter's at Godstow," she said. "My people . . ."

"I know, Rowley told me. Geoffrey knows, I told *him*. Stop wittering. I've seen snowmen with more defensive acumen than

Wolvercote. Leave it to young Geoffrey."

She supposed she'd have to.

He glanced round. "How is little Rowley-Powley, anyway? Got a tooth yet? Showing a flair for medicine?"

"She's well." He could always melt her. But it would be nice to get out of here. "These picked men of yours . . ." she said. This was Rowley all over again. Why didn't they *ever* bring massed troops?

"They're on their way," he said, "but I fear I outstripped them." He turned back to the window. "They'd told me she still wasn't buried, you see. My lads are bringing a coffin with them. Buggers couldn't keep up. "

They wouldn't have; he must have ridden like a fiend, melting the snow in front of him, to say good-bye, to mend the indecency inflicted on his woman.

"Hadn't long arrived before you turned up," he said. "Heard you coming up the stairs, so Dakers and I beat a retreat. First rule when one's outnumbered — learn the enemy's strength."

And learn that Rosamund, in her stupidity and ambition, had betrayed him. Like his wife, like his eldest son.

Adelia felt an awful pity. "The letters, my lord . . . I'm so sorry."

"Don't mention it." He wasn't being

polite; she mustn't refer to it again. Since he'd covered the corpse, he hadn't looked at it.

"So here we are," he said. Still cautious, he leaned out. "They're not keeping much of a watch, I must say. There's only a couple of men patrolling the courtyard — what in hell are the rest doing?"

"They're going to fire the tower," she told him, "and us in it."

"If they're using the wood in the hall, they'll have a job. Wouldn't light pussy." He leaned farther out of the window and sniffed. "They're in the kitchen, that's where they are . . . something's cooking. Hell's bollocks, the incompetent bastards are taking the time to eat." He loathed inefficiency, even in his enemies.

"I don't blame them." She was hungry, she was *ravenous*. A magic king had skewed this death chamber into something bearable. Without sympathy, without concession to her as a woman, by treating her as a comrade, he had restored her. "Have you got any food on you?"

He struck his forehead with the heel of his hand. "Well, there, and I left the festive meats behind. No, I haven't. At least, I don't think so. . . ." He had a pocket inside his jacket and he emptied its contents onto the table with one hand, his eyes still on the courtyard.

There was string, a bradawl, some withered acorns, needle and twine in a surprisingly feminine sewing case, a slate book and chalk, and a small square of cheese, all of them covered in oats for his horse.

Adelia picked out the cheese and wiped it. It was like chewing resin.

Now that she was more composed, events were connecting to one another. This king, this violent king, this man who, intentionally or not, had set on the knights that stirred Archbishop Becket's brains onto the floor of his cathedral, had sat quietly behind a hanging and listened, without sound, without moving, to treachery of extreme magnitude. And he'd been armed.

"Why didn't you come out and kill him?" she asked, not because she wished he had but because she truly wanted to know how he'd restrained himself from it.

"Who? Eynsham? Friend to the Pope? Legate *maleficus?* Thank you, he'll die, but not at my hand. I've learned my lesson."

He'd given Canterbury to Becket out of trust, because he loved him — and from that day his reforms had been opposed at every turn. The murder of the Jew-hating, venomous, now-sainted archbishop had set all Christendom against him. He'd done penance for it everywhere, allowing the monks of Canterbury to whip him in public, only just preventing his country from being placed under the Pope's interdict banning marriage, baptism, burial of the dead. . . .

Yes, he could control his anger now. Eleanor, Young Henry, even Eynsham, were safe from execution.

Adelia thought how strange it was that, locked in a chamber with a man as helpless as herself, at the top of a tower that any minute could be a burning chimney, she should be at ease.

He wasn't, though; he was hammering the mullion. "Where are they, in God's name? Jesus, if I can get here fast, why can't they?"

Because you outstripped them, Adelia thought. *In your impatience, you outstrip everybody, your wife, your son, Becket, and expect them to love you. They are people of our time and you are not; you see beyond the boundaries they set; you see me for what I am and use me for your advantage; you see Jews, women, even heretics, as human beings and use them for your advantage; you envisage justice, toleration, unattainable things. Of course nobody keeps up with you.*

Oddly enough, the one mind she could equate with his was Mother Edyve's. The world believed that what was now was permanent, God had willed it, there could be no alteration without offending Him.

Only a very old woman and this turbulent man had the sacrilegious impudence to question the status quo and believe that things could and should be changed for the betterment of all people.

"Come on, then," he said, "we've got time. Tell me. You're my investigator — what did you find out?"

"You don't pay me for being your investigator." She might as well point this out while she had the advantage.

"Don't I? I thought I did. Take it up with the Exchequer. Get on, get on." His stubby fingers drummed on the window sill. "Tell me."

So she told him, from the beginning.

He wasn't interested in the death of Talbot of Kidlington. "Silly bugger. I suppose it was the cousin, was it? Never trust the man who handles your money . . . Wolvercote? Vicious, that family. All rebels. My mother hanged the father from Godstow Bridge, and I'll do the same for the son. Go on, go on, get to the bits that *matter*."

He meant Rosamund's death, but it all mattered to Adelia, and she wasn't going to let him off any of it. She'd been clever, she'd been brave, it had cost too many lives; he was going to know everything. After all, he was getting it free.

She plowed on, occasionally nibbling at the cheese. Drops from melting icicles splashed on the sill. The king watched the courtyard. The body of the woman who'd begun it all lay on her bed and rotted.

He interrupted. "Who's that . . . *Saints' bollocks, he's stealing my horse.* I'll rip him, I'll mince his tripes, I'll . . ."

Adelia got up to see who was stealing the king's destrier.

A thickening mist hid the hill and gave an indistinct quality to the courtyard below, but the figure urging the horse into a gallop toward the maze entrance was recognizable, though he was bending low over its neck.

Adelia gave a yelp. "Not him, not him. He mustn't get away. Stop him, for God's sake, *stop him.*"

But there was nobody to stop him; some of Schwyz's men had heard the hooves and were running toward the maze, uselessly.

"Who was it?" the king asked.

"The assassin," she told him. "Dear God, he mustn't get away. I want him punished." For Rosamund, for Bertha . . .

Something had happened to frighten him if Jacques was deserting Eynsham and the second installment of his precious payment.

Then she was pulling at the king's sleeve. "It's your men," she said. "He must have heard them. They're here. Shout to them. Tell them to go after him. Will they catch him?"

"They'd better," he said. "That's a bloody good horse."

But if Henry's men *had* arrived and the assassin had heard them and decided to cut his losses, there was no sign of them in the courtyard and no sound.

Together, Adelia and the king watched the pursuers return, shrugging, to disappear toward the kitchen.

"Are you *certain* your men are on their way?" she asked.

"We won't see them til they're ready. They'll be coming through the rear of the maze."

"There's another entrance?"

The king smirked. "Imitate the mole, never leave yourself only one exit. Get on with it, tell me the rest."

Jacques's escape anguished her. She thought of the little unmarked grave in the nuns' cemetery. . . .

The king's fingers were tapping again, so she took up her tale where she'd left off.

There was another interruption. "Hello,

where's Dakers going?"

Adelia was beside him in an instant. The mist had begun to play tricks, ebbing and flowing in swirls that deceived the eye into seeing unmelted mounds of snow as crouching men and animals, but it didn't hide the thin black figure of Rosamund's housekeeper crawling toward the maze.

"What's that she's dragging?"

"God knows," the king said. "A sawing horse?"

It was something large and angular, too much for the human bundle of bones that collapsed after each pull but which managed to steady itself to pull again.

"She's mad, of course," the king said. "Always was."

It was agonizing to watch such effort, but watch they did, having to keep refocusing their eyes as Dakers inched her burden along like an ant through the shifting grayness.

Leave it, whatever it is, Adelia begged her. *They haven't seen you. Go and die at your own choosing.*

Another blink and there was only fog.

"So . . ." the king said. "You'd taken one of Eynsham's templates from this chamber to Godstow and given it to the priest. . . . Go on."

"His handwriting is distinctive, you see," she told him. "I've never seen another like it, very curly — beautiful, really — he uses classically square capitals but fills them in with whirls and his minuscule . . ."

Henry sighed, and Adelia hurried on. "Anyway, Sister Lancelyne, she's Godstow's librarian, once wrote to Eynsham asking if she might borrow the abbot's copy of Boethius's *Consolation* in order to copy it, and he'd written back, refusing . . ."

She saw again the learned little old nun among her empty shelves. "If ever we get out of here, I'd like Sister Lancelyne to have it."

"A whole *Philosophy*? Eynsham has a Boethius?" The Plantagenet eyes gleamed; he was greedy for books and totally untrustworthy when it came to other people's.

"*I should like,*" Adelia said clearly, "Sister Lancelyne to have it."

"Oh, very well. She'd better look after it. Get on, get on."

"And while we're about it" — there had to be some profit out of this — "if Emma Bloat should be widowed . . ."

"She will be," the king promised. "Oh, yes, she will be."

"She's not to be forced into marriage again."

531

With her own fortune and Wolvercote's lands, Emma would be a prize. She would also, as the widow of one of his barons, be in the king's gift, a valuable tradeable object in the royal marketplace.

"Is this a horse fair?" the king asked. "Are you haggling? With *me?*"

"Negotiating. Regard it as my fee."

"You'll ruin me," he said. "Very well. Can we proceed? I need evidence of Eynsham's calumny to show the Pope, and I doubt he'll regard curly handwriting as proof."

"Father Paton thought it was." Adelia winced. "Poor Father Paton."

"Anyway . . ." Henry was looking around the table. "The bastard seems to have taken his template with him."

"There are others. What we can't prove is that he employed an assassin to kill . . . who did kill."

"I shouldn't worry about that," the king said. "He'll probably tell us."

I've condemned a man to torture, she thought. Suddenly, she was tired and didn't want to say any more. If Schwyz managed to put a flame to the bonfire in the hall, there was no point to it, anyway.

She abridged what was left. "Then Rowley arrived. He told Walt, that's his groom, to look after me when the attack came. Walt, not knowing, told the assassin, who told Eynsham — who is very afraid of you and decided to run and take me with him." It sounded like the house that Jack built. That's all," she said, closing her eyes, "more or less."

Drips from the icicles were increasing, pattering like rain onto the windowsills of a silent room.

"Vesuvia Adelia Rachel Ortese Aguilar," the king said, musing.

It was an accolade. She opened her eyes, tried to smile at him, and closed them again.

"He's a good lad, young Geoffrey," Henry said. "Very loving. God bless him. I got him on a prostitute, Ykenai — strange name, the saints only know what race her parents were, because she doesn't. Big woman, comfortable. I still see her occasionally when I'm in London."

Adelia was awake now. He was telling her something, a tit for tat, payment for her trouble. This was about Rosamund without mentioning her name.

"I set her up in a pie shop, Ykenai, and very successful it's been, except it's making her bigger than ever. We talk about pies, there's a lot to making pies."

Big women, comfortable, bouncy mattresses, as Rosamund had been. Women who talked about little things, who didn't test him. Women as different from Eleanor as chalk to cheese — and maybe he'd loved both.

Wife and mistress both treacherous. Whether Rosamund had been ambitious herself or had been stirred into it by a devious abbot, the result was the same; she had nearly sparked a war. The only female refuge this man, this *emperor,* had left lived in a London pie shop where at least one loyal son had been born to him.

Henry's voice came from the window, nastily. "While he was with you, did the Bishop of Saint Albans tell you of his oath?" He wanted to hurt someone else who'd been betrayed.

"Yes," she said.

"He swore it in front of me, you know. Hand on the Bible, *'I swear by the Lord God and all the saints of Heaven that if You will guard her and keep her safe, I shall withhold myself from her.'* "

"I know," she said.

"Hah."

For the first time in days, she could hear the chatter of birds, as if small, frozen hearts were being thawed back to life.

Henry reached over and took the remnant of cheese out of her fingers, squashed it, and scattered the crumbs along the window-sill.

A robin flew down immediately to peck, its wings almost touching his hand before flying off again.

"I'll bring spring back to England," its king said. "They won't beat me, by Christ, they won't."

They have *beaten you,* Adelia thought. *Your men aren't coming. Everybody betrays you.*

Henry's head had gone up. "Hear that?"

"No."

"I did. They're here." His sword rasped from its scabbard. "Let's go down and fight the bastards."

They weren't *here.* It was birds he'd heard. The two of them would stay here forever and decompose alongside Rosamund.

She dragged herself to the window.

Alarmed men were emerging from the kitchen, turning this way and that, confused by the fog, running back to fetch weapons. She heard Schwyz's shout: "Round the other side. It came from the rear."

The Abbot of Eynsham was taking undecided steps toward the entrance to the maze, then away from it.

"Yes," Adelia said.

Henry's dagger that had cut her hands free was on the table. She took it up with a ferocious joy. She wanted to fight somebody.

But she couldn't. For one thing . . . "My lord, we're locked in."

He was standing on tiptoe, feeling around the top of the coronal that held the curtains of Rosamund's bed. His hand came away with a key in it. He waved it at her. "Never get into a hole without a second exit."

Then they were out of the door and pattering down the stairs, Henry leading.

Two landings down, they met one of Schwyz's men running up, sword drawn. Whether he was trying to find somewhere to hide or had come for her, Adelia never knew. His eyes widened as he saw the king.

"Wrong way," Henry told him, and stuck him through the mouth. The man fell. The king ran him through again, raising him on the swordpoint as if on a skewer, and flicked him off so that he was thrown round the next bend. Kept flicking him, a heavy man, round the next and the next, though he was long dead by the time they reached the hall.

The air outside was discordant with shouts and the clash of metal. The fog had thickened; it was difficult to make out who was fighting whom.

The king disappeared, and Adelia heard a gleeful howl of *"Dieu et Plantagenet"* as he found an enemy.

It was like being in the middle of battling unseen ghosts. With the dagger ready, she began walking cautiously forward to where she'd last seen Eynsham. One killer had escaped; she'd be damned if another thwarted justice. This one would if he could; not a courageous man, the abbot; he killed only through others.

Two heavy figures appeared on her left, their swords sparking as they fought. She jumped out of their way and they vanished again.

If I call him, he will come, she thought. She was still a bargaining counter; he'd want to use her as a shield. She had a knife, she could threaten him into standing still. "Abbot." Her voice was high and thin. "Abbot."

Something answered her in a voice even higher. In astonishment. In a crescendo of agony that rose into a falsetto beyond what was human. In shrieks that pulsed through the mist and overrode all noise of battle and silenced it. It overrode everything.

It was coming from the direction of the maze. Adelia began running toward it, sliding in the slush, falling, picking herself up, and blundering on. Whatever it was had to be helped; hearing it was unendurable.

Somebody splashed past her. She didn't see who it was.

A wall of bushes loomed up. Frantically, she used her hands to follow it round toward the maze entrance, toward the screaming. It was diminishing now; there were words in it. Prayer? Pleading?

She found the entrance and plunged inside.

Curiously, it was easier to see in here, merely gloomy, as if the tunnels were bewilderment enough and had regimented the mist into their own coils. The hedged doors were open, still giving straight passage.

He'd gone a long way in, almost to the exit that led to the hill. The sound was softening into mumbles, like somebody discontented. As Adelia came up, it stopped altogether.

The last paroxysm had sent the abbot arching backward over the mantrap so that his stomach curved outward. His mouth was stretched open; he looked as if he'd died roaring with laughter.

She edged round to the front. Schwyz was scrabbling at the mess where the machine's fangs had bitten into Eynsham's groin. "It's all right, Rob," he was saying. "It's all right." He looked up at Adelia. "Help me."

There was no point. He was dead. It would take two men to force the mantrap open. Only hate like the fires of hell had given Dakers the strength to lever the struts apart so that their jaws lay flat in the dirt, waiting to snap up the man who'd had Rosamund poisoned.

The housekeeper had sat herself a couple of feet away so that she could watch him die. And had died with him, smiling.

There was a lot of clearing up to do.

They brought the wounded down to Adelia on the landing stage, because she didn't want to return to the tower. There weren't many, and none were badly injured, most needing only a few stitches, which she managed with the contents of the king's sewing case.

All were Plantagenet men; Henry hadn't taken any prisoners.

She didn't ask what had happened to Schwyz; she didn't care much. Probably, he hadn't, either.

One of the barges that came upriver from Godstow contained Rosamund's much-traveled coffin. The Bishop of Saint Albans was aboard another. He'd been with Young Geoffrey at the storming of the abbey and looked tired enough to fall down. He kept his distance on seeing Adelia, though he thanked his God for her deliverance. Godstow had been liberated without loss on the

Plantagenet side. Wolvercote, now in chains, was the only one who'd put up any resistance.

"Allie's safe and well," Rowley said. "So are Gyltha and Mansur. They were cheering us on from the guesthouse window."

There was nothing else she needed to know. Yes, one thing. "Lawyer Warin," she said. "Did you find him?"

"Little sniveling fellow? He was trying to escape via the back wall, so we put him in irons."

"Good."

The thaw was proceeding quickly. Untidy plates of ice floating downriver and bumping into the landing stage became smaller and smaller. She watched them; each one carried its own little cloud of thicker fog through the mist.

It was still very cold.

"Come up to the tower," Rowley said. "Get warm."

"No."

He put his cloak around her, still without touching her. "Eleanor got away," he said. "They're hunting the woods for her."

Adelia nodded. It didn't matter one way or the other.

He shifted. "I'd better go to him. He'll need me to bless the dead."

"Yes," she said.

He walked away, heading for the tower and his king.

Another coffin was carried to the landing stage, assembled from pieces of the bonfire. Dakers would be accompanying her mistress to the grave.

The rest of the dead were left piled in the courtyard until the ground should be soft enough to dig a common grave.

Henry came, urging on the loading, shouting to the oarsmen that if they didn't row their hearts out, he'd have their bollocks; he was in a hurry to get to Godstow and then on to Oxford. He ushered Adelia aboard. The Bishop of Saint Albans, he told her, was staying behind to see to the burials.

The fog was too thick to allow a last glimpse of Wormhold Tower, even if Adelia had looked back, which she didn't.

The Plantagenet wouldn't go inside the cabin, being too concerned with piloting the rowers away from shoals, occasionally jotting notes on his slate book and studying the weather. "There'll be a breeze soon," he said.

He didn't let Adelia go inside, either; he said she needed air and sat her down on a thwart in the stern. After a while, he joined her. "Better now?"

"I'm going back to Salerno," she told him.

He sighed. "We've had this conversation before."

They had, after the last time he'd used her to investigate deaths. "I am not your subject, Henry, I'm Sicily's."

"Yes, but this is England, and I say who comes and goes."

She was silent, and he began wheedling. "I need you. And you wouldn't like Salerno now, not after England; it's too hot, you'd dry up like a prune."

She compressed her lips and turned her head away. *Damn him, don't laugh.*

"Eh?" he said. "Wouldn't you? Eh?"

She had to ask. "Did you know Dakers would set the mantrap for Eynsham?"

He was astonished, hurt. If he hadn't been trying to woo her, he'd have been angry. "How could I see what in hell the woman was dragging? It was too damn foggy."

She'd never know. For the rest of her life, she'd be questioned by the image of the two of them, him and Dakers, sitting together in the garderobe, planning. *"He'll die, but not by my hand,"* he had said. He'd been so certain.

"Nasty things, mantraps," he said. "Never use 'em." And paused. "Except for deer poachers." And paused. "Who deserve 'em."

542

He paused again. "And then only ones that take the leg."

She'd never know.

"I am returning to Salerno," she said, very clear.

"It'd break Rowley's heart, oath or not."

It would probably break hers, but she was going anyway.

"You'll stay." The nearest oarsmen turned round at the shout. "I've had enough of rebellion."

He was the king. The route to Salerno passed through vast tracts of land where nobody traveled without his permission.

"It's his oath, isn't it?" he said, wheedling again. "I wouldn't have made it myself, but then, I'm not bound to chastity, thank the saints. We'll have to see what we can do about that — I yield to nobody in my admiration for God, but He's no good in bed."

It was a quick journey; the thaw was putting the Thames into full spate, carrying the barge at speed. Henry spent the rest of the time making notes in his slate book. Adelia sat and stared into nothingness, which was all there was to see.

But the king was right, a light breeze had come up by the time they approached Godstow, and from some way off, the bridge became just visible. It appeared to be busy; the middle span was empty, but at each end people were milling around a single still figure.

As the barge passed the village, the activity among the group on this side of the bridge became clearer.

It was a hanging party. Taller than anybody else, Wolvercote stood in the middle of it with a noose around his neck while a man attached the other end of the rope to a stanchion. Beside him, the much smaller figure of Father Egbert muttered in prayer.

A young woman was watching the scene from the abbey end. The crowd of people behind her was keeping back, but one of them — Adelia recognized the matronly shape of Mistress Bloat — tugged at her daughter's hand as if she were pleading. Emma paid no attention. Her eyes never left the scene on the other side of the bridge.

Seeing the barge, a young man leaned over the bridge's parapet. His voice came clear and jolly. "Greetings, my lord, and my thanks to God for keeping you safe." He grinned. "I knew He would."

The oarsmen reversed their rowing stroke so that the boat could keep its position against the flow of the water and allow the exchange between king and son. Above them, Wolvercote kept his gaze on the sky. The sun was beginning to come out. A heron rose out of the rushes and flapped its gawky way farther downriver.

Henry put aside his slate book. "Well done, Geoffrey. Is everything secured?"

"All secure, my lord. And, my lord, the pursuers I put after the queen have sent word. She is caught and being brought back."

Henry nodded. Pointing up at Wolvercote, he said, "Has he made confession for his sins?"

"For everything except his treachery to you, my lord. He refuses to be absolved for rebellion."

"I wouldn't absolve the swine anyway," Henry said to Adelia. "Even the Lord'll have to think twice." He called back, "Tip him over, then, Geoffrey, and God have mercy on his soul." He gestured to his oarsmen to row on.

As the boat passed by, two of the men lifted Wolvercote up and steadied him so that he stood balanced on the parapet.

Father Egbert raised his voice to begin the absolution: *"Dominus noster Jesus Christus . . ."*

Adelia turned away. She was near enough

now to see Emma's face; it was completely expressionless.

". . . *Deinde, ego te absolvo a peccatis tuis in nominee Patris, et Filii, et Spiritus Sancti. Amen.*"

There was a thump of suddenly tightened rope. Jeers and cheering went up from both ends of the bridge.

Adelia couldn't watch, but she knew when Wolvercote had stopped struggling because it wasn't until then that Emma turned and walked away.

A crowd of soldiers, nuns, and serving people, nearly everybody in the abbey had gathered on the meadow below the convent to cheer King Henry in.

For Adelia there were only three, a tall Arab, an elderly woman, and a child whose small hand was being flapped up and down in welcome.

She bowed her head in gratitude at the sight of them.

After all, I have no need for any but these.

Allie seemed to have learned another word, because Gyltha was trying to make her say it, first encouraging the baby and then pointing toward Adelia, who couldn't hear it through the cheering.

There was a shout from the opposite bank that cut through the noise. "My lord, my

546

lord. We have recovered the queen, my lord."

At an order from Henry, the barge veered across the river toward a group of horsemen arriving through the trees. A man with the insignia of a captain of the Plantagenet guard was dismounting, while one of his soldiers helped the queen down from his horse where she'd been riding pillion.

A gate in the barge's taffrail was opened and a gangplank laid across the gap between it and the bank. The captain, a worried-looking man, came aboard.

"How did she get across the river?" Henry asked.

"There was an old wherry further down, my lord. We think Lord Montignard poled her across . . . my lord, he tried to delay her capture, he fought like a wolf, my lord . . . he . . ."

"They killed him," the queen called from the bank. She was brushing the soldier's restraining hand off her arm like a speck of dust.

The king went forward to help her aboard. "Eleanor."

"Henry."

"I like the disguise, you look well in it."

She was dressed like a boy, and she did look well in it, though as a disguise it would have fooled nobody; her figure was slim enough, but the muddy, short cloak and boots, the angle of the cap she'd stuffed her hair into, were worn with too much style.

The cheering from the abbey had stopped; there was an open-mouthed silence as if people on the far bank were watching a meeting between warring Olympians and waiting for the thunderbolts.

There weren't any. Adelia, crouched in the stern, watched two people who had known each other too well and been too long together to surprise now; they had conceived eight children and seen one of them die, ruled great countries together, made laws together, put down rebellions together, quarreled, laughed, and loved together, and if, now, all that had ended in a metaphorical attempt to disembowel each other, it was still in their eyes and hung in the air between them.

As if, even now, she couldn't bear to look anything but feminine for him, Eleanor took off her cap and sent it spinning into the river. It was a mistake; the boy's costume became grotesque as the long, graying hair of a fifty-year-old woman fell over its shoulders.

Gently, mercifully, her husband took off his cloak and put it around her. "There, my dear."

"Well, Henry," she said, "where's it to be this time? Back to Anjou and Chinon?"

The king shook his head. "I was thinking more of Sarum."

She tutted. "Oh, not Sarum, Henry, it's in England."

"I know, my love, but the trouble with Chinon was that you insisted on escaping from it."

"But Sarum," she persisted. "So dull."

"Well, well, if you're a good girl, I'll let you out for Easter and Christmas." He gestured to the rowers to take up their oars. "For now, though, we're making for Oxford. Some rebels there are waiting for me to hang them."

An enraptured Adelia woke up in panic. There was a river between her and her child. "My lord, my lord, let me off first."

He'd forgotten her. "Oh, very *well*." And to the rowers, "Make for the other bank."

Against fast running water, the procedure was lengthy, and the king tutted irritably all through it. By the time the barge was settled at a disembarking point on the requisite bank, it had gone long past the abbey, and Adelia was handed ashore on a deserted stretch of meadow into mud that she sank in up to the tops of her boots.

The king liked that. He leaned over the

taffrail, humor restored. "You'll have to squelch back," he said.

"Yes, my lord. Thank you, my lord."

The barge took off, its dipping and rising oars sending glittering droplets back onto the surface of the water.

Suddenly, the king was running along the barge's length to the stern so that he could tell her one more thing. "About the bishop's oath," he called, "don't worry about it. '. . . *if You will guard her and keep her safe . . .*' Very nicely phrased."

She called back. "Was it?"

"Yes." The rapidly increasing distance between them was forcing him to shout. "Adelia, you're my investigator into the dead, like it or not. . . ."

All she could see now was the Plantagenet three-leopard pennant fluttering as the barge rounded a wooded bend, but the king's voice carried cheerfully over its trees: "You're *never* going to be safe."

AUTHOR'S NOTE

Fair Rosamund Clifford holds a bigger place in legend than she does in historical records, which make only brief references to her, and I hope her shade does not haunt me for my fictional portrayal.

The English Register of Godstow Nunnery, edited by Andrew Clarke and published by the Early English Text Society, shows that the abbey was both highly regarded and efficiently administered at this time. It was also broad-minded enough to bury the body of Henry II's mistress, Rosamund Clifford, in front of the altar, where the tomb became a popular shrine. However, the great bishop, Hugh of Lincoln, though he had been a friend of Henry's, was shocked to find it there when he visited the convent in 1191, two years after the king's death, and ordered it to be disinterred and reburied somewhere less sacred in the convent grounds.

Most of the rebellion of Henry II's family

took place on the continent but, since the nice thing for a novel writer is the gap in medieval records, I have dared to interpose one such rising in England, where we do know at least that some of his discontented barons were quick to join in Young Henry and Eleanor's fight.

Eleanor of Aquitaine survived the death of Henry and the imprisonment he imposed on her. In fact, she survived all her sons as well, except King John. In her seventies, she crossed the Pyrenees to arrange the marriage of a granddaughter, and suffered an abduction and, later, a siege. She died at the age of eighty-two and was laid to rest beside her husband and Richard the First, their son, in the Abbey of Fontevrault, where their effigies are still to be seen in its beautiful church.

I make no apology for the way in which my characters go by water between Godstow and various places. The Thames around the island on which the remains of the convent stand is navigable to a fair way farther up even now, and there is every likelihood that its tributaries have changed their courses over the years, and those of the Cherwell, now disappeared, provided better going than the lesser roads. As Professor W. G. Hoskins, the father of landscape archaeology, says in his *Fieldwork to Local History* (Faber and Faber), "In medieval and later times a large proportion of inland trade went by river, far more than has ever been generally realised." Also, there are references to the Thames freezing during the very cold winters of the twelfth century.

Incidentally, beavers were common in English rivers during the twelfth century. It was later, in the 1700s, that they were hunted to extinction for their fur.

And, unlikely as it seems, opium *was* grown in the East Anglian fens, not only in the twelfth but in succeeding centuries — it is thought that the Romans brought the poppy to England, as they brought so much else. The tincture fen people called "Godfrey's Cordial" — a mixture of opium and treacle — was still in use in the twentieth century.

One by one, all of Henry's sons turned against him, and he died at Chinon in 1189, probably from bowel cancer, knowing that his youngest and most loved, John, had joined the rebellion of the elder brother, Richard.

I have given the manor of Wolvercote a fictitious lord for the purposes of this story; the real owner of the manor at this time was a Roger D'Ivri, and I have no evidence that

D'Ivri was involved in any rebellion against Henry II, though it is interesting that, whether he wanted to or not, he later gave the manor to the king, who gave it to Godstow Abbey.

The reference to paper as a writing material in chapter four may offend the general view that paper did not reach Europe, certainly northern Europe, until the fourteenth century. Granted, it wasn't used much in the twelfth century — scribes and monkish writers were snobbish about it and preferred vellum — but it was around, though probably of poor quality. Viz the interesting article posted on the Internet: "Medieval Ink" by David Carvalho.

The trick of getting out of a multicursal maze I owe to that lovely writer on landscape, Geoffrey Ashe, and his *Labyrinth and Mazes,* published by Wessex Books.

The real Abbot of Eynsham, whoever he was, must be absolved of the wickedness that I attribute to his fictional counterpart. As far as I know, he lived a blameless life and had high regard for women — though, in that case, he would have been a rare specimen among medieval churchmen.

The idea of God as both father and mother was famously encapsulated in the writings of the feminine mystic Julian of

Norwich in the fourteenth century, but the concept was deep in much Christian thinking long before that, and so the conversation between the Abbess of Godstow and Adelia in chapter eleven of this book is not necessarily anachronistic.

In the Middle Ages, the title of doctor was bestowed on followers of philosophy, not physicians, but I have applied it in the modern sense here to simplify meaning for readers and myself.

ACKNOWLEDGMENTS

As always, my gratitude to my agent, Helen Heller, for her wise judgment of plot and pace. And to Rachel Kahan, my editor at Penguin Group (USA), for the same. Also to the London Library, which contains everything an inquiring author needs to know, and to its staff.

And last but never least, to my husband, Barry, and the family for their patience — especially my daughter Emma, who shoulders secretarial burdens so well and leaves me free to write.

Thank you.

ABOUT THE AUTHOR

Ariana Franklin, a former journalist, is a biographer and author of the novels *City of Shadows* and *Mistress of the Art of Death*. She is married with two daughters and lives in England.